The Lost Lady of Lone

E.D.E.N. Southworth

Contents

THE LOST LADY OF LONE

BY

E.D.E.N. Southworth

THE LOST LADY OF LONE
By MRS. E.D.E.N. SOUTHWORTH

Author of "Nearest and Dearest,"
"The Hidden Hand," "Unknown,"
"Only a Girl's Heart,"
"For Woman's Love," etc.

1876

PUBLISHERS' NOTICE.

"THE LOST LADY OF LONE" is different from any of Mrs. Southworth's other novels. The plot, which is unusually provocative of conjecture and interest, is founded on thrilling and tragic events which occurred in the domestic history of one of the most distinguished families in the Highlands of Scotland. The materials which these interesting and tragic annals place at the disposal of Mrs. Southworth give full scope to her unrivalled skill in depicting character and developing a plot, and she has made the most of her opportunity and her subject.

CHAPTER I.
THE BRIDE OF LONE.

E h, Meester McRath? Sae grand doings I hae na seen sin the day o' the queen's visit to Lone. That wad be in the auld duke's time. And a waefu' day it wa'." "Dinna ye gae back to that day, Girzie Ross. It gars my blood boil only to think o' it!"

"Na, Sandy, mon, sure the ill that was dune that day is weel compensate on this. Sooth, if only marriages be made in heaven, as they say, sure this is one. The laird will get his ain again, and the bonnyest leddy in a' the land to boot."

"She *is* a bonny lass, but na too gude for him, although her fair hand does gie him back his lands."

"It's only a' just as it sud be."

"Na, it's no all as it sud be. Look at they fules trying to pit up yon triumphal arch! The loons hae actually gotten the motto 'HAPPINESS' set upside down, sae that a' the blooming red roses are falling out o' it. An ill omen that if onything be an ill omen. I maun rin and set it right."

The speakers in this short colloquy were Mrs. Girzie Ross, housekeeper, and Mr. Alexander McRath, house-steward of Castle Lone.

The locality was in the Highlands of Scotland. The season was early summer. The hour was near sunset. The scene was one of great beauty and sublimity. The occasion one of high festivity and rejoicing.

The preparations were being completed for a grand event. For on the morning of the next day a deep wrong was to be made right by the marriage of the young and beautiful Lady of Lone to the chosen lord of her heart.

Lone Castle was a home of almost ideal grandeur and loveliness, situated in one of the wildest and most picturesque regions of the Highlands, yet brought to the utmost perfection of fertility by skillful cultivation.

The castle was originally the stronghold of a race of powerful and warlike Scottish chieftains, ancestors of the illustrious ducal line of Scott-Hereward. It was strongly built, on a rocky island, that arose from The midst of a deep clear lake, surrounded by lofty mountains.

For generations past, the castle had been but a picturesque ruin, and the island a barren desert, tenanted only by some old retainer of the ancient family, who found shelter within its huge walls, and picked up a scanty living by showing the famous ruins to artists and tourists.

But some years previous to the commencement of our story, when Archibald-Alexander-John Scott succeeded his father, as seventh Duke of Hereward, he conceived the magnificent, but most extravagant idea of transforming that grim, old Highland fortress, perched upon its rocky island, surrounded by water and walled in by mountains--into a mansion of Paradise and a garden of Eden.

When he first spoke of his plan, he was called visionary and extravagant; and when he persisted in carrying it into execution, he was called mad.

The most skillful engineers and architects in Europe were consulted and their plans examined, and a selection of designs and contractors made from the best among them. And then the restoration, or rather the transfiguration, of the place was the labor of many years, at the cost of much money.

Fabulous sums were lavished upon Lone. But the Duke's enthusiasm grew as the work grew and the cost increased. All his unentailed estates in England were first heavily mortgaged and afterwards sold, and the proceeds swallowed up in the creation of Lone.

The duchess, inspired by her husband, was as enthusiastic as the duke. When his resources were at an end and Lone unfinished she gave up her marriage settlements, including her dower house, which was sold that the proceeds might go to the completion of Lone.

But all this did not suffice to pay the stupendous cost.

Then the duke did the maddest act of his life. He raised the needed money from usurers by giving them a mortgage on his own life estate in Lone itself.

The work drew near to its completion.

In the meantime the duke's agents were ransacking the chief cities in Europe in search of rare paintings, statues, vases, and other works of art or articles of virtu to decorate the halls and chambers of Lone; for which also the most famous manufacturers in France and Germany were elaborating suitable designs in upholstery.

Every man directing every department of the works at Lone, whether as engineer, architect, decorator, or furnisher, every man was an artist in his own speciality. The work within and without was to be a perfect work at whatever cost of time, money, and labor.

At length, at the end of ten years from its commencement, the work was completed.

And for the sublimity of its scenery, the beauty of its grounds, the almost tropical luxuriance of its gardens, the magnificence of its buildings, the splendor of its decorations, and the luxury of its appointments, Lone was unequalled.

What if the mad duke had nearly ruined himself in raising it?

Lone was henceforth the pride of engineers, the model of architects, the subject of artists, the theme of poets, the Mecca of pilgrims, the eighth wonder of the world.

Lone was opened for the first time a few weeks after its completion, on the occasion of the coming of age of the duke's eldest son and heir, the young Marquis of Arondelle, which fell upon the first of June.

A grand festival was held at Lone, and a great crowd assembled to do honor to the anniversary. A noble and gentle company filled the halls and chambers of the castle, and nearly all the Clan Scott assembled on the grounds.

The festival was a grand triumph.

Among the thousands present were certain artists and reporters of the press, and so it followed that the next issue of the **London News** contained full-page pictures of Castle Lone and Inch Lone, with their terraces, parterres, arches, arbors and groves; Loch Lone, with its elegant piers, bridges and boats; and the surrounding mountains, with their caves, grottoes, falls and fountains.

Yes, the birthday festival was a perfect triumph, and the fame of Lone went forth to the uttermost ends of the earth. The English Colonists at Australia, Cape of Good Hope, and New Zealand, read all about it in copies of the **London News**, sent out to them by thoughtful London friends. We remember the day, some years since, when we, sitting by our cottage fire, read all about it in an illustrated paper, and pondered over the happy fate of those who could live in paradise while still on earth. Five years later, we would not have changed places with the Duke of Hereward.

But this is a digression.

The duke was in his earthly heaven; but was the duke happy, or even content?

Ah! no. He was overwhelmed with debt. Even Lone was mortgaged as deeply as it could be--that is, as to the extent of the duke's own life interests in the estate. Beyond that he could not burden the estate, which was entailed upon his heirs male. Besides his financial embarrassments, the duke was afflicted with another evil--he was consumed with a fever too common with prince and with peasant, as well as with peer--the fever of a land hunger.

The prince desires to add province to province; the peer to add manor to manor; the peasant to own a little home of his own, and then to add acre to acre.

The Lord of Lone glorying in his earthly paradise, wished to see it enlarged, wished to add one estate to another until he should become the largest land-owner in Scotland, or have his land-hunger appeased. He bought up all the land adjoining Lone, that could be purchased at any price, paying a little cash down, and giving notes for the balance on each purchase. Thus, in the course of three years, Lone was nearly doubled in territorial extent.

But the older creditors became clamorous. Bond, and mortgage holders threatened foreclosure, and the financial affairs of the "mad duke," outwardly and apparently so prosperous, were really very desperate. The family were seriously in danger of expulsion from Lone.

It was at this crisis that the devoted son came to the help of his father--not wisely, as many people thought then--not fortunately, as it turned out. To prevent his father from being compelled to leave Lone, and to protect him from the persecution of creditors, the young Marquis of Arondelle performed an act of self-sacrifice and filial devotion seldom equalled in the world's history. He renounced all his own entailed rights, and sold all his prospective life interest in Lone. His was a young, strong life, good for fifty or sixty years longer. His interest brought a sum large enough to pay off the mortgage on Lone and to settle all others of his father's outstanding debts.

Thus peaceable possession of Lone might have been secured to the family during the natural life of the duke. At the demise of the duke, instead of descending to his son and heir, it would pass into the possession of other parties, with whom it would remain as long the heir should live.

Thus, I say, by the sacrifice of the son the peace of the father might have been secured--for a time. And all might have gone well at Lone but for one unlucky event which finally set the seal on the ruin of the ducal family.

And yet that event was intended as an honor, and considered as an honor.

In a word the Queen, the Prince Consort, and the royal family, were coming to the Highlands. And the Duke of Hereward received an intimation that her majesty would stop on her royal progress and honor Lone with a visit of two days. This was a distinction in no wise to be slighted by any subject under any circumstances, and certainly not by the duke of Hereward.

The Queen's visit would form the crowning glory of Lone. The chambers occupied by majesty would henceforth be holy ground, and would be pointed out with reverence to the stranger in all succeeding generations.

In anticipation of this honor the "mad" Duke of Hereward launched out into his maddest extravagances.

He had but ten days in which to prepare for the royal visit, but he made the best use of his time.

The guest chambers at Lone, already fitted up in princely magnificence, had new splendors added to them. The castle and the grounds were adorned and decorated with lavish expenditure. The lake was alive with gayly-rigged boats. Triumphal arches were erected at stated intervals of the drive leading from the public road, across the bridge connecting the shore with the island, and--maddest extravagance of all--the ground was laid out and fitted up for a grand tournament after the style of the time of Richard Coeur de Lion, to be held there during the queen's visit--that fatal visit spoken of in the early part of this chapter.

Yes, fatal!--for a hundred thousand pounds sterling, won by the son's self-sacrifice, which should have gone to satisfy the clamorous creditors of the duke, was squandered in extravagant preparations to royally entertain England's expensive royal family.

A second time Lone was the scene of unparalleled display, festivity, and rejoicing. Once more all the country round about was assembled there; again the artists and reporters of the London press were among the crowd; and again full-page pictures of the ceremonies attending the queen's reception and entertainment were published in the illustrated papers, and the fame of that royal visit went out to the uttermost parts of the earth.

But mark this: Every footman that waited at the grand state-dinner table was a bailiff in disguise, in charge of the plate and china, which, together with all the fabulous riches of art, literature, science and *virtu* collected at Lone had been taken in execution, by the officers secretly in possession.

The royal party, with their retinue, left Lone on the afternoon of the third day.

And then the crash came? The blow was sudden, overwhelming and utterly destructive.

The shock of the fall of Lone was felt from one end of the kingdom to the other.

For the last time a crowd gathered around Castle Lone. But they came not as festive guests but as a flock of vultures around a carcass, bent on prey. For the last time artists and reporters came not to illustrate the triumphs, but to record the downfall of the great ducal house of Scott-Hereward; to make sketches, take photographs and write descriptions of the magnificent and splendid halls and chambers, picture-galleries and museums, before they should be dismantled by the rapacious purchasers who flocked to the vendue of Lone, to profit by the ruin of the proprietor.

And for the last time illustrations of Lone and its glories went forth over every part of the world where the English language is spoken, or the English mails penetrate.

Another heavy blow fell upon the doomed duke. Even while the grand vendue was still in progress the duchess died of grief.

When all was over, and the good duchess was laid in the family vault, the duke and the young marquis disappeared from Lone and none knew whither they went. Some said that they had gone to Australia; some that they were in America; some that they were on the Continent. Others declared that they had hidden themselves in the wilderness of London, where they were living in great poverty and obscurity, and even under assumed names.

Opinions and rumors differed also concerning the character and conduct of the young marquis. Many called him a devoted son, filled with the spirit of heroic self-sacrifice. Many others affirmed that he was a hypocrite and a villain, addicted to drinking, gambling, and other vices and even cited times, places, and occasions of his sinning.

There never lived a man of whom so much good and so much evil was said as of the young Marquis of Arondelle. A stranger coming into the neighborhood of Lone, would hear these opposite reports and never be able to decide whether the absent and self-exiled young nobleman was a model of virtue or a monster of vice.

But there was one whose faith in him was firm as her faith in Heaven.

Rose Cameron was the daughter of a Highland shepherd, living about ten miles north of Ben Lone. No court lady in the land was fairer than this rustic Highland beauty. Her form was tall, fine, and commanding. Her step was stately and graceful as the step of an antelope. Her features were large, regular, and clear cut, as if chiseled in marble, yet full of blooming and sparkling life as ruddy health and mountain air could fill them. Her hair was golden brown, and clustered in innumerable shining ringlets closely around her fair open forehead and rounded throat. Her eyes were large, and clear bright blue. Her expression full of innocent freedom and joyousness.

Rumor said that the fast young Marquis of Arondelle, while deer-stalking from his hunting lodge in the neighborhood of Ben Lone, had chanced to draw rein at the gate of Rob. Cameron's sheiling, and had received from the shapely hand of the beautiful shepherdess a cup of water, and had been so suddenly and forcibly smitten by her Juno-like beauty, that thenceforth his visits to his hunting lodge became very frequent, both in season and out of season, and that he was a very dry soul, whose thirst could be satisfied by nothing but the spring water that spouted close by the shepherd's sheiling, dipped up and offered by the hands of the beautiful shepherdess.

Much blame was cast by the rustic neighbors upon all parties concerned--first of all, upon the young marquis, who they declared "meant nae guid to the lass," and then to the old shepherd, who they said, "suld tak mair care o' his puir mitherless bairn," and lastly, to the girl, who, as they affirmed, "suld guide hersel' wi' mair discretion."

None of these criticisms ever came to the ears of the parties concerned: they never do, you know.

Besides the lovers seemed to be infatuated with each other, and the shepherd seemed to be blind to what was going on in his sheiling. To be sure, he was out all day with his sheep, while his lass was alone in the sheiling. Or, if by sickness *he* was forced to stay home, then *she* was out all day with the sheep alone.

Gossip said that the young marquis visited the handsome shepherdess in her sheiling, and met her by appointment, when she was out with her flock.

And as the occasion grew, so grew the scandal, and so grew indignation against the marquis and scorn of the shepherdess.

"He'll nae mean to marry the quean! If she were my lass, I'd kick him out, an' he were twenty times a markis!" said the shepherd's next neighbor, and many approved his sentiment. These were among the detractors of the young nobleman.

But he had warm defenders--who affirmed that the Marquis of Arondelle would never seek a peasant girl to win her affections, unless he intended to make her his marchioness--which was an idea too preposterous to be entertained for an instant--therefore there could be no truth in these rumors.

And at length, when the great thunderbolt fell that destroyed Lone and banished the ducal family, there were not wanting "guid neebors" who taunted Rose Cameron with such words as these:

"The braw young markis hae made a fule o' ye, lass. Thou't ne'er see him mair. And a guid job, too. Best ye'd ne'er see him at a'!"

But the handsome shepherdess betrayed no sign of mortification or doubt. When such prognostics were uttered, she crested her queenly head with a smile of conscious power, and looked as though--"she could, an if she would,"--tell more about the Marquis of Arondelle, than any of these people guessed.

Meanwhile, princely Lone passed into the possession of Sir Lemuel Levison, a London banker of enormous wealth. He had not always been Sir Lemuel Levison. But he had once been Lord Mayor of London, and for some part that he had taken in a public demonstration or a royal pageant, (I forget which,) he had been knighted by her Majesty.

He was, at this time, a tall, spare, fair-faced, gray-haired and gray bearded man of sixty-five. He was a widower, with "one only daughter," the youngest and sole survivor of a large family of children.

This daughter, Salome, had never known a mother's love nor a father's care. She was under three years old when her mother passed away.

Then her father, hating his desolate home, broke up his establishment on Westbourne Terrace, London, and placed his infant daughter under the care of the nuns in the Convent of the Holy Nativity in France.

Here Salome Levison passed the days of her dreamy childhood and early youth. Her father seldom found time to visit her at her convent school, and she never went home to spend her holidays. She had no home to go to.

When Salome was eighteen years of age, the Superior of the convent wrote to Sir Lemuel Levison, enclosing a letter from his daughter that considerably startled the absorbed banker and forgetful father. He had not seen his daughter for two years, and now these letters informed him that she wished to become a Nun of the Holy Nativity, and to enter upon her novitiate immediately! But that being a minor, she could not do so without his consent.

His sole surviving child! The sole heiress of his enormous wealth! On whom he depended, to make a home for him in his declining years, when he should have made a few more millions of millions upon which to retire!

And now this long neglected daughter had found consolation in devotion, and wished to take the vail which was to hide her forever from the world!

Sir Lemuel Levison hastened to France, and brought his daughter back to England. He took apartments at a quiet London hotel, and looked about for a suitable country-seat to purchase.

At this time Lone was advertised. He went thither with the crowd.

He saw Lone, liked it, wanted it, and determined to "pay for it and take it."

He stopped the vandalish dismantling of the premises by outbidding everybody else and purchasing all the furniture, decorations, plate, pictures, statues, vases, mosaics, and everything else, and ordering them to be left in their old positions.

He then engaged the house-steward, the housekeeper, and as many more of the servants of the late proprietor as he could induce to remain at Lone.

And when the princely castle was cleared of its crowds, and once more restored to order, beauty and peace, Sir Lemuel Levison went back to London to bring his daughter home.

Salome, submissive to her father's will, yet disappointed in her wish to take the vail, met every event in life with apathy.

Even when the splendors of Lone broke upon her vision she regarded them with an air of indifference that amused, while it mortified, her father.

"I see how it is, my girl," he said. "You have renounced the world, and are pining for the convent. But you know nothing of the world. Give it a fair trial of three years. Then you will be twenty-one years old, of legal age to act for yourself, with some knowledge of that which you would ignorantly renounce; and then if you persist in your desire to take the vail--well! I shall then have neither the power nor the wish to prevent you," added the wise old banker, who felt perfectly confident that at the end of the specified time his daughter would no longer pine to immure herself in a convent.

Salome, grateful for this concession, and feeling perfectly self-assured that she would never be won by the world, kissed her father, and roused herself to be as much of a comfort and solace to him as she might be in the three years of probation. And she took her place at the head of her father's magnificent establishment at Lone with much of gentle quiet and dignity.

And now it is time to give you some more accurate knowledge of the outward appearance and the inner life of this motherless, convent-reared girl, who, though a young and wealthy heiress, was bent on forsaking the world and taking the vail. In the first place, she was not beautiful at all in repose. There can be no physical beauty without physical health. And Salome Levison partook of the delicate organization of her mother, who had passed away in early womanhood, and of her brothers and sisters, who had gone in infancy or childhood.

Salome, when still and silent, was, at first sight plain. She was rather below the medium height, slight and thin in form, pale and dark in complexion, with irregular features, and quiet, downcast, dark-gray eyes, whose long lashes cast shadows upon pallid cheeks, and which were arched with dark eyebrows on a massive forehead, shaded with an abundance of dark brown hair, simply parted in the middle, drawn back and wound into a rich roll. Her dress was as simple as her station permitted it to be.

Altogether she seemed a girl unattractive in person and reserved in speech.

The very opposite of the handsome shepherdess of Ben Lone.

And yet when she looked up or smiled, her face was transfigured into a wondrous beauty; such intellectual and spiritual beauty as that perfect piece of flesh and blood never could have expressed. And she was a "sealed book." Yet the hour was at hand when the "sealed book" was to be opened--when her dreaming soul, like the sleeping princess in the wood, was to be awakened by the touch of holy love to make the beauty of her person and the glory of her life.

CHAPTER II.
AN IDEAL LOVE.

A few weeks after their settlement at Lone, Sir Lemuel Levison returned to London on affairs connected with his final retirement from active business.

Salome was left at the castle, with the numerous servants of the establishment, but otherwise quite alone. She had neither governess, companion, nor confidential maid. She suffered from this enforced solitude. She had seen all the splendors of the interior of Lone, and there was nothing new to discover--except--yes, there was Malcom's Tower, which tradition said was the most ancient portion of the castle, whose foundations had been dug from the solid rock, hundreds of feet below the surface of the lake.

The tower had been restored with the rest of the castle, but had never been fitted up for occupation.

Salome determined to spend one morning in exploring the old tower from foundation to top.

She summoned the housekeeper to her presence, and made known her purpose.

"Macolm's Watch Tower, Miss! Weel, then, it's naething to see within, forbye a few auld family portraits and sic like, left there by the auld duke; but there'll be an unco' foine view frae the top on a braw day like this," said Dame Ross, as she detached a bunch of keys from her belt, and signified her readiness to attend her young mistress.

I need not detail the explorations of the young lady from the horrible dungeon of the foundation--up the narrow, winding steps, cut in the thickness of the outer wall, which was perforated on the inner side by doorways on each landing, leading into the strong, round stone rooms or cells on each floor, lighted only by long narrow slits in the solid masonry. All the lower cells were empty.

But when they reached the top of the winding steps and opened the door of the upper cell, the housekeeper said:

"Here are deposited some o' the relics left by the auld duke until such time as he shall be ready to tak' them awa'."

Salome followed her into the room and suddenly drew back in surprise.

She saw standing out from the gloom, the form of a young man of majestic beauty and grace.

A second look showed her that this was only a full-length life-sized portrait--but of whom?

Her gaze became riveted on the glorious presence.

The portrait represented a young man of about twenty-five years of age, tall, finely formed, broad-shouldered, deep-chested, with a well-turned, stately head, a Grecian profile, a fair, open brow, dark, deep blue eyes, and very rich auburn hair and beard. He wore the picturesque highland dress--the tartan of the Clan Scott.

But it was not the dress, the form, the face that fascinated the gaze of the girl. It was the air, the look, the SOUL that shone through it all!

A sun ray, glancing through the narrow slit in the solid wall, fell directly upon the fine face, lighting it up as with a halo of glory!

"It is the face of the young St. John! Nay, it is more divine! It is the face of Gabriel who standeth in the presence of the Lord! But it expresses more of power! It is the face of Michael rather, when he put the hosts of hell to flight! Oh! a wondrously glorious face!" said the rapt young enthusiast to herself, as she gazed in awe-struck silence on the portrait.

"Ye are looking at that picture, young leddy? Ay it weel deserves your regards! It is a grand one!" said Dame Ross, proudly.

" ***Who is it? One of the young princes?***" inquired Salome, in a low tone, full of reverential admiration.

"Ane o' the young princes? Gude guide us! Nae, young leddy; I hae seen the young princes ance, on an unco' ill day for Lone! And I dinna care if I never see ane mair. But they dinna look like that," said the housekeeper, with a deep sigh.

"Who is it, then?" whispered Salome, still gazing on the portrait with somewhat of the rapt devotion with which she had been wont to gaze on pictured saint, or angel, on her convent walls. "Who is it, Mrs. Ross?"

"Wha is it? Wha suld it be, but our ain young laird? Our ain bonny laddie? Our young Markis o' Arondelle? Oh, waes the day he ever left Lone!" exclaimed Dame Girzie, lifting her apron to her eyes.

"The Marquis of Arondelle!" echoed Salome, catching her breath, and gazing with even more interest upon the glorious picture.

Even while she gazed, the ray that had lighted it for a moment was withdrawn by the setting sun, and the picture was swallowed up in sudden darkness.

"The Marquis of Arondelle," repeated Salome in a low reverent tone, as if speaking to herself.

"Ay, the young Markis o' Arondelle; wae worth the day he went awa'!" said the housekeeper, wiping her eyes.

Salome turned suddenly to the weeping woman.

"I have heard--I have heard--" she began in a low, hesitating voice, and then she suddenly stopped and looked at the dame.

"Ay, young leddy, nae doubt ye hae heard unco mony a fule tale anent our young laird; but if ye would care to hear the verra truth, ye suld do so frae mysel. But come noo, leddy. It is too dark to see onything mair in this room. We'll gae out on the battlements gin ye like, and tak' a luke at the landscape while the twilight lasts," said Dame Girzie.

Salome assented with a nod, and they climbed the last steep flight of stairs, cut in the solid wall, and leading from this upper room to the top of the watch-tower.

They came out upon a magnificent view.

The bright, long twilight of these Northern latitudes still hung luminously over island, lake and mountain.

While Salome gazed upon it Dame Girzie said:

"All this frae the tower to the horizon, far as our eyes can reach, and far'er, was for eight centuries the land of the Lairds of Lone. And noo! a' hae gane frae them, and they hae gane frae us, and na mon kens where they bide or how they fare. Wae's me!"

"It was indeed a household wreck," said Salome, with sigh of sincere sympathy.

"Ye may say that, leddy, and mak' na mistake."

"What is that lofty mountain-top that I see on the edge of the horizon away to the north, just fading in the twilight?" inquired Salome, partly to divert the dame from her gloomy thoughts.

"Yon? Ay. Yon will be, Ben Lone. It will be twenty miles awa', gin it be a furlong. Our young laird had a braw hunting lodge there, where in the season he was wont to spend weeks thegither wi' his kinsman, Johnnie Scott, for the young laird was unco' fond of deer stalking, and sic like sport. I dinna ken wha owns the lodge now, or whether it went wi' the lave of the estate," said Dame Girzie, with a deep sigh.

"It is growing quite chilly up here," said Salome, shivering, and drawing her little red shawl more closely around her slight frame. "I think we will go down now, Mrs. Ross. And if you will be so good as to come to me after tea, this evening, I shall like to hear the story of this sorrowful family wreck," she added, as she turned to leave the place.

That evening, as the heiress sat in the small drawing room appropriated to her own use, the housekeeper rapped and was admitted.

And after seating herself at the bidding of her young mistress, Girzie Ross opened her mouth and told the true story of the fall of Lone, as I have already told to my readers.

"And this devoted son actually sacrificed all the prospects of his whole future life, in order to give peace and prosperity to his father's declining days," murmured Salome, with her eyes full of tears and her usually pale cheeks, flushed with emotion.

"He did, young leddy, like the noble soul, he was," said Dame Girzie.

"I never heard of such an act of renunciation in my life," murmured Salome.

"And the pity of it was, young leddy, that it was a' in vain," said the housekeeper.

"Yes, I know. Where is he now?" inquired the young girl, in a subdued voice.

"I dinna ken, leddy. Naebody kens," answered Girzie Ross, with a deep sigh, which was unconsciously echoed by the listener.

Then Dame Ross not to trespass on her young mistress's indulgence, arose and respectfully took her leave.

Salome fell into a deep reverie. From that hour she had something else to think about, beside the convent and the vail.

The portrait haunted her imagination, the story filled her heart and employed her thoughts. That night she dreamed of the self-exiled heir, a beautiful, vague, delightful dream, that she tried in vain to recall on the next morning.

In the course of the day she made several attempts to ask Mrs. Girzie Ross a simple question. And she wondered at her own hesitation to do it. At length she asked it:

"Mrs. Ross, is that portrait in the tower very much like Lord Arondelle?"

"Like him, young leddy? Why, it is his verra sel'! And only not sae bonny because it canna move, or smile, or speak. Ye should see him *alive* to ken him weel," said the housekeeper, heartily.

That afternoon Salome went up alone to the top of the tower, and spent a dreamy, delicious hour in sitting at the feet of the portrait and gazing upon the face.

That evening, while the housekeeper attended her at tea, she took courage to make another inquiry, in a very low voice:

"Is Lord Arondelle engaged, Mrs. Ross?"

She blushed crimson and turned away her head the moment she had asked the question.

"Engaged? What--troth-plighted do you mean, young leddy?"

"Yes," in a very low tone.

"Bless the lass! nay, nor no thought of it," answered the housekeeper.

"I was thinking that perhaps it would be well if he were not, that is all," explained Salome, a little confusedly.

That night, as she undressed to retire to bed, she looked at herself in the glass critically for the first time in her life.

It was not a pretty face that was reflected there. It was a pale, thin, dark face, that might have been redeemed by the broad, smooth forehead, shaped round by bands of dark brown hair, and lighted by the large, tender, thoughtful gray eyes, had not that forehead worn a look of anxious care, and those eyes an expression of eager inquiry.

"But then I am so plain--so very, very plain," she said to herself, as if uttering the negation of some preceding train of thought.

And with a deep sigh she retired to rest.

The next day Girzie Ross herself was the first to speak of the young marquis.

"I hae been thinking, young leddy, what garred ye ask me gin the young laird, were troth plighted. And I mistrust ye must hae heard these fule stories anent his hardship, having a sweetheart at Ben Lone. There's nae truth in sic tales, me leddy. No that I'm denying she's a handsome hizzy, this Rose Cameron; but she's nae one to mak' the young laird forget his rank. Ye'll no credit sic tales, me young leddy."

"I have heard no tales of the sort," said Salome, looking up in surprise.

"Ay, hae ye no? Aweel, then, its nae matter," said the dame.

"But what tales are there, Mrs. Ross?" uneasily inquired the heiress. And then she instantly perceived the indiscretion of her question, and regretted that she had asked it.

"Ou aye, it's just the fule talk o' thae gossips up by Ben Lone. They behoove to say that's its na the game that draws the young laird sae often to Ben Lone; but just Rab Cameron's handsome lass, Rose, and she *is* a handsome quean as I said before; but nae 'are to mak' the young master lose his head for a' that! Sae ye maun na beleiv' a word of it, me young leddy," said Dame Girzie.

And she hastened to change the subject.

"Ah! what a power beauty is! It can make a prince forget his royal state, and sue to a peasant girl," sighed Salome to herself. "I wonder--I wonder, if there *is* any truth in that report? Oh, I hope there is not, for his own sake. I wonder where he is--what he is doing? But that is no affair of mine. I have nothing at all to do with it! I wonder if I shall ever meet him. I wonder if he would think me very ugly? Nonsense, what if he should? He is nothing to me. I--I *do* wonder if a young man so noble in character, so handsome in person as he is, ever could like a girl without any beauty at all, even if she--even if she--Oh, dear! what a fool I am! I had better never have come out of the convent. I will think no more about him," said Salome, resolutely taking up a volume of the "Lives of the Saints," and turning to the page that related how--

"St. Rosalie, Darling of each heart and eye, From all the youth of Italy

Retired to God."

"That is the noblest love and service, after all," she said--"the noblest, surely, because it is Divine!"

And she resolved to emulate the example of the young and beautiful Italian virgin. She, too, would retire to God. That is, she would enter her convent as soon as her three probationary years should be passed.

But though she so resolved to devote herself to Heaven in this abnormal way, the natural human love that now glowed in her heart, would not be put down by an unnatural resolve.

Days and nights passed, and she still thought of the banished heir all day, and dreamed of him all night--the more intensely as well as purely perhaps, because she had never looked upon his living face.

To her he was an abstract ideal.

Later in the month her father returned to Lone--on business of more importance than that which had hurried him away.

He had only retired from one phase of public life to enter upon another.

There was to be a new Parliament. And at the solicitations of many interested parties, and perhaps also at the promptings of his own late ambition, Sir Lemuel Levison consented to stand for the borough of Lone. In the absence of the young Marquis of Arondelle there was no one to oppose him, and he was returned by an almost unanimous vote.

Early in February, Sir Lemuel Levison took his dreaming daughter and went up to London to take his seat in the House of Commons at the meeting of Parliament.

He engaged a sumptuously furnished house on Westbourne Terrace, and invited a distant relative, Lady Belgrave, the childless widow of a baronet, to come and pass the season with him and chaperone his daughter on her entrance into society.

Lady Belgrade was sixty years old, tall, stout, fair-complexioned, gray-haired, healthy, good-humored, and well-dressed--altogether as commonplace and harmless a fine lady as could be found in the fashionable world.

Salome had never seen her, scarcely ever heard of her before the day of her arrival at Westbourne Terrace.

Salome met Lady Belgrade with courtesy and kindness, but with much indifference.

Lady Belgrade, on her part, met her young kinswoman with critical curiosity.

"She is not pretty, not at all pretty, and one does not like to have a plain girl to bring out. She is not pretty, and what is worse than all, she seems **to know it**. And she can only grow pretty by believing that she is so. A girl with such a pair of eyes as hers can always get the reputation of beauty if she can only be made to believe in herself," was Lady Belgrade's secret comment; but--

"What beautiful eyes you have, my dear!" she said with effusion, as she kissed Salome on both cheeks.

The girl smiled and blushed with pleasure, for this was the first time in all her life that she had been credited with any beauty at all.

Lady Belgrade was partly right and partly wrong.

A girl with such a physique as Salome could never be pretty, never be handsome, but, with such a soul as hers, might grow beautiful.

At her Majesty's first drawing-room, Salome Levison was presented at court, where she attracted the attention, only as the daughter of Sir Lemuel Levison, the new Radical member for Lone, and as the sole heiress of the great banker's almost fabulous wealth.

Then under the experienced guidance of Lady Belgrade, she was launched into fashionable society. And society received the young expectant of enormous wealth, as society always does, with excessive adulation.

Salome was admired, followed, flattered, feted, as though she had been a beauty as well as an heiress. She was petted at home and worshiped abroad. Her father gave unlimited pocket-money in form of bank-cheques, to be filled up at her own discretion. For she was his only daughter, and he wished to get her in love with the world and out of conceit of a convent. And surely the run of his bank, and of all the fine shops of London, would do that, he thought, if anything could.

But Salome remained a "sealed book" to the wealthy banker, and a great trial to the fashionable chaperon who had her in training. Salome **would not** grow pretty, in spite of all that could be done for her. Salome would not make a sensation, for all her father's wealth and her own expectations. She remained quiet, shy, silent, dreamy, even in the gayest society, as in the Highland solitudes, with one worship in her soul--the worship of that self-devoted son--that self-banished prince, whose "counterfeit presentment" she had seen in the tower at Lone, and who had become the idol of her religion.

But all this did not hinder the heiress from receiving some very matter of fact and highly eligible offers of marriage; for though Salome, in the holiness of her dreams, was almost unapproachable, the banker was not inaccessible. And it was through her father that Salome, in the course of the season, had successively the coronet of a widowed earl, the title of a duke's younger son, and the fortune of a baronet who was just of age, laid at her feet.

She rejected them all--to her father's great disappointment and disturbance.

"I fear--I do much fear that her mind still runs on that convent. She does nothing but dream, dream, dream, and absolutely ignore homage that would turn another girl's head. I wish she were well married, or--I had almost said ill married! anything is better than the convent for my only surviving child! If she will not accept an earl or a baronet, why cannot her perversity take the form of any other girl's perversity? Why can she not fall in love with some penniless younger son, or some dissipated captain in a marching regiment? I am sure even under such circumstances I should not perform the part of the 'cruel parent' in the comedies! I should say, 'Bless you my children,' with all my heart! And I should enrich the impecunious young son, or reform the tipsy soldier. Anything but the convent for my only child!" concluded the banker, with a sigh.

But Salome had ceased to think of the convent. She thought now only of the missing marquis.

The offers of marriage that had been made to Salome, rejected though they were, had this good effect upon her mind. They encouraged her to think more hopefully of herself. Salome was too unworldly, too pure, and holy, to suspect that these offers had been made her from any other motive than personal preference. It was possible, then, that she might be loved. If other men preferred her, so also might he on whom she had fixed. And now it had come to this with the dreaming girl--she resolved to think no more of retiring to a convent, but to live in the world that contained her hero; to keep herself free from all engagements for his sake, to give *herself* to him, if possible, if not to give his land back to him some day, at least. So in her secret soul she consecrated herself in a pure devotion to a man she had never seen, and who did not even know of her existence.

When Parliament rose at the end of the London season, Sir Lemuel Levison took his daughter on an extended Continental tour, showing her all the wonders of nature, and all the glories of art in countries and cities. And Salome was interested and instructed, of course. Yet the greatest value her travels had for her was in the possibility of their bringing her to a meeting with the missing heir. It had been said that the mad duke and his son were somewhere on the Continent. A wide field! Yet, on the arrival of Sir Lemuel and Miss Levison at any city, Salome's first thought was this:

"Perhaps they are living here, and I shall see him."

But she was always disappointed. And at the end of a seven months' sojourn on the Continent, Sir Lemuel Levison brought his daughter back to London, only in time for the meeting of Parliament.

Only two years of Salome's probation was left--only two more seasons in London. Her father's anxiety increased.

He sent for her chaperone again, and opened his house in Westbourne Terrace to all the world of fashion. Again the young heiress was followed, flattered, feted as much as if she had been a beauty as well. Again she received and rejected several eligible offers of marriage. And so the second season passed.

Sir Lemuel Levison took his daughter to Scotland, and invited a large company to stay with them at Lone, thinking that, after all, more matches were made in the close daily intercourse of a country house, than in the crowded ball-rooms of a London season.

But though the banker's daughter received two or three more eligible offers of marriage, she politely declined them all, and stole away as often as she could to worship the pictured image in the old tower.

Her chaperone was in despair.

"How many good men and brave has she refused, do you know, Lemuel?" inquired Lady Belgrade.

"Seven, to my certain knowledge," angrily replied the banker.

"Perhaps she likes some one you know nothing about," suggested the dowager.

"She does not; I would let her marry almost any man rather than have her enter a convent, as she is sure to do when she is of age. I would let her marry any one; aye, even Johnnie Scott, who is the most worthless scamp I know in the world."

"And pray who is Johnnie Scott!"

"Oh, a handsome rascal; is sort of kinsman and hanger-on of the young Marquis of Arondelle; he used to be. I don't know anything more about him."

"Perhaps he *is* the man."

"Oh, no, he is not. There is no man in the convent. Well, we go up to London again in February. It will be her last season. If she does not fall in love or marry before May, when she will be twenty-one years of age, she will immure herself in a convent, as I am pledged not to prevent her."

The conversation ended unsatisfactorily just here.

In the beginning of February Sir Lemuel Levison, with his daughter and her chaperone, went up to London for her third season. They established themselves again in the sumptuous house on Westbourne Terrace, and again entered into the whirl of fashionable gayeties.

It was quite in the beginning of the season that Sir Lemuel and Miss Levison received invitations to a dinner party at the Premier's.

It was to be a semi-political dinner, at which were to be entertained certain ministers, members of Parliament, with their wives, and leading journalists.

Sir Lemuel accepted for himself and Miss Levison. On the appointed day they rendered themselves at the Premier's house, where they were courteously welcomed by the great minister and his accomplished wife.

After the usual greetings had been exchanged with the guests that were present, and while Sir Lemuel and Miss Levison were conversing with their hostess, the Premier came up with a stranger on his right arm.

Salome looked up, her heart gave a great bound and then stood still.

The original of the portrait in the tower, the self-devoted son, the self-exiled heir, the idol of her pure worship, the young Marquis of Arondelle stood before her.

And while the scene swam before her eyes, the Premier bowed, and presenting him, said:

"Sir Lemuel, let me introduce to you, Mr. John Scott of the **National Liberator**. Mr. Scott, Sir Lemuel Levison, our new member for Lone."

Mr. John Scott!

CHAPTER III.
THE RUINED HEIR.

Where, meanwhile, was the "mad" duke with his loyal son?

Various reports had been circulated concerning them, so long as they had been remembered. Some had said that they had emigrated to Australia; others that they had gone to Canada; others again that they were living on the Continent. All agreed that wherever they were, they must be in great destitution.

But now, three years had passed since the fall of Lone and the disappearance of the ruined ducal family, and they were very nearly forgotten.

Meanwhile where were they then?

They were hidden in the great wilderness of London.

On leaving Lone, the stricken duke, crushed equally under domestic affliction and financial ruin, and failing both in mind and body, started for London, tenderly escorted by his son.

It was the last extravagance of the young marquis to engage a whole compartment in a first-class carriage on the Great Northern Railway train, that the fallen and humbled duke might travel comfortably and privately without being subjected to annoyance by the gaze of the curious, or comments of the thoughtless.

On reaching London they went first to an obscure but respectable inn in a borough, where they remained unknown for a few days, while the marquis sought for lodgings which should combine privacy, decency and cheapness, in some densely-populated, unfashionable quarter of the city, where their identity would be lost in the crowd, and where they would never by any chance meet any one whom they had ever met before.

They found such a refuge at length, in a lodging-house kept by the widow of a curate in Catharine street, Strand.

Here the ruined duke and marquis dropped their titles, and lived only under their baptismal name and family names.

Here Archibald-Alexander-John Scott, Duke of Hereward and Marquis of Arondelle in the Peerage of England, and Baron Lone, of Lone, in the Peerage of

Scotland, was known only as old Mr. Scott.

And his son Archibald-Alexander-John Scott, by courtesy Marquis of Aron-delle, was known only as young Mr. John Scott.

Now as there were probably some thousands of "Scotts," and among them, some hundreds of "John Scotts," in all ranks of life, from the old landed proprietor with his town-house in Belgravia, to the poor coster-monger with his donkey-cart in Covent Garden, in this great city of London, there was little danger that the real rank of these ruined noblemen should be suspected, and no possibility that they should be recognized and identified. They were as completely lost to their old world as though they had been hidden in the Australian bush or New Zealand forests.

Here as Mr. Scott and Mr. John Scott, they lived three years.

The old duke, overwhelmed by his family calamity, gradually sank deeper and deeper into mental and bodily imbecility.

Here the young marquis picked up a scanty living for himself and father by contributing short articles to the columns of the *National Liberator*, the great or-gan of the Reform Party.

He wrote under the name of "Justus." After a few months his articles began to attract attention for their originality of thought, boldness of utterance, and bril-liancy of style.

Much speculation was on foot in political and journalistic circles as to the au-thor of the articles signed "Justus." But his incognito was respected.

At length on a notable occasion, the gifted young journalist was requested by the publisher of the *National Liberator*, to write a leader on a certain Reform Bill then up before the House of Commons.

This work was so congenial to the principles and sentiments of the author, that it became a labor of love, and was performed, as all such labors should be, with all the strength of his intellect and affections.

This leader made the anonymous writer famous in a day. He at once became the theme of all the political and newspaper clubs.

And now a grand honor came to him.

The Premier--no less a person--sent his private secretary to the office of the *Na-tional Liberator* to inquire the name and address of the author of the articles by "Justus," with a request to be informed of them if there should be no objection on the part of author or publisher.

The private secretary was told, with the consent of the author, what the name and address was.

"Mr. John Scott, office of the *National Liberator*."

Upon receiving this information, the Premier addressed a note to the young journalist, speaking in high terms of his leader on the Reform Bill, predicting for him a brilliant career, and requesting the writer to call on the minister at noon the following day.

The young marquis was quite as much pleased at this distinguished recognition of his genius as any other aspiring young journalist might have been.

He wrote and accepted the invitation.

And at the appointed hour the next day he presented himself at Elmhurst House, the Premier's residence at Kensington.

He sent up his card, bearing the plain name:

"Mr. John Scott."

He was promptly shown up stairs to a handsome library, where he found the great statesman among his books and papers.

His lordship arose and received his visitor with much cordiality, and invited him to be seated.

And during the interview that followed it would have been difficult to decide who was the best pleased--the great minister with this young disciple of his school, or the new journalist with this illustrious head of his party.

This agreeable meeting was succeeded by others.

At length the young journalist was invited to a sort of semi-political dinner at Elmhurst House, to meet certain eminent members of the reform party.

This invitation pleased the marquis. It would give him the opportunity of meeting men whom he really wished to know. He thought he might accept it and go to the dinner as plain Mr. John Scott, of the *National Liberator*, without danger of being recognized as the Marquis of Arondelle.

For in the days of his family's prosperity he had been too young to enter London society.

And in these days of his adversity he was known to but a limited number of individuals in the city, and only by his common family name.

On the appointed evening, therefore, he put on his well-brushed dress-suit, spotless linen, and fresh gloves, and presented himself at Elmhurst House as well dressed as any West End noble or city nabob there.

He was shown up to the drawing-room by the attentive footman, who opened the door, and announced:

"Mr. John Scott."

And the young Marquis of Arondelle entered the room, where a brilliant little company of about half a dozen gentlemen and as many ladies were assembled.

The noble host came forward to welcome the new guest. His lordship met him with much cordiality, and immediately presented him to Lady ----, who received him with the graceful and gracious courtesy for which she was so well known.

Finally the minister took the young journalist across the room toward a very tall, thin, fair-skinned, gray-haired old gentleman, who stood with a pale, dark-eyed, richly-dressed young girl by his side.

They were standing for the moment, with their backs to the company, and were critically examining a picture on the wall--a master-piece of one of the old Italian painters.

"Sir Lemuel," said the host, lightly touching the art-critic on the shoulder.

The old gentleman turned around.

"Sir Lemuel, permit me to present to you Mr. John Jones--I beg pardon--Mr. John Scott, of the **National Liberator**--Mr. Scott, Sir Lemuel Levison, our member for Lone," said the minister.

Sir Lemuel Levison saw before him the young Marquis of Arondelle, whom he had know as a boy and young man for years in the Highlands, and of whom, indeed, he had purchased his life interest in Lone. But he gave no sign of this recognition.

The young marquis, on his part, had every reason to know the man who had succeeded, not to say supplanted, his father at Lone Castle. But by no sign did he betray this knowledge.

The recognition was mutual, instantaneous and complete. Yet both were gravely self-possessed, and addressed each other as if they had never met before.

Then the banker called the attention of the young lady by his side:

"My daughter."

She raised her eyes and saw before her the idol of her secret worship, knowing him by his portrait at Lone. She paled and flushed, while her father, with old-fashioned formality, was saying:

"My daughter, let me introduce to your acquaintance, Mr. John Scott of the *National Liberator*. You have read and admired his articles under the signature of Justus, you know!--Mr. Scott, my daughter, Miss Levison."

Both bowed gravely, and as they looked up their eyes met in one swift and swiftly withdrawn glance.

And before a word could be exchanged between them the doors were thrown open and the butler announced:

"My lady is served."

"Sir Lemuel, will you give your arm to Lady ----, and allow me to take Miss Levison in to dinner?" said the noble host, drawing the young lady's hand within his arm.

"Mr. John Scott" took in Lady Belgrave.

At dinner Miss Levison found herself seated nearly opposite to the young marquis. She could not watch him, she could not even lift her eyes to his face, but she could not chose but listen to every syllable that fell from his lips. It was the cue of some of the leading politicians present to draw out this young apostle of the reform cause. And of course they proceeded to do it.

The young journalist, modest and reserved at first, as became a disciple in the presence of the leaders of the great cause, gradually grew more communicative, then animated, then eloquent.

Among his hearers, none listened with a deeper interest than Salome Levison. Although he did not address one syllable of his conversation to her, nor cast one glance of his eyes upon her, yet she hung upon his words as though they had been the oracles of a prophet.

If the high ideal honor and reverence in which she held him, could have been increased by any circumstance, it must have been from the sentiments expressed, the principles declared in his discourse.

She saw before her, not only the loyal son, who had sacrificed himself to save his father, but she saw also in him the reformer, enlightener, educator and benefactor of his race and age.

Of all the men she had met in the great world of society, during the three years that she had been "out," she had not found his equal, either in manly beauty and dignity, or in moral and intellectual excellence.

His brow needs no ducal coronet to ennoble it! *His* name needs no title to illustrate it. The "princely Hereward!" "If all the men of his race resembled him, they well deserved this popular soubriquet. And whether this gentleman calls himself Mr. Scott or Lord Arondelle, I shall think of him only as the 'princely Hereward.'" mused Salome, as she sat and listened to the music of his voice, and the wisdom of his words.

She was sorry when their hostess gave the signal for the ladies to rise from the table and leave the gentlemen to their wine.

They went into the drawing-room, where the conversation turned upon the subject of the brilliant young journalist. No one knew who he was. Scott, though a very good name, was such a common one! But the noble host's endorsement was certainly enough to pass this gifted young gentleman in any society. The ladies talked of nothing but Mr. Scott, and his perfection of person, manner and conversation, until the entrance of the gentlemen from the dining-room.

The host and the member for Lone came in arm in arm, and a little in the rear of the other guests, and lingered behind them.

"This most extraordinary young man, this Mr. Scott--you have known him some time, my lord?" said Sir Lemuel Levison, in a low tone.

"Ay, probably as long as you have, Sir Lemuel," replied the Premier, with a peculiarly intelligent smile.

"Ah, yes! I see! Your lordship has possibly detected my recognition of this young gentleman," said Sir Lemuel.

"Of course. And I, on my part, knew him when I first saw him again after some years."

"His name was common enough to escape detection."

"Yes, but his face was not, my dear sir. The profile of the 'princely Hereward' could never be mistaken. Our first meeting was purely accidental. He was pointed out to me one evening at a public meeting, as the 'Justus' of the *National Liberator*.' I looked and recognized the Marquis of Arondelle. Nothing surprises or *should* surprise a middle-aged man. Therefore, I was not in the least degree moved by what I had discovered. I sent, however, to the office of the *Liberator* to inquire the address, not of the Marquis of Arondelle, but of the writer, under the signature of 'Justus.' Received for answer that it was Mr. John Scott, office of the *Liberator*. I wrote to Mr. John Scott, and invited him to call on me. That was the beginning of my more recent acquaintance with this gifted young gentleman. Why he has chosen to drop his title I cannot know. He has every right to be called by his family name, only, if he so pleases. And, Sir Lemuel, we must regard his pleasure in this matter. Not even to my wife have I betrayed him," said the Premier, as they passed into the drawing-room.

"Umph, umph, umph," grunted the banker, who, surfeited with wealth though he was, could think of but one cause to every evil in the world, and that the want of money, and of but one remedy for that evil, and that was--plenty of money. "Umph, umph, umph! It is his poverty has made him drop the title that he cannot support. If he would only marry my girl now, it would all come right."

The entrance of the tea-service occupied the guests for the next half hour, at the end of which the little company broke up and took leave.

Salome Levison went home more thoughtful and dreamy than ever before--more out of favor with herself, more in love with her "paladin," more resolved never to marry any man except he should be John Scott, Marquis of Arondelle.

She almost loathed the hollow world of fashion in which she lived. Yet she went more into society than ever, though she enjoyed it so much less. She had a powerful motive for doing so. She attended all the balls, parties, dinners, concerts, plays, and operas to which she was invited, only with the hope of meeting again with him whose image had never left her heart since it first met her vision.

But she never was gratified. She never saw him again in society. John Scott was unknown to the world of fashion.

The season drew to its close. Constant going out, day after day, and night after night, would have weakened much stronger health than that possessed by Salome Levison. And, when added to this was constant longing expectation, and constant sickening disappointment, we cannot wonder that our pale heroine grew paler still.

Her chaperone declared herself "worn out" and unable to continue her arduous duties much longer.

Sir Lemuel Levison was puzzled and anxious.

"I cannot see what has come to my girl! She goes out all the time; she accepts every invitation; gives herself no rest; yet never seems to enjoy herself anywhere. She grows paler and thinner every day, and there is a hectic spot on her cheeks and a feverish brightness in her eyes that I do not like at all. I have seen them before, and I have too much reason to know them! I do believe she is fretting herself into a decline for her convent. I do believe she only goes out as a sort of penance for her imaginary sins! Poor child! I must really have a talk and come to an understanding with her!" said the anxious father to himself, as he mused on the condition of his daughter.

CHAPTER IV.
SALOME'S CHOICE.

Sir Lemuel Levison was taking his breakfast in bed. The London season was near its close. Parliament sat late at night, and often all night. Sir Lemuel, a punctual and diligent member of the House, seldom returned home before the early dawn.

So Sir Lemuel was taking his breakfast in bed, and "small blame to him."

It was a very simple breakfast of black tea, dry toast, fresh eggs, and cold ham.

"Take these things away now, Potts. Go and find Miss Levison's maid, and tell her to let her mistress know that I wish to see my daughter here, before she goes out," said the banker, as he drained and set down his tea-cup.

"Yes, Sir Lemuel," respectfully answered the servant, as he lifted the breakfast tray and bore it off.

"Umph! that is the manner in which I have to manoeuvre for an interview with my own daughter, before I can get one," grumbled the banker, as he lay back on his pillow and took up a newspaper from the counter-pane.

Before he had time to read the morning's report of the night's doings at the House, Salome entered the room.

The banker darted a swift keen look at her, that took in her whole aspect at a glance.

She was dressed for a drive. She wore a simple suit of rich brown silk, with hat, vail and gloves to match, white linen collar and cuffs, and crimson ribbon bow on her bosom, and a crimson rose in her hat. Her face was pale and clear, but so thin that her broad, fair forehead looked too broad beneath its soft waves of dark hair, and her deep gray eyes seemed too large and bright under their arched black eye-brows.

"You wished to see me, dear papa?" she said, gently.

"Yes, my love. But--you are going out? Of course you are. You are always going out, when you are not gone. I hope, however, that I have not interfered with any very important engagement of yours, my dear?" said the banker, half impatiently, half affectionately.

"Oh, no, papa, love! I was only going with Lady Belgrade to a flower-show at the Crystal Palace. I will give it up very willingly if you wish me to do so," said Salome, gently, stooping and pressing her lips to his, and then seating herself on the side of his bed.

"I do not wish you to do so, my child. I shall be going out myself in a couple of hours. But I want to have a little conversation with you. I suppose a few minutes more or less will make no difference in your enjoyment of the flower-show."

"None whatever, papa, dear."

"Humph! Salome, now that I look at you well, I do not believe you care a penny for the flower-show. Come, tell me the truth, girl. Do you care one penny to go to the flower-show?" he inquired, looking keenly into her pensive face.

"No, papa, dear," she answered, in a very low tone.

"Humph! I thought not. Now do you care for **any** of the shows, plays, balls, and other tom-fooleries that occupy you day and night? I pause for a reply, my daughter."

"No, papa, I do not," she answered, in a still lower tone.

"Then why the deuce do you go to them?" demanded the banker.

His daughter's soft, gray eyes sank beneath his scrutinizing gaze, but she did not answer. How **could** she confess that she went out into company daily and nightly only in the hope of seeing again the one man to whom she had given her unsought heart, and for whose presence her very soul seemed famishing.

"What is it that you **do** care for, then, Salome?" demanded her father, varying his question.

Her head sank upon her bosom, but still she did not answer. How could she tell him that she cared only for a man who did not care for her.

"This is unbearable!" burst forth the banker. "Here you are with every indulgence that affection can yield you, every luxury that money can give you, and yet you are not well nor content. What ails you girl? Are you pining after your convent? Set fire to it. Are you pining after your convent, I ask you, Salome?"

"Indeed, **no**, papa!"

"What!" demanded her father, starting up at her reply and gazing with doubt into her pale, earnest face.

"I am not thinking of the convent, dear papa. Indeed I had forgotten all about it. If it will give you any pleasure to hear it, dear papa, let me tell you that I have quite given up all ideas of entering a convent," added Salome, with a pensive smile.

"What!" exclaimed the banker, starting up in a sitting position and bending toward his daughter as if in doubt whether to gaze her through and through or to catch her to his heart.

She met that look and understood her father's love for his only child, and reproached herself for having been so blind to it for these three years past.

"Dearest papa," she said, with tender earnestness, "I have no longer the slightest wish or intention of ever entering a convent. And I wonder now how I ever could have been so insane as to think I could live all my life contentedly in a convent, or so selfish as to forget that by doing so I should leave my father alone in the world!"

"My darling child! Is this truly so? Are these really your thoughts?" exclaimed the banker, with such a look of delight as Salome had not believed possible in so aged a face.

"Really and truly, my father! And does it give you so much pleasure?"

"Pleasure my daughter! It gives me the greatest joy! Hand me my dressing-gown, my dear. I must get up. I cannot lie here any longer. You have put new life into me!"

Salome handed him his gown, socks, and slippers, and then went to clear off his big easy-chair, which was burdened with his yesterday's dress suit, and draw it up for his use.

And in a few minutes the banker, wrapped in his gown, with his feet in his slippers, was seated comfortably in his arm-chair.

"Now, shall I ring for Potts, papa, dear?" inquired Salome.

"No, my love, I don't want Potts, I want you. Sit down near me, Salome, and listen to me. You have made me very happy this morning, my darling; and now I wish to make you happy; you are not so now; but I am your father; you are my only child; all that I have will be yours; but in the meantime, you are not happy. What can I do, my beloved child, to make you so?" said the banker, drawing her to his side and kissing her tenderly, and then releasing her.

"Papa, dear, I should be a most ungrateful daughter if I were not happy," answered the girl.

"Then you *are* a very thankless child, my little Salome, for you are very far from happy," said her father, gravely shaking his head, yet looking so tenderly upon her as to take all rebuke from his words.

Salome dropped her eyes under his searching, loving gaze.

"My child, I know that I have the power to bless you, if you will only tell me how. Tell me, my dear," persisted her father.

But still she dropped her eyes and hung her head.

"If your mother were here, you could confide in her. You cannot confide in your father, my poor, motherless girl, and he cannot blame you," said Sir Lemuel, sadly.

"Father, dear father, I *do* love you; and I will confide in you," said Salome, earnestly.

For just then a mighty power of faith and love arose in her soul, casting out fear, casting out doubt, subduing pride and reserve.

"What is it, then, my love? Have you formed any attachment of which you have hesitated to tell me? Hesitate no longer, my dearest Salome. Tell me all about it. It is nothing to be ashamed of. Love is natural. Love is holy. Oh, it is your mother that should be telling you all this, my poor girl, not your awkward, blundering old father," suddenly said the banker, breaking off in his discourse as his daughter hid her crimson face upon his shoulder.

"My dear, gentle father, no mother could be tenderer than you," murmured Salome.

"Tell me all, then, my darling. It is the first wish of my heart to see you happily married. And no trifling obstacle shall stand in the way of its accomplishment. *Who is he, Salome?*" he inquired, in a low whisper, as he passed his hand around her neck.

She did not answer, but she kissed and fondled his hand.

"You cannot bring yourself to tell me yet? Well, take your own time, my love. You will tell me some time or another," he continued, returning her soft caresses.

"Yes, I will tell you sometime, dear, good, tender father. But now--when do we leave town papa?"

"In less than three weeks, my dear."

"And where do we go?"

"To Lone Castle, if you like; if not, anywhere you prefer, my dear."

"Then we *will* go to Lone, if you please, papa."

"Certainly, my dear."

"Papa?"

"Yes, love."

"Will you do something for me before we leave town?"

"I will do anything on earth that you wish me to do for you, my dear," said the banker, looking anxiously toward her.

She hesitated for a few moments, and then said:

"Papa, I want you to give just such a semi-political dinner party as that given by the Premier in the beginning of the season."

"What! my little, pale Salome taking an interest in politics!" exclaimed the banker, in droll surprise.

"Yes, papa; and turning politician on a small, womanish scale. You will give this semi-political dinner?"

"Why of course I will! Whom shall we invite?"

"Papa, the very same party to a man, whom we met at the Premier's dinner."

"Let me see. Who was there? Oh! there were three members of Parliament and their wives; two city magnates and their daughters; you and myself, Lady Belgrade, and--and the Marquis of--John--Mr. John Scott, I mean."

"Yes, papa, that was the company. Send the invitations out to-day, for this day week please--if no engagement intervenes to prevent you."

"Very well, my dear. You see to it. I leave it all in your hands. Now you may ring for Potts, my dear. I have to dress and go down to the House. I am chairman of a committee there, that meets at two. And you, my love, must be off to your flower-show. You must not keep Lady Belgrade waiting."

Salome touched the bell, and on the entrance of the valet, she kissed her father's hand and retired.

"Now I wonder," mused the old gentleman, "who it is she wants to meet again, out of that dinner company? It cannot be either of the old M.P.'s or their wives; nor the two elderly city magnates, or their tall daughters; that disposes of ten out of the fourteen invited guests. The remainder included Lady Belgrade, myself, Salome herself, and--Lord, bless my soul, alive!" burst forth the banker, with such a start, that his valet, who was brushing his hair, begged his pardon, and said that he did not mean it.

"Lord, bless my soul alive," mentally continued the banker, without paying the slightest attention to the apologizing servant. "The Marquis of Arondelle! He was the fourteenth guest, and the only young man present! And upon my word and honor, the very handsomest and most attractive young fellow I ever saw in all the days of my life! Come!" he added to himself, as the full revelation of the truth burst upon his mind; "*that* can be easily enough arranged. If he is the sensible, practical man I take him to be, he will get back his estates and the very best little wife that ever was wed into the bargain; and my girl will be a marchioness, and in time a duchess. But stay--what is that I heard up at Lone about the young marquis and a handsome shepherdess? Chut! what is that to us? That is probably a slander. The marquis is a noble young fellow; and I will bring him home with me this evening. I will not wait a week until that dinner comes off. We cannot afford to lose so much time at the end of the season," mused the banker, through all the time his valet was dressing him.

And now we must glance back to that evening when John Scott, Marquis of Arondelle, first met Salome Levison. He had met many statuesque, pink and white beauties in his young life; and he had admired each and all with all a young man's ardor. But not one of them had touched his heart, as did the first full gaze of those large, soft gray eyes that were lifted to his and immediately dropped as the old banker had presented him to--

"My daughter, Miss Levison."

She was not statuesque. She was not pink and white. She was not at all handsome, or even pretty; yet something in the pale, sweet, earnest face, something in the soft clear gray eyes touched his heart even before he was presented to her. But when she lifted those eloquent eyes to his face, there was such a world of sympathy, appreciation and devotion in their swift and swiftly-withdrawn gaze, that her soul seemed then and there to reveal itself to his soul.

He never again met the full gaze of those spirit eyes. He never exchanged a word with her after the first few formal words of greeting. He had only bowed to her, in taking leave that evening.

Yet those eyes had haunted him in their meek appealing tenderness ever since. He did not meet her anywhere by accident, and he did not try to meet her by design. He only thought of her constantly. But what had he to do with the banker's wealthy heiress, the future mistress of Lone? If he were so unwise as to seek her acquaintance, the world would be quick to ascribe the most mercenary motives to his conduct. But like weaker minded lovers, he comforted himself by writing such transcendental poetry as "The Soul's Recognition," "The Meeting of the Spirits," "What Those Eyes Said," etc. He did not publish these. After having relieved his mind of them, he put them away to keep in his portfolio. So you see the handsome, "princely" Hereward was as much in love with our pale, gray-eyed girl as She could possibly be with him.

And so with the young marquis also the season passed slowly and heavily away, until the day came when into his den at the office of the *Liberator* walked Sir Lemuel Levison.

His heart really beat faster, although it was only her father who entered.

He arose, and placed a chair for his visitor.

"Lord Arondelle, you **know** I knew you when I met you at Lord P.'s dinner-party, and I saw that you knew me. It was not my business to interfere with your incognito, and so I met you as you met me--as a stranger. But surely here and now we may meet as friends without disguise," said the banker, as he slowly sank into his seat.

"We must do so, Sir Lemuel, since we are *tete-a-tete*. It would be idle and useless to do otherwise," replied the young marquis, courteously.

"And now, my young friend, you are wondering what has brought me here," continued the banker.

"I am at least most grateful to any circumstance that gives me the pleasure of your company, Sir Lemuel," courteously replied the young marquis.

"Well, my lord, I come to beg you to waive ceremony, and go home with me to dinner this evening. I hope you have no engagement to prevent you from coming," added Sir Lemuel, with more earnestness than the occasion seemed to call for.

"I have no engagement to prevent me," answered the young man frankly, but slowly and thoughtfully, for he was wondering not only at the invitation but at the suddenness and earnestness with which it was given.

"Then I *hope* you will come?" said the banker.

"You are very kind, Sir Lemuel. Yes, thanks, I will come," said the marquis.

"So happy! Will you allow me to call for you--at--at your lodgings?"

"Thanks, Sir Lemuel, if you will kindly call *here* at your own hour, it will be more directly in your way home, and you will find me ready to accompany you."

"Quite right. I will be here at seven. Good morning."

And with this the banker went away.

"He wants me to make an article about something, I suppose," mused the young man when the elder had gone. "I will go. I will see that sweet girl again, even if I never see her afterwards."

The temptation was certainly very strong. And so, at the appointed hour, when the banker called at the office of the *National Liberator* he found the young gentleman in evening dress ready to accompany him home.

Salome Levison was dressed for dinner, and seated in the drawing-room with her chaperone, Lady Belgrade.

Salome was certainly not expecting any guest. But she intended to go to the opera that evening with Lady Belgrade, to hear the last act of Norma. Luckily for Sir Lemuel's plan, it was not a peremptory engagement, and could easily be set aside.

On this evening she was beautifully dressed. She wore a delicate tea-rose tinted rich silk skirt, with an over skirt of point lace, looped up with tea-rose buds, a tea-rose in her dark hair, a necklace of opals set in diamonds, and bracelets of the same beautiful jewels. Refined, elegant, and most interesting she certainly looked.

Meanwhile, the banker came home, and himself conducted the unexpected guest to the drawing-room.

"Mr. John Scott, my dear," said Sir Lemuel, bringing the young gentleman up to his daughter.

The young marquis caught the sudden lighting up of those soft, gray eyes, and the sudden flushing of those delicate cheeks.

It was but for an instant; for even as he bowed before her, her eyes fell and her color faded.

It was but for an instant, yet in that glance those eyes had again revealed her soul to his.

The young marquis was not a vain man. He could not at once believe the evidence of his own consciousness. But he found it rather more awkward to sit down and open a conversation with this pale, shy girl, than he ever had in his palmiest days to make himself agreeable to the brightest beauty that ever honored Castle Lone with a visit.

For once the presence of a chaperone was not unwelcome to a pair of young people secretly in love with each other.

Lady Belgrade chattered of the weather, the opera the park, and what not, and relieved the embarrassment of the lovers during the interval in which Sir Lemuel Levison had gone to change his dress.

The young marquis seldom spoke to Salome, but when he did, his voice sank to a low, tender, reverential tone that thrilled her inmost spirit. She replied to him only in soft monosyllables, but her drooping eyelids, and kindling cheeks, told him all he wished to know. He might have wondered more at the interest he had seemed to excite in a girl he had met but once before, had he not had a corresponding experience himself. He knew that he himself had been deeply impressed by this sweet, shy, pale girl, on the first meeting of her soft gray eyes, with their soul of love shining through them.

He did not know that this "soul of love" had first been awakened in her, by hearing his story and seeing his portrait, and that it was which so powerfully attracted him--for love creates love.

Sir Lemuel Levison hurried over his toilet, and soon entered the drawing-room.

Dinner was immediately announced.

"Mr. Scott, will you take my daughter to the table?" said the banker, as he gave his own arm to Lady Belgrade.

It was an elegant little dinner for four, arranged upon a round table. There was no possibility of estrangement, in so small a party as that.

Sir Lemuel talked gayly, and without effort, for he was very happy. Lady Belgrade chattered, because she was spiritually a magpie. And as both constantly appealed to "Mr. Scott," or to Salome, it was impossible for either of the lovers to relapse into awkward silence. The conversation was general and lively.

Sir Lemuel Levison and Lady Belgrade would have talked in the most flattering manner of "Mr. Scott's" leaders, if that young gentleman had not laughingly waived off all such direct compliments.

When dinner was over, Lady Belgrade gave the signal, and arose from the table. Salome followed her, and left the two gentlemen to their wine.

"It afflicts me to have to call you Mr. Scott, my lord," said Sir Lemuel, when he found himself alone with his guest.

"Then call me John, as you used to do when I rode upon your foot in my childhood, and when I used to come to you in all my worst scrapes in boyhood--I shall never resume my title, Sir Lemuel," replied the young man.

"Never!" exclaimed the banker.

"Never, Sir Lemuel. A pauper lord is rather a ridiculous object. I will never be one."

"You **could** not be one. I won't hear you say such things about yourself. See here, John. Do you know why I bought Lone when I knew it was to be sold?"

"I suppose because you wanted it."

"Now what did I want with Lone? I, an old widower, without family, except one little girl at school? I did not want Lone. I wanted you to have it. But I knew that if I did not buy it some one else would. And--I had this only daughter, who would have Lone after me. And I thought perhaps--But then you disappeared, you know, and no one on earth could tell for three years what had become of you, when you suddenly turned up as Mr. John Scott at the Premier's dinner."

The banker paused, and ran his hand through his gray hair.

The young man looked at him with curiosity and interest.

"Plague take it all! her mother, if she has one, could manage this matter so much better than I can," muttered the banker, as he poured out a glass of wine and drank it. "Well, Lord Arondelle--I will give myself the pleasure of calling you so while we are **tete-a-tete** 'over the walnuts and wine.' Lord Arondelle, there is my daughter;

what do you think of her?" he demanded, bending down his gray brows and fixing his keen blue eyes scrutinizingly upon the young man's face which flushed at the suddenness of the question. But he quickly recovered himself, and replied in a low, reverent tone:

"I think Miss Levison the loveliest young creature I have ever had the happiness to know."

"You do! So do *I*! I think so too. And the man who gets my girl to wife will get a pearl of price."

"I truly believe that," said the young man, with an involuntary sigh.

"That is right! Ahem! Bother it! a woman could do this so much better than such a blundering old fellow as I! Well, there! Salome has, in the three years since her first entrance into society, refused half a score of eligible men. She is, and always has been, perfectly free from any such engagement. If you are equally free, my dear marquis--(If I could only be her mother for three seconds)--Ahem! if you are equally free, and if you admire my girl as you say you do, and if you can win her affections--she--she shall be yours, and I will settle Lone upon her. There, her mother would have done this better, I know. So much better that you would have proposed to my daughter without ever dreaming that the suggestion came from our side. But as for me, I have flung my girl at your head, nothing less!" grumbled the banker.

"My dear Sir Lemuel," said the young man, with some emotion, as he left his seat and came and stood by the banker's chair, leaning affectionately over him; "when I first met your lovely daughter, I was so deeply impressed by her rare sweetness, gentleness, intelligence--ah! Heaven knows what it was! It was something more than all these. In a word, I was so deeply impressed by her perfect loveliness, that had I been as really the heir of Lone as I was the Marquis of Arondelle, I should at once have cultivated her further acquaintance, and, before this, have laid my heart and hand, titles and estates, at her feet."

"Well, well, my boy? Well, my dear lad, why didn't you do it?" inquired the banker, with tears rising to his kind eyes.

"I have just told you, because I was a ruined man," said the marquis with mournful dignity.

"'A ruined man?'" echoed the banker, with almost angry earnestness. "*I* know that you are ***not*** a ruined man! And you know, even better than I do, because you have more brains than I have; YOU know that no young man, sound in body and sound in mind, can be ruined by any financial calamity that can fall upon him. You love my daughter, you say. Well, then, you have my authority to ask her to be your wife. There, what do you say?"

The young marquis sat down and covered his face with his hand for one thoughtful moment, and then replied:

"This is a happiness so unexpected that it seems unreal. Sir Lemuel, do you really appreciate the fact that I am a man without a shilling that I do not earn by my labor?"

"I really appreciate the fact, and most highly appreciate the fact that you are Marquis of Arondelle, and to be Duke of Hereward--and that you are personally as noble in nature as you are fortunately noble in descent. And although my first motive in favoring this marriage is the pure desire for yours and for my daughter's happiness, still I assure you, my lord, I am keenly alive to its eligibility in a mere worldly point of view. Your ancient historical title is, (to speak as a man of the world,) much more than an equivalent for my daughter's expectations. But it is not, as I said before, as a highly eligible, conventional marriage that I most desire it, but as a marriage that I feel sure will secure the happiness of yourself and my daughter, whom I shall, nevertheless, be very proud to see, some day, Duchess of Hereward. Come, now, I never saw a gallant young man hesitate so long. I shall grow angry presently."

"Sir Lemuel," said the marquis, with some irrepressible emotion, "were I now really the Duke of Hereward, and the owner of Lone, and were your lovely daughter as dowerless as I am penniless at this moment, and did you give her to me, my deepest gratitude would be due you, and you have it now. When may I see Miss Levison and put my fate to the test?"

"That's right. Upon my word, my boy, if I were a galvanic foreigner instead of a staid Englishman, I should jump up and embrace you. Consider yourself embraced. When shall you see her? We will go into the dining room now and get a cup of tea from the ladies; after which, you shall see her as soon and as often as you please. And after you win her, as I am sure you will, we will have a blithe wedding and you and your bride will do the Continent for a wedding-tour, and then come back and spend the Autumn at Lone. We two old papas, the duke and myself, will join you there, and everything will be quite as it used to be in the old days."

"Ah! my poor father!" sighed the young man.

"What of the duke, my dear boy? You told me he was well," said the banker, anxiously.

"Yes, he is well in body, better in body than he has been for years; but I think that is only because his mind is failing."

"I am very sorry to hear that! In what respect does this failure show itself--in loss of memory?"

"In partial loss of memory; but chiefly in a hallucination that possesses him. He thinks that he is still the master of Lone as well as the Duke of Hereward. He thinks that he lives in London, and in the most Objectionable part of London, only to gratify my 'eccentric whim' of being a journalist. And he daily and hourly urges me to return with him to Lone!"

"In the name of Heaven, then gratify him! Take him to Lone as my guest, until you can keep him there as your own. Let him be happy in the illusion that he is still its master. I will see that the servants there, who are most of them his own old people, do not say or do anything to dispel the illusion! Come, my son-in-law, that is to be, will you take your father at once to Lone?"

For all answer the young marquis grasped and wrung the hand of his old friend.

"But will you do it?" persisted the banker, who wanted to be satisfied on that point.

"I will think of it. I will think most gratefully of your kind invitation, Sir Lemuel. And now shall we join the ladies?"

"Certainly," said the banker.

They went into the drawing-room.

Lady Belgrade was presiding over the tea urn.

Salome, who was seated near her, looked up and saw him. Again the marquis noted the sudden, beautiful lighting up of those soft, gray eyes, as they were lifted for a moment to his face. Again they fell beneath his glance, as her pale cheeks flushed up. He could not be mistaken. This sweet girl whom he loved, loved him in return.

"I was just about to send for you. You lingered long at table, Sir Lemuel," said Lady Belgrade, as the two gentlemen bowed and seated themselves.

"Oh, important political and journalistic matters to discuss," said Sir Lemuel. ("Only they were *not* discussed,") he added, mentally.

"So I supposed," said Lady Belgrade, as she handed him a cup of tea, which he immediately passed to his guest.

After tea, when the service was removed, Sir Lemuel challenged Lady Belgrade for a game of chess, and told his daughter to show Mr. Scott those chromoes of the Madonnas of Raphael which had arrived in the last parcel from Paris.

Salome flushed to the edges of her dark hair as she arose, glanced shyly at her guest for an instant, and walked to the other end of the drawing-room.

There, on a gilded stand, under a brilliant gasolier, lay a large and handsome volume, which Salome indicated as the one referred to by her father.

The marquis brought two chairs to the stand, and they sat down to go over the book.

Meanwhile, the banker and the dowager commenced their game of chess. But from time to time, each looked furtively in the direction of the young people. *They* were looking at the Madonnas of Raphael, and, once in a while, shyly into each other's eyes. All that Sir Lemuel saw there pleased him. All that Lady Belgrade saw there *dis*pleased her.

At length she put her hand over that of her antagonist, and stopped his move while she said:

"Sir Lemuel, a conflagration may be arrested by stamping out a spark of fire."

"Whatever do you mean, my lady!" inquired the perplexed banker.

"An inundation may be prevented by stopping up a small leak."

"I am more mystified than ever!"

"Look at Salome and Mr. Scott, then," said her ladyship, solemnly.

"Well, what of them? They seem to be very happy and very well pleased with each other."

"Ah! that is it, and worse may come of it."

"What worse can come of it?"

"Sir Lemuel, this Mr. Scott, you must remember, is nothing but an adventurer, who only gains an entrance into respectable circles on account of his journalistic reputation. He is probably also a pauper, but being a very handsome and attractive man, he is certainly a very dangerous, and likely to be a very successful fortune-hunter."

"You mean he may try to marry my heiress?"

"Yes, Sir Lemuel."

"He has my full consent to do so."

"Sir Lemuel!"

"Listen, my good lady, I have a secret to tell you. That gentleman whom we have known as Mr. John Scott only, is really Archibald-Alexander-John Scott, Marquis of Hereward."

A woman of the world is hardly ever "taken aback." Lady Belgrade gave no exclamation. But she caught her breath and stared at the speaker.

"It is as I have told you. He is the Marquis of Arondelle. He is going to marry my daughter. He will get back Lone through her. And she will be Marchioness of Arondelle, and in due time Duchess of Hereward."

"You--don't--say--so!" breathed her ladyship, slowly.

"And now, you know how to manage it. You must aid the young couple as much as you can by giving them as much as possible of each other's society."

"Yes, I see," said her ladyship. "And now--don't look toward them again."

The banker nodded intelligently. And they gave their attention to the game.

And the two young people seemed to find inexhaustible interest in the volume they were bending over.

It was eleven o'clock before the young marquis arose to take leave.

"I have asked Miss Levison to ride with me in the Park to-morrow, and she has kindly consented--with your approbation, Sir Lemuel," said the young man.

"Certainly, Mr. Scott. I consider horseback riding one of the most healthful of exercises," said the banker, heartily.

The young marquis then bowed and took his leave.

Lady Belgrade gathered up her embroidery work and bade them good-night.

"My girl, what do you think of Mr. Scott?" asked the banker, when he was left alone with his daughter.

"Oh, papa," she breathed in an embarrassed manner.

"Do you know who he really is, my dear?"

"Yes, papa, I knew him when I first met him at the Premier's dinner. I knew him by his portrait that I saw at Castle Lone!"

"Oh, you did!" said the banker, musing.

His daughter looked at him for a moment, and then suddenly threw herself into his arms, clasped his neck and kissed him fervently, exclaiming, with her face radiant with delight:

"Oh, papa! this is all your doing! I understand it all, dear papa! Bless you! bless you! bless you, my own, own dear papa! You have made your child so happy!"

CHAPTER V.
ARONDELLE'S CONSOLATION.

On the next day, at the appointed hour, Salome came down to the drawing-room dressed for her ride.

She wore a rich habit of dark blue summer-cloth, fastened with small gold buttons, fine, tiny white linen cuffs and collar, dark blue gloves, dark blue velvet hat with a short, white ostrich plume secured by a small gold butterfly, and she carried in her hand a slender ivory-handled riding-whip, set with a sapphire. Her dress was neat, elegant, and appropriate; and her face was for the moment radiant and beautiful from inward joy.

In due time, the young marquis presented himself, and the lovers went forth for their ride.

It is not necessary to linger over this courtship, in which "the course of true love" ran so smooth as to seem monotonous to all but the lovers themselves.

The ride was followed by the small dinner party. And after that the young marquis became a daily visitor at Elmthorpe House, where he was ever received with fatherly affection by Sir Lemuel, and with subdued delight by Salome.

The lovers had come to a mutual understanding for days before the marquis made a formal proposal for Miss Levison's hand.

But it happened one evening that they found themselves alone in the drawing-room. They were seated at a table, loaded with books of engravings, photographs, and so forth.

Salome was turning over the pages of Dore's Milton.

"Close the volume, now, Miss Levison," Lord Arondelle said at length, uttering the formal words with a tone and look of such reverential tenderness as to seem a caress.

Salome shut the book, and looked up to read the open volume of his eloquent face; but her eyes instantly sank beneath the gaze of ardent passion that met them.

"Listen to me, Salome, my beloved; for I love you, and have loved you ever since the first moment when I met the beautiful spirit beaming through your sweet eyes--'Sweetest eyes were ever seen!' Dear eyes! look on me!"

Salome, for all her profound and ardent affections, was still a very shy maiden. She wished to raise her eyes to his; she wished to pour her heart out to him; to let him have the comfort of knowing how perfectly she loved him, how utterly she was his own. But she could not look at him, she could not speak to him as yet. Her dark eyelashes drooped to her crimson cheeks.

"My beloved, do you hear me? I am telling you how I have loved you since I first met your heavenly eyes. This is no lover's rhapsody, my own, for your eyes are heavenly in their spiritual beauty. And they have haunted me, Salome, like the eyes of a guardian angel ever since they first looked upon me. Daily they would have drawn me to your side but for my wrecked and ruined state," he said, with a half suppressed sigh.

His look, his tone, and, more than all, his allusion to the calamity of his house, reached her soul, and broke the spell of reserve by which she was bound.

"Oh, do not say that you are ruined!" she cried, in a voice thrilled and thrilling with profound emotion. "Do not think that you are ruined. *You* could *never* be ruined. *Nothing* could ruin *you*. It is not in the power of fate to ruin a man like YOU. And if you loved me when you first met my eyes it was because you read in them the soul that was created yours! And if these eyes have haunted you ever since it was because this soul has been always longing, yearning, aspiring towards yours!" And she dropped her face in her hands and wept for pure joy.

"Salome, Salome, can this be indeed true? Can I have been so blessed? Am I indeed so happy? Then is this abundant compensation for all that I have lost in this world! Heavenly consolation for all I have suffered on earth! Speak again, oh, my dearest! Tell me once more, for I can scarcely realize my happiness! Speak again, beloved, for your words are life to me!" he exclaimed, with profound emotion.

"Yes, I will tell you all!" she said, wiping away her joyful tears and looking up. "I will tell you everything for it is your right! You have made me so happy to-day! I loved you from the beginning. First, I loved the magnanimous, self-sacrificing man who, at the age of twenty-one years, with a brilliant future before him, could renounce all his prospects to give peace to his father's latter years. I loved you then, Lord Arondelle, before I knew what manner of man you looked!"

"How blessed, how surely blessed I am in hearing you," he breathed, in a low and reverent tone.

"Afterward I saw your portrait in Malcolm's Tower at Lone," she continued, in a soft voice. "And I saw a beauty and a grandeur in the face and form that seemed the fitting manifestation of a soul like yours. And I loved you more than ever. My mornings were passed in the tower near the glory of that picture. But I gazed on it so hopelessly! You were missing, you were lost to your world! And then I was so plain, so pale, and dark and gray-eyed. If I should ever be so fortunate as to meet you, I thought you would never be likely to love me!"

"My consolation! You are most lovely from your spirit, and now you ***know*** that I loved you from my first meeting with you," he breathed, in a low, earnest tone, pouring his whole soul's devotion through the gaze that he fixed on her face.

Again her eyes drooped as she murmured:

"If I am lovely in the very least, it must be that my love for you has made me so; for, even then, when I had only heard your story and seen your portrait, I loved you so, that I could not think of marriage with any other man."

"And that was the reason why you refused so many excellent offers?" he inquired, with a smile.

"Perhaps that was the reason," she replied, lowly bending her head.

"Tell me more, my consolation! I thirst for your words; they are as the words of life to me," he murmured, eagerly.

She continued, still speaking in a low, thrilling voice:

"At last--at last--at last--after three long years of waiting, longing, aspiring, I met you face to face. Oh!" she exclaimed, and as she spoke her hand for the first time went out to meet his, which closed upon it with a close clasp, and her eyes lifted themselves to his in a full blaze of love that seemed to blend their spirits into one.

"Oh! if in that moment you loved me, it must have been because you read my soul, for in that moment I consecrated my life to you for acceptance or rejection. I recorded a vow in heaven to be no man's wife unless I could be yours; but to live unmarried so that when, in the course of nature, my dear father should pass to the higher life and leave me Castle Lone, I might be free to transfer it to its rightful owner."

"Ah! my beloved! you would have been capable of such an act of renunciation as that! But I could not have accepted the sacrifice, Salome."

"In that case I should have made a will and bequeathed it to you, and then prayed to the Lord to take me from the earth, that you might have it all the sooner. But let that pass. Thanks be to Heaven, there is no need of that. It would have been sweet to die for you, but it is so much sweeter to *live* for you, dearest!" she said, lifting up a face in which rosy blushes, radiant smiles, and beaming eyes were blended in dazzling beauty.

"Oh! angel of my destiny, what can I render you for all the blessings you have brought me?" exclaimed her lover, clasping her to his bosom in a close embrace.

"Your love--your love! which will crown me a queen among women!" she whispered, softly.

The morning succeeding this scene, Lord Arondelle called and asked for a private interview with Sir Lemuel Levison.

He was invited up into the library, where he found the banker alone among his books.

"Good morning, Arondelle. Glad to see you. Take this chair," said the old gentleman, rising, shaking hands with his visitor, and placing a seat for him.

The young marquis returned the hearty shake of the banker's hand, and took the offered chair.

"Now, I suppose that you have come to tell me that you have taken up the girl I flung at your head about a month ago?" said the banker, rubbing his hands.

"No, nothing of the sort," replied the young marquis, effectually declining to understand the jest of his host. "I do not remember that you ever flung any girl at my head. I came, Sir Lemuel, to tell you that I am so happy as to have won Miss Levison's consent to be my wife, if we have your approbation," he added, with a bow.

"Humph! It amounts to about the same thing. Well, my dear boy, you have my consent and blessing on two conditions."

"Name them, Sir Lemuel."

"The first is, that you can assure me on your honor that you really do love my daughter. I would not give her to an emperor who did not love her as she deserves to be loved," said the banker, emphatically.

"Love her!" repeated the young man, in a deep and earnest tone. "Love is scarcely the word, nor adoration, nor worship! She is the soul of my soul! She lives in my life, and my life is the larger, higher, holier for her!"

"Humph! I don't understand one word of what you are talking about, but I suppose it means that you really do love Salome. So the first condition will be fulfilled," said the banker, with a smile.

"And the second, sir. What is the second?"

"The second is, that the marriage shall take place within a month from this time."

"Agreed, sir. The sooner the better. The sooner I may call your lovely daughter mine, the sooner I shall be the most blessed among men," exclaimed the young marquis, earnestly clapping his palm into the open hand of the banker, and shaking it heartily.

"There! well, the second condition will be fulfilled. And now I will tell you what I never told you in so many words before, namely, that on the day Salome Levison becomes Marchioness of Arondelle, I will give her Lone as a marriage portion. There, now, not a word more upon that subject. I will send a message to my attorney to meet us here to-morrow morning," said the banker, rising and ringing the bell.

"You will let me thank--" began the marquis.

"No, I won't!" exclaimed the banker, cutting short the young gentleman's acknowledgements. "Excuse me now half a minute, I want to write a line," he added, as he hastily scribbled off a note.

A footman entered in answer to the bell.

"Take this to the office of the Messrs. Prye, Lincoln's Inn Fields, and wait an answer," said Sir Lemuel, handing the folded note to the man, who bowed and retired.

"Prye must meet us here to-morrow morning to see to the marriage settlements. And I must see to Prye! Even lawyers may be hurried if they be well paid for making haste!" concluded the banker, rubbing his hands. "But now go and find Salome, and tell her it is all right! She has not got a stern father to ruffle the course of her true love, but a spooney old fellow who spreads out his hands over your heads and says: 'Bul-less you, my chee-ild-der-en!'"

Lord Arondelle smiled at the dry banker's imitation of the heavy stage-father, but made no comment.

"Yes, go see Salome; and then go to the duke, your father, and acquaint him with the result of your proposal. I take it for granted that you had his grace's authority for making it."

"I had, sir. He told me to be guided by my own judgment."

"Well tell him all about the settlements as I have told them to you. Agree to any amendment he may propose, for I will make it all right."

"That is allowing a very large margin, indeed. I thank you, Sir Lemuel; but I must reflect before taking advantage of it."

"Well, well; perhaps the duke will meet my solicitor here to-morrow morning in regard to the settlements. I consider the fact that he has steadily declined every invitation I have sent him to come to us on any occasion. Still, I hope he may be induced to honor us with his presence to-morrow in the interest of these marriage settlements, and to remain and dine with us in honor of this betrothal," said the banker.

"I hope you will kindly continue to excuse my father, sir. His age, his infirmities, his failing mind and body, will, I trust, be his sufficient apologies," said the young marquis gravely.

"You think that he will not come, then!"

"I fear that he cannot."

"I'm sorry for that. However, tell him all that I have told you, and agree to any alterations in the settlements that he may see fit to suggest. There! Go to Salome! Go to Salome! I must be off to the House," said the conscientious M.P. rising, and putting an end to the interview.

It was subsequently arranged that the marriage should be celebrated at Castle

Lone on that day three weeks.

Two weeks out of the three, Sir Lemuel Levison remained in town to give his daughter and her chaperon an opportunity of getting up as good a trousseau as could be prepared in so short a time. But jewellers, milliners, and dressmakers may be hurried as well as lawyers, when they are well paid to make haste. And so, in two weeks, the banker's heiress, the future Marchioness of Arondelle and Duchess of Hereward, had a trousseau as magnificent and splendid as if it had been in preparation for two years. When it was all carefully packed and sent down to Lone, Sir Lemuel Levison and his household prepared to follow.

On the day before their departure a very curious thing happened.

Sir Lemuel was waiting in his library, when a footman entered and laid a card before him. It was not a visiting card, but a business card. And it bore the name of a firm:

Dazzle and Sparkle, jewellers, Number Blank, Bond street.

"What is the meaning of this?" inquired the banker.

"If you please, sir, the person who brought it directed me to say, that he craves to speak with you on the most important business," answered the man.

"Important to himself most likely, and not in the least so to me. Well, show him up," said Sir Lemuel.

The servant withdrew and, after a few moments, reappeared and announced:

"Mr. Dazzle, of Dazzle and Sparkle, Bond street."

A little, round-bodied, bald-headed man entered the library.

Sir Lemuel Levison received him with some surprise, but with much politeness.

"I have come, sir, on a little business," began the visitor, who forthwith proceeded and explained his business at length.

It seemed that the imbecile Duke of Hereward, being well pleased with his son's marriage, and imagining himself still to be the master of Lone and of a princely revenue, went to Messrs. Dazzle and Sparkle, and ordered a splendid set of diamonds for his prospective daughter-in-law.

The firm, who, as well as all the world of London, had heard of the forthcoming marriage between the son of the pauper duke and the daughter of the wealthy banker, gravely accepted the order, pondered over it, and finally determined to lay the whole matter before the banker himself.

"You have acted with much discretion, Mr. Dazzle. Fill the duke's order, and hold me responsible for the amount. And say nothing of the affair," was the banker's answer to the tradesman, who bowed and left the room.

The next morning Sir Lemuel Levison, his daughter, her chaperon, and their household, went down to Castle Lone.

Active preparations were at once commenced for the wedding, which was to take place at Lone on the Tuesday of the following week.

The first thing that Salome did on reaching the castle was to have the portrait of the Marquis of Arondelle brought down from the tower and mounted in state between the two lofty front windows of her favorite sitting-room.

Among the servants at Lone, none received the bride elect with more effusive love than the old housekeeper, Girzie Ross.

"Eh, me leddy! Heaven, sent ye to redeem Lone. My benison on ye, me leddy! and my ban on yon hizzie, wha hae been makin' sic' an ado, ever sin the report o' your betrothal has been noised about!" said the dame.

"But who are you talking about, my dear Mrs. Ross?" inquired Salome.

"Ou just that handsom hizzie, Rosy Cameron, wha will hae it that she, her vera sel', is troth-plighted to our young laird--the jaud!" replied the housekeeper.

"But, Mrs. Ross, surely that must be a mistake of yours. No girl could have the impertinence to say such a false thing of Lord Arondelle," exclaimed Salome, in disgust and abhorrence of the very idea presented.

"Indeed, then, my young lady, *she* ha' the impertinence to say just that thing--not in a whisper and in a corner, but loudly in the vera castle court, to whilk she cam yestreen, sae noisily that I was fain to threaten her wi' the constable before I could get shet o' her," said the housekeeper nodding her head.

"What can the girl mean by it? What excuse can she possibly have to justify such a mad charge?" inquired Salome, in a painful anxiety that she could neither conquer nor yet explain to herself. She did not doubt the honor of her promised husband. She would have died rather than doubt him. Why, then, should this sudden anguish wring her heart. "What excuse can she have, Mrs. Ross?" repeated Salome.

"Eh, me leddy, wha kens? Boys will be boys. And whiles the best o' them will be wild where a bonny lassie is concerned. No that's I'm saying sic a thing anent our young laird. But ye ken he used to be unco fond o' the sport o' deer stalking up by Ben Lone, where this handsome hizzie, Rose Cameron, bides wi' her owld feyther. And I e'en think the young laird, may whiles, hae putten a speak on the lass. Nae mair nor less than just that," said the housekeeper as she left the room to look after some important household work.

A few minutes after her exit, Sir Lemuel Levison entered.

Finding his daughter almost in tears, he naturally inquired:

"What on earth is the matter with you, my child?"

"Nothing, papa! At least nothing that should trouble me!"

"But what is it?"

"Well then, papa, dear, here has been a foolish girl--**very** foolish, I think she must be, going about, intruding even into the Castle, and telling all that will listen to her, that **she** is betrothed to the Marquis of Arondelle."

"Oh! Just as I feared!" muttered the banker, in a tone that instantly riveted the attention of his daughter.

"**What** did you fear, my father?" she inquired, fixing her eyes upon his face.

The banker hesitated.

His daughter repeated her question:

"**What** did you fear, my dear father?"

"Why, just what has happened, my love!" impatiently answered the banker. "That this silly report would reach your ears and give you uneasiness. It **has** reached you; but do not, I beseech you, let it trouble you!"

"There is no truth in it of course, papa?" said Salome, in a tone of entreaty.

"No, no, at least none that need concern you. Lord bless my soul, girl, young men will be young men! Arondelle is now about twenty-five years of age. And he was not brought up in a convent, as you were. He has lived for a quarter of a century in the world! Surely, you do not expect that a young man should live as long as that without ever admiring a pretty face, and even telling its owner so, do you?"

"I never once thought about that, at all, papa," said Salome, in a mournful tone.

"No, I'll warrant you didn't! Well, don't think anything more of it now. And don't expect too much of human nature. In this year of grace there are no saints left alive! Believe that, and accept it, my girl!"

CHAPTER VI.
A HORRIBLE MYSTERY ON THE WEDDING DAY.

On the day before the wedding all the preparations were completed.

The grounds around the castle, paradisial in their own natural beauty under this heavenly blue sky of June, were adorned with all that art and taste and wealth could bring to enhance their attractions in honor of the occasion.

Triumphal arches of rare exotic flowers were erected at intervals along the avenue leading from the castle courtyard down to the bridge that spanned Loch Lone from the island, to the mountain hamlet on the main land. The bridge itself was canopied with evergreens, and starred with roses. Every house in the little hamlet of Lone was so wreathed and festooned with flowers as to look like a fairy bower. The little gothic church, said to be coeval in history with the castle itself, was decorated within and without as for an Easter or Christmas festival. And the only inn of the place, an antiquated but most comfortable public house, known for centuries as the "Hereward Arms," was almost covered with flags, banners and bushes, in honor of the presence of the Duke of Hereward, and the Marquis of Arondelle, especially, and of other noble guests who had arrived there to assist at the wedding of the next day.

Yes, the expectant bridegroom and his aged father were at the Hereward Arms. Etiquette did not admit of their being guests at the Castle on the day before the expected marriage. And much ado had the young marquis to keep the duke quietly at the inn. The old man enjoying his pleasing hallucination of being still the proprietor of Lone, and the possessor of a princely revenue, fretted against the delay that detained him at the Hereward Arms, when he was so anxious to go on to Castle Lone. And his son did not venture to leave him until late at night, when he left him in bed and asleep.

Then the young marquis walked out and crossed the evergreen covered bridge leading to the Castle grounds. He knew that custom did not sanction his visit to his bride-elect on the night before their wedding, but he could at least gaze on the walls that sheltered her, while he rambled over the rich lawns, parterres, shrubberies, and terraces.

Within the Castle, meanwhile, all the arrangements for the morning's festivity were completed.

Halls, drawing-rooms, parlors, chambers, and dining-rooms, all sumptuously furnished and beautifully decorated, were ready for the wedding guests.

In the dining-room the luxurious wedding-breakfast was set. The service was of solid gold and finest Sevres china; the viands comprised every foreign and domestic delicacy fitting the feast.

In the drawing-room the magnificent bridal presents were displayed--coronets, necklaces, earrings, brooches, bracelets, rings, of pearls, diamonds, opals, emeralds, sapphires, and amethysts; jewel caskets, dressing cases, work boxes, and writing desks, of ormolu, of malachite, of pearl, and of ivory, of silver, and of gold; illuminated prayer-books and Bibles, with antique covers and clasps set with precious stones; tea and dinner sets of solid gold; camel's hair and Cashmere shawls and scarfs; sets of lace in Honiton, Brussels, Valencia. Irish point and old point--on to an endless list of the most splendid offerings.

"The wealth of Ormus and of Ind"

seemed to load the tables in costly gifts to the banker's daughter, and marquis' bride.

In the bride's own luxurious dressing-room, the elegant bridal costume was displayed. It consisted of a fine point-lace dress over a trained-skirt of rich white satin, a full-length vail of priceless cardinal point-lace; white kid boots, embroidered with small pearls; white kid gloves, trimmed at the wrists with lace; wreath and bouquet of orange flowers; necklace and pendant earrings and bracelets of rich Oriental pearls, set with diamonds. These jewels were the imaginary gift of the mad duke to the bride-elect of his son, and were paid for, as has been already explained, by the bride's own father. A sentiment of tender reverence for the unfortunate old duke had inspired Salome to select these jewels from all the others that had been lavished upon her, to wear on her wedding day.

To the credit of the good banker's delicacy and discretion let it be said, that not even Salome knew but that this elegant gift had been given by the duke in reality as it was in intention.

The Castle was now full of guests, friends of the bride and of her father's family. The eight young ladies who were to attend her to the altar, had arrived early in the afternoon, each chaperoned by her mother, aunt, or some matronly friend. These had all been shown to their separate apartments.

They assembled again at the seven o'clock dinner in the family dining-room, and afterwards made a little tour of inspection through the rooms, looking with approval and admiration upon the sumptuous wedding-breakfast table, set in the great dining-room, and with surprise and enthusiasm at the splendid wedding presents displayed in the drawing-room. Finally, after a social cup of tea, they separated and retired to their several rooms, that they might be up in good time the next morning.

When Salome entered her own bed-chamber, she found the old housekeeper, Girzie Ross, awaiting her.

"I took the liberty, me leddy, to come to see ye, gin ye hae ony commands for me the night," said the dame, courtesying.

"No, Mrs. Ross, I have no orders to give. All is done, as I understand. If there be anything left undone, you will use you own discretion about it. I can thoroughly trust you," said Salome.

"Guid-night, then, me leddy. And a guid rest and a blithe waking till ye," said the dame, courtesying again, and turning to leave the room.

"One moment, Mrs. Ross, if you please," said the young lady, gently arresting her steps.

"Ay, me leddy, as mony as ye'll please," promptly replied the dame, returning to her place.

"I wish to ask you a question," began Salome, in a slow and hesitating manner. "Have you seen or heard anything more of that girl, Mrs. Ross?"

"Meaning that ne'er-do-weel light o' love Rose Cameron, me leddy!" inquired the housekeeper.

"Yes, Rose Cameron. There have been such crowds of people on the island to-day to inspect the decorations, that I thought--I thought--"

"As that handsome jaud might be amang 'em, me leddy? Ou, ay, and sae she waur! But when I caught her prowling about here, I sent Mr. McRath to warn her off the place, and threaten her wi' the constable gin she didna gang!" said the housekeeper.

"But that was cruel, Mrs. Ross."

"Na, na, me leddy. It waur unco well dune! She was after no guid prowling about here, and making an excuse o' luking at the deekorated grounds. She didna care for the sight a bodle! Aweel she's gane, and a guid riddance."

"What does the girl look like, Mrs. Ross?"

"Eh, leddy, she's a strapping wench! tall and broad-shouldered, and full-breasted, with a handsome head that she carries unco high, and big, bold blue eyes, and a heap o' long, red hair. That's Rosy Cameron, me leddy."

This was a rather rough portrait of the Juno-like Highland beauty; but then, it was drawn by an enemy, you know.

"But dinna fash yersel' about yon hizzie ony mair, me young leddy. She'll na be permitted to trouble ye," concluded the housekeeper.

"That will do, Mrs. Ross. Thanks. But pray do not let anyone be harsh with that poor girl. If she is a little crazy, she is all the more to be pitied. Good-night," said Salome, thus gently dismissing her talkative attendant.

"Guid night, me young leddy. Guid rest and blithe waking to ye," repeated the old woman, as she courtesied and left the room.

"Poor girl!" mused Salome. "I cannot help sympathizing with her tonight. What if Arondelle who is so courteous to all, were courteous to her also. And she, unused to courtesy in her rude Highland home, mistook such gentle courtesy for preference, for love, and gave him her love in return? He would not be in the least to be blamed, while she would be much to be pitied. What a cruel sight these wedding preparations must be to her! What a miserable night this must be for her! I must see to that poor girl's welfare," concluded Salome.

A low rap at her door disturbed her.

"Come in."

Her maid entered.

"What is it, Janet?"

"If you please, Miss, Sir Lemuel's man has just brought me a message for you. Sir Lemuel requests, Miss, that you will come to his room before you retire."

"Dear papa, I will go at once. You need not wait for me here, Janet. Just turn the lights down low--they make the room so warm--and leave the windows partly open, and then go to bed, my girl, I shall not want you again tonight," said Salome, as she passed out of the chamber and went down to the long hall, at the opposite extremity of which was her father's room.

She entered silently, and found the banker wrapped in his gray silk dressing-gown and seated in his large resting-chair.

"Come and sit by me, my dear. I only wanted to have a little talk with you to-night," he said, holding out his hand to her.

She went up to him, clasped and kissed the out-stretched hand, and then seated herself, not on the chair by his side, for that would not have brought her near enough to him, but on the footstool at his feet, so that she could lay her head upon his knees.

"Salome, my darling, I have not been a good father to you," he said, sadly, as he ran his long white fingers through the tresses of the little dark-haired head that lay upon his knees.

"Oh, papa! the best and dearest papa that ever lived!" she answered, drawing his hand to her lips and kissing it fondly.

"No, no; I have not been a good father to you, my poor motherless child. I feel it to-night. I left you fourteen years in a foreign convent, and scarcely ever saw you. Was that being a good father to you, my child?"

"Yes, dear, it was. I had to be educated. And the nuns did their whole duty by me, did they not?" said Salome, soothingly.

"They sent me home a sweet and lovely child, who in the three years that she has been my greatest blessing and comfort has made me feel and know how much I lost in banishing her from my presence so long--fourteen years!--a time never to be redeemed!" said the banker, with a sigh.

"Yes, papa, dear. It can and shall be redeemed. For now you know I shall live with you as long as you live. My marriage will not deprive you of your daughter, but give you a dear and noble son. You know it is settled that after our brief wedding we shall return to Lone, and you and the duke, and Arondelle and myself, will all live here together until the meeting of Parliament in February, and then we shall go up to London together. So cheer up, papa. All the coming years shall compensate for all we have lost in the past," said Salome, gayly caressing him.

"'The coming years?' Ah, my darling! do you forget that I am quite an old man to be your father? You were the child of my old age, Salome! I was nearly fifty when you were born. I am nearly seventy now!"

"*Dear father!*" murmured Salome, caressing him with ineffable tenderness.

"Do not let me sadden you, my darling. I would not be a day younger. It is well to be old. It is well to have lived a long time in this world, for it is a good world. But good as it is, it is but rudimentary. It is to the human being only what the soil is to the seed--the germinating bed; the full and perfect world is beyond. Young Christians believe this. Aged Christians know it. There, brighten up! And think that this marriage of yours and Arondelle's if it be as true as I feel assured it is--will be not for time only but for all eternity! Believe this and be happier than you were ever before! There now, my darling! I called you in here to make my little confession. I have received absolution. Now go to your rest. Good night," said the banker, bending and kissing her forehead.

"Dear, dearest father! bless your daughter before she goes," said Salome, in a voice thrilling with emotion, as she raised from her seat and knelt at her father's feet.

The old man laid his hand upon her bowed head and solemnly invoked a blessing upon her.

"May the Lord look down on you, my daughter. May He give you health and grace to bear your burdens and do your duties as wife and mother, and save and bless you and yours, now and ever more, for Christ's dear sake. AMEN."

She arose in silence from her knees, put her arms around his neck, kissed him, and glided from the room.

And now a terrible and mysterious thing happened to the bride-elect.

The lights had been turned very low in the hall. The household had all retired to rest. The stillness and the sense of darkness awed her as she glided noiselessly along in the deep shadows. Suddenly she saw the form of a man approaching from the direction of her own room. He might be some belated servant on some legitimate business for one of the guests, yet he startled her. She looked intently toward him, but in the obscure light she could only see that he was a tall man in dark clothing, and with a very white face. She shrank back in the shadow of the wall as he swiftly and silently approached her.

Then with amazement she recognized the face and form of her betrothed husband. But the face was deadly pale, and the form was shaking as with an ague fit.

"ARONDELLE! *You here!*" she exclaimed, starting towards him.

But she met only the empty air, the form had vanished.

In unbounded amazement she stared all around to see where it could have gone, and in what part of the darksome hall she herself then stood.

She found herself opposite to the entrance of a long, narrow passage opening from the hall and leading to the door of a staircase communicating with the dungeons of Malcolm's Tower.

She looked down that passage. It was black as the mouth of Hades!

A nameless terror seized her, and she fled precipitately down the hall, nor stopped until she had reached her own room, rushed in, and shut and bolted the door. Then she sank down into the nearest chair, feeling cold as ice, and trembling from head to foot.

Her maid had over-acted her instructions, and had not only turned the lights low, but had turned them out entirely.

There was no need of artificial light, however; for the windows were open and the room was flooded with the brilliant moonshine of these northern latitudes.

Salome did not know or care how the room was lighted. She sat there thrilled with awe of what she had just experienced.

Had she really seen the marquis?--or his spirit? Or had she been the victim of an optical illusion?

If she had seen the marquis, what could have brought him secretly into the house and up into the hall of the bed-rooms, at that hour of the night? And why did he not answer her, when she called him?

It surely could not have been the marquis whom she saw! He never would have crept into the house and up to their private-rooms, at that hour of the night, or fled from her, when she called him?

What was it then that she had seen in the likeness of her lover?

Was it the disembodied spirit of Arondelle? *Could* the spirit of a living man appear in one place, while the body of the man was present in another? She had heard and read of such wonders, yet she could not accept them as facts.

No, this was no spirit.

What then? Had she been the subject of an optical illusion? She had heard of those wonders also!

But no! This was too real, too solid, too substantial for an optical illusion!

Was the form she had seen possibly that of some other person, some guest of the house, who had lost his way.

No, and a thousand noes! She knew every guest staying at the castle, and knew that not one of them bore the slightest resemblance to the Marquis of Arondelle.

No, the form that she had seen in the murky hall seemed that of her betrothed husband, or it was his spirit.

She could not tell which, nor could she test the question now. The house was full of wedding guests, who were now most probably sound asleep in their beds. And the household all had long since retired. She could not rouse them only to satisfy her own doubts without any other practical result. For what if the intruder were Lord Arondelle? He was not in the least an objectional guest. And in the morning he would explain his strange presence.

By this time Salome had reasoned herself into some degree of calmness. But she was still too much excited to feel sleepy or to think of retiring to bed.

The mid-summer night was warm and close, even there in the Highlands--or in her nervous condition it seemed to her to be so. She wanted more air. She went to the window, and seated herself in an easy-chair, and looked out.

A heavenly night!

The deep-blue sky was spangled with myriads of sparkling stars. The full harvest moon was at the zenith and pouring down a flood of silvery radiance over mountain, lake and island.

Right opposite the window was the elegant little bridge that spanned the lake between the island and the mountain, at the base of which stood the little Gothic church with the cottages of the hamlet clustered around it.

A beautiful scene!

This morning it had been gay and noisy with a rejoicing crowd come to inspect the decorated grounds, and to triumph over the approaching marriage of their disinherited young lord, with the present heiress of his lost estate.

To-morrow this scene would be even more gay and more noisy, with a greater and more rejoicing crowd. For all the Clan Scott were to gather here to do honor to the nuptials of their hereditary chieftain.

But to-night the beautiful scene was holy in its solitude and stillness.

Hark!

A sound of voices beneath the window.

Salome started, and drew back. And the next moment, paralyzed by consternation and despair, she overheard the following conversation:

"*Hist!* are you there, Rose?" inquired a dear familiar voice.

"Ay, I'm here, me laird! After being turnit frae the castle like a thief, or a beggar, or a dog! after being threatened wi' a constable and a prison if I ever showed my face here; but once mair I hae come agen, in obedience to your bidding! Come creeping, creeping, creeping ander the castle wa', by night, like ony puir cat afeared o' scauding water! Ay, me laird, I'm here, mair fule I!" replied a woman's voice.

"Hush, Rose! Do not say so, my girl. And do not call me 'lord;' I am your slave and not your 'lord,' my lady queen! You know I love you--you only of all women."

"Luve me? Ou, ay, sae ye tell me. But this gran' wedding is coming unco near to be naething but a jest. How far will ye carry the jest? Up till the altar railings? Into the bridal chamber? It's deceiving and fuling me, ye are, me laird! But I'll tell ye weel! Ye sail no marry yon girl, I say! Gin ye gae sae far as to lead her to the kirk mesel' will meet you at the altar and forbid the marriage. And *then* see wha will put me out!"

"Hush, hush, you wild Highland witch, and listen to me. I shall not marry that girl! How can I, when I am married to you? I have had an object in letting this thing go on thus far. My plans could not all be accomplished until to-night. But to-night something will happen that will put all thoughts of marrying and giving in marriage effectually out of the heads of all parties concerned, I will warrant. And to-morrow, you and I will be far away from this place--together, and never to part again. Wait here for me, my love; I shall not be long away. But on your life, do not stir, or speak, or scarcely breathe until you see me again."

"How long will you be gone?"

"Perhaps an hour. Perhaps two hours. You can be patient?"

"Ay, I can be patient."

Here the low, whispering voice ceased. And Salome?

Before that conversation was half through, Salome had fallen back in her chair in a deadly swoon.

CHAPTER VII.
THE MORNING'S DISCOVERY.

When Miss Levison recovered her consciousness it was broad daylight. The rising sun glancing over the top of the Eastern mountain sent arrows of golden light in through the window at which she sat.

Music filled the morning air!

Salome passed her hands over her eyes, and gazed around. So long and deep had been her swoon that, for the time, she had utterly lost her memory, and now found difficulty in trying to recover it. Bewildered, she looked about, and listened to the strange, wild music sounding under her window--a sort of morning serenade or reveille, it seemed.

Next her eyes fell upon her magnificent bridal array, displayed on stands near the elegant dressing-table.

Then she remembered that this was her wedding-day, and a flush of joy lighted up her face.

But it passed in a moment.

What was this that lay so heavy at her heart! Was it the remnant of an evil dream?

What had happened? Something must have happened! Else why should she find herself seated in that easy-chair at the open window, and see that her bed had not been occupied?

Then, slowly, she recollected the events of the previous night--her retirement to her chamber; her talk there with the housekeeper about Rose Cameron, the "handsome hizzie," who had been haunting the premises and giving trouble all that day; the message from her father; her affecting interview with him in his bedroom; her return to her own apartment through the dimly-lighted, deserted hall, where she met the pale and spectral form of Lord Arondelle, who vanished as she called to him! her terrified flight into her own chamber!

All these incidents she clearly remembered.

Then her excited vigil in the easy-chair, by the open window, and the two voices that broke upon it--that of her betrothed husband and that of a woman--of this same Rose Cameron, whose name had been so disreputably connected with Lord Arondelle's; who then and there claimed to be his wife and was not contradicted!

There! that was the weight that lay so heavy at her heart!

"And yet it must have been a dream!" she said to herself. Of course she had fallen asleep there in the easy-chair, and with her thoughts running on the apparition she had met in the hall, and on the country people's gossip about Lord Arondelle and Rose Cameron, she had had that evil dream. Unquestionably it was only a dream! Lord Arondelle could never play so base a part as he had seemed to do in her dream! She reproached herself for having even involuntarily been the subject of it.

And yet! and yet! the weight lay heavy at her heart, and although this was a warm June morning, she shivered as though it had been January.

She arose to close the window.

Then--

What a magnificent and beautiful scene burst upon her vision! The eastern horizon was ablaze with glory. Lovely morning clouds, soft, transparent white, tinted with rose, violet and gold, tempered the dazzling splendor of the rising sun, and half vailed the opal-hued mountain tops, and even hung upon the emerald mountain side. Morning sky, rosy clouds, and opal mountains, were all reflected as by a mirror in the clear water of the lake below.

The hamlet at the foot of the mountain was gay with flags and banners and festoons of flowers. The bridge spanning the lake and connecting the hamlet with the island, was grand with triumphal arches. The lake was alive with gayly-trimmed pleasure-boats of every description. The island, with its groves, shrubberies, parterres, arbors, terraces, statues, was decorated with flags and banners, innumerable colored lamps and floral mottoes and devices.

The streets of the hamlet, the bridge and the island was each alive with a merry crowd of tenantry and peasantry in their picturesque holiday suits, coming to see the wedding pageant.

Gayer than all was the gathering of the Clan Scott, in their brilliant tartans, and with their national music to do honor to the nuptials of the heir of their chief.

As Miss Levison looked and listened, the shadows of the night vanished from her mind as clouds before the sun!

How strange the thought that the evil dream should have troubled her at all! But the dream had seemed as real as any waking experience. But then, again, dreams often do seem so! She would think no more of it, except to repent having been so unjust to Lord Arondelle, even though it was but in an involuntary dream.

It was as yet very early in the morning--not seven o'clock. Her serenaders had waked her betimes, and the country people had clearly determined to lose not one hour of that festive day. But Miss Levison was still shivering in the mild June morning. She thought she would ask for a cup of coffee to warm her.

She rang her bell.

Her maid entered the room, courtesied, and stood waiting

"Janet, tell the housekeeper to send me a strong, hot cup of coffee," she said.

"Yes, Miss. If you please, Miss, my lord's gentleman is below with a note and a parcel for you, Miss."

"Very well, Janet. Do you bring it up and ask the man to wait. There may be answer," replied Miss Levison, as the rose clouds rolled over her clear, pale cheeks.

The girl courtesied and withdrew.

"To think of my being so wicked as to have such a dream about him--**him**!" she said to herself, as again she shivered with cold.

Presently the housekeeper entered with a tiny cup of coffee on a small silver tray in her hand, and with many cordial congratulations on her lips.

Fortunately the lace curtains of the bed were down, so that she could not see that it had not been slept in, and annoy her young mistress with exclamations and questions.

"Eh, me young leddy! a blithe bridal morn ye hae got; and a braw sight on the ramparts of a' the Scotts, wi' their tartans and bag-pipes, come to do ye honor!" said the housekeeper, as she held the tray to her mistress.

Miss Levison drank the coffee, returned the cup, and then inquired:

"Where is Janet? I sent her with a message; she should have returned by this time."

"Ou, aye, sae she should. She's clacking her clavvers wi' yon lad frae the 'Hereward Arm.' But here she is now, me young leddy," answered the housekeeper, as the maid entered the room and placed in her mistress' hand a note and a small parcel, tied up in white paper with narrow white ribbon, and sealed with the Hereward crest.

Miss Levison opened the note and read:

"HEREWARD ARMS INN, Tuesday Morning.

"I greet you, my only beloved, on this our bridal morning--the commencement of a long and happy union for both of us! Yes, a long union, for it will stretch into eternity, and a happy one, for come what will, we shall be happy in each other. I send you the richest jewel that has ever been in our possession, the only one which has survived the wreck of our fortunes. It has been preserved more on account of its traditionary interest than for its intrinsic value. Tradition tells us that at the taking of Jerusalem, in the first crusade, this jewel was snatched from the turban of Saladin, the Sultan, in single combat, by our wild crusading ancestor, Ranulph d' Arondelle. It adorned his own hemlet at the siege of St. Jean d' Acre, some years later. In short, it has been handed down from father to son through six centuries and sixteen generations. It has "in the thickest carnage blazed" on battle-fields, and in the maddest merriment flashed in festive scenes. Yet it is an offering all too poor for my great love to make, or your great worth to receive. But take it as the best I have to give.

"ARONDELLE."

She read this note with tearful eyes, roseate cheeks' and smiling lips. And then she untied the white ribbon and opened the white paper. It first disclosed a golden casket about four inches square, richly chased and bearing the Hereward arms set in small precious stones. The tiny key was in the lock. She opened it and found, lying on a bed of rich white satin, a large, burning, blazing ruby heart--the famous ruby of the Hereward, said to be the largest in the world. Miss Levison had read of this jewel as one of the most valuable among precious stones. She had heard also, what evidently the young marquis did not think worth while to tell her in connection with its history, namely, that it had been held as an amulet of such power that it was believed the ducal house of Hereward would never be without a male heir as long as it possessed that priceless ruby heart. Miss Levison supposed this to be the reason why it had been preserved by the old duke from the total wreck of his fortune. And the marquis had given it to her! Well, that was not giving it out of the family, since she was to be his wife. While offering it he had undervalued the royal gift. But how highly she appreciated it, rating it far above all the other jewels that blazed upon her table.

"And to think I should have had such an evil dream about him, and even suffered myself to be troubled by it!" she said, pressing his note to her lips.

Then she shivered so hardly that her old housekeeper exclaimed:

"Me dear young leddy, ye hae surely taken cauld. Let me order a fire kindled here."

"Nonsense, Mrs. Ross--a fire on this warm summer morning? I could not bear it. Besides if I shiver with cold one moment, I glow with heat the next," said Miss Levison, smiling.

"Ay; I am sair afeard ye's gaun to be ill, wi' all thae shivers and glows," replied the dame, shaking her head.

"Nonsense again, Mrs. Ross, dear woman. I am well enough. Now, Janet, did you tell his lordship's messenger to wait?"

"Yes, Miss."

Miss Levison drew a little writing-stand to her side, opened the desk, took out materials and penned the following note:

"LONE CASTLE, Tuesday.

"MY MOST BELOVED AND HONORED: Your right royal gift is beyond all price for richness, beauty, traditional interest, and symbolism, and as such I shall hold it above all other gifts, and cherish it to the end of my life. But it is not only to speak of your invaluable gift I write; it is also to ask you to do a strange thing to please me this morning. It is now eight o'clock. We are appointed to meet at the church at eleven. Will you meet me *here* first at half-past nine? I wish to tell you something before we go to the altar. It is nothing important that I have to tell you-- you will probably only laugh at it; but I must get it off my mind; for it weighs there like a sin. Come and receive my little confession, and give absolution to YOUR OWN SALOME."

She enveloped and directed this note, and gave it to Janet, with orders to hand it to Lord Arondelle's man.

When the girl had left the room, Miss Levison turned to the housekeeper and inquired:

"Has my father's bell rung yet, do you know?"

"Na, me young leddy, it has na rung yet. Sir Lemuel's man, Mr. Peter, is downstairs, waiting for the summons."

"Perhaps he had better call his master," suggested Miss Levison.

"Na, Miss, sae I tauld him; but he said his orders were no to call his master the morn', but to wait till he heard his bell ring. He's waiting for that e'en noo."

"Very well, Mrs. Ross. Papa was up late last night, I know, and is probably tired this morning. So we must let him sleep as long as possible. But as soon as his bell rings, be sure to take him up a cup of coffee."

"Verra weel, Miss."

"And, Mrs. Ross, I hope that all our guests are cared for, and served in their own rooms with tea and toast, or coffee and muffins, as they choose?"

"Ou, ay, me dear young leddy, I hae ta'en care of a' that. And what will I bring yersel', Miss, before ye begin to dress?"

"Nothing; I have had a cup of coffee. That is sufficient for the present."

"Neathing but ae wee bit cup o' coffee, my dear young leddy?"

"No; I have no appetite. I suppose no girl ever did have on her wedding morning," said Miss Levison, shivering and then flushing.

The housekeeper contemplated her young mistress with growing anxiety.

"I am sure ye are no weel," she ventured again to suggest.

"I am quite well, my dear Mrs. Ross. Do not disturb yourself. But go now and send Janet and Kitty to me. I must begin to dress."

The housekeeper left the room, and was soon replaced by the lady's maid and the upper house-maid.

"Is my bath ready, Kitty?"

"Yes, Miss; and I have poured six bottles of ody collone intil it," said the girl, with a very self-approving air.

"You needn't have done that," said Miss Levison, with an amused smile, "but you meant well, and I thank you."

She took her customary morning bath, and slipping on a soft, white, cashmere wrapper, placed herself in the hands of her maidens to be dressed for the altar.

Janet combed, and brushed and arranged the shining dark brown hair. Kitty laced the dainty white velvet boots. Janet arrayed her in her bridal robes, and Kitty clasped the costly jewels around her neck and arms. One placed the bridal vail and wreath upon her head, while the other drew the pretty pearl-embroidered gloves upon her hands.

At length her toilet was complete, and she stood up, beautiful in her youth, love, and joy, and imperial in her array.

She wore a long trained dress of the richest white satin, trimmed with deep point lace flounces, headed with trails of orange flower buds; an over-dress of fine cardinal point lace, looped up with festoons of orange buds; a point lace berthe and short sleeve ruffles; a necklace, pendant, and bracelets of pearls set in diamonds, white kid gloves, embroidered with fine white silk; white satin boots worked with pearls. On her head the rich, full orange flower wreath. And over all, like mist over frost and snow, fell the long bridal vail of finest point lace, softening the whole effect.

"The young ladies, your bridesmaids, bid me tell you, Miss, that they are quite ready to come to you, when you are so to receive them," said Kitty, as she placed the bouquet of orange flowers in its jewelled holder, and handed it to her mistress.

"Very well. I will send for them in good time," answered Miss Levison, glancing at the little golden clock upon the mantel-piece, and noticing that it was nearly half-past nine, the hour at which she expected Lord Arondelle. "But now, Kitty, my good girl, go and inquire if my father is up, and return and let me know. I would like to see him in his room."

The house-maid courtesied and went out, and after a few minutes' absence returned running.

"If you please, Miss, Sir Lemuel hasn't rung his bell yet, and Mr. Peters says, with his duty to you, Miss, as it is so late, hadn't he better call his master?"

"By no means! Let Mr. Peters obey his master's orders not to disturb him until his bell rings," answered the young lady.

"Yes, Miss; and if you please, Miss, here is a card, and his lordship, Lord Arondelle, is down stairs asking for you, Miss," said the girl, laying the pasteboard in question before her young mistress.

"Lord Arondelle! Yes, I expected his lordship. Where is he?"

"Mr. McRath showed him into the library, Miss."

"Quite right. None of our guests have left their rooms yet?"

"No, Miss, they be all busy a dressing of themselves, as I think."

"Ah! then go before me and open the door, and tell his lordship that I shall be with him in a moment," said Miss Levison.

The girl dropped another courtesy and preceded her mistress down stairs. In going down the great upper hall, Miss Levison passed the door of the dark, narrow passage at right angles with the hall, and leading to the tower stairs, where she had seen the apparition of the night before. She shivered and hurried on. She paused a moment before the door leading to the ante-room of her father's bed-chamber, and listened to hear if he were stirring; but all within seemed as still as death. She went on and descended the stairs and reached the library-door, just as Kitty opened it and said:

"Miss Levison, my lord," and retired to give place to the young lady.

Miss Levison entered the library.

Lord Arondelle, in his wedding dress, stood by the central book-table. As his costume was the regulation uniform of a gentleman's full dress, it needs no description here. Gentlemen array themselves much in the same style for a dinner or a ball, a wedding or a funeral--the only difference to mark the occasion being in the color of the gloves.

Lord Arondelle advanced to meet his bride.

"My love and queen! this meeting is a grace granted me indeed! How beautiful you are!" he exclaimed, taking both her hands and carrying them to his lips. "But you are shivering, sweet girl! You are cold!" he added anxiously, as he looked at her more attentively.

"I have been shivering all the morning. I sat at my open window late last night and got a little chilled; but it is nothing," she answered, smiling.

"You shall not do such suicidal things, when I have the charge of you, my little lady," he said, half jestingly, half seriously, as he led her to a sofa and seated her on it, taking his own seat by her side.

"Come, now," he gayly continued, "was that indiscreet star-gazing which has resulted in a cold the little sin for which you wish me to give you absolution?"

"No, my lord. My sin was an evil dream."

"A dream!"

"Ay, a dream."

"But a dream cannot be a sin!"

"Hear it, and then judge. But first--tell me--were you in the castle late last night?" she gravely inquired.

He paused and gazed at her before he replied:

"*I* in the castle late last night? Why, most certainly not! Why ever should you ask me such a question, my love?"

"Because if you were not in the castle last night--"

"Well?"

"I met your 'fetch,' as the country people would call it."

"My--I beg your pardon."

"Your 'fetch,' your double, your spectre, your spirit, whatever you may call it."

"Whatever do you mean, Salome?"

"Shall I tell you all about it?"

"Of course--yes, do."

Miss Levison began and related all the circumstances in detail of her night visit to her father's room, and her meeting with an appearance which she took to be that of her betrothed husband, but which, on being called by her, instantly vanished.

Lord Arondelle mused for awhile. Miss Levison gazed on him in anxious suspense for a few minutes, and then inquired:

"What do you think of it?"

"My love, if I were a transcendental visionary, I might say, that at the hour you saw my image before you, my thoughts, my mind, my spirit, whatever you choose to call my inner self, was actually with you, and so became visible to you; but--" he paused.

"But--what?" she inquired.

"Not being a transcendentalist or a visionary, I am forced to the conclusion that what you thought you saw, was, really nothing but an optical illusion!"

"You think that?"

"Indeed I do!"

"I assure you, that the image seemed as real, as substantial, and as solid to me then as you do now."

"No doubt of it! Optical illusions always seem very real--perfectly real."

"It was an optical illusion then! That is settled! And now!" exclaimed Salome. Then she paused.

"Yes, and now! About the sinful dream! What did you dream of? Throwing me over at the last moment and marrying a handsomer man?" gayly inquired the young marquis.

"I will tell you presently what I dreamed; but first tell me, were you in our grounds last night?" she gravely inquired.

"Yes, my little lady; but how did you know of it?" inquired the young marquis in surprise.

"I did not know it. Were you under my window?" she asked, in a low, tremulous tone.

"Yes, love. How came you to suspect me?" he inquired, more than ever astonished.

"I did not suspect you. Had you a companion with you?" she murmured.

"No, Salome. Certainly not. Why, sweet, do you ask me?"

"I thought I heard your voice speaking to some one who answered you under my window."

"But, love, there was no one with me. I was quite alone. And I did not speak at all--not even to myself. I am not in the habit of soliloquizing."

"Please tell me, if you can, at what hour you were under my window."

"It was between ten and eleven o'clock. I was walking in the grounds, and I went under your wall and looked up. I saw three shadows pass the lighted windows, which I took to be those of yourself and your attendants, and then suddenly the lights were turned off and all was dark. I knew then that you had retired to rest, and of course I turned away and walked back to the hamlet. But, love, instead of telling the little story you promised, it seems that you have put me through a very sharp examination," said his lordship, laughing. "Now, what do you mean by it? There is something behind all this," he added, gravely.

"Of course there is something behind. Did I not tell you that I had a confession to make concerning a wicked dream? Listen, Lord Arondelle. At the time you stood under my window and saw the light turned off, and supposing that I had gone to rest, you turned away and left the grounds, at that time I had *not* gone to rest, but had gone to my father's room, in returning from which I experienced that strange optical illusion. My nerves must have been strangely disordered, for when I reached my own chamber again, and finding it quite dark, opened the window and sat down to look out upon the moonlit lake, I immediately fell asleep, and had a terrible, and a terribly real and distinct dream--a dream, dear, that nearly overturned my reason, I do believe."

"What was it, love?" he inquired.

She told him without the least reserve.

He listened to her with interest, and then laughed aloud.

"The idea of your having such a dream about me as that! I do not wonder it weighed upon your mind. Yes, it was very wicked of you, my sinful child--very. But since you sincerely repent, I freely absolve you. ***Benedicite!***"

Salome looked and listened to him with surprise; for as she spoke of dreaming that he called Rose Cameron his wife, he not only laughed at that idea, but really appeared as if the very existence of the girl was unknown to him.

Then Salome ventured another question:

"Do you know any one of the name of Rose Cameron?"

"No, not personally. I believe one of our shepherds, up at Ben Lone, has a very handsome daughter of that name, but I have never seen her," said the young marquis, with an open sincerity that carried conviction with it.

Salome was amazed, but convinced. What could have started the false reports concerning the young marquis and the handsome shepherdess? Clearly Rose's own hallucination. She had seen the marquis somewhere, without having been seen by him; she had fallen in love with him, and had partly lost her reason and imagined all the rest, she thought.

"And so you have never even looked upon the beauty of that dream?" she said, with a smile.

"Never even looked upon her," assented the marquis.

"Then I do, in downright earnest, beg your pardon for my dream," said Salome, gravely.

"But I have already given you absolution, my erring daughter? ***Benedicite! Benedicite!***" replied the marquis still laughing.

At that moment there was a light rap at the library door, followed by the entrance of a footman who placed a small, twisted note in the hands of Miss Levison.

She opened it and read:

"MY DEAR CHILD: It is after ten o'clock. We go to church at eleven. Sir Lemuel has not yet rung his bell. His valet having received his orders last night not to call him this morning, has declined to do so. What is to be done under these circumstances? Send me a verbal message by the bearer. Your loving Aunt,

"SOPHIE BELGRADE."

"My father not yet risen!" exclaimed Salome in surprise. "He must have overslept himself with fatigue. Tell Lady Belgrade, with my thanks, that I will go to my father's room and waken him," she added, turning to the footman, who bowed and went to deliver his message.

"I hope Sir Lemuel is quite well?" said the young marquis, earnestly.

"He is quite well. My father regulates his habits so well as to live in perfect harmony with the laws of life and health. If he fatigues himself over night, he always takes a compensating rest in the morning. That is what he is doing now. But I think he is sleeping even longer than he intended to do, so I really must arouse him now, if we are to keep our appointment with the minister. Good-by, until we meet at the church, Lord Arondelle," she said, as she floated from the room in her bridal robe, and vail.

"Who says that she is not beautiful, belies her? She is lovely in person and in spirit," murmured the young marquis, as he took up his hat to leave the house.

CHAPTER VIII.
A HORRIBLE DISCOVERY.

In order not to attract the attention of the crowds of people who swarmed in the village, on the bridge, and on the island, Lord Arondelle had driven over to the castle in a closed cab that now waited at the gates to take him back again.

He left the library and went out into the great hall.

The hall porter, an elderly, stout, and important-looking functionary, slowly arose from his chair to honor the young marquis by opening the doors with his own official hands instead of leaving that duty to the footman.

And Lord Arondelle was just in the act of passing out when his steps were suddenly arrested.

A WILD AND PIERCING SHRIEK RANG THROUGH THE HOUSE, STAR-TLING ALL ITS ECHOES!

It was followed by a dead silence, and then by the sound of many hurrying feet and terrified exclamations.

"Salome! my bride! Oh, what has happened!" thought the startled young marquis, rushing back into the hall and up the stairs.

In the upper hall he found a crowd of terrified people, all hurrying in one direction--toward the bedroom of the banker.

"The dear old gentleman has got a fit, I fear, and his daughter has discovered him in it," was the next thought that flashed upon the mind of the marquis as, without waiting to ask questions, he rushed through and distanced the crowd, and reached the door of the banker's bedroom, which was blocked up by men and women, wedding guests, and servants, some questioning and exclaiming, some weeping and wailing, some standing in panic-stricken silence.

"What has happened?" cried the young marquis pushing his way with more violence than ceremony through all that impeded his entrance into the chamber.

No one answered him. No one dared to do so.

"It is Lord Arondelle--let his lordship pass," said one of the wedding guests, recognizing the expectant bridegroom as he entered the room.

An awe-struck group of persons was gathered around some object on the floor; they made way in silence for the approach of the marquis.

He passed in and looked down.

HORROR UPON HORRORS! There lay the dead body of the banker, full-dressed as on the evening before, but with his head crushed in and surrounded by a pool of coagulated blood! The face was marble white; the eyes were open and stony, the jaws had dropped and stiffened into death. Across the body lay the swooning form of his daughter, with her bridal vail and robes all dabbled in her father's blood.

"HEAVEN OF HEAVENS! Who has done this?" cried the marquis, a cold sweat of horror bursting from his pallid brow as he stared upon this ghastly sight!

A dozen voices answered him at once, to the effect that no one yet knew.

"Run! run! and fetch a doctor instantly! Some of you! any of you who can go the quickest!" he cried, as he stooped and lifted the insensible form of his bride and laid her on the bed--the bed that had not been occupied during the night. Evidently from these appearances, the banker had been murdered before his usual hour of retiring.

"Who has gone for a doctor?" inquired Lord Arondelle, in an agony of anxiety, as he bent over the unconscious form of his beloved one.

"I have despatched Gilbert, yer lairdship. He will mak' unco guid haste," answered the steward, who stood overcome with grief as he gazed upon the ghastly corpse of his unfortunate master.

"My lord," said Lady Belgrade, who stood by too deeply awed for tears, and up to this moment for action either--"my lord, you had better go out of the room for the present, and take all these men with you, and leave Miss Levison to the care of myself and the women. This is all unspeakably horrible! But our first care should be for her. We must loosen her dress, and take other measures for her recovery."

"Yes, yes! Great Heaven! yes! Do all you can for her! This is maddening!" groaned the marquis, smiting his forehead as he left the bedside, yielding his place to the dowager.

"Do try to command yourself, Lord Arondelle. This is, indeed, a most awful shock. It would have been awful at any time, but on your wedding day it comes with double violence. But do summon all your strength of mind, for *her* sake. Think of her. She came to this room in her bridal dress to call her father, that he might get ready to take her to the altar, to give her to you, and she found him here murdered--weltering in his blood. It was enough to have killed her, or unseated her reason forever," said the lady, as she busied herself with unfastening the rich, white, satin bodice of the wedding robe.

"Oh, Salome! Salome! that I could bear this sorrow for you! Oh, my darling, that all my love should be powerless to save you from a sorrow like this!" cried the young man, dropping his head upon his clenched hands.

"My lord," continued Lady Belgrade, who was now applying a vial of sal ammonia to her patient's nostrils: "my dear Lord Arondelle, rouse yourself for her sake! She has no father, brother, or male relative to take direction of affairs in this awful crisis of her life. You, her betrothed husband, should do it--must do it! Rouse yourself at once. Look at this stupefied and gaping crowd of people! Do not be like one of them. Something must be done at once. Do WHAT OUGHT TO BE DONE!" she cried with sudden vehemence.

"I know what should be done, and I will do it," said the young man, in a tone of mournful resolution. Then turning to the crowd that filled the chamber of horror, he said:

"My friends we must leave this room for the present to the care of Lady Belgrade and her female attendants."

Then to the dowager he said:

"My lady, let one of your maids cover that body with a sheet and let no one move it by so much as an inch, until the arrival of the coroner. As soon as it is possible to do so, you will of course have Miss Levison conveyed to her own chamber. But when you leave this room pray lock it up, and place a servant before the door as sentry, that nothing may be disturbed before the inquest."

Lastly addressing the stupefied house-steward, he said:

"McRath, come with me. The castle doors must all be closed, and no one permitted to learn the arrival of a police force, which must be immediately summoned."

So saying, after a last agonized gaze upon the insensible form of his bride, he left the room of horrors, followed by the house-steward and all the male intruders.

The news of the murder spread through the castle and all over the island, carrying consternation with it. Yet the wedding guests outside, who were quite at liberty to go, showed no disposition to do so. They had come to take part in a joyous wedding festival--they remained, held by the strange fascination of ghastly interest that hangs over the scene of a murder--and such a murder!

So, the crowd, instead of diminishing, greatly increased. Peasants from the hills around, who, having had no wedding garments, had forborne to appear at the feast, now came in their tattered plaids, impelled by an eager curiosity to gaze upon the walls of the castle, and see and hear all they could concerning the mysterious murder that had been perpetrated within it.

The country side rang with the terrible story. And soon the telegraph wires flashed it all over the kingdom.

The coroner hastened to the castle, inspected the corpse, and ordered that everything should remain untouched. He then empanelled a jury for the inquest, whose first session was held in the chamber of death, from which the suffering daughter of the deceased banker had been tenderly removed.

Such among the guests who were not detained as witnesses, found themselves at liberty to depart. But very few availed themselves of the privilege. They preferred to stop and see the end of the inquest.

Skillful and experienced detectives were summoned by telegraph from Scotland Yard, London, and arrived at the castle about midnight.

The house was placed in charge of the police while the investigation was pending.

But the materials for the formation of a decided verdict seemed very meagre.

A careful examination of the body showed that the banker had been killed by one mortal blow inflicted by a blunt and heavy instrument that had crushed in the skull. The instrument was searched for, and soon found in a small but very heavy bronze statuette of Somnes that used to stand on the bedroom mantel-piece; but was now picked up from the carpet, crusted with blood and gray hair. But the miscreant who had held that deadly weapon, and dealt that mortal blow, could not be detected.

Investigation further brought to light that an extensive robbery had been committed. From the banker's person his diamond-studded gold watch, chain, and seals, his gold snuff-box, set with emeralds, a heavy cornelian seal ring set in gold, and his diamond studs and sleeve buttons were taken. A patent safe, which stood in his room, and contained valuable documents as well as a large amount of money, had been broken open, the documents scattered, and the money carried off.

Yet no trace of the robber could be found.

The broken safe was the only piece of "professional" burglary to be seen anywhere about the house. The fastenings on every door and every window were intact.

The most plausible theory of the murder was, that some burglar, or burglars, attracted and tempted by the rumor of almost fabulous treasure then in the castle in the form of wedding offerings to the bride, had gained access to the building, and penetrated to the upper chambers, where, finding the banker still up and awake, they had killed him by one fell blow, to prevent discovery.

True, the priceless wedding presents had not been disturbed. They still blazed in their open caskets upon the drawing-room table--a splendid spectacle. But then they had been guarded all through the night by two faithful men-servants armed with revolvers and seated at the table under a lighted chandelier. It was supposed that the robbers, seeing this lighted and guarded room, had crept past it and mounted to the banker's chamber to pursue their nefarious purpose there; that simple robbery was their first intention, but being seen by the watchful banker, they had instantly killed him to prevent his giving the alarm.

For no alarm had been given!

Every inmate of the house who was examined testified to having passed a quiet night, undisturbed by any noise.

The hall porter and footmen whose duty it was to see to the closing of the castle at night, and the opening of it in the morning, testified to having fastened every door at eleven o'clock on the previous night, and to having found them still fastened at six in the morning.

How, then, did the murderers and robbers gain access to the house, since there was no sign of a broken lock or bolt to be seen anywhere, except in the safe in the banker's room.

Suspicion seemed to point to some inmate of the castle, who must have let the miscreants in.

Yes, but what inmate?

No member of the small family, of course; no visitor, certainly; no servant, probably! Yet, for want of another subject, suspicion fell upon Peters, the valet. He was always the last to see his master at night, and the first to see him in the morning. He had a pass-key to the ante-room of his master's chamber. It was believed to be a very suspicious circumstance, also that he had so persistently declined to call his master that morning, asserting as he did to the very last that Sir Lemuel had given orders that he should not be disturbed until he rang his bell.

This story of the valet was doubted. It was suspected that he might have been in league with the robbers and murderers, might have admitted them to the house that night after the family had retired, and concealed them until the hour came for the commission of their crime; and that he made excuses in the morning not to call his master so as to prevent as long as possible the discovery of the murder, and give the murderers time to get off from the scene of their awful crime.

The valet was not openly accused by any one. The officers of the law were too discreet to permit that to be done.

But he was detained as a witness, and subjected to a very severe examination.

Peters was a very tall, very spare, middle-aged man, with a slight stoop in his shoulders, with a thin, flushed face, sharp features, weak, blue eyes, and scanty red hair and whiskers, dressed with foppish precision. He looked something like a fool; but as little like the confederate of robbers and murderers as it was possible to imagine.

Witness testified that his name was Abraham Peters, that he was born in Drury Lane, London, and was now forty years of age; that he had been in the service of Sir Lemuel Levison for the last five years; that he loved and honored the deceased banker, and had every reason to believe that his master valued him also. He said that it was his service every night to assist his master in undressing and getting to bed, and every morning in getting up and dressing.

A juror asked the witness whether he was in the habit of waiting every morning for his master's bell to ring before going to his room.

The witness answered that he was not; that he had standing orders to call his master every morning at seven o'clock, except otherwise instructed by Sir Lemuel.

Another juror inquired of the witness whether he had received these exceptional instructions on the previous night.

The witness answered that he had received such; that his master had sent him with a message to his daughter, Miss Levison, requesting her to come to his room, as he wished to have a talk with her. He delivered his message through Miss Levison's maid, and returned to his master's room. But when Miss Levison was announced Sir Lemuel dismissed him with permission to retire to bed at once, and not to call his master in the morning, but to wait until Sir Lemuel should ring his bell.

"I left Miss Levison with her father, your honor, and that was the last time as ever I saw my master alive," concluded the valet, trembling like a leaf.

"I presume that Miss Levison will be able to corroborate this part of your testimony. Where *is* Miss Levison? Let her be called," said the coroner.

The family physician, who was present at the inquest, arose in his place and said:

"Miss Levison, sir, is not now available as a witness. She is lying in her chamber, nearly at the point of death, with brain fever."

"Lord bless my soul, I am sorry to hear that! But it is no wonder, poor young lady, after such a shock," said the kind-hearted coroner.

"But here, sir," continued the doctor, "is a witness who, I think, will be able to give us some light."

CHAPTER IX.
AFTER THE DISCOVERY.

"Sir, if you please, I request that this witness be immediately placed under examination," said Lord Arondelle, who sat, with pale, stern visage, among the spectators, now addressing the coroner.

"Yes, certainly, my lord. Let the man be called," answered the latter.

A short, stout, red-haired and freckle-faced boy, clothed in a well-worn suit of gray tweed, came forward and was duly sworn.

"What is your name, my lad?" inquired the coroner's clerk.

"Cuddie McGill, an' it please your worship," replied the shock-headed youth.

"Your age?"

"Anan?"

"How old are you?"

"Ou, ay, just nineteen come St. Andrew's Eve, at night."

"Where do you live?"

"Wi' my maister, Gillie Ferguson, the saddler, at Lone."

"Well now, then, what do you know about this case?" inquired the clerk, who, pen in hand, had been busily taking down the unimportant, preliminary answers of the witness under examination.

"Aweel, thin your worship, I ken just naething of ony account; but I just happen speak what I saw yestreen under the castle wa', and doctor here, he wad hae me come my ways and tell your honor; its naething just," replied Cuddie McGill, scratching his shock head.

"But tell us what you saw."

"Aweel, then, your worship, I had been hard at wark a' the day, and could na get awa to see the wedding deecorations. But after my wark was dune and I had my bit aitmeal cake and parritch, I e'en cam' my way over the brig to hae a luke at them."

"Well, and what did you see besides the decorations?"

"An it please your worship, as I cam through the thick shrubbery I spied a lassie, standing under the balcony on the east side o' the castle wa'."

"At what hour was this?"

"I dinna ken preceesely. It may hae been ten o'clock; for I ken the moon was about twa hours high."

"Ay, well; go on."

"I hid mysel' in the firs and watchit the lassie; for I said to mysel' it wair a tryste wi' her lad, and I behoove to find out wha they were. Sae I watchit the lassie. And presently a tall gallant cam' up till her, and they spake thegither. I could na hear what they said. But anon the tall mon went his ways, and the lassie bided her lane under the balcony. I wondered at that. And I waited to see the end. I waited, it seemed to me, full twa hour. The moon was weel nigh overhead, when at lang last the gallant cam' on wi' anither tall mon. And they passed sae nigh that I heard their talk. Spake the gallant: 'I would na hae had it happened for a' we hae gained.' Said the ither ane: 'It could na be helpit. The auld mon skreekit. He would hae brocht the house upon us, and we hadna stappit his mouth.' And the twa passit out o' hearing, and sune cam' to the lassie under the balcony. And the three talkit thegither, but I just couldna hear a word they spake. And sae I went my ways home, wondering what it a' meant. But I thocht nae muckle harm until the morn when I heerd o' the murder."

"Would you know the tall man again if you were to see him?" inquired the coroner.

"Na, for ye ken I could na see a feature o' his face."

"Would you know the girl again?"

"Na. I could na see the lass ony mair than the gallant."

"Nor the third man?"

"Na, nor the ither ane."

"Did you hear any name or any place spoken of between the parties?"

"Na, na name, na pleece. I hae tuld your honor all I heerd. I heerd no mair than

I hae said," replied the witness.

And the severest cross-examination could not draw anything more from him.

The officials put their heads together and talked in whispers.

This last witness gave, after all, the nearest to a clue of any they had yet received.

The notes of the testimony were put in the hands of the London detective then present.

"Allow me to remind you, sir," said Lord Arondelle, "that this interview testified to by the last witness, was said to have taken place between ten and twelve at night, and that there is a train for London which stops at Lone at a quarter past twelve. Would it not be well to make inquiries at the station as to what passengers, if any, got on at Lone?"

"A good idea. Thanks, my lord. We will summon the agent who happened to be on duty at that hour," said the coroner.

And a messenger was immediately dispatched to Lone to bring the railway official in question.

In the interim, several of the household servants were examined, but without bringing any new facts to light.

After an absence of two hours, the messenger returned accompanied by Donald McNeil, the ticket-agent who had been in the office for the midnight train of the preceding day.

He was a man of middle age and medium size, with a fair complexion, sandy hair and open, honest countenance. He was clothed in a suit of black and white-checked cloth.

He was duly sworn and examined. He gave his name as Donald McNeil, his age forty years, and his home in the hamlet of Lone.

"You are a ticket-agent at the Railway Station at Lone?" inquired the coroner's clerk.

"I am, sir."

"You were on duty at that station last night, between twelve midnight and one, morning?"

"I was, sir."

"Does the train for London stop at Lone at that hour?"

"The up-train stops at Lone, at a quarter past twal, sir, and seldom varies for as muckle as twa minutes."

"It stopped last night as usual, at a quarter past twelve?"

"It did, sir, av coorse."

"Did any passengers get on that train from Lone?"

"**One** passenger did, sir; whilk I remarked it more particularly, because the passenger was a young lass, travelling her lane, and it is unco seldom a woman tak's that train at that hour, and never her lane."

"Ah! there was but one passenger, then, that took the midnight train from Lone for London?"

"But one, sir."

"And she was a woman?"

"A young lass, sir."

"Did she take a through ticket?"

"Ah, sir, to London."

"What class?"

"Second-class."

"Had she luggage?"

"An unco heavy black leather bag, sir, that was a'."

"How do you know the bag was heavy?"

"By the way she lugged it, sir. The porter offered to relieve her o' it, but she wad na trust it out o' her hand ae minute."

"Ah! Was it a large bag?"

"Na, sir, no that large, but unco heavy, as it might be filled fu' o' minerals, the like of whilk the college lads whiles collect in the mountains. Na, it was no' large, but unco heavy, and she wad na let it out o' her hand ae minute."

"Just so. Would you know that young woman again if you were to see her?"

"Na, I could na see her face. She wore a thick, dark vail, doublit over and over her face, the whilk was the moir to be noticed because the nicht was sae warm."

"You say her face was concealed. How, then, did you know her to be a young woman?"

"Ou, by her form and her gait just, and by her speech."

"She talked with you, then?"

"Na, she spak just three words when she handed in the money for her ticket: 'One--second-class--through.'"

"Would you recognize her voice again if you should hear it?"

"Ay, that I should."

"How was this young woman dressed?"

"She wore a lang, black tweed cloak wi' a hood till it, and a dark vail."

A few more questions were asked, but as nothing new was elicited the witness was permitted to retire.

Other witnesses were examined, and old witnesses were recalled hour after hour and day after day, without effect. No new light was thrown upon the mystery.

No one, except Cuddie McGill, the saddler's apprentice, could be found who had seen the suspicious man and woman lurking under the balcony.

Certainly Lord Arondelle remembered the "dream" Miss Levison had told him of the two persons whom she mistook to be himself and Rose Cameron talking together under her window. But Miss Levison was so far incapable of giving evidence as to be lying at the point of death with brain fever. So it would have been worse than useless to have spoken of her dream, or supposed dream.

The coroner's inquest sat several days without arriving at any definite conclusion.

The most plausible theory of the murder seemed to be that a robbery had been planned between the valet and certain unknown confederates, who had all been tempted by the great treasures known to be in the castle that night in the form of costly bridal presents; that no murder was at first intended; that the confederates had been secretly admitted to the castle through the connivance of the valet; that the strong guard placed over the treasures in the lighted drawing-room had saved them from robbery; that the robbers, disappointed of their first expectations, next went, with the farther connivance of the valet, to the bedchamber of Sir Lemuel Levison, for the purpose of emptying his strong box; that being detected in their criminal designs by the wakeful banker, they had silenced him by one fatal blow on the head; that they had then accomplished the robbery of the strong box, and of the person of the deceased banker; and had been secretly let out of the castle by the valet.

Finally, it was thought that the man and the woman discovered under the balcony by Cuddie McGill on the night of the murder, were confederates in the crime, and the woman was the midnight passenger to whom Donald McNeil sold the second-class railway ticket to London, and that the heavy black bag she carried contained the booty taken from the castle.

On the evening of the third day of the unsatisfactory inquest a verdict was returned to this effect.

That the deceased Sir Lemuel Levison, Knight, had come to his death by a blow from a heavy bronze statuette held in the hands of some person unknown to the jury. And that Peters, the valet of the deceased banker, was accessory to the murder.

A coroner's warrant was immediately issued, and the valet was arrested, and confined in jail to await the action of the grand jury.

An experienced detective officer was sent upon the track of the mysterious, vailed woman, with the heavy black bag, who on the night of the murder had taken the midnight train from Lone to London.

Then at length the coroner's jury adjourned, and Castle Lone was cleared of the law officers and all others who had remained there in attendance upon the inquest.

And the preparations for the funeral of the deceased banker were allowed to go on.

In addition to the long train of servants there remained now in the castle but seven persons:

The young lady of the house, who lay prostrate and unconscious upon the bed of extreme illness or death; Lady Belgrade, who in all this trouble had nearly lost her wits; the Marquis of Arondelle, who had been requested to take the direction of affairs; the old Duke of Hereward, who had been brought to the castle in a helpless condition; the family physician, who had turned over all his other patients to his assistant, and was now devoting himself to the care of the unhappy daughter of the house; and lastly the family solicitor, and his clerk, who were down for the obsequies.

Beside these, the undertaker and his men came and went while completing their preparations for the funeral.

There had been some talk of embalming the body, and delaying the burial, until the daughter of the deceased banker should view her father's face once more; but the impossibility of restoring the crushed skull to shape rendered it advisable that she should not be shocked by a sight of it. So the day of the funeral was set.

But before that day came, another important event occurred at Lone Castle. It was not entirely unexpected. The old Duke of Hereward, since his arrival at the castle, had sunk very fast. He had been carefully guarded from the knowledge of the tragedy which had been enacted within its walls. He knew nothing of the murder of Sir Lemuel Levison, or even of the banker's presence in the castle. His failing mind had gone back to the past, and he fondly imagined himself, as of yore, the Lord of Lone and of all its vast revenues. The presence and attendance of all his old train of servants, who, as I said before, had been kindly retained in the service of the banker's family, helped the happy illusion in which the last days of the old duke were passed, until one afternoon, just as the sun was sinking out of sight behind Ben Lone, the old man went quietly to sleep in his arm-chair, and never woke again in this world.

A few days after this, in the midst of a large concourse of friends, neighbors and mourners, the mortal remains of Archibald-Alexander-John Scott, Duke of Hereward and Marquis of Arondelle, in the peerage of England, and Lord of Lone and Baron Scott, in the peerage of Scotland, were laid side by side with those of Sir Lemuel Levison, Kt., in the family vault of Lone.

The reading of the late banker's will was deferred until his daughter and sole heiress should be in a condition to attend it.

And the family solicitor took it away with him to London to keep until it should be called for.

The crisis of Salome's illness passed safely. She was out of the imminent danger of death, though she was still extremely weak.

The family physician returned to his home and his practice in the village of Lone, and only visited his patient at the castle morning and evening.

Now, therefore, besides the train of household servants, there remained at the castle but three inmates--Salome Levison, reduced by sorrow and illness to a state of infantile feebleness of mind and body; Lady Belgrade, nearly worn out with long watching, fatigue, and anxiety; and the young Marquis of Arondelle, whom we must henceforth designate as the Duke of Hereward, and whom even the stately dowager, who was "of the most straitest sect, a Pharisee" of conventional etiquette, nevertheless implored to remain a guest at the castle until after the recovery of the heiress, and the reading of the father's will.

The young duke who wished nothing more than to be near his bride, readily consented to stay.

But Salome's recovery was so slow, and her frame so feeble, that she seemed to have re-entered life through a new infancy of body and mind.

Strangely, however, through all her illness she seemed not to have lost the memory of its cause--her father's shocking death. Thus she had no new grief or horror to experience.

No one spoke to her of the terrible tragedy. She herself was the first to allude to it.

The occasion was this:

On the first day on which she was permitted to leave her bedchamber and sit for awhile in an easy resting chair, beside the open window of her boudoir, to enjoy the fresh air from the mountain and the lake, she sent for the young duke to come to her.

He eagerly obeyed the summons, and hastened to her side.

He had not been permitted to see her since her illness, and now he was almost overwhelmed with sorrow to see into what a mere shadow of her former self she had faded.

As she reclined there in her soft white robes, with her long, dark hair flowing over her shoulders, so fair, so wan, so spiritual she looked, that it seemed as if the very breeze from the lake might have wafted her away.

He dropped on one knee beside her, and embraced and kissed her hands, and then sat down next her.

After the first gentle greetings were over, she amazed him by turning and asking:

"Has the murderer been discovered yet?"

"No, my beloved, but the detectives have a clue, that they feel sure will lead to the discovery and conviction of the wretch," answered the young duke, in a low voice.

"Where have they laid the body of my dear father?" she next inquired in a low hushed tone.

"In the family vault beside those of my own parents," gravely replied the young man.

"Your own--**parents**, my lord? I knew that your dear mother had gone before, but--your father--"

"My father has passed to his eternal home. It is well with him as with yours. They are happy. And we--have a common sorrow, love!"

"I did not know--I did not know. No one told me," murmured Salome, as she dropped her face on her open hands, and cried like a child.

"Every one wished to spare you, my sweet girl, as long as possible. Yet I **did** think, they had told you of my father's departure, else I had not alluded to it so suddenly. There! weep no more, love! Viewed in the true light, those who have passed higher are rather to be envied than mourned."

Then to change the current of her thoughts he said:

"Can you give your mind now to a little business, Salome?"

"Yes, if it concerns you," she sighed, wiping her eyes, and looking up.

"It concerns me only inasmuch as it affects your interests, my love. You are of age, my Salome?"

"Yes, I was twenty-one on my last birthday."

"Then you enter at once upon your great inheritance--an onerous and responsible position."

"But you will sustain it for me. I shall not feel its weight," she murmured.

"There are thousands in this realm, my love, good men and true, who would gladly relieve me of the dear trust," said the duke, with a smile. "We must, however, be guided by your father's will, which I am happy to know is in entire harmony with your own wishes. And that brings me to what I wished to say. Kage, your late father's solicitor, is in possession of his last will. He could not follow the custom, and read it immediately after the funeral, because your illness precluded the possibility of your presence at its perusal. But he only waits for your recovery and a summons from me to bring it. Whenever, therefore, you feel equal to the exertion of hearing it, I will send a telegram to Kage to come down," concluded the duke.

"My father's last will!" softly murmured Salome. "Send the telegram to-day, please. To hear his last will read will be almost like hearing from him."

"There is beside the will a letter from your father, addressed to you, and left in the charge of Kage, to be delivered with the reading of the will, in the case of his, the writer's, sudden death," gravely added the duke.

"A letter from my dear father to me? A letter from the grave! No, rather a letter from Heaven! Telegraph Mr. Kage to bring down the papers at once, dear John," said Salome, eagerly, as a warm flush arose on her pale, transparent cheek.

"I will do so at once, love; for to my mind, that letter is of equal importance with the will--though no lawyer would think so," said the duke.

"You know its purport then?"

"No, dearest, not certainly, but I surmise it, from some conversations that I held with the late Sir Lemuel Levison."

As he spoke the door opened and Lady Belgrade entered the room, saying softly, as she would have spoken beside the cradle of a sick baby:

"I am sorry to disturb your grace; but the fifteen minutes permitted by the doctor have passed, and Salome must not sit up longer."

"I am going now, dear madam," said the duke, rising.

He took Salome's hand, held it for a moment in his, while he gazed into her eyes, then pressed it to his lips, and so took his morning's leave of her.

The same forenoon he rode over to the Lone Station, and dispatched a telegram to the family solicitor, Kage.

CHAPTER X.
THE LETTER AND ITS EFFECT.

Mr. Kage arrived at Lone, within twenty-four hours after having received the duke's telegram. He reached the castle at noon and had a private interview with the duke in the library, when it was arranged that the will and the letter should be read the same afternoon in the presence of the assembled household.

"The letter also? Is not that a private one from the father to his daughter?" inquired the duke.

"No, your grace. There are reasons why it must be public, which you will recognize when you hear it read," answered the lawyer.

"Then I fear I have been mistaken in my private thoughts concerning it. Pray, will it give us any clue to the perpetrators of the murder?"

"None whatever! It certainly was not a violent death that the banker anticipated for himself when he prepared that letter to be delivered in the event of his sudden decease."

"Has any clue yet been found to the murderer?"

"None that I have heard of."

"Or to the mysterious woman who was supposed to have carried off the booty?"

"None, Detective Keightley called on me yesterday for some information regarding the stolen property, and I furnished him with a photograph of that snuff-box given to Sir Lemuel Levison by the Sultan of Turkey--the gold one richly set with precious stones. Sir Lemuel had it photographed by my advice, for identification in case of its being stolen. And he left several duplicate copies with me. I gave one to Keightley. But the man could give me no information in return. The missing woman seemed lost in London. And the proverbial little needle in the haystack might be as easily found," said the lawyer.

The announcement of luncheon put an end to the interview.

The two gentlemen passed on into the smaller dining-room where Lady Belgrade awaited them. She received the solicitor politely and invited him to the table.

After the three were seated and helped to what they preferred, her ladyship turned to the lawyers and said:

"My niece understands that you have a letter for her, left in your charge by her father. She wishes you to send it to her immediately. Her maid is here waiting to take it."

"Pardon me, my dear lady, the letter must remain in my possession until after the reading of the will, when, for certain reasons, it must be read, as the will, in the presence of the household. Pray explain this to Miss Levison, and tell her that I shall be ready to read and deliver both at five o'clock this afternoon, if that will meet her convenience," said the lawyer, respectfully.

"That will suit her; but I hope the forms will not occupy more than an hour.

Miss Levison is still extremely feeble, and ought not to sit up longer," said the dowager.

"It will not require more than half an hour, madam," replied Mr. Kage.

Lady Belgrade gave the message to the maid for her mistress. And when the girl retired, the conversation turned upon the proceedings of the London detectives in pursuit of the unknown murderers.

At the appointed hour the household servants were all assembled in the dining-room. At the head of the long table sat the family attorney and his clerk. Before them lay a japanned tin box, secured by a brass padlock. It contained the last will, the letter, and other documents appertaining to the deceased banker's estate. They were only waiting for the entrance of Miss Levison and her friends. No one else was expected. There was not the usual crowd of poor relatives who "crop up" at the reading of almost every rich man's will. The late Sir Lemuel Levison had no poor relations whatever. His people were all rich, and all scattered over Europe and America, at the head of banks, or branches of banks, in every great capital, of the almost illustrious house of "Levison, Bankers."

The assembled household had not to wait long. The door opened and the young lady of Lone entered, supported on each side by the Duke of Hereward and the dowager, Lady Belgrade.

Her fair, transparent, spiritual face looked whiter than ever, in contrast to her deep black crape dress, as she bowed to the lawyer, and passed to her seat at the table.

The duke and the dowager seated themselves on either side of her.

"Are you quite ready, Miss Levison, to hear the will of the late Sir Lemuel Levison?" inquired the attorney.

"I am quite ready, Mr. Kage, thanks," replied the young lady, in a low voice, and speaking with an effort.

The attorney unlocked the box, took out the will, unfolded and proceeded to read it.

The document was dated several years back. It was neither long nor complex. After liberal bequests to each one of his household servants, rich keepsakes to his dear friends, an annuity to the dowager Lady Belgrade, and a princely endowment to found an orphan asylum and children's hospital in the heart of London, he bequeathed the residue of his vast estates, both real and personal, without reserve and without conditions, to his only and beloved child, Salome.

After the reading of the will was finished, the attorney arose, came around to where the ladies sat, and congratulated Miss Levison and Lady Belgrade, on their rich inheritance.

"How could he do it?" thought the unconventional and weeping heiress. "Oh, how could he congratulate me on an inheritance which came, and could only have come, through my dear father's decease!" Then in a voice broken with emotion, she said:

"Thanks, Mr. Kage. Will you please now to read my dear papa's letter?--since you *are* to read it aloud, I think," she added.

"Such was the deceased Sir Lemuel's direction, my dear Miss Levison," said the lawyer. And returning to his place at the head of the table, he took the letter from the japanned box, opened it, and said:

"This letter from my late honored client to his daughter was committed by the late Sir Lemuel Levison to my charge to be retained and read after the will, in the event of a circumstance which has already occurred--I mean the sudden and unexpected death of the writer. The letter will explain itself."

Here the lawyer cleared his throat, and began to read:

"ELMHURST HOUSE, Kensington, London,

"Monday, May 1st, 18--.

"MY DEAREST ONLY CHILD: Blessings on your head! Nothing could have made me happier, than has your betrothal to so admirable a young man as the Marquis of Arondelle. Had I possessed the privilege of choosing a husband for you, and a son-in-law for myself, from the whole race of mankind, I should have chosen him above all others. But, my dearest Salome, the satisfaction I enjoy in your prospects of happiness is shadowed by one faint cloud. It is not much, my love; it is only the consciousness of my age and of the precarious state of my health. I may not live to see you united to the noble husband of your choice. Therefore it is that I have urged your speedy marriage with what your good chaperon, Lady Belgrade, evidently considers indecorous haste. She must continue to think it indecorous, because unreasonable. I cannot, and will not, darken your sunshine of joy, by giving to you *now* the real reason of my precipitation--the extremely precarious state of my health. Yet, in the event of my being suddenly taken from you, I must prepare this letter to be delivered to you after my death, that you may know my last wishes. If I live to see you wedded to the good Lord Arondelle, this paper shall be torn up and destroyed; if not, if I should be suddenly snatched away from you before your wedding-day, this letter will be read to you, after my will shall have been read, in the presence of your betrothed husband, your good chaperon and your assembled household, that you and they and all may know my last wishes concerning you, and that none shall dare to blame you for obeying them, even though in doing so you have to pursue a very unusual course. My wish, therefore, is that your marriage with Lord Arondelle may not be delayed for a day upon account of my death; but that it take place at the time fixed or as soon thereafter as practicable. In giving these directions, I feel sure that I am consulting the wishes of Lord Arondelle, the best interests of yourself, and the happiness of both. Follow my directions, therefore, my dearest daughter, and may the blessing of our Father in Heaven rest upon you and yours, is the prayer of

"Your devoted father, LEMUEL LEVISON."

During the reading of the letter the face of Salome was bathed in tears and buried in her pocket-handkerchief.

The duke sat by her, with his arm around her waist, supporting her.

At the end of the reading, without looking up, she stretched out her hand and whispered softly:

"Give me my dear father's letter now."

The attorney, who was engaged in re-folding the documents and restoring them to the japanned box, left his seat, and came to her side, and placed the letter in her hands.

"Thanks, Mr. Kage," she said, wiping her eyes and looking up. "But now will you tell me if you know what my dear father meant by writing of the precarious state of his health? He seemed to enjoy a very vigorous and green old age."

"Yes, he '*seemed*' to do so, my dear young lady; but it was all seeming. He was really affected with a mortal malady, which his physicians warned him might prove fatal at any moment," gravely replied the lawyer.

"And he never hinted it to us!"

"He did not wish to sadden your young life with a knowledge of his affliction."

"My own dear papa! My dear, dear papa! loving, self-sacrificing to the end of his earthly life! never thinking of his own happiness--always thinking of mine or of others! My dear, dear father!" murmured the still weeping daughter.

"He thought of your happiness, and of the happiness of your betrothed husband, my dear young lady, when he committed that letter to my care, to be delivered to you in case of his sudden death, and when he charged me to urge with all my might, your compliance with its instructions. And now permit me to add, my dear Miss Levison, that to obey your father's will in this matter would be the very best and wisest course you could pursue."

"Thanks, Mr. Kage; I know that you are a faithful friend to our family; but--I must have a little time to recover," murmured Salome, faintly.

"Here, you may remember my dear Salome, that when I told you of this letter in the possession of Mr. Kage, I said that I thought I knew its purport from certain conversations I had held with your late father. He had hinted to me the dangerous condition of his health, and he had expressed a hope that no accident to himself should be permitted to postpone our marriage; and then he told me that he had left a letter with his solicitor to be read in case of his sudden death, and that the letter would explain itself. He concluded by begging me if anything should happen to him to necessitate the delivery of that letter to you, to urge upon you the wisdom and policy of following its direction. He could not have given me a commission I should be more anxious or earnest in executing. My dear Salome, will you obey your good father's wishes? Will you give me at once a husband's right to love and cherish you?" he added in a low whisper.

"Oh, give me a little time," she murmured--"give me a little time. There is nothing I wish more than to do as my dear father directed me, and as you wish me; but my heart is so wounded and bleeding now, I am still so weak and broken-spirited. Give me a little time, dear John, to recover some strength to overcome my sorrow."

Here she broke down and wept.

"I think we had best take her back to her room," said Lady Belgrade, rising.

Mr. Kage locked up the documents in the japanned box, put the key in his pocket-book, and consigned the box to the care of his clerk.

Lady Belgrade dismissed the assembled servants to their several duties, and then, assisted by Lord Arondelle, led the bereaved and suffering girl from the room.

The lawyer and his clerk, who were to dine and sleep at the castle, were left alone.

The lawyer rang and asked for a bottle of wine and a couple of glasses, and lighted his cigar, to pass away the time until the dinner hour.

The next morning Mr. Kage and his clerk went back to London.

It now became an anxious question, whether the marriage of the young Duke of Hereward and the heiress of Lone should proceed according to her father's wishes.

Mr. Kage, the family attorney, urged it: Dr. McWilliams, the family physician, urged it: above all the expectant bridegroom, the Duke of Hereward; only the bride-elect, Salome, and her chaperon, Lady Belgrade, objected to it.

Salome, ill and nervous from the severe shock she had received, could decide upon nothing hastily and pleaded for a short delay.

Lady Belgrade argued etiquette and conventionalities--the impropriety of the daughter's marriage so soon after the father's murder.

Meanwhile the summer had merged into early autumn; the season of the Highlands was over, and the cold Scotch mists were driving summer visitors to the South coast, or to the Continent.

The climate was telling heavily upon the delicate organization of Salome Levison. She contracted a serious cough.

Then the family physician, (so to speak,) "put down his foot" with professional authority so stern as not to be contested or withstood.

"This is a question of life or death, my lady," he said to the dowager--"a question of life and death, ye mind! And not of conventionality and etiquette! Let conventionality and etiquette go to the D., from whom they first came. This girl must die, or she must marry immediately, and go off with her husband to the islands of the Grecian Archipelago. That is all that can save her. And as for you, my laird duke," continued the honest Scotch doctor, breaking into dialect as he always did whenever he forgot himself under strong excitement, "as for you, me laird duke, if ye dinna overcome the lassie's scruples, and marry her out of hand, the de'il hae me but I'll e'en marry her mysel', and tak' her awa to save her life! Now, then will I tak' her mysel' or will you?"

"I will take her!" said the young duke, smiling. Then turning to the dowager, he added, gravely: "Lady Belgrade, this marriage must and shall take place immediately. You must add your efforts to mine to overcome your niece's scruples. Your ladyship has been working against me heretofore. I hope now, after hearing what the doctor has said, that you will work with me."

"Of course, if the child's life and health are in question: and, indeed, this climate is much too severe for her, and she certainly does need rousing; and as it has been three months now since Sir Lemuel Levison's funeral, I don't see--But, of course, after all, it is for you and Salome to decide as you please;" answered Lady Belgrade, in a confused and hesitating manner, for when the dowager went outside of her conventionalities she lost herself.

Salome Levison was again besieged by the pleadings of her lover, the counsels of her solicitor, and the arguments of her physician, all with the co-operation of her chaperon.

"I do not see what else can be done, my dear," she said to her protegee. "The ceremony can be performed as quietly as possible, and you two can go away, and the world be no wiser."

"As if I cared for the world! I will do this in obedience to my dear father's directions and my betrothed husband's wishes, and I do not even think of the world," gravely replied Salome.

"Now, then, to the details, my dear. What day shall we fix? And shall the ceremony be preformed here at the castle or at the church at Lone?"

"Oh, not here! not here! I could not bear to be married here, or at the Lone church either. No, Lady Belgrade. We must go up to our town house in London, and be married quietly at St. Peter's in Kensington, where I used to attend divine service with my dear papa," said Salome, becoming agitated.

"Very well, my love. But don't excite yourself. We will go. And the sooner the better. These horrid Scotch mists are aggravating my rheumatism beyond endurance," concluded the dowager.

It was now the last week in September. But so diligently did the dowager, and the servants under her orders exert themselves both at Castle Lone and in London, that before the first of October, Miss Levison, with her chaperon and their attendants, were all comfortably settled in the luxurious town-house in the West End.

The Duke of Hereward took lodgings near the home of his bride-elect.

As the marriage settlements had been executed, and the bridal paraphernalia prepared for the first marriage day set three months before, there was really nothing to do in the way of preparation for the wedding, and no reason for even so much as a week's delay. An early day was therefore set. It was decided that the ceremony should be performed without the least parade.

Since her departure from Castle Lone and her arrival at their town house, the change of scene and of circumstances, and the preliminaries of her wedding and her journey, had the happiest effects upon Miss Levison's health and spirits.

She recovered her cheerfulness, and even acquired a bloom she had never possessed before. And her attendants took care to keep from her all that could revive her memory of the tragedy at Lone.

One morning the Duke of Hereward came to the house and asked to see Lady Belgrade alone.

The dowager received him in the library.

"Has Miss Levison seen the morning papers?" he inquired, as soon as the usual greetings were over.

"No, they have not yet come," answered her ladyship.

"Thank Heaven! Do not let her see them on any account! I would not have her shocked. The truth is," he added, in explanation of his words to the wondering dowager, "I have important news to tell you. The mysterious vailed woman, supposed to be connected with the robbery and murder at Lone Castle, has been found and arrested. The stolen property has been discovered in her possession. And she-- you will be infinitely shocked--she proves to be Rose Cameron, the daughter of one of our shepherds, living near Ben Lone."

CHAPTER XI.
THE VAILED PASSENGER.

We must return to the night of the murder, and to the man and woman whom Salome Levison heard, and did not merely "dream" that she heard, conversing under her balcony at midnight.

When left alone in her dark and silent hiding-place, the woman waited long and impatiently. Sometimes she crept out from her shadowy nook, and stole a look up to the casements of the castle, but they were all dark and silent, and closely shut, save one immediately above her head, which stood open, though neither lighted nor occupied.

She had waited perhaps an hour when stealthy footsteps were heard approaching, and not one, but two men came up whispering in hurried and agitated tones. She caught a few words of their troubled talk.

"You have betrayed me! I never meant, under any circumstances, that you should have done such a deed!" said one.

"It was necessary to our safety. We should have been discovered and arrested," said the other.

"You have brought the curse of Cain upon my head!" groaned the first speaker.

"Come, come, my lord, brace up! No one intended what has happened. It was an accident, a calamity, but it is an accomplished fact, and 'what is done, is done,' and 'what is past remedy is past regret.' If the old man hadn't squealed--"

"Hush! burn you! the girl will hear!" whispered the first speaker, as they approached the woman under the balcony.

"Rose, here; don't speak. Take this bag; be very careful of it; do not let it for a moment go out of your sight, or even out of your hand. Go to Lone station. The train for London stops there at 12:15. Take a second-class ticket, keep your face covered with a thick vail until you get to London, and to the house. I will join you there in a few days," said the first speaker, earnestly.

"Why canna ye gae now, my laird?" impatiently inquired the girl.

"It would be dangerous, Rose."

"I'm thinking it is laughing at me ye are, Laird Arondelle. You'll bide here and marry yon leddy," said the girl, tossing her head.

"No, on my soul! How can I, when I have married you? Have you not got your marriage certificate with you?"

"Ay, I hae got my lines, but I dinna like ye to bide here, near your leddy, whiles I gang my lane to London."

"Rose, our safety requires that you should go alone to London. You cannot trust me; yet see how much I trust you. You have in that bag, which I have confided to your care, uncounted treasures. Take it carefully to London and to the house on Westminster Road. Conceal it there and wait for me."

"Who is yon lad that cam' wi' ye frae the castle?" inquired the girl, pointing to the other man who had withdrawn apart.

"He is one of the servants of the castle, who is in my confidence. Never mind him. Hurry away now, my lass. You have just time to cross the bridge and reach the station, to catch the train. You are not afraid to go alone?"

"Nay, I'm no feared. But dinna be lang awa' yersel', my laird, or I shall be think-ing my thoughts about yon leddy," said the girl, as she folded the dark vail around and around the hat, and without further leave-taking, started off in a brisk walk toward the bridge.

She passed through the castle grounds and over the bridge, and went on to the station, without having met another human being.

She secured her ticket, as has been related, and when the train stopped, she took her place on a second-class car.

Being very much of an animal, and very much fatigued, she could not be kept awake even by the excitement of her novel and perilous position, but, holding on to her booty, and lulled by the swift motion of the train, she fell asleep, and slept until eight o'clock next morning, when she was awakened by the stopping of the train and the bustle of the arrival at Euston Square Station. Her first thought was for the safety of her bag. With a start of dismay she missed it from her lap, where she had been holding it so tightly.

"An' it 's yer little valise yer a looking for, my dear, there it be at yer feet, where it fell, with a crash, while ye slept. An' there was anything in it would break, sure it 's broken entirely," said a kindly man, pointing to the bag upon the floor.

She hastily picked it up.

"Oh! if any one had known what it contains, would it have been left there in safety all the time I slept?" she asked herself, as her hands closed tightly upon her recovered treasure.

But the passengers were all leaving the train, and so she got out with the rest.

She was too cunning to take a cab from the station. She left it on foot and walked a mile or two, making many turns, before, at length she hailed a "four wheeler," hired it and directed the cabman to drive to Number ---- Westminster Road.

CHAPTER XII.
THE HOUSE ON WESTMINSTER ROAD.

An hour's ride through some of the most crowded streets of London brought her to her destination--a tall, dingy, three-storied brick house, in a block of the same.

She paid and dismissed the cab at the door, and then went up and rang the bell.

It was answered by an old woman, in a black skirt, red sack, white apron, and white cap.

"Well, to be sure, ma'am, you have taken me unexpected; but I'm main glad to see you so soon. Come in, and I'll make you comfortable in no time," said the woman, with kindly respect, as she held the door wide open for her mistress.

"Any one been here sin' we left Mrs. Rogers?" inquired the traveller.

"No, ma'am--no soul. It is very lonely here without you. Let me take your bag, ma'am. It do seem heavy," said Mrs. Rogers, as she held out her hand and took hold of the handle of the satchel.

"Na, I thank ye. It's na that heavy neither," exclaimed the girl, nervously jerking back the bag, and following her conductor into the house and up stairs.

An unlikely house to be the shelter of thieves and the receptacle of stolen goods. There was a look of sober respectability about its dinginess that might have appertained to a suburban doctor with a large family and a small practice. An old oil cloth, whole, but with its pattern half washed off, covered the narrow hall--an old stair-carpet of originally good quality, but now thread-bare in places, covered the steps. This was all that could be seen from the open door by any chance caller. But upstairs all was very different.

As the girl reached the landing, the old woman opened a door on her left and ushered her into a bright, glaring room, filled up with cheap new furniture, in which blinding colors and bad taste predominated. Carpets, curtains, chair and sofa covers, and hassocks, all bright scarlet; cornices, mirrors, and picture frames, (framing cheap, showy pictures,) all in brassy looking gilt. Through this sitting-room the girl passed into a bedroom, where, also, the furniture was in scarlet and gilt, except the white draperied bed and the dressing-table. Here the girl threw herself down in an easy-chair saying:

"I'll just bide here a bit and wash my face and hands, while ye'll gae bring my breakfast."

"Yes, ma'am. What would you like to have?" inquired the woman.

"Ait meal parritch, fust of a', to begin wi' twa kippered herrings; a sausage; a beefsteak; twa eggs; a pot o' arange marmalade; a plate of milk toast, some muffins, and some fresh rolls," concluded the girl.

"Anything more, ma'am?" dryly inquired Mrs. Rogers.

"Nay--ay! Ye may bring me a mutton chop, wi' the lave."

"Tea or coffee, ma'am?"

"Baith, and mak' haste wi' it," answered the girl.

The old woman, smiling to herself, went out.

The girl being left alone, fastened both doors of her room, hung napkins over the key-holes, drew close the scarlet curtains of her windows, and then sat down on the floor and opened the bag and turned out its contents on the carpet.

Fortunatus! what a sight! Well might her fellow-passenger have heard a crash when the bag slipped from her lap to the bottom of the car!

About twelve little canvas bags filled with coins, and marked variously on the sides--L50, L100, L500, L1,000.

She gazed at the treasure in a sort of rapture of possession! How fast her heart beat! She did not think that there was so much money in the whole world! She began to count the bags, and add up their marked figures, to try to estimate the amount. There were two bags marked one thousand, four marked five hundred, three marked one hundred, and three marked fifty pounds--in all twelve little canvas bags containing altogether four thousand four hundred and fifty pounds.

What a mine of wealth! How she gloated over it! She longed to cut open the little canvas bags and spread the whole glittering mass of gold and silver on the carpet before her, that she might gaze upon it--not as a miser to hoard it, but as a vain beauty to spend it. How many bonnets and dresses and shawls and laces and jewels this money would buy? How she longed to lay it out! But she dared not do it yet.

She dared not even open the canvas bags. She must conceal her riches.

She began to put the bags back in the satchel.

In doing so, she perceived that she had not half emptied it--there was something in each of the buttoned pockets on the inside. She opened the pockets and turned out their contents.

Rainbows and sunbeams and flashes of lightning!

Her eyes were dazzled with splendor. There was set in a ring a large solitaire diamond in which seemed collected all the light and color of the sun! There was a watch in a gold hunting case, thickly studded with precious stones, and bearing in the center of its circle the initials of the late owner, set in diamonds, and which was suspended to a heavy gold chain. There was a snuff-box of solid gold encrusted with pearls, opals, diamonds, rubies, emeralds, amethysts and sapphires, in a design of Oriental beauty and splendor.

There were also diamond studs and diamond sleeve-buttons--each a large solitaire of immense value, and there were other jewels in the form of seals, lockets, and so forth; and all those delighted her woman's eyes and heart. But, above all, the golden box, set with all sorts of flaming precious stones, with its splendid colors and blazing fires dazzled her sight and dazed her mind.

"I *will* keep this for mysel'," she said, as she put it in the bosom of her dress--"I will, I *will*, I WILL! He shall na hae this again. I'll tell him it was lost or sto'en."

Then she opened the satchel and began to put away the other jewels, until she took up the watch, looked at it longingly, put it in the bag, took it out again, and finally, without a word, slipped it into her bosom beside the box.

Next she trifled with the temptation of the diamond ring. She slipped it on and off her finger. She had large beautiful hands in perfect proportion to her large beautiful form, and the ring that had fitted the banker's long thin finger fitted her round white one perfectly. So, she took the jewelled box from her bosom, opened it, put the diamond ring in it, then closed and returned it to its hiding place.

Finally retaining the box, the watch and the rings, she replaced all the jewels and the money-bags in the satchel, and put the satchel for the present between the mattresses of her bed. While thus engaged she heard her old attendant moving about in the next room, and she knew that she was setting the table for her breakfast.

So she hastened to smooth the bed again, and snatch the napkins off the keyholes, and unlock the doors lest her very caution should excite suspicion.

Then at length she took time to wash the railroad dust from her face, and brush it from her hair.

And finally she passed into her sitting-room where she found the table laid for her single breakfast.

Presently her housekeeper entered bringing one tray on which stood tea and coffee with their accompaniments, and followed by a young kitchen maid with another tray on which stood the bread, butter, marmalade, meat, fish, etc., with *their* accompaniments.

When all these were arranged upon the table, Rose Cameron sat down and fell to.

Being a very perfect animal, she was blessed with an excellent appetite and a healthy digestion. She was therefore, a very heavy feeder; and now bread, butter, fish, meat, marmalade disappeared rapidly from the scene, to the great amusement of the housekeeper and kitchen maid, who had never seen "a lady" eat so ravenously.

When the breakfast service was removed, she went back into her bedroom, locked the door, and covered the keyholes as before, and took the satchel from between the mattresses, and opened it to gloat over her treasures; for she quite considered them as her own. Again she was "tempted of the devil." She thought of the fine shops in London, and the fine ready-made dresses she could buy with the very smallest of these bags of money.

"Why should I no'? What's his is mine! I'll e'en tak the wee baggie, and gae till the fine shops," she said to herself. And selecting one of the fifty pound bags, she replaced the others in the satchel, and put the satchel in its hiding place.

She got ready for her expedition by arraying herself in a cheap, dark-blue silk suit, and a straw hat with a blue feather. Then she carefully locked her bedroom door, and took the key with her when she left the house.

Her ambition did not take any very high flights, although she did believe herself to be a countess. She knew nothing of the splendid shops of the West End. She only knew the Borrough and St. Paul's churchyard, both of which she thought, contained the riches and splendors of the whole world. She went to the nearest cab-stand, took a cab, and drove to St. Paul's churchyard, (in ancient times a cemetery, but now a network of narrow, crowded streets, filled with cheap, showy shops.) She spent the best part of the day in that attractive locality.

When she returned, late in the afternoon, the canvas bag was empty and the cab was full, for Rose Cameron, the country girl, ignorant of the world, but having a saving faith in the dishonesty of cities, refused to trust the dealers to send the goods home, but insisted on fetching them herself.

She displayed her purchases--mostly gaudy trash--to the wondering eyes of Mrs. Rogers, and then, tired out with her long night's journey and her whole day's shopping, she ate a heavy supper and went to bed. Such excesses never seemed to over-task her fine digestive organs or disturb her sleep. After an unbroken night's rest she awoke the next morning with a clear head and a keen appetite, and rang for the housekeeper to bring her a cup of tea to her bedside.

While waiting for her tea she wondered if her "guid mon" would arrive during the next twenty-four hours.

And that revived in her mind the memory of her supposed rival. During the preceding day she had been so absorbed in the contemplation of her newly-acquired treasures in jewelry and money that she had scarcely thought of what might then be going on at Castle Lone.

Now she wondered what happened there; whether the marriage had failed to take place; but, of course, she said to herself, it had failed. Lord Arondelle would never commit bigamy--but *how* had it failed? What had been made to happen to prevent it from going on? And what had the bride and her friends said or thought?

Above all, why had Lord Arondelle, married to herself as she fully believed him to be, *why* had Lord Arondelle allowed the affair to go so far, even to the wedding-morning, when the wedding-feast was prepared, and the wedding guests arrived?

It must have been done to mortify and humiliate those city strangers who sat in his father's seat, she thought.

Oh, but she would have given a great deal to have seen her hated rival's face on that wedding-morning when no wedding took place?

No doubt "John" would tell her all about it when he arrived. And oh! How impatient she became for his arrival!

Her reflections were interrupted by the entrance of the housekeeper with a cup of tea in one hand and the *Times* in the other.

"Good morning, ma'am. And hoping you find yourself well this morning! Here is your tea, ma'am. And here is the paper, ma'am. There's the most hawful murder been committed, ma'am, which I thought you might enjoy along of your tea," said the worthy woman, as she drew a little stand by the bedside and placed the cup and the newspaper upon it.

"A murder?" listlessly repeated Rose Cameron, rising on her elbow, and taking the tea-cup in her hand.

"Ay, ma'am, the most hawfullest murder as ever you 'eard of, on an' 'elpless old gent, away up at a place in Scotland called Lone!"

"EH!" exclaimed Rose Cameron, starting, and nearly letting fall her tea-cup.

"Yes, ma'am, and the most hawfullest part of it was, as it was done in the night afore his darter's wedding-day, and his blessed darter herself was the first to find her father's dead body in the morning."

"Gude guide us!" exclaimed Rose Cameron, putting down her untasted tea, and staring at the speaker in blank dismay.

"You may read all about it in the paper, ma'am," said the housekeeper.

"When did it a' happen?" huskily inquired the girl, whose face was now ashen pale.

"On the night before last, ma'am. The same night you were traveling up to London by the Great Northern. And bless us and save us, the poor bride must have found her poor pa's dead body just about the time you arrived at home here, ma'am, for the paper says it was ten o'clock."

"Ou! wae's me! wae's me! wae's me!" cried Rose, covering her ashen-pale face with her hands and sinking back on her pillow.

"Oh, indeed I'm sorry I told you anything about it, ma'am, if it gives you such a turn. I *did* hope it would amuse you while you sipped your tea. But la! there! some ladies do be *so* narvy!"

"An' that's the way the braw wedding was stappit!" cried Rose, without even hearing the words of her attendant.

"Yes, ma'am," replied Mrs. Rogers, not understanding the allusion of the speaker, "*that* was the way the wedding was stopped, in course. No wedding could go on after *that*, you know, ma'am, anyhow, let alone the bride falling into a fit the minute she saw the bloody corpse of her murdered father, and being of a raving manyyack ever since. Instead of a wedding and a feast there will be an inquest and a funeral."

"Was--there--a--robbery?" inquired Rose Cameron in a low, faint, frightened tone.

"Ay, ma'am, a great robbery of money and jewelry, and no clue yet to the vily-uns as did it! But won't you drink your tea, ma'am?"

"Na, na, I dinna need it now. Ou! this is awfu'! Wae worth the day!" exclaimed the horror-stricken girl, shivering from head to foot as with an ague.

"Indeed, I am very sorry I told you anything about it, ma'am. But I thought it would interest you. I didn't think it would shock you. But, indeed, if I were you, I wouldn't take on so about people I didn't know anything about. And you didn't know anything about *them*. You haven't even asked the names," urged the worthy woman.

"Na, na, I did na ken onything anent them; but it is unco awfu'!" said Rose, in hurried, tremulous tones.

Not for all her hidden treasures would she have had it suspected that she even remotely knew anything about the murder or the man who was murdered.

"And yet you take on about them. Ah! your heart is too tender, ma'am. If you are going to take up everybody else's crosses as well as your own, you'll never get through this world, ma'am. Take an old woman's word for that."

"Thank'ee, Mrs. Rogers. Noo, please gae awa and leave me my lane. I'll ring for ye if I want ye," said Rose, nervously.

"Very well, ma'am. I'll go and see after your breakfast."

"Oh, onything at a'! The same as yestreen. Only gae awa!" exclaimed the ex-cited girl, too deeply moved now even to care what she should eat for breakfast.

When the housekeeper had left her alone she gave way to the emotions of horror and fear which prudence had caused her to restrain in the presence of the woman. She wept, and sobbed, and cried out, and struck her hands together. She was, in truth, in an agony of terror.

For now she understood the hidden meaning of her lover's words, when on the night of the murder he had said to her, under the balcony, "Something will hap-pen to-night that will put all thoughts of marrying and giving in marriage out of the heads of all concerned." And she comprehended also how the meaning of the fragmentary conversation she had overheard between her lover and his companion, as they approached her from the house: "You have brought the curse of Cain upon me." "It could not be helped." "If the old man had not squealed out," and so forth.

Sir Lemuel Levison had been robbed and murdered, and she--Rose Cameron--had been accessory to the robbery and the murder! She had lain in wait under the balcony while the burglars went in and slaughtered the old banker, and emptied his money chest. She had received the booty, and carried it off, and brought it to London. She had it even then in her possession!

She was liable to discovery, arrest, trial, conviction, execution.

With a cry of intense horror she covered up her head under the bedclothes and shook as with a violent ague. She had suspected, and indeed, she had known by circumstance and inference, that the money and jewels contained in the bag she had brought from Castle Lone, had been taken from the house, but she had tried to ignore the fact that they had been stolen. But now the knowledge was forced upon her.

She had been accessory both before and after the facts to the crime of robbery and murder, and she was subject to trial and execution. It all now seemed like a horrible nightmare, from which she tried in vain to wake.

While she shivered and shook under the bedclothes, the housekeeper came up and opened the door and said:

"Mr. Scott have come, ma'am. Will he come up?"

"Ay, bid him come till me at ance!" cried the agitated woman, without uncovering her head.

A few minutes passed and the door opened again and her lover entered the room still wearing his travelling wraps.

"Rose, my lass, what ails you?" he inquired, approaching the bed, and seeing her shaking under the bedclothes.

"It's in a cauld sweat, I am, frae head to foot," she answered.

"You have got an ague! Your teeth are chattering!" said Mr. Scott, stooping over her.

"Keep awa' frae me! Dinna come nigh me!" she cried, cuddling down closer under the clothing. She had not yet uncovered her face or looked at him.

"What is the meaning of all this, Rose?" he inquired, in a tone of displeasure.

"Speer that question to yoursel'! no' to me!" she answered, shuddering.

"Look at me!" said the man, sternly.

"I canna look at you! I winna look at you! I hae ta'en an awfu' scunner till ye!"

"What have I done to you, you exasperating woman, that you should behave to me in this insolent manner?" demanded the man.

"What hae ye dune till me, is it? Ye hae hanggit me! nae less!" cried the girl, with a shudder.

"*Hanged* you? Whatever do you mean? Are ye crazy, girl?"

"Ay, weel nigh!"

"But what do you mean by saying that I have hanged you? Come, I insist on knowing!"

"Oh, then I just ken a' anent the murder up at Lone Castle! Ye hae drawn me in till a robbery and murder, without me kenning onything anent it until a' was ower, and me with the waefu' woodie before me!"

"Rose, if I understand you, it seems that you think I was in some sort concerned in the death of Sir Lemuel Levison?"

"Ay, that is just what I *be* thinking!" said the shuddering girl.

"Then you do me a very foul and infamous injustice, Rose! Look at me! Do I look like an assassin? Look at me, I say!" sternly insisted the man.

"I canna luke at ye! I winna luke at ye! I hae lukit at ye ower muckle for my ain gude already!" cried the girl, cowering under the clothes.

"See here, lass? I say that you are utterly wrong! I had no connection whatever with the death of the banker! I would not have hurt a hair of his gray head for all that he was worth! Come! I answer you seriously and kindly, although your grotesque and horrible suspicion deserves about equally to be laughed at or punished. Come, look into my face now and see whether I am not telling you the truth."

"And sae ye did na do the deed?" she inquired at length, uncovering her head and showing a pale affrighted face.

"My poor lass, how terrified you have been! No, of course, I did not. But how came you to know anything about that horrible affair?"

Rose took up the morning paper and put it in his hands.

"Ah! confound the press!" muttered the man between his teeth.

"What did ye say?"

"These papers, with their ghastly accounts of murders, are nuisances, Rose!"

"Ay sae they be! But ye didna do the deed?"

The man made a gesture of impatience.

"Aweel, then sin ye had na knowledge o' the deed until after it was done, what did ye mean by saying that something wad happen, wad pit a' thoughts o' marriage and gi'eing in marriage out the heads o' a' concerned?--when ye spak till me under the balcony that same night?"

"I meant--I meant," said the man, hesitating, "that I would let the preparations for the wedding go on to the very altar, and then before the altar I would reject the bride! I had heard something about her."

"Ah! I thought ye did it a' for spite!"

"But Rose, I never thought you were such an utter coward as I have found you out to be to-day!" said the man reproachfully.

"Ay' I can staund muckle; but I canna staund murder!"

"It is not even certain that there has been any murder committed. The coroner's jury have not yet brought in their verdict. Many people think that the old man fell dead with a sudden attack of heart-disease, and in falling, struck his head upon the top of that bronze statuette, which was found lying by him."

"Ay! and that wad be likely eneuch! for na robber wou'd gae to kill a man wi' siccan a weepon as that," said Rose, who had begun to recover her composure.

Then the man began to question her in his turn:

"You brought the satchel safely?"

"Ay, I brought it safely."

"Where is it?"

"Lock the door and I'll get it."

The man locked the door. While his back was turned, Rose jumped out of bed and slipped on a dressing-gown. Then she put her hand in between the mattresses and drew out the bag.

"Have you examined its contents?" inquired the man.

"Na, I hanna opened it once," replied the girl, unhesitatingly telling a falsehood.

"Oh! then I have a surprise for you. Sir Lemuel Levison was my banker. He had my money, and also my jewels, in his charge. He delivered them to me last night a few minutes before I brought them out and gave them to you. You know I wished you to take them to London because--I meant to reject Miss Levison at the altar, and after that, of course, I could not return to the castle for anything. Don't you see?"

"Ay, I see! But stap! stap! Noo you mind me about the bag. When you brought out the bag that night, I heard you and a man talking. You said to the man, 'You hae brocht the curse o' Cain upon me.' Noo, an ye had naething to do wi' the murder, what did ye mean by that?"

The man's face grew very dark. "She cross-questions me," he muttered to himself. Then controlling his emotions, he affected to laugh, and said:

"How you do twist and turn things, Rose! One would think you were interested in convicting me. But I had rather think that you are a little cracked on this subject. I never used the words you think you heard. The servant had brought me the wrong walking-stick, one that was too short for me, and so I said, 'You have brought that cursed cane to me.'"

"Ou, *that* indeed!" said the credulous girl, "But what did *he* mean when he said, 'It could na be helpit. The auld man squealed?'"

"I don't know what he meant, nor do I know whether he used those words. Probably he did not; and you mistook him as you have mistaken me. But I am really tired of being so cross-questioned, Rose. Look me in the face, and tell me whether you really believe me to be guilty or not?" he said, in his most frank and persuasive manner.

"Na, na, I canna believe ony ill o' ye, Johnnie Scott," replied the girl.

And, in fact, the man had such magnetic power over her that he could make her believe anything that he wished.

"Now let us look into this satchel," he said, proceeding to open it.

He took out the bags of money.

"There is one bag gone! fifty pounds gone!" he exclaimed.

"Na, that canna be, gin it was in the bag. I hanna opened it ance," said the girl, unhesitatingly.

The man paid no attention to her words, but took out the jewels and began to examine them.

"Confound it! The watch and chain are gone, and the solitaire diamond ring is gone, and--" here the man broke out into a volley of curses forcible enough to right a ship in a storm, and said: "The jewel snuff-box, worth ten times all the other jewels put together, is gone! How is this, Rose?"

"I dinna ken. How suld I ken? I took the bag frae your hands, and I put it back intil your hands, e'en just as I took it, without ever once seeing the inside o' it," boldly replied the girl.

A volley of curses from the man followed, and then he inquired:

"Was the bag out of your possession at any time since you received it?"

"Na, not ance."

"Then that infernal valet has taken the lion's share of the prog! I wish I had him by the throat!" exclaimed the man, with a torrent of imprecations.

"What do ye mean by a' that?" inquired Rose.

"I mean, that servant I believed in has robbed me, that is all," said the man.

With her recovered spirits Rose had regained her appetite. She now rang the bell loudly.

The housekeeper answered it.

"*Is* breakfast ready?" inquired the hungry creature.

"Yes, madam; and I will put in on the table just as soon as you are ready for it," answered the old woman.

"Put it on now, then," replied the girl.

The housekeeper left the room.

Rose made a hasty toilet while her husband was washing the railway dust from his face and head.

And then both went into the adjoining parlor, where the morning meal was by this time laid.

After breakfast the man went out.

The woman remained in the house. She was in a very unenviable state of mind. She was not yet quite easy on the subject of the murder at Lone Castle. For although her husband and herself might have no connection with the crime, still they had undoubtedly been lurking secretly about the house on the very night of its perpetration, and therefore might get into great trouble. And, besides, she was frightened at having secreted the costly watch and chain, snuff-box, and other jewels, from her Scott, and then told him a falsehood about them. What if he should find her out in her dishonesty and duplicity?

She did not dream of giving up her stolen property. She would risk all for the possession of that precious golden box, whose brilliant colors and blazing jewels fascinated her very soul; but where could she securely hide it from her husband's search? At that moment it was with the watch and the diamond ring under the bolster of her bed. But there it was in danger of being discovered, should a search be made.

She went into her bedroom and looked about for a hiding-place.

At length she found one which she thought would be secure.

The gilt cornice at the top of her bedroom window was hollow. She climbed up on top of her dressing bureau, and reaching as far as she could she pushed first the snuff-box, (which also contained the diamond ring,) and then the watch and chain, far into the hollow part of the cornice, over the window.

There she thought they would be perfectly safe.

The next few days passed without anything occurring to disturb the peace of this misguided peasant girl.

Every morning the man who called himself Lord Arondelle, but who was known at the house he occupied only as Mr. Scott, and who professed to be the husband of the young woman--went out in the morning and remained absent until evening.

Every day the girl, known to her servants as Mrs. Scott, spent in dressing, going out riding in a cab, and freely spending the money that her husband lavished upon her, and in gormandizing in a manner that must have destroyed the digestive organs of any animal less sound and strong than this "handsome hizzie" from the Highlands.

On the Monday of the week following the tragedy at Castle Lone, however, Mr. Scott came home in the evening in a state of agitation and alarm.

"Where is that satchel with the money?" he inquired as he entered the bedroom of his wife.

She stared at him in astonishment, but his looks so frightened her that she hastened to produce the bag.

He took from it a little bag of gold marked L500, and threw it in her lap, saying:

"There, take that!" And before she could utter a word, he hurried out of the room.

She ran down stairs after him, calling:

"John! John! what ails you? What hae fashed ye sae muckle?"

But he banged the hall door and was gone.

"That's unco queer!" said Rose, as she retraced her steps, up stairs, feeling a vague anxiety creeping upon her.

"He'll be back sune. He has na gane a journey, for he has na ta'en e'en sa mickle as a change o' linnen, or a second collar," she said, as she regained her room, and sank down breathless into a chair.

The bag of gold he had left her next attracted her attention. L500--ten times as much as she had ever possessed in her life. The contemplation of this fortune drove all speculations about the movements of "John" out of her head. "John" was always queer and uncertain, and *would* go off suddenly sometimes and be gone for days.

"I winna fash mysel' anent him! He may tak' his ain gait, and I'll tak' mine!" she said to herself, as she resolved to go out the very next day and buy what her heart had long been set upon--a cashmere shawl!

The next morning's papers however contained news from Lone, which, had Rose taken the trouble to look at them, must have thrown some light upon the sudden departure of Mr. Scott.

They contained this telegraphic item, copied from the evening papers:

"The coroner's inquest that has been sitting at Lone, returned last night a verdict of murder against Peters, the valet of the late Sir Lemuel Levison, and against some person or persons unknown. The valet has been arrested and committed to gaol to await the action of the grand jury. It is said that he is very much depressed in spirits, and it is supposed that he will make a full confession, and save himself from the extreme penalty of the law by giving up the names of his confederates in the crime, and turning Queen's evidence against them."

Rose did not read the papers at all. They did not interest that fine animal.

She went shopping that day, and bought a blazing scarlet cashmere shawl. Mr. Scott did not return in the evening, but she was not troubled. She had a roast pheasant, champagne, and candied fruits for supper, and she was happy.

She went shopping the next day, and bought a flashing set of jewels.

Mr. Scott did not return in the evening, but she had another luxurious supper, and was still happy. In this way a week passed, and still Mr. Scott did not come back. But Rose shopped and gormandized and enjoyed her healthy animal life.

Then she felt tempted to wear her gold watch and chain when she dressed to go abroad. So one morning she put it on, and went out. She had not the slightest suspicion of the danger to which she exposed herself by wearing it. She was not afraid of any one finding it in her possession, except her husband. So she wore it proudly day after day.

One morning, about ten days after the departure of "Mr. Scott," the postman left a letter for her. It was a drop-letter. She opened it and read.

It was without date or signature, and merely contained these lines:

"Business detains me from you longer than I had expected to stay. Do not be anxious. I will return or send very soon."

Rose was not anxious. She was enjoying herself. Now after shopping and eating and drinking all day, she went to the theatre at night. The theatre--one of the humblest in the city--was a new sensation to her, and her first visit to one was so delightful that she resolved to repeat it every evening.

"I shanna fash mysel' anent Johnnie ony mair. He'll come hame when he gets ready," she said in her heart.

But weeks grew into months, and "Johnnie" did not come home.

Rose's five hundred pounds had sunk down to fifty pounds, and then indeed she did begin to grow impatient for the return of her husband. Suppose the money should give out before he came back?

One day, while she was disturbing herself by these questions, she went out shopping as usual. When she had made her purchases she looked at her watch, and found that it had stopped. She was too ignorant to know what was the matter with it. She only knew that when she wound it up it would not go.

So she asked the dealer from whom she had bought her goods to direct her to a watchmaker.

The dealer gave her the address of a jeweller not far off.

She took her watch to "Messrs. North and Simms, Watchmakers and Jewellers," and asked an elderly man behind the counter, who happened to be one of the firm, if he could make her watch "gae" while she waited for it in the shop. And she detached it from its chain and handed it to him.

Mr. North received the rich, diamond-studded, gold repeater, and looked at the tawdry, ignorant, vain creature that presented it, with astonishment.

Then he examined the initials set in diamonds, and a change came over his face. He went to his desk, taking the watch with him. He drew out a small drawer, took from it a photograph, and compared it with the watch in his hand. Then he placed both together in the drawer and locked it and beckoned a young man from the opposite counter, scribbled a few words on a card and sent him out with it.

Rose, who had watched all these movements without the least suspicion of their meaning, now moved toward the jeweller and said:

"Aweel then, hae ye lookit at my watch and can ye na mak it ga?"

"The spring is broken, Miss, and it will take a little time to repair it. You can leave it with me, if you please," replied Mr. North.

"Indeed, then, and I'm nae sic a fule! I'll na leave it with you at a'. If you canna mak it gae just gie it till me," she said.

Now Mr. North did not wish his customer to leave his shop yet a while. The truth was that photographs of the late Sir Lemuel Levison's watch and snuff-box, in the possession of his legal steward, had been copied and the copies distributed by London directory to every jeweller in the city, as a means of discovering the stolen property, and finally detecting the criminals.

Messrs. North and Simms had received a copy of each.

And when Rose presented the rich watch to be repaired, Mr. North had at first suspected and then identified the article as the missing watch of the late Sir Lemuel Levison. And he had locked it in the drawer with the photographs, and dispatched a messenger to the nearest police station for an officer.

His object now was to detain Rose Cameron until the arrival of that officer.

"Will you look at something in my line this morning, Miss?" he inquired.

"Na. Gi'e me my watch, and I will gae my ways home," she answered.

"I have a set of diamonds here that once belonged to the Empress Josephine. They are very magnificent. Would you not like to see them?"

"Ou, ay! an empress's diamonds? ay, indeed I wad!" cried the poor fool, vivaciously.

Mr. North drew from his glass case a casket containing a fine set of brilliants, which probably the Empress Josephine had never even heard of, and displayed it before the wondering eyes of the Highland lass.

While she was gazing in rapt admiration upon the blazing jewels, the messenger returned, accompanied by a policeman in plain clothes.

"Excuse me, Miss, I wish to speak to a customer," said the jeweller, as he met the officer and silently took him up to the farther end of the shop to his desk, opened a little drawer and showed him the watch and the photographs.

Then they conferred together for a short time. The jeweller told the policeman how the watch had fallen into his hands; but that the pretended owner, finding that he could not repair it while she waited, had refused to leave it, and insisted on taking it home with her.

"Give it to her. Let her take it home. She can then be followed and her residence ascertained. I think, without doubt, that we have now got a certain clue to the perpetrators of the robbery and murder at Castle Lone."

CHAPTER XIII.
A SURPRISE FOR MRS. SCOTT.

"Will ye gie me my watch or no?" exclaimed Rose, growing impatient of the whispered colloquy between the jeweller and the policeman in plain clothes, although she was quite unsuspicious of its subject.

"Here it is, madam," said the jeweller, with the utmost politeness, as he came and placed the watch in her hand.

She attached it to her chain and then left the shop.

The policeman sauntered carelessly toward the door and kept his eye covertly upon her.

She got into a four-wheeled cab and drove off.

The policeman hailed a "Hansom," sprang into it, and directed the driver to keep the first cab in sight and follow it to its destination.

Rose, as it was now late in the afternoon, and she was longing for her turbot, green-turtle soup, and roast pheasants and champagne, drove directly home.

Her housekeeper met her at the door with good news.

"A letter from the master, ma'am. The postman brought it soon after you left home," she said, putting another "drop" letter in the hand of her mistress.

"Is dinner ready?" inquired Rose, who was more interested in her meals than in her lover.

"Just ready, ma'am," replied the housekeeper.

"Put it on the table directly, then," said Rose, as she ran up stairs to her own room.

She threw herself into a chair and opened the letter to read it, at her ease.

It was without date and very short. It only informed her that the writer was still detained by "circumstances beyond his control," and enjoined her to wait patiently in her house on Westminster Road, until she should see him.

It was also without signature.

"And there's nae money in it. I dinna ken why he should write to me at a', if he will send me nae money," was the angry comment of Rose, as she impatiently threw the letter into the fire.

Her "improved" circumstances had not taught the peasant girl any refinement of manners. She did not think it at all necessary to change her dress, or even to wash her face after her dusty drive. But when dinner was announced, she went to the table as she had come into the house. And she enjoyed her dinner as only a young person with a perfectly healthful and intensely sensual organization could. She lingered long over her dessert of candied fruits, creams, jellies, and light wines. And when the housekeeper came in at length with the strong black coffee, she made the woman sit down and gossip with her about London life.

While they were so employed, "the boy in buttons," whose duty it was to attend the street door and answer the bell, entered the room and said:

"A gemman down stairs axing to see the missus. I told 'im 'er was at dinner, and mussent be disturbed at meals, which 'e hanswered, and said as 'is business were most himportant, and 'e must see you whether or no, ma'am, which I beg yer parding for 'sturbing yer agin horders."

"It will be a mon frae Johnnie Scott. He'll be fetching me a message or some money. Gae tell him to come in," said Rose, in hopeful excitement.

"Must I bring the gemman up here, missus?" inquired Buttons.

"Ay, ye fule! Where else? Wad ye ask the gentlemon intil the kitchen? And we had na that money rooms to choose fra!" said Rose, impatiently.

And indeed, in that great empty old house, she had but three to her own use--the tawdry scarlet parlor, which was also her dining room; the equally tawdry scarlet chamber; and the dressing-room behind it.

The boy vanished and soon reappeared, ushering in the policeman in plain clothes.

"You will be coming frae Mr. Scott, wi' a message?" said Rose, without rising to receive him.

"No, mum; haven't the pleasure of that gent's acquaintance, though I would like to enjoy it. I come to *Mrs.* Scott, however, and on particular unpleasant business. What is your full name, mum?" gruffly inquired the policeman, approaching her.

"And what will my name be to you, ye rude mon? And wha ga'ed ye commission to force yersel, on my company at my dinner?" indignantly inquired Rose.

"My commission, as you call it, mum, lies in this warrant, which authorizes me to make a thorough search of these premises for property stolen from Lone Castle on the night of the first of June last."

As the policeman spoke, Rose stared at him with eyes that grew larger, and a face that grew whiter every minute. And as she stared, she suddenly recognized the visitor as the man she had seen in the jeweller's shop, talking with the proprietor while the latter was pretending to be examining the watch she had put in his hand for repairs.

And now the whole truth burst upon her. The watch had been recognized by the jeweller, who perhaps had seen it in Sir Lemuel Levison's possession, or perhaps had had it in his own for cleaning, and he had sent for this policeman in plain clothes, who had followed her home, "spotted" the house, and then taken out a search-warrant. Fright and rage possessed her soul. And oh! in the midst of all, how she cursed her own folly in secreting those dangerous jewels in the house, and her madness in wearing the watch abroad.

"I hope you will submit quietly to the necessary search, mum. It will be the better for you," said the officer.

Then rage got the better of fright in Rose Cameron's distracted bosom.

"I'll tear your e'en out, first, ye--" here followed a volley of expletives not fit to be reported here--"before ye s' all bring me to sic an open shame! Search my house, will ye? Ye daur!" and here the handsome Amazon struck an attitude of resistance.

The policeman went to the front window, threw it up, and beckoned to some persons below.

In two minutes, the sound of footsteps was heard upon the stairs, the door was opened, and a couple of officers entered the room.

Rose Cameron gazed at them in terror and defiance.

"Mrs. Scott, you are my prisoner. We arrest you on the charge of complicity in the murder of Sir Lemuel Levison, and the robbery of Castle Lone!" said the first policeman, laying his hand on the girl's shoulder.

"Tak' yer claws affen me, ye de'il!" exclaimed Rose, springing from under his hand, and then shrinking, shuddering, into the nearest chair.

"Perkins, look after this woman, while I direct the search of the house. You come with me, Thompson. We will go through this room now," said the first police-man, putting his hand on the lock of the chamber door.

"Ye sell na gae into my bedroom, ye de'il! It is na decent for a strange mon to gae into a leddy's chamber!" cried Rose, springing before him to bar his entrance.

"Never mind her, Mr. Pryor; I'll take care of her," said the man called Perkins, as with a firm hand he laid hold of his prisoner, and forced her, screaming, scratching, and resisting with all her might from the door.

"Excuse me, my girl, but this is a murder case, and we must not stand upon po-liteness to the fair sex; here," added Perkins, as he forced her down upon her chair and held her there so firmly that all she could do was to spit, glare, and rail at him.

"Oh, my dear, good lady, do be quiet. You are in the hands of the law, which I believe you to be as innersent as the dove unborn; but it will be the best for you to submit quietly," said the housekeeper, who had hitherto sat in appalled silence, taking note of the proceedings.

"I will na submit to ony sic indignity," screamed Rose, with an additional tor-rent of very objectionable language.

Meantime officers Pryor and Thompson passed into the bedroom and began the search. Bureau and bureau drawers, wardrobes, boxes, caskets, cases, were opened, ransacked, and their contents turned out, but no sign of the stolen property was discovered. Closets, wash-stands, and chair cushions next underwent a thorough examination, with a similar result. Then the bed was pulled to pieces, and the mattresses were closely scrutinized, to detect any sign of a recent ripping and re-sewing of any part of the seams through which the stolen jewels might have been pushed in among the stuffing, but evidently the mattresses had not been tampered with.

Then the two officers of the law stopped and looked at each other.

"Before proceeding further in our search, we must be sure as the stolen goods are not in this room," said Pryor.

"I don't know where they can be concealed in this room," said Thompson.

"We must apply our infallible square inch rule, now. Take the inside of this room from floor to ceiling, and search in succession *every square inch of it*. No matter whether the part under review seems a likely or an unlikely, or even a possible or an impossible place of concealment, search it whether or no. Stolen goods are often found in impossible places, or in what seems to be such," said Pryor.

The search was re-commenced on the new principle, and following the square inch system into an impossible place, they at last came upon the stolen treasure, hidden in the hollow of the cornice at the top of the scarlet window curtains, near the bedstead.

"Here we are! all right! The jewel snuff box, and the solitaire diamond ring. The watch and chain will be found upon her person. This will be sufficient for to-day. We must close and seal these rooms, and place a couple of men on guard here before we take the girl to the station-house," said Pryor, as he carefully bestowed the recovered jewels in the deep breast-pocket of his coat.

The two officers returned to the parlor, where they found Perkins sitting by the prisoner, who was now pallid and quiet, merely because she had raged herself into a state of exhaustion.

"Go and fetch a close cab, Thompson. And you, good woman, fetch your missus' hat and wraps, and whatever else you may think she will need to go to the Police Station-House, and spend the night there. I will also trouble you for that watch and chain, my dear," said Pryor, turning lastly to his prisoner.

"I will na gie my bonny watch! And I will na gae to your filthy station-house, ye--!"

Whew! Inspector Pryor was used to storms of abuse from female prisoners, and could stand them well on most occasions; but now he turned as from a shower of fire, and walked rapidly to the window, while Perkins forcibly took from her the watch and chain, and put them for the present into his own pocket.

Thompson came in to announce the cab, and the housekeeper entered with her mistress's hat and shawl, and a small bundle tied up in a handkerchief.

But Rose stormed and wept, and utterly refused either to put on the hat and shawl, or to enter the cab. Nor could any amount of pursuasion or threats move her obstinacy until she found that the officers of the law were about to take her by force, and without her proper out-door dress.

Then, indeed, she yielded to the coaxing of her housekeeper, and allowed the old woman to prepare her for her compulsory drive.

When she was ready, Inspector Pryor would have escorted her down stairs, but she shook off his hand with angry scorn, and with an expletive that made even his case-hardened ears burn and tingle again.

"If I maun gae, I will gae; but I willna hae your filthy hand on me, ye beastly de'il!" she added, as she reached the cab. She paused an instant, with her foot upon the step, and looked up and down the street, as if she contemplated for a moment a flight for liberty and life; but probably she did not like the prospect of the hue and cry, the pursuit and recapture sure to ensue, for the next instant she stepped into the cab.

That night Rose Cameron passed in the Police Station-House of the Westminster precinct. She had slept in much less comfortable, if more respectable quarters, when she lived in the Highland hut at the foot of Ben Lone.

The officers who had her in charge overlooked all her viciousness in consideration of her youth and beauty, and afforded her every indulgence which their own duty and her safe-keeping permitted. They gave her a cell and a clean cot to herself; and one of them, to whom she gave a sovereign, went out at her orders and bought for her a luxurious and abundant supper.

And Rose--a perfect animal, as I beg leave to remind you--ate heartily and slept soundly, notwithstanding her perils and terrors.

The next morning Rose Cameron was taken before the sitting magistrate of the Police Court at Vincent Square.

The two witnesses from Lone, McNeil, the saddler, who had seen her lurking under the window of the castle at midnight on the night of the murder; and Ferguson, the railway clerk, who had sold her the ticket for the twelve-fifteen express to London, had been summoned by telegraph on the day before, had come up by the night train, and were now in court ready to identify the prisoner. Sir Lemuel Levison's house-steward, also summoned by telegraph, was there to identify the stolen jewels which were produced in court. The examination was brief and conclusive. McNeil and Ferguson swore to the woman as being Rose Cameron, and also as being the very woman they had each seen on the night of the murder, under the suspicious circumstances already mentioned.

And McRath swore to the watch and chain, the jewelled snuff-box, and the solitaire diamond ring as the property of his deceased master, worn upon his person on the same night of the murder.

The three policemen swore to finding the stolen property in the possession of the prisoner.

Rose Cameron was incapable of inventing a plausible defence.

When asked how this property came into her possession, she said she had picked up the watch and chain found upon her person, on the sidewalk, on Westminster Road, where she supposed the owner must have dropped it, and as she did not know who the owner might be, she had kept it, to her sorrow. But as for the gold snuff-box and the solitaire diamond ring, she did not know anything about them; she had never seen them in her life, until they were drawn out of the hollow cornice by Inspector Pryor, and where they must have been hidden by somebody else.

This explanation was not received. And before the morning was over, Rose Cameron was remanded to her cell in the police station-house to wait until she could be taken back to Scotland for trial.

When she reached her cell, she gave herself up to a passion of hysterical weeping and sobbing.

She was interrupted by a visit from her friendly housekeeper.

"My poor, dear, injured lady, I was here early this morning to see you, but could not get in," said the woman, after the first exciting greetings were over.

"Sit ye down. Dinna staund, and tire yersel'," said the poor creature, glad to see any familiar face.

"Oh, my good young lady, you were always very kind to me. And I never can believe as you've had anything to do with what you are accused of," said the good woman, weeping.

"And sae I hadna. I dinna ken onything anent it. As for yon braw boxie, I ne'er set een on it, na, nor the fine ring, till the policeman pu'ed it doon frae the tap o' the window curtain. And the fine watch, they fund on me, and said belongit to Sir Lemuel Levison; that watch waur gied to me by a gude freend," said Rose, wiping the great tears from her stormy eyes.

"I will believe it, my good young lady. I can very well believe it. I see how you have been imposed upon by bad people; but do you keep a stiff upper lip, madam, and don't be in no ways cast down, and your innercence will come like pure gold from the furniss, as the saying is. And now, my dear young lady, I have some news for you, as will help to divert your mind from your troubles, I hope," said the well-meaning woman, soothingly.

"Is it about Johnnie Scott? Is it about my gude mon?" eagerly inquired Rose.

"No, my dear young lady, it is not about him. You remember the marriage that was broken off, for the time between the young Marquis of Arondelle and the heiress of Lone?"

"Yes! broken off by the murder of the bride's feyther, the nicht before the wedding day--the murder o' Sir Lemuel Levison, wi' whilk I now staund accusit. Ou, aye, I mind it! I am na likely to forget it!" sharply answered Rose Cameron.

"Well, my dear young lady, the marriage is on again."

"*Eh!*" exclaimed Rose Cameron, springing up.

"Yes, my dear young lady. You know I always take time to look over the morning papers that are left at the house for you, and this morning I read that a grand marriage would take place at St. George's, Hanover Square, between the young Duke of Hereward--he who was Marquis of Arondelle before his father's death-- and the heiress of the late Sir Lemuel Levison. And how, after the ceremony, there would be a breakfast at the bride's house, and then how the happy pair would set out for their wedding tower."

While the well-meaning housekeeper was speaking, Rose Cameron was staring at her in dumb amazement.

"I brought the paper in my pocket, ma'am, thinking, under all the circumstances, it would interest you and help to make you forget your own troubles. Would you like to read it for yourself?"

"Yes! gie me the paper," cried Rose, snatching it from the housekeeper before the latter could hand it.

"Where's the place? Where's the place?" cried the impatient young woman, wildly turning the pages.

"Here it is ma'am. At the top of the 'FASHIONABLE NEWS,'" said the landlady, pointing out the item.

Rose pounced upon it, and read aloud:

"The marriage of His Grace, the Duke of Hereward, with Miss Levison, only daughter and heiress of the late Sir Lemuel Levison, will be celebrated at twelve, noon, to-day, at St. George's, Hanover Square. After the ceremony the noble party will adjourn to Elmhurst House, Westbourne Terrace, the home of the bride, to partake of the wedding breakfast, after which the happy pair will leave town by the tidal train for Dover, ***en route*** for their continental tour."

Rose Cameron threw down the paper and sprang to her feet with the bound of a tigress.

"Oh, the villain! Oh, the shamfu', fause, leeing villain! This wad be the important business that kept him awa' frae me! This wad be the reason why he got me lockit up in prison here--for I ken weel that he pit the dogs o' the law on my track noo, if I dinna ken before--to keep me fra getting out to ban his marriage noo, as I wad ha banned it then hadna something else dune it for me. But it isna too late yet! I'll ban his wedding travels, gin I couldna ban his wedding! I'll bring him down to disgrace and shame afore a' his graund wedding guests--the fause-hearted, leeing, shamefu' villain! I will pu' him down frae his grandeur yet, gin ye will only help me!" exclaimed Rose Cameron, pouring out this torrent of words, as she strode up and down the narrow floor of her cell with the stride of an enraged lioness.

"My dear, good young lady, I don't know, the least in the world, why you should get so excited over the young duke's marriage," said the housekeeper, gazing in amazement and terror upon the face of the infuriated young creature.

"Why suld I get excited o'er it, indeed?" exclaimed Rose, stopping suddenly in her furious stride, and confronting her unoffending visitor with a scowl of rage.

"Come now; come now;" murmured the woman, soothingly, for she began to fear that she was in the presence, and in the power, of a lunatic.

"Dinna yo ken then, ye auld fule, that the Dooke o' Hareward is my ain gude mon?" imperiously demanded Rose.

"Oh, her poor head! Her poor head is going, and no wonder, poor lass!" murmured the old woman, compassionately.

"But how suld ye ken?" cried Rose, scornfully throwing herself down into her seat again. "He ca'ed himsel' Mr. John Scott. Mr. John Scott! And mysel' Mrs. John Scott. And sae ye kenned us, and nae itherwise."

"Poor girl! Poor girl!" murmured the housekeeper. "She's far gone! Far gone! Poor girl!"

"Puir girl, is it? It will be puir dooke before a' is ended! I'll hae him hanggit for trigomy, or what e'er ye ca' the marryin' o' twa wives at ance. Twa wives! Ou! I'll nae staund it! I'll nae staund it!" cried Rose, suddenly bounding to her feet.

"Come now! Come now! my dear, good young lady," said the housekeeper, coaxingly.

"Ye'll nae believe it! Ye'll nae believe he's my ain gude mon wha has marrit the heiress the morn? Look here, then! And look here! And look here!" continued the girl, impetuously, as she took a small morocco letter-case from her bosom and opened it, and took out one after another--a parchment, a letter, and a photograph.

"Yes, dear, I'll look at anything you like," said the housekeeper, with a sigh, for she thought she was only humoring a lunatic.

"Here's my marritge lines. And I was marrit here, in Lunnun town, at a kirk ye ca' St. Margaret's, by a minister ca'ed Smith. It's a' doon here in the lines. Look for yoursel'. Ye can read. See! Here will be my name, Rose Cameron. And here will be my gudeman's--de'il ha'e him!--Archibald-Alexander-John Scott, Marquis of Arondelle. And here will be the minister's name at the fut--James Smith; and the witnesses--John Jones, clerk, and Ann Gray, (she waur an auld body in a black bonnet and shawl). Noo! is that a' richt and lawfu'?" demanded Rose, triumphantly.

"Indeed, ma'am, it looks so!" said the perplexed housekeeper. And these indiscreet words burst from her lips, almost without her own volition--"But the idea of the young Marquis of Arondelle marrying of you in downright earnest is beyond belief! It is, indeed!"

"And what for nae?" cried Rose, angrily. "What for nae, wad he nae marry me, if he lo'ed me? He wad na hae me without marritge ye suld ken."

"No offence, my dear young madam. None at all. I was only astonished, that's all," said the housekeeper, deprecatingly, though she wondered and doubted whether all she heard and saw was truth.

"And, here! See here! Here is a letter I got frae him sune after the wedding. Ye ken the Dooke o' Harewood was Markiss o' Arondelle time when he married me?"

"Yes, so it seems," said the housekeeper.

"Aweel then, see here. This letter begins--'***My ain dear Wifie***,' ye mind?--'***My ain dear Wifie***'--and gaes on wi' a lot o' luve, and a' that, whilk I need na read, till ye. And it ends, look here--'***Your devoted husband***--ARONDELLE.' There! what do ye think o' that?"

"I'm so astonished, ma'am, I don't know what to think."

"But ye ken weel noo, that my gude mon wha ca'ed himsel' John Scott, was the Markiss o' Arondelle, and is noo the Dooke of Harewood?"

"Yes, ma'am, I know that!--that is, if I'm awake and not dreaming," added the woman.

"And ye ken weel that the Dooke of Harewood hae get me lappet up here in prison sae I canna get out to prevent him ha'eing his wicked will, in marrying the heiress o' Lone?"

"I know that, too, ma'am--that is, if I'm not dreaming, as I said before," answered the bewildered old woman.

"Aweel, noo, I canna get out to forestal this graund wickedness. The shamefu' villain took gude care to prevent that, but I can circumvent him, for a' that, gin ye will help me, Mrs. Brown. Will ye?"

"You may be sure o' that, my poor young lady; for if things be as they seem, you have suffered much wrong," earnestly answered the woman.

"Aweel, then, tak' my marritge lines, my letter, and this likeness o' my laird-- and may the black de'il burn him in--"

"Oh, my dear child, don't say that. It is dreadful. Tell me what I am to do with these papers and this picture."

"First of a', ye'll be very carefu' o' 'em, and be sure to bring them back safe to me."

"Yes, surely, my dear; but what am I to do with them?"

"Ye'll get a cab, and tak' the papers and the picture to the bride's house, and ask to see the bride alone, on a matter o' life and death. And ye maun tak' nae denial. Ye maun see her, and tell her anent mysel' here, betrayed into prison sae I canna come to warn her. And show her my marritge lines, and my letter, and my laird's pictur'--the foul fien' fly awa' wi' him!--and tell her, gin she dinna believe them, to gae to the auld kirk o' St. Margaret's, Wes'minster, and look at the register, and see the minister, Mr. Smith, and the clerk, Mr. Jones, and the auld bodie, Mrs. Gray, and she'll find out anent it! Will ye do this for me?"

"Yes, I will, my dear child."

"Here is a half-sovereign then to pay for the cab hire. And, oh! be sure ye tak' unco gude care o' my papers! They's a' my fortun', ye ken."

"Yes, indeed, I know how important they are to you, and I will bring them back safe," said the housekeeper, as she put the marriage certificate, the letter, the portrait, and the money in her pocket, and arose to leave the cell.

"And noo, we'll see, an' I dinna bring ye to open shame, ye graund de'il!" exclaimed Rose.

"I don't blame your anger, my poor dear, but don't use bad words. And now I am off. Good-day to you until I see you again," said the woman, as she left the cell.

Mrs. Brown was a good woman, but she did delight in hearing and retailing gossip, and in making and seeing a sensation; so she rather enjoyed her errand to Westbourne Terrace. She was also a brave woman, so she did not shrink from meeting the high-born bridegroom and the bride with her overwhelming revelations.

CHAPTER XIV.
THE SECOND BRIDAL MORN.

We must return to Elmhurst House and take up the thread of Salome's destiny, where we left it on the morning on which the young Duke of Hereward had called on Lady Belgrade and informed her ladyship of the arrest of the mysterious, vailed passenger, and implored her to keep all the papers announcing that arrest, or in any manner referring to the tragedy at Castle Lone, from the sight of the bereaved daughter and betrothed bride.

"And so the mysterious vailed woman had been discovered, and she turns out to be Rose Cameron!" repeated Lady Belgrade, reflectively. Then, after a pause, she said: "I wonder who was her confederate in that atrocious crime--or, rather, who was her master in it? for she is too weak and simple to have been anything but a blind tool, poor creature!"

"You knew her, then?" said the duke.

"Only by report while I was staying at Castle Lone. But the report came from the tenantry, who had known her from childhood--a handsome, ignorant, vain and credulous fool of a peasant girl, more likely to become the victim of some godless man, than the confederate of murderers. Did *you* know her, duke?" meaningly inquired the lady, as she remembered the reports in circulation at Castle Lone, that connected the name of the handsome shepherdess with that of the young nobleman.

"No, I never saw the girl in my life. I have heard her beauty highly praised by some of the late companions of my hunting expeditions at Ben Lone; but I had no opportunity of judging for myself; and, moreover, I always discouraged such conversation among my comrades. But there, that is quite enough of the unhappy girl. I mentioned her arrest not as a most important fact only, but in order to warn you not to let our dear Salome get a sight of the daily papers, until you have looked over them, and assured yourself that they contain no reference to this arrest."

"I see the wisdom of your warning, and I will endeavor to be guided by it; but it may be difficult to do so. My very sequestration of the papers may excite Salome's suspicions."

"Then lose them; tear them; but do not let her see any part of them which may contain any reference to this girl. I thank Heaven that to-morrow I shall be able to take her out of the country and guard her peace and safety with my own head and hand. I shall take care also to keep her away until the trial and conviction of the criminals shall be over and done with, so that she may not be in any way harassed or distressed by the proceedings."

"Yes, that will be very wise. If she were in England or Scotland during the time of the trial, she might be subpoenaed as a witness for the prosecution. She was the first, poor child, to discover the dead body of her father, you know," said Lady Belgrade.

"I do not forget that circumstance, or what distress it may yet cause her," replied the young duke.

And very soon after he took leave and went away.

Lady Belgrade's task in keeping the day's papers from the sight of Salome Levi-son was easier than she had anticipated.

Salome, deeply interested and absorbed in the final preparations for her marriage, did not even think of the newspapers, much less ask for them.

The bridal day dawned, once more, for the heiress of Lone.

Salome, with her attendant, was up early. The young girl, since her departure from Lone Castle, the scene of her father's murder, and her arrival at Elmhurst House, and occupations with her wedding preparations, had wonderfully recovered her health and spirits.

Yet on this, her bridal day, she arose with a heavy heart. A vague dread of impending evil weighed upon her spirits.

This occasion might well have brought back vividly cruelly to her memory, that fatal bridal morn when, going to invoke her father's presence and blessing on her marriage, she found him lying stiff and stark in the crimson pool of his own curdled blood. She had no father here on earth, now, to give her to the man she loved, and to bless her union with him.

That, in itself might have been enough to account for the gloom that darkened her wedding day. But that was not all. For, though her father was not visibly present here on earth, she knew that he watched and blessed her from his eternal home. No! but her prophetic soul was darkened by the shadow of some approaching misfortune.

Margaret, her new maid, brought her a cup of coffee in her chamber. After she had drank it, she went sadly in her dressing-room, to make her toilet for the altar.

Margaret was her only attendant and dresser.

Salome was still in the deepest mourning for her murdered father. In leaving it off, for the marriage altar only, she had resolved to replace it only by such a simple dress as might have been worn by any portionless bride in the middle class of society.

She wore a plain white tulle dress, over a lustreless white silk, an Illusion vail, a wreath of orange buds, and white kid gloves and gaiters. She wore no jewels of any sort.

Her bridesmaids, only two in number, were dressed like herself, except that they wore no vails, and that their wreaths were of white rose buds.

At eleven o'clock in the morning, a handsome but very plain coach drew up before the gate of Elmhurst Terrace.

The bride, attended by her two bridesmaids and Lady Belgrade, entered it, and was driven off quietly to St. George's, Hanover square.

No invitations had been issued for the wedding, except to the nearest family connections of the bride and bridegroom.

But unfortunately the news of the approaching marriage had crept out, and got into the morning papers, and consequently the street before the church, the churchyard, and the church itself, were crowded with spectators.

Way was made for the small bridal procession, which was met at the entrance by the bridegroom's party, consisting of himself, his "best man," and his second groomsman.

There, with reverential tenderness, the young Duke of Hereward greeted his bride. And the small procession passed up the central aisle, and formed before the altar.

Around them stood the nearest friends of the two families.

Behind them, extending back to the farthest extremity of the church, crowded a miscellaneous mass of spectators.

This must have happened through the oversight of those parties whose duty it was to have had the church doors closed and guarded, so that the marriage of the so recently and cruelly orphaned daughter might be as private and decorous as it was intended to be.

Baron Von Levison, the head of the Berlin branch of the great European banking firm of Levison, had come over to act the part of father to his orphan niece, and stood near the chancel to give her away.

The Bishop of London, assisted by two clergymen, all in their sacred robes of office, stood within the chancel to perform the marriage ceremony.

After the short preliminary exhortation, the ceremony was commenced. The bride was very pale, paler than she had ever been, even in those dread days when she stood always face to face with death. In making the responses her voice faltered, fainted, and died away with every new effort. No one would have thought from her look, tone or manner, that she was giving her hand, where her heart had so long and so entirely been bestowed. She seemed rather like a victim forced unwillingly to the altar by despotism or by necessity, than a happy bride about to be united to the man of her choice.

At length the trial was over. The benediction was pronounced, and the young husband sealed the sacred rites by a kiss on the cold lips of his youthful wife.

Friends crowded around with congratulations; but all who took the hand of Salome, Duchess of Hereward, felt its icy chill even through her glove and theirs.

"No wonder poor child," they said to themselves; "she is thinking of her father, murdered on her first appointed wedding-day."

But it was not that. Salome had too clear a spiritual insight not to know that her father was more alive than he had been while on earth, and that he was bending down and blessing her, even there.

No; but the dark shadow of the approaching ill drew nearer and nearer. She could not know what it was. She could only feel it coming and chilling and darkening her soul.

After a few minutes passed in the vestry, during which the marriage of Archibald-Alexander-John Scott, Duke of Hereward, and Salome Levison was duly registered and signed and witnessed, the newly-married pair were at liberty to return home.

The young duke handed his youthful duchess into his own handsomely appointed carriage.

Baron Von Levison took her vacated place in the carriage with Lady Belgrade and the bridesmaids.

The few invited guests, being only the nearest family connections of the bride and bridegroom, got into their carriages and followed to the bride's residence on Westbourne Terrace, where the wedding breakfast awaited.

There were now no decorated halls and drawing-rooms, no bands of music, no display of splendid bridal presents, no parade whatever.

To be sure, an elegant breakfast-table was laid for the guests. It was decorated only with fragrant white flowers from the home conservatory, furnished with white Sevres china and silver, and provided with a luxurious and dainty repast. That was all. All magnificence and splendor of display was carefully avoided in the feast as in the ceremony.

Only ten in all sat down to the table, viz., the bride and bridegroom, two brides-maids, two groomsmen, Lady Belgrade, Baron Von Levison, the Bishop of London, and the Rector of St. George's.

A graver wedding party never was brought together. Even the youthful brides-maids and groomsmen, expected to be "the life of the company," were awed into silence by the preponderance of age and clerical dignity in the little assembly, for the bishop was not ready with his usual harmless little jest, and the rector did not care to take precedence over his superior.

The conversation was serious rather than merry, and the speeches earnest rath-er than witty.

Near the end of the breakfast, the bride's health was proposed by the first groomsman in a complimentary speech, which was acknowledged in a few appro-priate remarks by her nearest relative, the Baron Von Levison. The bridegroom's health was then proposed by the baron, and acknowledged by a deep and silent bow from the duke.

Then the health of the bridesmaids, the clergy, Lady Belgrade, and the Baron Von Levison were duly honored.

And then the young bride arose, courtesied to her guests, and attended by her bridesmaids, retired to change her wedding dress for a traveling suit.

"How deadly pale she looks! Is my niece really happy in this marriage?" in-quired the Baron Von Levison, in a low tone, of Lady Belgrade, as the guests left the table.

"She is very happy in this marriage, which she has set her heart on for years. In a word, this young wife is madly in love with her husband. But you must consider what an awful shock she had on her first appointed wedding-day, and how it must recur to her mind in this," answered the dowager.

"Ah, to be sure! to be sure! poor child! poor child!" muttered the German head of the family.

Meanwhile the young Duchess of Hereward reached her apartments.

Her dresser, Margaret, was in attendance. Her travelling suit of black bomba-zine, trimmed with black crape, was laid out. With the assistance of her maid she slowly divested herself of her white vail and robes, and put on the black travelling dress. A black sack and a black felt hat, both deeply trimmed with crape, and black gloves, completed her toilet.

When she was quite ready she kissed her two bridesmaids and said:

"Leave me alone now for a few minutes, dear girls, and wait for me in the drawing-room. I will join you very soon."

The young ladies returned her kisses and retired.

Then Salome dismissed her maid, that Margaret should prepare to accompany her mistress.

Finally, as soon as she found herself alone, she sank on her knees to pray, that, if possible, this dark shadow might be permitted to pass away from her soul; that light and strength and grace might be given her to do all her duties and bear all her burdens as Christian wife and neighbor; that she and her husband might be blessed with true and eternal love for each other, for their neighbor, and above all for their Lord.

As she finished her prayer, and arose from her knees, her maid re-entered the room, dressed to attend her mistress on her journey.

The girl did not forget to honor the bride with her new title.

"I beg pardon, your grace," she said, "but there is a strange-looking old woman down stairs who says she is a widow from Westminster Road, and that she must see your grace on a matter of life and death, before you start on your wedding tour."

"I do not know any such person," said the young duchess, slowly, while that vague shadow of impending calamity gathered over her spirit more darkly and heavily than before.

"Thomas, the hall footman, brought me the message from the woman, your grace, and I went down to see her myself before troubling you. I thought she might be only a bolder begger than usual. But she is no begger, your grace. She looks respectable," answered the girl.

"Go to the woman and explain to her that I have no time to see her now, and ask her if she cannot intrust her business to you to be brought to me," said the duchess.

The maid courtesied and left the room.

"What is it? What is it? Why does every unusual event strike such deadly terror to my heart?" inquired the bride, as she sank, pale and trembling, into her resting-chair.

In a few minutes the door opened and Margaret re-appeared.

"I beg your grace's pardon, but the old woman is very obstinate and persistent. She will not tell me her business. She says it is with your grace alone; that it concerns your grace most of all; that it is a matter of more importance than life or death; and that--indeed I beg your pardon, your grace--but I do not like to deliver the rest of her message, it seems so impertinent," said the girl, blushing and casting down her eyes.

"Nevertheless, deliver it. I will excuse you. The impertinence will not be yours," said the bride, as a cold chill struck her heart.

"Then, your grace, she seized me by the two shoulders and looked me straight in the face, and said--'Tell your mistress, if she would save herself from utter ruin, she will see me and hear what I have to tell her, before she sees the Duke of Hereward again!'" answered the girl, in a low tone.

"'*Before I see the Duke of Hereward again*.' Ah, what is it? What is it?" murmured the bewildered bride to herself. Then she spoke to Margaret. "Bring the woman up here. I will see her at once."

Once more the girl obediently left the room.

The young bride covered her pale face with her hands, and trembled with dread of--she knew not what!

A few minutes passed. The door opened again, and Margaret re-appeared, ushering in Rose Cameron's housekeeper.

Salome looked up.

CHAPTER XV.
THE CLOUD FALLS.

When Rose Cameron's emissary entered the bride's chamber, the young duchess arose from her chair, but almost instantly sank back again, overpowered by an access of that mysterious foreshadowing of approaching calamity which had darkened her spirit during the whole of this, her bridal day.

And it was better, perhaps, that this should be so, as it prepared her to sustain the shock which might otherwise have proved fatal to one of her nervous and sensitive organization.

She looked up from her resting-chair, and saw, standing, courtesying before her, a weary, careworn, elderly woman, in a rusty black bonnet, shawl, and gown. No very alarming intruder to contemplate.

The woman, on her part, instead of the proud and insolent beauty she had expected to see, in all the pomp and pride of her bridal day and her new rank, beheld a fair and gentle girl, still clothed in the deepest mourning for her murdered father.

And her heart, which had been hardened against the supposed triumphant rival of the poor peasant girl, now melted with sympathy.

And she, who had persistently forced her way into the bride's chamber, with the grim determination to spring the news upon her without hesitation or compassion, now cast about in her simple mind how to break such a terrible shock with tenderness and discretion.

"You look very much fatigued. Pray sit down there and rest yourself, while you talk to me," said the young duchess, gently, and pointing to a chair near her own.

"Ay, I am tired enough in mind and body, my lady, along of not having slept a wink all last night on account of--what I'll tell you soon, my lady. So I'll even take you at your kind word, my lady, and presume to sit down in your ladyship's presence," sighed the woman, slowly sinking into the indicated seat, and then adding: "I know as ladyship is not exactly the right way to speak to a duke's lady as is a duchess; but I don't know as I know what is."

"You must say 'your grace' in speaking to the duchess," volunteered Margaret, in a low tone.

"Never mind, never mind," said the bride, with a slight smile. "I am quite ready to hear whatever you may have to say to me. What can I do for you?"

The visitor hesitated and moaned. All her eager desire to overwhelm Rose Cameron's rival with the shameful news of her bridegroom's previous marriage and living wife had evaporated, leaving only deep sympathy and compassion for the sweet young girl, who looked so kindly, and spoke so gentle. Yet deeply she felt that, even for this gentle girl's sake, she must reveal the fatal secret! It was dreadful enough and humiliating enough to have had the marriage ceremony read over herself and an already married man, the husband of a living woman; but it would be infinitely worse, it would be horrible and shameful, to let her go off in ignorance, believing herself to be that man's wife--to travel with him over Europe.

All this, the honest woman from Westminster Road knew and felt, yet she had not the courage now to shock that gentle girl's heart by telling the news which must stop her journey.

"Please excuse me; but I must really beg you to be quick in telling me what I can do to serve you. My time is limited. Within an hour we have to catch the tidal train to Dover. And--I have much to do in the interim," said the young duchess, speaking with gentle courtesy to this poor, shabby woman in the rusty widow's weeds.

"Ah, my lady--grace, I mean! there is no need of being quick! When you hear all I have to tell you--to my sorrow as well as yours, my grace!--your hurry will all be over; and you will not care about catching the tidal train--not if you are the lady as I take my--*your* grace to be!"

"What do you mean?" inquired Salome, in low, tremulous tones.

"My lady--grace, I mean! will you send your maid away? What I have to tell you, must be told to you alone," whispered the visitor.

"Margaret, you may retire. I will ring when I want you," said the young duchess.

And her maid, disgusted, for her curiosity had been strongly aroused, left the room and closed the door. And, as Margaret had too much self-respect to listen at the key-hole, she remained in ignorance of what passed between the young duchess and the uncanny visitor.

"Your strange words trouble me," said Salome, as soon as she found herself alone with her visitor.

"Ay, my lady, your grace, I know it. And I am sorry for it. But I cannot help it. And, indeed, I'm very much afeared as I shall trouble you more afore I am done."

"Then pray proceed. Tell me at once all you have to tell. And permit me to remind you that my time is limited," urged the young duchess.

"Ay, madam, my lady--grace, I mean. But grant me your pardon if I repeat that there is indeed no hurry. You will not take the tidal train to Dover. Not if you be the Christian lady as I take you for," gravely replied the visitor.

"I must really insist upon your speaking out plainly and at once," said Salome, with more of firmness than she had as yet exhibited, although her pale cheeks grew a shade paler.

"My lady--your grace, I should say--when I started to come here this morning, to bring you the news I have to tell, my heart was *that* full of anger against him and you, for the deep wrongs done to one I know and love, that I did not care how suddenly I told it, or how awfully it might shock you. But now that I see you, dear lady--grace, I mean--I do hate myself for having of such a tale to tell. But, for all that--for your sake as well as for hers, I must tell it," said the woman, solemnly.

"For Heaven's sake, go on! What is it you have to tell me?" inquired the bride, in a fainting voice.

"Well, then, your lady, my grace--Oh, dear! I know that ain't the right way to speak, but--"

"No matter! no matter! Only tell me what you have to tell and have done with it!" said Salome, impatiently at last.

"Well, then--I beg ten thousand pardons, my lady, but did your ladyship ever hear tell, up your way in Scotland, of a very handsome young woman of the lower orders, by the name of Rose Cameron?"

"Yes, I have heard of such a girl," answered the bride, in a low tone, averting her face.

"I thought your ladyship must have heard of her. And now--I beg a million of pardons, my lady--but did your ladyship ever happen to hear of a certain person's name mentioned alongside of hers?"

"I decline to answer a question so improper. What can such a question have to do with your present business?" inquired the bride, with more of gentle dignity than we have ever known her to assume.

"It has a great deal to do with it, your ladyship. It has everything to do with it, as I shall soon prove to your grace. Take no offence, dear lady. I won't use any name to trouble you. And I won't say anything but what I can prove. Will you let me go on on them terms, your ladyship?" humbly inquired the messenger.

"Yes, yes, if you only WILL be quick. I *wish* you to go on. I believe you to mean well, though I do not exactly know what you really *do* mean," said Salome, nervously.

"Well, then, my lady, if you ever heard of this handsome Highland peasant girl, called Rose Cameron, you must have heard that she lived long of her old father, a shepherd, dwelling at the foot of Ben Lone, near by where--a--a certain person had his shooting-lodge. My dear lady, it is the same wicked old story as we hear over and over again, and a many times too often. Well, the young man--a certain person, I mean--while at his shooting-box, foot of Ben Lone, happened to see this handsome lass, and fell in love with her at first sight, as certain persons sometimes do with young peasant girls as they oughtn't to marry. But mayhap your ladyship have heard all this before."

Salome had heard it all before; and now, in silence and sadness, she was wondering what she had to hear more; but certainly not expecting to hear the degrading revelation her visitor had still to make.

"Well, my lady," resumed the visitor, "a certain person courted handsome Rose Cameron a long time, trying to coax her to accept of his heart without his hand, after the manner of certain persons, to poor and pretty young girls. But the handsome peasant was as proud as a princess, and so she was. And she would see him hanged first, and so she would, before she would degrade herself for him, especially as she wasn't overmuch in love with him herself, but only pleased with his preference, and proud to show him off. She didn't worship him at all. She worshiped herself, my lady. And she could take care of herself and keep him in his place, even while she sort of encouraged his attentions. That was the secret of her power over him, my lady. She would neither take him on his terms nor let him go. And the more she resisted him the more he fell down and worshiped her, until, at length, he was ready to give up everything for her sake, and offer her marriage. That was what she really wanted to fetch him to, for she was ambitious as well as honest--that she was! Are you listening to me, my lady?"

"I am listening," breathed the bride, in a faint voice.

She had turned her chair around, so that her weary head could rest upon the corner of the dressing-table, where she now leaned, face downward, on her spread hands.

"Well, my lady, when she had fetched him to that pass as to offer her marriage, she took him at his word, and he brought her up to London. And they were married, sure enough, in the old church at St. Margaret's near by where I live, in Westminster."

"It is false! It is false! It is false as--Oh! Heaven of Heavens!" cried Salome, wildly, throwing back her head and hands, and then dropping them again with a low, heart-broken moan.

"I am cut to the soul, my lady, to say this; but I must say it, even for your sake, my lady, and I only say what I can easy prove," spoke the woman, humbly.

"Go on, go on," moaned Salome, without lifting her head.

"Well, my lady, after their marriage, they came to my house to live, which this was the way of it; I had a three-story brick house on Westminster Road, and I took lodgers. But what between getting only a few lodgers, and them being bad pay, I got myself over head and ears in debt, and was in danger of being sold up by my creditors, when a certain person, as called hisself Mr. John Scott, come and took the whole house right offen my hands just as it was, and engaged me as his house-keeper, telling of me as he was just married, and was agoing to bring home his wife. Well, my lady, he advanced me money to pay my debts, and then he fetched Mrs. John Scott, which was no other than Rose Cameron, my lady, as I soon after found out from herself. Well, he fetches Mrs. John Scott to look at the first floor which he was agoing to refit complete for her, and according to her taste. Well, your ladyship, she, having of a very glarish sort of her own, she chooses furniture all scarlet and gold, enough to put your eyes out. And when all was fixed up onto that first floor, then he brought her home sure enough."

Without lifting her face, Salome murmured some words in so low and smothered a tone that they were inaudible to her visitor.

"I beg pardon, my lady. What did you please to say?" inquired the woman, bending toward the bowed head of the bride.

"I asked how long ago was it?" she repeated, in a faint voice.

"Just about a year, my lady."

"Go on."

"Well, then, my lady, first along he seemed very fond of her, seemed to doat on her, and loaded her with dresses, and trinkets, and sweetmeats, and nick-nacks of all sorts, and never came home without bringing of her something. And she never got anything very nice but what she would call me up and give me some; for she made quite a companion of me, my lady. But after a few weeks, Mr. John Scott was frequent away from home for days together. But this didn't trouble Mrs. John

Scott much. I soon saw as she wasn't that deep in love with him as she couldn't live without him. And so he kept her well supplied with finery and dainties, or with the money to get them, he might go off as often, and stay as long as he liked. She lived an idle, easy, merry life, and frequent went to the play-house, and took me. 'And all was merry as a marriage bell,' as the old saying says, until this summer, when Mr. John Scott went off, and stayed longer then he ever stayed before. Well, my lady, while he was still away, one morning in last June, Mrs. John Scott takes up the *Times* to look over. She didn't often look over the papers, and when she did it was only to see what was going to be played at the theatres. But *that* morning her eyes happened to light down on something in the paper as put her into a perfect fury. She was so beside herself as to let out a good deal that she meant to have kept in. And by her own goings on I found out that it was the announcement of the marriage, that was to come off in two days at Lone Castle, between the young Marquis of Hereward and the daughter and heiress of Sir Lemuel Levison, as had set her on fire. I tried my best to quiet her, and even asked her what it was to her? She said she would soon let 'em all know what it was to her. I begged her to explain. But she would give me no satisfaction. She seemed all cock-a-whoop, begging your lady-ship's pardon, to go somewhere and do something. And that same night she packed her carpet-bag and off she went. I asked her what I should say to Mr. John Scott if he should come home before she did. And she told me never to mind. I shouldn't have any call to say anything. *She* should see him before *I* could. And so off she went that same night."

"What night was that?" slowly and faintly breathed Salome, without lifting her fallen head.

"Two nights before--before the marriage was to have been, my lady," answered the woman, in a low and hesitating tone.

"Proceed, please."

"And now, my lady, I must tell you what happened at Lone, as I received it from her own lips this very morning, before I came here. She went down to Scotland by the night express of the Great Northern, and arrived at Lone early in the morning of the day before the wedding-day that should have been. She found great preparations going on for the marriage of the markis and the heiress. She went over to the castle with the crowd of the country people who gathered there to see the grand decorations for the wedding. But she saw nothing of the bride or of the bride-groom; and, moreover, she was warned off with threats by the servants of the castle. But at length, towards night-fall, my lady, she saw Mr. John Scott, as he called him-self, hanging about the Hereward Arms, and she 'went for him,' as the saying is. But he drew her apart from the crowd. And there she charged him with perfidy, and threatened to appear at the church the next day with her marriage lines and forbid the banns. He did all he could to quiet her, said that she was deceived and mistaken, and that he could not marry any one, being already married to herself, and that if she would meet him that night at the castle, just under the balcony, near Malcolm's Tower, he would explain everything to her satisfaction."

"*It was no dream, then!* Oh, Heaven! it was no dream! And my own senses witness against him!" exclaimed Salome again, throwing up her face and hands with a cry of anguish, and then dropping them, as before, upon the table in an attitude of abject despair.

"My lady, this is too much for you! too much!" said the compassionate woman, weeping over the distress she had caused.

"No, no; go on, go on; I will hear it all. My own senses, pitying Heaven! my own senses bear witness to it," moaned Salome, in a smothered voice.

"Ah, my lady, it grieves me deeply to go on, as you bid me. They met, Mr. John Scott, as he called himself, and Rose Cameron, at the time and place agreed on--at midnight at Castle Lone, under the balcony near Malcolm's Tower. And there, my lady, he repeated to her that he was not going to marry anybody, reminding her that he was already married to herself; and he explained that something would happen before morning, which would put all thoughts of marrying and giving in marriage out of the heads of all parties concerned. And then he--"

A groan of anguish burst from the almost breaking heart of the wretched bride, as she lifted a face convulsed and deathly white with her soul's great agony.

"My lady! oh, my lady!" exclaimed the woman, in much alarm.

"I heard it all! I heard it all!" cried Salome, as if speaking to herself and uncon-scious of the presence of a hearer. "I heard it all! I heard it all! Yea! my own senses were witnesses of my own dishonor and despair!" she groaned, as she threw her arms and her head violently forward upon the table.

"My lady, for mercy's sake, my lady!" exclaimed the widow, standing up and bending over her.

"Oh, what a hell! what a hell is this world we live in! And what devils walk to and fro upon the earth!--devils beautiful and deceitful as the fallen archangel himself!" moaned Salome, all unconscious of the words.

"Ah, my dear lady, for goodness' sake, now don't talk so, that's a darling," coaxed the good woman.

"DO NOT HEED ME! Go on! go on! Give me the death-blow at once, and have done with it!" cried Salome, lifting her blanched and writhen face and wringing hands, and then dashing them down again.

The appalled visitor seemed stricken dumb.

"Go on, go on," moaned the poor bride in a half smothered tone.

"Lord help me! I have forgotten where I was! I wish it had befallen anybody but me to have this here hard duty to do! Where was I again? Ah! under the balcony. My lady, he told her to wait there for him until he came back. And he went away, and was gone an hour or more. Then he came back, and another man along of him. The night was so still, she heard them coming before they got in sight. And she heard them a talking in a low voice. And Mr. John Scott he seemed awful put out about something or other as the other man had done agin his orders. And he said, hoarse like, 'I wouldn't have had it done, no, not for all we have got by it!' And the other one said, 'It couldn't be helped. The old man squealed, and we had to squelch him.' Says Mr. John Scott: 'You've brought the curse of Cain upon me!' Says t'other one, 'It was chance. What's done is done, and can't be undone. What's past remedy is past regret. And what can't be cured must be endured. The old man squealed, and had to be squelched, or he'd have brought the house about our ears--'"

"Oh, my father! my dear father! my poor, murdered father! And *you*! oh *you*! with the beauty and glory of the archangel, and the cruelty and deceit of the arch fiend, I can never look upon your face again--never! The sight would blast me like a flame of fire," raved Salome, throwing back her head, wringing her hands, and gasping as if for breath of life.

"Ah, my dear lady, I know how hard it is! Pardon me, my lady, but I feel a mother's heart in my bosom for you. Try to be patient, sweet lady, and do not despair. You are so young yet, hardly more than a child you seem. You have a long life before you yet. And if you be good, as I am sure you will be, it will be a happy life, in which these early sorrows will pass away like morning mists," said the woman, soothingly.

"Oh, never more for me will morning dawn! Eternal night rests on my soul! For myself I do not care! But, oh, my ruined archangel!" she wailed, burying her face in her hands.

A dead silence fell between the two, until Salome, without changing her position, murmured;

"Go on to the end; I will not interrupt you again. Oh, that I could wake from this night-mare!--or--expire in it! Go on and finish."

"My lady, while the two men were speaking, they came in sight of the woman who was waiting under the balcony. Then Mr. John Scott says: 'Hush! my girl will hear us.' And they hushed, but it was too late--she had heard them. Mr. John Scott came up to her in a hurry, and put a small but heavy bag in her hand, saying that she must take it and take care of it, and never let it go out of her possession, and that she must hurry back to Lone Station and catch the midnight express train back to London, and that he himself would follow her, and join her at home the next night."

"And all that, too, was proved--yes, proved by the mouths of two witnesses at the inquest, though they did not either of them recognize the man or the woman," moaned Salome.

"Mrs. John Scott returned to my house about breakfast time the next morning, my lady, bringing that bag with her, which I noticed she wouldn't let out of her sight, no, nor even out of her hand, while I was near her. She wouldn't answer any of my questions, or give me any satisfaction then, even so far as to tell me where she had been, or if she had seen Mr. John Scott. So I knew nothing until the next morning, when I got the *Times*. I don't in general care about reading the papers myself, but opened it that morning to see if there was anything in it about the grand wedding at Lone. And oh! My lady, I saw how the wedding had been stopped on account of--on account--of what happened to Sir Lemuel Levison that night, my lady, as I don't like to talk of it, or even t think of it. But when Mrs. John Scott rang her bell that morning, my lady, I took up the paper with her cup of tea, which she always took in bed. And oh, my lady, when she came to know what had happened at Lone, she went off into the very worst hysterics I ever saw. I was struck all of a heap! I couldn't imagine why she should take it so awfully to heart as that. But that's neither here nor there. I know ***now*** why she took it so to heart. In the midst of all the hubbub, Mr. John Scott returned. And she fairly flew at him! She said, among other bitter, things, that he would bring her to the gallows yet! And she charged him with what she had overheard. But somehow or other he laughed at her, and explained it all away to her satisfaction. He could always make her believe whatever he pleased. If he had told her the rainbow was only a few yards of striped Leamington ribbon, she would have believed him! He didn't stay more than an hour, and was off again in a hurry. We didn't see him again until the last of the week. It was the news of the coroner's verdict on the Lone murder case was telegraphed to London, when he came rushing in at the door and up the stairs like a mad-man. And in ten minutes he came rushing down stairs again and out of the street door like a madman, but he carried the heavy little bag off with him in his hand. And he has never been back since. But, from time to time, he wrote to her, and sent her money, and told her that business still kept him away. But, mind you, my lady, his letters were all without date or signature, and were drop letters, now from one London post-office, and now from another, so that she never knew where to address him. Not that she cared. As long as her money lasted she was, perfectly satisfied. She lived comfortably, and she amused herself, and often went to the play and took me with her, and all went merry again until yesterday, when, all on a sudden, the police made a descent on the house, and arrested Mrs. John Scott on a charge of being implicated in the robbery and murder at Castle Lone, and proceeded to search the house, where they found the watch-chain, snuff-box, and other valuable property belonging to the late Sir Lemuel Levison!"

"Great Heaven! they found these things in the house rented by--by--"

Salome could say no more, but ended with a groan that seemed to rend body and soul apart.

"They found the stolen jewels there, my lady. My unhappy mistress denied all knowledge of them, but her words availed her nothing. She was carried off to prison that same night. This morning she was taken before the sitting magistrate, and examined, and remanded to prison, until she can be carried back to Scotland for trial. Neither she nor I know at what hour she may be removed, or by what train she may be taken to Scotland. She may be gone now, for aught I know."

"Where is the poor creature now confined?" inquired Salome, in a dying voice.

"In the Westminster police station-house, my lady, if she has not been already removed. But I must tell your ladyship--your grace, I mean--how I happen to come to you now. I was at the West End this morning, my lady, and in returning to the city I passed St. George's Church, Hanover Square, and I saw the pageant of your wedding. And when I got back to Westminster and looked into the station-house to see my unfortunate mistress, and to help her mind often her own troubles, I told her about the wedding of the Duke of Hereward with the heiress of Sir Lemuel Levison, at St. George's Church, my lady. She went off into the most terrible fit of excitement I ever seen her in yet, and I have seen her in some considerable ones, now I do assure your ladyship. And in her raving and tearing, my lady, I first heerd that Mr. John Scott and the young Marquis of Arondelle and the Duke of Hereward was all one and the same gentleman, and he was the lawful husband of Rose Cameron. My lady, I thought her troubles had turned her head, and so I did not believe a word she said. And, my lady, I do not expect *you* to believe *me* without proof, any more than I believed *her*."

"Oh, Heaven of Heavens! I have the proof! I have the proof in the evidence of my own senses, too fatally discredited until now. But if you have further proof, give it me at once," groaned Salome.

"Here is the marriage certificate. Look at that first, my lady, if you please," said Mrs. Brown, putting the document in her hands.

Salome gazed at it with beclouded vision, but she saw that it was a genuine certificate of marriage between Archibald-Alexander-John Scott, Marquis of Arondelle, and, Rose Cameron, signed by James Smith, Rector of St. Margaret's Church, Westminster, and witnessed by John Thomas Price, Sexton, and Ann Gray, Pew-opener.

"The man must have been mad! mad! to have done this, in the first instance, and then--done what he has just this morning," moaned Salome, as she returned the certificate to the woman.

"My lady, he thought as he had got Rose Cameron lagged, he would never be found out. Here, my lady, is the first letter he wrote to her after they were married. I reckon it is a foolish love-letter enough, not worth reading; but what I want you to notice is, his handwriting, and the way he commences his letter--'My Darling

Wife,' and the way he ends it--'Your Devoted Husband, Arondelle.'"

"I recognize the handwriting, and I note the signature. I do not wish to read the letter," muttered Salome, waving it away.

"Well, then, my lady, here is a photograph of his grace, given to his wife a few days before their marriage," said the widow, offering a small card.

Salome took it, looked at it, and dropped it with a long, low wail of anguish.

It was a duplicate of one presented to herself by the Duke of Hereward, from the same negative.

Silence again fell between the lady and her visitor until it was broken by a rap at the door, and the voice of the maid without, saying:

"Beg pardon, your grace, but Lady Belgrade desires me to say that you have but fifteen minutes to catch the train."

"Very well," replied the young duchess; but her voice sounded strangely unlike her own.

"Your ladyship will not go on your bridal tour?" said the visitor, imploringly.

"No, I shall not go on a bridal tour. How can I?--I am not a bride. I am not a wife. I am not the Duchess of Hereward. I am just Salome Levison, as I was before that false marriage ceremony was performed over me! But do you be discreet. Say nothing below stairs of what has passed between us here," said Salome, speaking now with such amazing self-control that no one could have guessed the anguish and despair of her soul but for the marble whiteness and rigidity of her face.

"Be sure I shall not say one word, my lady," answered Mrs. Brown.

There was another low rap at the door, and again the voice of the maid was heard:

"Please your grace, what shall I say to Lady Belgrade?"

"Tell her ladyship that I am nearly ready," answered the young duchess. "And, Margaret," she added, "show this good woman out. And then, do not return here until I ring."

The visitor courtesied and went to the door, where she was met by the maid, who conducted her down stairs.

Salome locked and double-locked and bolted the doors leading from her apartments to the front corridor, and then she retreated to her dressing-room, alone with her terrible trial.

Who can conceive the mortal agony suffered by that young, overburdened heart and overtasked brain.

Who can estimate the force of the conflict that raged in her bosom, between her passion and her conscience? Between her love and her duty? Between what she knew of her worshiped husband, from daily association, and what she had just heard proved upon him by overwhelming testimony, confirmed also by the evidence of her own too long discredited senses!

He--her Apollo--her ideal of all manly excellence--her archangel, as in the infatuation of her passion she had called him--he a bigamist, and an accomplice in the murder of her father!

It was incredible! incomprehensible! maddening!

Or surely it was some awful nightmare dream, from which she must soon awake.

What should she do? How meet again the people below?

She would not look upon *his* face again. She could not. She felt that to do so would be perdition.

In the darkness of her despair a great temptation assailed her.

But we must leave her alone to wrestle with the demon, while we join the wedding-party below.

CHAPTER XVI.
VANISHED.

After the withdrawal of the bride and her attendant from the breakfast-table, the bridegroom and his friends remained a few moments longer, and then joined Lady Belgrade and the bridesmaids in the drawing-room.

They passed some fifteen or twenty minutes in pleasant social chat upon the event of the morning, the state of the weather, and the political, financial, or fashionable topics of the day.

In half an hour they felt disposed to yawn, and some surreptitiously consulted their watches.

Then one of the bridesmaids, at the request of Lady Belgrade, sat down to the piano and condescended to favor the company with a very fine wedding march.

Three quarters of an hour passed, and then the Baron Von Levison--(Paul Levison, the head of the great Berlin branch of the banking-house of "Levison," had been ennobled in Germany, as his brother had been knighted in England)--Baron Von Levison then inquired of the bridegroom what train he intended to take.

"The tidal train, which leaves London Bridge Station at three-thirty," answered the duke.

"Then your grace should leave here in fifteen minutes, if you wish to catch that train," said the baron.

The bridegroom spoke aside to Lady Belgrade.

"Had we not better send and see if Salome is ready? We have but little time to lose."

"Yes," said her ladyship, who immediately rang the bell, and dispatched a message to the young duchess's dressing-maid.

A few minutes elapsed, and an answer was returned to the effect that her grace would be ready in time to catch the train.

The travelling carriage was at the door, and all the lighter luggage, such as dressing-bags, extra shawls and umbrellas, were put in it.

And they waited full fifteen minutes, without seeing or hearing from the loitering bride.

"I will go up to Salome myself," said Lady Belgrade, impatiently.

"No, pray do not hurry her; if we miss this train we can take the next, and though we cannot catch the night-boat from Dover to Calais, we can stop at the 'Lord Warden' and cross the Channel to-morrow morning," urged the duke.

"At least I will send another message to her, and let her know that the time is more than up," said her ladyship.

And again she rang the bell and sent a servant with a message to the lady's maid.

Full ten minutes passed, and then Margaret, the maid, came herself to the drawing-room door, begged pardon for her intrusion, and asked to speak with Lady Belgrade.

Lady Belgrade went out to her.

"What is it? The time is up! This delay is perfectly disgraceful. They will never be able to catch the tidal train now--never!" said her ladyship in a displeased tone.

"If you please, my lady, I am afraid something has happened," said the girl, in a frightened tone.

"What do you mean?" inquired the dowager, sharply.

"If you please, my lady, I went up and found all the doors leading from the corridor into her grace's suite of apartments locked fast. I knocked and called, at first softly, then loudly, but received no answer. I listened, my lady, but I heard no sound nor motion in the rooms."

"I will go up myself," said Lady Belgrade, uneasily.

And she hurried, as fast as her age and her size would permit, to the part of the house comprising the apartments of the duchess. Three doors opened from the corridor, relatively, into the boudoir, bed-room, and dressing-room, which were also connected by communicating doors within.

Lady Belgrade rapped and called at each in succession, but in vain. There was no response.

"She has fainted in her room! That is what has happened! This day of fatigue and excitement has been too much for her, in the delicate state of her health. Every one noticed how ill she looked when she came up stairs. Margaret, there is a back door, you are aware, leading from your lady's bath-room down to the flower garden. Go around and go up the back stairs and see if that door is open--if so, enter the rooms by it and open this," said her ladyship, never ceasing, while she talked, to rap at and shake the door at which she stood.

Margaret flew to obey, and made such good haste, that in about two minutes she was heard within the rooms hurrying to open the closed door. In two seconds bolts were withdrawn, keys turned, and the door was opened.

"How is she?" quickly demanded the dowager, as she stepped into the dressing-room.

"My lady, I haven't seen her grace. If you please, perhaps she is in her chamber," replied the maid.

Lady Belgrade bustled into the bed-room, looking all around for the bride, then into the boudoir, calling on her name.

"Salome! Salome, my dear! Where are you?" No answer; all in the luxurious rooms still and silent as the grave.

"This is very strange! She *may* be in the garden," said her ladyship, passing quickly into the bath-room, and descending the stairs that led directly into a small flower-garden enclosed by high walls.

The garden was now dead and sear in the late October frost. No sign of the missing girl was there.

"This is very strange! Can she have gone down into the drawing-room, after all? I will see. There is no possibility of catching the tidal train now. It is already three o'clock; the train leaves London Bridge Station at three thirty, and it is a good hour's ride from Kensington!" said Lady Belgrade, speaking more to herself than to her attendant, as she came out of the rooms.

"Shall I go through the house and inquire if any one has seen her grace, my lady?" respectfully suggested Margaret.

"Yes; but first shut and lock that garden door of your lady's bath-room. It is not safe to leave it open," replied Lady Belgrade, as she again descended the stairs.

As she entered the drawing-room, the young Duke of Hereward came to meet her.

"I hope nothing is the matter. Salome was not looking strong this morning. And this delay? I trust that she is well?" he said, in an anxious, inquiring tone.

"Salome is not in her apartments. I have sent a servant to seek her through the house. Her delay has made you miss the train, your grace," said Lady Belgrade, in visible annoyance.

"That does not much matter, so that the delay has not been caused by her indisposition," said the young duke, earnestly.

"No indisposition could possibly excuse such eccentricity of conduct at such a time. Salome is moving somewhere about the house, according to her crazy custom," said Lady Belgrade.

"I really cannot hear that sweet girl so cruelly maligned, even by her aunt," said the duke, with a deprecating smile.

As they spoke, the Baron Von Levison appeared and said:

"I should have been very glad to have seen you off, duke, and to have thrown a metaphorical old shoe after you; but your bride seems to have taken so long to tie her bonnet strings, that she has made you miss your train. And now you can't go until the night express, and I really can't wait to see you off by that. I have an appointment at the Bank of England at four. God bless you, my dear duke. Make my adieux to my niece, and tell her that if the men of her family had been as unpunctual as the women seem to be, they never would have established banks all over Europe."

And with a hearty shake of the bridegroom's hand, and a deep bow to Lady Belgrade, the Baron Von Levison took leave.

His example was followed by the bishop and the rector, who now came up and expressed regret at the inconvenience the bridegroom would experience by having missed his train, but agreed that it was much better to know that fact before starting for it, and having the long drive to London Bridge Station and back again for nothing. And they extolled the comfort of the night express, and the elegance of accommodations to be found at the Lord Warden Hotel. And upon the whole, they concluded that his grace had not missed much, after all, in missing the "tidal."

Then again they wished much happiness to attend the married life of the young couple, and so bade adieux and departed.

There now remained of the wedding guests only the two bridesmaids and the groomsmen.

These were grouped near one of the bay-windows, and engaged in a subdued conversation.

The Duke of Hereward and Lady Belgrade still stood near the door, waiting for news of the lingering bride.

To them, at length, came the maid, Margaret, with pallid face and frightened air.

"If you please, my lady, we have searched all over the house and inquired of everybody in it. But no one has seen her grace, nor can she be found."

CHAPTER XVII.
THE LOST LADY OF LONE.

"Cannot be found? Whatever do you mean, girl? You cannot mean to say that the Duchess of Hereward is not in this house?" demanded Lady Belgrade, in amazement.

"I beg pardon, my lady; but we have made a thorough search of the premises, without being able to find her grace," respectfully answered the maid.

"Oh, but this is ridiculous! The duchess is in some of the rooms; she must be! Go and renew your search, and tell her grace, when you find her, that she has made the duke miss the tidal train; but that we are waiting for her here," commanded the lady.

The girl went, very submissively, on her errand.

Lady Belgrade dropped wearily into her chair, muttering:

"I do think servants are so idiotic. They can't find her because she happens to be out of her own room. I would go and hunt her up myself, but really the fatigue of this day has been too much for me."

The Duke of Hereward did not reply. He walked restlessly up and down the floor, filled with a vague uneasiness, for which he could not account to himself--for surely, he reflected, Salome must be in the house somewhere; it could not possibly be otherwise; and there were a dozen simple reasons why she might be missed for a few minutes; doubtless she would soon appear, and smile at their impatience.

Ay, but the minutes were fast growing into hours, and Salome did not re-appear.

The maid returned once more from her fruitless search.

"Indeed, I beg your pardon, my lady; but we cannot find her grace, either in the house or in the garden," she said, with a very solemn courtesy.

"Now this is really beyond endurance! I suppose I must go and look for her myself," answered Lady Belgrade, rising in displeasure.

"Will you let me accompany your ladyship?" gravely inquired the duke.

Lady Belgrade hesitated for a few moments, and then said:

"Well,--yes, you may come. We will go down stairs first."

They descended to the first floor, and went through the dining-room, sitting-room, library and little parlors; but without finding her they sought.

Then they ascended to the next floor and went through the picture-gallery, the music-room, the dancing-saloon, the hall, and lastly, the three drawing-rooms, in case that she might have returned there while they were absent. But their search was still without success.

Then they ascended to the upper floors, and looked all through the handsome suites of private apartments, but still without discovering a trace of the missing bride.

And so all over the house, from basement to attic, and from central hall to garden wall, they went searching in vain for the lost one.

The dowager and the duke returned to the drawing-room and looked each other in the face.

The dowager was stupefied with bewilderment. The duke was pale with anxiety.

The mystery was growing serious and alarming.

"What do you think of it, Lady Belgrade?" inquired the duke.

"I cannot think at all. I am at my wit's end," answered the lady. "What do *you* think?" she inquired, after a moment's pause.

"I think--that we had better call the servants up, one at a time, and put them separately through a strict examination," answered the duke.

Lady Belgrade rang the bell.

A footman appeared in answer to it.

"Examine him first, your grace," said the lady.

The duke put the young man through a strict catechism, without satisfactory results. John was the hall footman, whose business it was to answer the street-door bell and announce visitors. And he assured his grace that no one had entered or left the house that morning, to *his* knowledge, except the wedding party and their attendants.

The hall-porter was next summoned and examined, and his report was found to correspond exactly to that of the footman.

The butler was sent for and questioned, but could throw no light on the mystery of the lady's disappearance.

The pantry footman was next called up. His duty was to wait on the butler and attend the servants' door, to take in provisions delivered there. And the first plausible clue to the mystery of Salome's disappearance was received from him.

"Yes, my lady," he said, "there have been a stranger to the servants' door this morning--an elderly old widow woman, my lady, dressed in black, and werry much in earnest about seeing her grace; would take no denial, my lady, on no account; which compelled me to go to her grace's lady's-maid, Miss Watson, my lady, and send a message to her grace," said the young footman.

"Did the duchess see this strange visitor?" inquired the duke.

"Miss Watson come down and seen her first, your grace, and told her how she mustn't disturb the duchess. But the visitor was so dead set on seeing her grace, and used such strong language about it, that at last Miss Watson took up her message and in a few minutes come back and took up the visitor."

"She did? And what next?" inquired Lady Belgrade.

"Please, my lady, there was nothing next. In about an hour Miss Margaret brought the elderly old lady down, and I showed her out of the servants' door."

"Did she leave the house alone?" inquired the duke.

"Yes, your grace, just as she came, alone."

"Go and tell Margaret Watson to come here," said Lady Belgrade.

The man bowed and retired.

In a few minutes the girl made her appearance again.

"How is it, Watson, that you did not mention the visitor you showed up into your lady's room this morning?" inquired Lady Belgrade, in a severe tone.

"If you please, my lady, I did not think the visitor signified anything," meekly answered the maid.

"How could you tell *what* signified at a time like this?"

"I beg pardon, my lady; but it was the time itself that made me forget the visitor."

"Who was she? What time did she come? What did she want?" sharply demanded the lady.

"Please, my lady, she said her name was Smith, or Jones, or some such common name as that. I think it was Jones, my lady. And she lived on Westminster Road--or it might have been Blackfriars Road. Least-ways it was one of those roads leading to a bridge because I remember it made me think of the river."

"Extremely satisfactory! At what hour did this Mrs. Smith or Jones, from Westminster or Blackfriars, come?" inquired Lady Belgrade.

"Just as her grace went up to her room to change her dress. She had just finished changing it when the woman was admitted."

"And now! what did the woman want of the duchess?"

"I do not know, my lady. Her business was with her grace alone. And she requested to have me sent out of the room. I did not see the woman again, until her grace called me to show her, the woman, out again."

"And you did so?"

"Yes, my lady. And I have not seen the woman since. And--I have not seen her grace since, either, my lady."

"You may go now," answered Lady Belgrade.

And the girl withdrew.

The Duke of Hereward and Lady Belgrade were once more left alone together.

Again their eyes met in anxious scrutiny.

"What do you think now, Duke?" inquired her ladyship.

"I think the disappearance of the duchess is connected with the visit of that strange woman. She may have been an unfortunate beggar, who, with some story of extreme distress, so worked upon Salome's sympathies as to draw her away from home, to see for herself, and give relief to the sufferers. Or--I shudder to think of it--she may have been a thief, or the companion of thieves, and with just such a story, decoyed the duchess out for purposes of plunder. This does not certainly seem to be a probable theory of the disappearance, but it does really seem the only possible one," concluded the duke, in a grave voice.

And though he spoke calmly, his soul was shaken with a terrible anxiety that every moment now increased.

"But is it at all likely that Salome, even with all her excessive benevolence, could have been induced to leave her home at such a time as this, even at the most distressing call of charity? Would she not have given money and sent a servant?" inquired Lady Belgrade.

"Under normal conditions she would have done as you say. But remember, dear madam, that Salome is not in a normal condition. Remember that it is but three months since she suffered an almost fatal nervous shock in the discovery of her father's murdered body on her own wedding morning. Remember that it is scarcely six weeks since her recovery from the nearly fatal brain fever that followed--if indeed she has ever fully recovered. *I* do not believe that she has, or that she will until I shall have taken her abroad, when total change of scene, with time and distance, may restore her," sighed the duke.

"I thought she was looking very well for the last few weeks," said Lady Belgrade.

"Yes, until within the last few days, in which she seems to have suffered a relapse, easily accounted for, I think, by the association of ideas. The near approach of her wedding day brought vividly back to her mind the tragic events of her first appointed wedding morning, and caused the illness that has been noticed by all our friends this day. The excitement of the occasion has augmented this illness. Salome has been suffering very much all day. Every one noticed it, although, with the self-possession of a gentlewoman, she went calmly through the ceremonies at the church, and through the breakfast here. But I think she must have broken down in her room, and while in that state of nervous prostration she must have become an easy dupe to that beggar, or thief, whichever her strange visitor may have been," said the duke; and while he spoke so calmly on such an anxious and exciting subject, he, too, under circumstances of extreme trial and suspense, exhibited the self-possession and self-control which is the birthright of the true gentleman no less than of the true gentlewoman.

"It may be as you think. It would be no use to question the servants further. They know no more than we do. We can do nothing more now but wait, with what patience we may, for the return of that eccentric girl," said Lady Belgrade, with a deep sigh, as she settled herself down in her chair.

Another hour passed--an hour of enforced inactivity, yet of unspeakable anxiety. Three hours had now elapsed since the mysterious disappearance of the bride; and yet no news of her came.

"She does not return! This grows insupportable!" exclaimed Lady Belgrade, at length, losing all patience, and starting up from her chair.

"She *may* be detained by the sick bed, or the death bed, of some sufferer who has sent for her," replied the duke, huskily, trying to hope against hope.

"As if she would so absent herself on her wedding day, on the eve of her wedding tour!" exclaimed the lady, beginning to walk the floor in a thoroughly exasperated state of mind.

"Of course she would not, in her normal mental condition; but, as I said before--"

"Oh, yes, I know what you said before. You insinuated that Salome may be insane from the latent effects of her recent brain fever, developed by the excitement of the last few days. And, Heaven knows, you may be right! It looks like it! Mysteriously gone off on her wedding day, in the interim between the wedding breakfast and the wedding tour! Gone off alone, no one knows where, without having left an explanation or a message for any one. What can have taken her out? Where can she be? Why don't she return? And night coming on fast. If she does not return within half an hour, you will miss the next train also, Duke," exclaimed Lady Belgrade, pausing in her restless walk, and throwing herself heavily into her chair again.

"Perhaps," said the Duke, in great perplexity, "we had better have the lady's maid up again, and question her more strictly in regard to the strange visitor's name and address; for I feel certain that the disappearance of the duchess is immediately connected with the visit of that woman. If we can, by judicious questions, so stimulate the memory of the girl as to obtain accurate information about the name and residence, we can send and make inquiries."

For all answer, Lady Belgrade arose and rung the bell for about the twentieth time that afternoon.

And Margaret Watson was again called to the drawing-room and questioned.

"Indeed, if you please, my lady, I am very sorry. I would give anything in the world if I could only remember exactly what the old person's name was, and where she lived. But indeed, my lady, what with being very much engaged with waiting on her grace, and packing up the last little things for the journey, and getting together the dressing-bags and such like, and having of my mind on them and not on the woman, and no ways expecting anything like this to happen, I wasn't that interested in the visitor to tax my memory with her affairs. But I know her name was a common one, like Smith or Jones, and I **think** it was Jones. And I know she said she lived on Westminster Road or Blackfriars Road, or some other road leading over a bridge, which I remember because it made me think about the river. But I couldn't tell which," said the girl in answer to the cross-questioning.

"And is that all you can tell us?" inquired Lady Belgrade.

"I beg pardon, my lady, but that is all I can remember," meekly replied the girl.

"Then you might as well remember nothing. You can go!" said Lady Belgrade, in deep displeasure.

The girl retired, a little crestfallen.

"Is there any other fool you would like to have called up and cross-examined, Duke?" sarcastically inquired the lady.

The duke made a gesture of negation. And the lady relapsed into painful silence.

And now another weary, weary hour crept by without bringing news of the lost one.

The watchers seemed to "possess their souls" in patience, if not "in peace." There was really nothing to be done but to wait. There was no place where inquiries could be made. At this time of the year nearly all the fashionable world of London was out of town. Nor at any time had Salome any intimate acquaintances to whom she would have gone. Nor would it have been expedient just yet to apply to the detective police for help to search abroad for one who might of herself return home at any moment.

The Duke of Hereward and Lady Belgrade could only wait it in terrible anxiety, though with outward calmness, for what the night might bring forth.

But in what a monotonous and insensible manner all household routine continues, "in well regulated families," through the most revolutionary sort of domestic troubles.

The first dinner bell had rung; but neither of the anxious watchers had even heard it.

The groom of the chambers came in and lighted the gas in the drawing-rooms, and retired in silence.

Still the watchers sat waiting in a state of intense, repressed excitement.

The second dinner bell rang. And almost immediately the butler appeared at the door, and announced, with his formula:

"My lady is served," and then:

"Will your grace join me at dinner?" courteously inquired Lady Belgrade, thinking at the same time of the unparalleled circumstance of the bridegroom dining without his bride upon his wedding day--"Will your grace join me at dinner?" she repeated, perceiving that he had not heard, or at least had not answered her question.

"I beg pardon. Pray, excuse me, your ladyship. I am really not equal--"

"I see! I see! Nor am I equal to going through what, at best, would be a mere form," said her ladyship. Then turning toward the waiting butler, she said--"Remove the service, Sillery. We shall not dine to-day."

The man bowed and withdrew.

And the two watchers, whose anxiety was fast growing into insupportable anguish, waited still, for still, as yet, they could do nothing else but wait and control themselves.

"Your grace has missed the last train," said Lady Belgrade, at length, as the little cuckoo clock on the mantel shelf struck ten.

"Yes the night express leaves London Bridge station for Dover at ten-thirty, and it is a full hour's drive from Kensington," replied the duke.

And both secretly thanked fortune that the wedding guests had all departed before the bride's mysterious absence from the house at such a time had become known; and they knew not but that "the happy pair had left by the tidal train for Dover, *en route* for their continental tour,"--as per wedding programme. And both silently hoped that the household servants would not talk.

The time crept wearily on. The clock struck eleven.

"I cannot endure this frightful suspense one moment longer! I never heard of such a case in all the days of my life! A bride to vanish away on her bridal day! Duke of Hereward you are her husband! WHAT IS TO BE DONE?" exclaimed Lady Belgrade, starting up from her seat and giving full sway to all the repressed excitement of the last few hours.

"My dear lady," said the duke, controlling his own emotions by a strong effort of will, and speaking with a calmness he did not feel--"My dear lady, the first thing you should do, should be to command yourself. Listen to me, dear Lady Belgrade. I have waited here in constrained quietness, hoping for our Salome's return from moment to moment, and fearing to expose her to gossip by any indiscreet haste in seeking her abroad. But I can wait no longer. I must commence the search abroad at once. I shall go immediately to a skillful detective, whom I know from reputation, and put the case in his hands. What seems to us so alarming and incomprehensible, may be to a man of his experience simple and clear enough. We are too near the fact to see it truly in its proper light. This man I understand to be faithful and discreet, one who may be intrusted with the investigation of the most delicate affairs. I will employ him immediately, in the confidence that no publicity will be given to this mystery. In the meanwhile, my dear Lady Belgrade, I counsel you to call the household servants all together. Do not inform them of the nature of my errand out, but caution them to silence and discretion as to the absence of their lady. You will allow me to confide this trust to you?"

"Assuredly, Duke! And let me tell you that these servants are all so idolatrously devoted to their mistress, that they would never breathe, or suffer to be breathed in their presence, one syllable that could, in the remotest degree, reflect upon her dignity," said the lady.

"I will return within an hour, madam," replied the duke, as he bowed and left the room.

He went directly to the nearest police station at Church Court, Kensington.

He asked to see Detective Collinson of the force.

Fortunately, Detective Collinson was at the office, and soon made his appearance.

The duke asked for a private interview.

The detective invited him to sit down in an empty side-room.

There the duke put the case of the missing lady in his hands, giving him all the circumstances supposed to be connected with her disappearance.

The detective exhibited not the slightest surprise at the hearing of this unprecedented story, nor did he express any opinion. Detectives never are surprised at anything that may happen at any time to anybody, nor have they ever any opinions to venture in advance.

Mr. Collinson said he would take the case and give it his undivided attention, but would promise nothing else.

The Duke of Hereward, obliged to be contented with this answer, arose to leave the room. In passing out he met the chief, who had not been present when he first entered.

"Oh, I beg your grace's pardon, but I consider this meeting very fortunate," said that officer, respectfully touching his hat.

"Upon what ground?" gravely inquired the duke.

"Your grace is wanted as a witness for the Crown, on the trial of John Potts and Rose Cameron, charged with the murder of the late Sir Lemuel Levison. The girl, who was arrested at a house in Westminster Road a few days ago, has been sent down to Scotland, and the trial will commence, on the day after to-morrow, at the Assizes now open at Bannff. But, according to the newspaper report, we thought your grace to be now on your way to Paris, and we were just about to dispatch a special messenger to you. So your grace will perceive how fortunate this meeting turns out to be."

"Yes, I perceive," said the duke, dryly.

"And your grace will not be inconvenienced, I hope," said the chief, as he bowed and placed a folded paper in the duke's hand.

It was a subpoena commanding the recipient, under certain pains and penalties, to render himself at the Town Hall of Bannff as a witness for the Crown, in the approaching trial of John Potts, alias Abraham Peters, and Rose Cameron.

CHAPTER XVIII.
THE FLIGHT OF THE DUCHESS

When the emissary of Rose Cameron had gone, the young Duchess of Hereward, in a whirlwind of long-repressed excitement, slammed, locked and bolted all the doors leading from her apartments into the hall, and then fled into her dressing-room and cast herself head long down upon the floor in the collapse of utter, infinite despair--despair in all its depth of darkness, without its benumbing calmness!

Her soul was shaken by a tempest of warring passions! Amazement, indignation, grief, horror, raged through her agonized bosom!

It was well that no human eye beheld her in this deep degradation of woe! For in the madness of her anguish, she rolled on the floor, and tore the clothing from her shoulders and the dark hair from her head! She uttered such groans and cries as are seldom heard on this earth--such as perhaps fill the murky atmosphere of hell. She impiously called on Heaven to strike her dead as she lay! She was indeed on the very brink of raving insanity.

There was but one thought that held her reason on its throne--the necessity of immediate flight and escape--escape from the man whom she had just vowed at the altar to love, honor, and obey until death--the man whom she had worshiped as an archangel!

The man?--the fiend, rather!

What had she just now found him proved to be?

Yes **proved** to be, beyond the merciful possibility of a saving doubt!--proved to be by the most overwhelming and convicting testimony, corroborated also by the evidence of her own eyes and ears, too long discredited for his sake.

Her eyes had seen him lurking stealthily in the dark hall, near her father's bed-room door, late on the night of that father's murder. She had spoken to him, and at the sound of her voice he had shrunk silently out of sight.

Yet she had discredited the evidence of her own eyes, and persuaded herself that she had been the subject of an optical illusion.

Her ears had heard a part of his midnight conversation with his female confed-erate under the balcony--had heard his prediction that something would happen that night to prevent the marriage that he promised her should never take place--a prediction so awfully fulfilled in the morning by the discovery of the dead body of her murdered father! She had fainted at the sound of his voice, uttering such treach-erous and cruel words; yet on her return to consciousness she had disbelieved the evidence of her own ears, and convinced herself that she had been the victim of a nightmare dream!

Yes! she had disallowed the direct evidence of her own senses rather than be-lieve such diabolical wickedness of her idol! But now the evidence of her own eyes and ears was corroborated by the most complete and convincing testimony--the conversation under the balcony, as reported by Rose Cameron's messenger, corre-sponded exactly with the conversation overheard by herself at the time and place it was said to have occurred, but which she dismissed from her mind as an evil dream! This corroborating testimony proved it to be an atrocious reality! And the man to whom she had given her hand that morning was an accomplice in the murder of her father! unintentionally perhaps, for the witness testified to the horror he expressed on learning from his confederate that a murder had been committed: "The old man squealed and we had to squelch him!" How she shuddered at the memory of these horrible words!

But this man was not her husband, after all! Although a marriage ceremony had been performed between them by a bishop, he was not her husband, but the husband of Rose Cameron. She had overwhelming and convincing proof of this also!

The letters written to Rose Cameron, calling her his dear wife, and signing himself her devoted husband "Arondelle," were in the handwriting of the Duke of Hereward! She could have sworn to that handwriting, under any circumstances.

And the photograph shown as the likeness of Rose Cameron's husband, was a duplicate of one in her own possession, given her by the duke himself.

And, above all, the certificate of marriage between them, signed by the offici-ating clergyman and witnessed by the officers of the church, was unquestionably genuine, regular, and legal!

No! there was not one merciful doubt to found a hope of his innocence upon! It was amazing, stupefying, annihilating, but it was true. Her idol was a fiend, glori-ous in personal beauty, diabolical in spirit, as the fallen archangel Lucifer, Son of the Morning!

He was deeply, atrociously, insanely guilty!

Yes, insanely! for how could he have acted so recklessly, as well as so crimi-nally, if he had not been insane? Would he not have known that swift discovery and disgrace were sure to follow the almost open commission of such base crimes? And if no feeling of honor or conscience could have deterred him, would not the fear of certain consequences have done so?

His insanity was *her* only rational theory of the case! But his supposed insan-ity did not vindicate him to her pure and just mind. For he was not an insane *man* so much as an insane devil! He had only been mad in his recklessness, not in his crimes.

Then quickly through her storm-tossed soul passed the thought that both sa-cred and profane history recorded instances of crimes committed by righteous and honorable men. Amazing truth! She remembered the piety and the *sin* of David, when he stole the wife of Uriah, and betrayed that loyal servant and brave soldier to a treacherous and bloody death! She remembered the loyalty and the *treason* of that chivalrous young Scottish prince who headed a fratricidal rebellion, in which his father and his king was slain, and who, as James IV., lived a life of remorse and penance, until, in his turn, he was slain on the fatal field of Flodden. She thought of these, and other instances, in which it might seem as if an angel and a devil lived together, animating one man's body. This would, of course, produce inconsistency of conduct, insanity of mind.

But among all the harrowing thoughts that hurried through her tortured mind, one feeling was predominant--the necessity of instant flight. There was no other cause for her to pursue. The bridal train was awaiting her down stairs. Soon they would send to summon her again. How could she meet them? What could she say to them? How could she ever look upon the face of the Duke of Hereward and *live*?

She must fly at once. No, there was no time to write a note and leave it pinned on her dressing-table cushion. Besides, what could she say in her note? Nothing; or nothing that she would say.

She must go and make no sign. She forced herself to rise from the floor and commence hurried preparations for immediate flight.

In all the tumult of her soul, some intuition guided her through her hasty arrangements to take the most effectual means to elude pursuit and baffle discovery.

She took off her handsome mourning dress of black silk and crape that she had put on to travel in, and she packed it, with the black felt hat, vail, sack and gloves that belonged to the suit, in one of her trunks, which she carefully locked.

Then from some receptacle of her left-off colored dresses, she selected a dark-gray silk suit, with sack, hat, vail and gloves to match. And in that she dressed herself.

Then she reflected.

"They will think that I went away in my mourning dress, which they will miss. If they describe me, they will describe a lady in deep mourning. If any one comes in pursuit, they will look for a young woman in black, and pass me by, because I shall wear gray and keep my vail down."

Then she concealed in her bosom all the cash she had in hand, being about fifteen hundred pounds in Bank of England notes, which she had previously drawn out for her own private uses during her bridal tour. This she thought would go far to meet the unknown expenses of her future. She also took her diamonds. She might have to sell them, she thought, for support.

Then, when she was quite ready, dressed in the dark gray suit, sack, hat, vail and gloves, and with a small valise in her hand, she went into her bath-room, and to the back door at the head of the private stairs leading down to the little garden of roses that was her own favorite bower.

She watched for a few seconds, to be sure that no one was in sight, and then she slipped swiftly down the stairs and crossed the garden to a narrow back door, which she quickly opened and passed through, shutting it after her. It closed with a spring and cut off her re-entrance there, even if she had been disposed to turn back.

But she was not.

She glanced nervously up and down the lane at the back of the garden wall, but saw no one there.

Then she walked rapidly away, and turned into a narrow street, keeping her gray vail doubled over her face all the time.

She purposely lost herself in a labyrinth of narrow streets, getting farther and farther from her home, before she ventured near a cab-stand.

At length she hailed a closed cab, engaged it, entered it, closed all the blinds, and directed the driver to take her to the Brighton, Dover, and South Coast Railway Station at London Bridge, and promised him a half-sovereign if he would catch the next train.

Yes! after a few moments of rapid reflection, as to whither she would go, she resolved to leave London by that very same tidal-train on which she and her husband were to have commenced their bridal tour, for there, of all places, she felt that she would be safest from pursuit; that, of all directions, would be the last in which they would think of seeking her!

And while they should be waiting and watching for her at Elmhurst House, she would be speeding towards the sea coast, and by the time they should discover her flight, she would be on the Channel, *en voyage* for Calais.

Beyond this she had no settled plan of action. She did not know where she would go, or what she should do, on reaching France.

She only longed, with breathless anxiety, to fly from England, from the Duke of Hereward, and all the horrors connected with him. She felt that she was not his wife, could never have been his wife, and that the mockery of a marriage ceremony, which had been performed for them by the Bishop of London that morning, at St. George's Hanover Square, had made the duke a felon and not a husband!

If she should remain in England she might even be called upon, in the course of events, to take a part in his prosecution. And guilty as she believed him to be, she could not bring herself to do that!

No! she must fly from England and conceal herself on the Continent!

But where?

She knew not as yet!

Her mind was in a fever of excitement when she reached London Bridge.

She paid and discharged her cab, giving the driver the promised half sovereign for catching the train.

Then, with her thick vail folded twice over her pale face, and her little valise in her hand, she went into the station, made her way to the office and bought a first-class ticket.

Then she went to the train, and stopping before one of the first carriages called a guard to unlock the door and let her enter.

"Oh, you can't have a seat in this compartment, Miss," said a somewhat garrulous old guard, coming up to her. "This whole carriage is reserved for a wedding party--the Duke and Duchess of Hereward, as were married this morning, and their graces' retinue, which they are expected to arrive every minute, Miss. But you can have a seat in *this* one, Miss. It is every bit as good as the other," concluded the old man, leading the way to a lady's carriage some yards in advance.

"Reserved for a wedding party--reserved for the Duke and Duchess of Hereward and their retinue!"

How her heart fainted, almost unto death, with a new sense of infinite disappointment and regret at what might have been and what was! Reserved for the Duke and Duchess of Hereward! Ah, Heaven!

"Here you are, Miss!" said the guard, opening the door of an empty carriage.

"How long will it be before the train starts?" inquired the fugitive in a low voice.

The guard looked at his big silver watch and answered:

"Time'll be up in three minutes, Miss."

"But if the--the--wedding party should not arrive before that?" hesitatingly inquired Salome.

"Train starts all the same, Miss! Can't even wait for dukes and duchesses. 'Gin the law!" answered the old guard, as he touched his hat and closed and locked the door.

Salome sank back in her deeply-cushioned seat, thankful, at least, that she was alone in the carriage.

And in three minutes the tidal train started.

CHAPTER XIX.
SALOME'S REFUGE.

Salome was scarcely sane. Married that morning, with the approval and congratulations of all her friends, by one of the most venerable fathers of the church, to one of the most distinguished young noblemen in the peerage, who was also the sole master of her heart, and--

Flying from her bridegroom this afternoon as from her worst and most hated enemy!

She could not realize her situation at all.

All seemed a horrible nightmare dream, from which she was powerless to arouse herself; in which she was compelled to act a painful part, until some merciful influence from without should awaken and deliver her!

In this dream she was whirled onward toward the South Coast, on that clear, autumnal afternoon.

In this dream she reached Dover, and got out at the station amid all the confusion attending the arrival of the tidal train, and the babel of voices from cabmen, porters, hotel runners, and such, shouting their offers of:

"Carriage, sir!"

"Carriage, ma'am!"

"Steamboat!"

"Calais steamer!"

"Lord Warden's!"

"Victoria!" and so forth.

Acting instinctively and mechanically, she made her way to the steamboat.

There seemed to be an unusually large number of people going across.

She saw no one among the passengers, whom she recognized; but still she kept her vail folded twice across her face, as she passed to a settee on deck.

She was scarcely seated before the boat left the pier.

Wind and tide was against her, and the passage promised to be a slow and rough one.

And soon indeed the steamer began to roll and toss amid the short, crisp waves of Dover Straits, now whipped to a froth by wind against tide.

Most of the passengers succumbed and went below.

Now, whether intense mental pre-occupation be an antidote to sea-sickness, we cannot tell. But it is certain that Salome did not suffer from the violent motion of the boat. She was indeed scarcely conscious of it.

She sat upon the deck, wrapped in a large shepherd's plaid shawl, with her gray vail thickly folded over her face, which was turned toward the west, where the setting sun was sinking below the ocean horizon, and drawing down after him a long train of glory from over the troubled waters.

But it is doubtful if Salome even saw this, or knew what hour, what season it was!

A rough night followed. Wrapped in her shawl, absorbed in her dream, Salome remained on deck, unaffected by the weather, and indifferent to its consequences, although more than once the captain approached and kindly advised her to go below.

It was after midnight when the boat reached her pier at Calais.

In the same dream Salome left her seat and landed among the sea-sick crowd.

In the same dream she allowed the custom-house officers to tumble out the contents of her little valise, and satisfied, without cavil, all their demands, and answered without hesitation all the questions put to her by the officials.

In the same dream she made her way to a carriage on the railway train just about to start for Paris.

There were three other occupants of the carriage, which was but dimly lighted by two oil lamps. Salome did not look toward them, but doubled her vail still more closely over her face as she sat down in a corner and turned toward the window, on the left side of her seat.

The night was so dark that she could see but little, as the train flashed past what seemed to be but the black shadows of trees, fields, farm-houses, groves, villages, and lonely chateaux.

A weird midnight journey, through a strange land to an unknown bourne.

Occasionally she stole a glance through her thick vail toward her three fellow passengers, who sat opposite to her, on the back seat--three silent, black-shrouded figures who sat mute and motionless as watchers of the dead.

Very terrifying, but very appropriate figures to take part in her nightmare dream.

She turned her eyes away from those silent, shrouded, mysterious figures, and prayed to awake.

She could not yet.

But as she peered out through the darkness of the night, and saw the black shadows of the roadway flying behind her as the train sped southward, her physical powers gradually succumbed to fatigue, and her waking dream passed off in a dreamless sleep.

She slept long and profoundly. She slept through many brief stoppages and startings at the little way stations. She slept until she was rudely awakened by the uproar incident upon the arrival of the train at a large town.

She awoke in confusion. Day was dawning. Many passengers were leaving the train. Many others were getting on it.

She rubbed her eyes and looked around in amazement and terror. She did not in the least know where she was, or how she had come there.

For during her deep and dreamless sleep she had utterly forgotten the occurrences of the last twenty-four hours.

Now she was rudely awakened, bewildered, and frightened to find herself in a strange scene, amid alarming circumstances, of which she knew or could remember nothing; connected with which she only felt the deep impression of some heavy preceding calamity. She saw before her the three silent, black, shrouded forms of her fellow-passengers, but their presence, instead of enlightening, only deepened and darkened the gloomy mystery.

She pressed her icy fingers to her hot and throbbing temples, and tried to understand the situation.

Then memory flashed back like lightning, revealing all the desolation of her storm-blasted, wrecked and ruined life.

With a deep and shuddering groan she threw her hands up to her head, and sank back in her seat.

"Is Madame ill? Can we do anything to help her?" inquired a kindly voice near her.

In her surprise Salome dropped her hands, and at the same time her vail fell from before her face.

Suddenly she then saw that the three mute, shrouded forms before her were Sisters of Mercy, in the black robes of their order, and knew that they had only maintained silence in accordance with their decorous rule of avoiding vain conversation.

Even now the taller and elder of the three had spoken only to tender her services to a suffering fellow-creature.

The fugitive bride and the Sister of Mercy looked at each other, and at the instant uttered exclamations of surprise.

In the sister, Salome recognized a lay nun of the Convent of St. Rosalie, in which she had passed nearly all the years of her young life, and in which she had received her education, and to which it had once been her cherished desire to return and dedicate herself to a conventual service.

In Salome the nun saw again a once beloved pupil, whom she, in common with all her sisterhood, had fondly expected to welcome back to her novitiate.

"Sister Josephine! You! Is it indeed you! Oh, how I thank Heaven!" fervently exclaimed the fugitive.

"Mademoiselle Laiveesong! You here! My child! And alone! But how is that possible?" cried the good sister in amazement.

Before Salome could answer the guard opened the door with a party of passengers at his back. But seeing the compartment already well filled by the three Sisters of Mercy and another lady, he closed the door again and passed down the platform to find places for his party elsewhere.

The incident was little noticed by Salome at the time, although it was destined to have a serious effect upon her after fate.

In a few minutes the train started.

"My dear child," recommended Sister Josephine, as soon as the train was well under way--"my dear child, how is it possible that I find you here, alone on the train at midnight! Were you going on to Paris, and alone? Was any one to meet you there?"

"Dear, good Sister Josephine, ask me no questions yet. I am ill--really and truly ill!" sighed Salome.

"Ah! I see you are, my dear child. Ill and alone on the night train! Holy Virgin preserve us!" said the sister, devoutly crossing herself.

"Ask me no questions yet, dear sister, because I cannot answer them. But take me with you wherever you go, for wherever that may be, there will be peace and rest and safety, I know! Say, will you take me with you, good Sister Josephine?" pleaded Salome.

"Ah! surely we will, my child. With much joy we will. We--(Sister Francoise and Sister Felecitie--Mademoiselle Laiveesong,)" said Sister Josephine, stopping to introduce her companions to each other.

The three young persons thus named bowed and smiled, and pressed palms, and then sat back in their seats, while the elder Sister, Josephine, continued:

"We have come up from Fontevrau, and are now going straight on to our convent. With joy we will take you with us, my dear child. Our holy mother will be transported to see you. Does she expect you, my dear child?" inquired the sister, forgetting her tacit promise to ask no more questions.

"No, no one expects me," sighed the fugitive, in so faint a voice that the good Sister forbore to make any more inquiries for the moment.

The train rushed onward. Day was broadening. The horizon was growing red in the east.

The party travelled on in silence for some ten or fifteen minutes, and then, Sister Josephine growing impatient to have her curiosity satisfied, made a few leading remarks.

"And so you were coming to us unannounced by any previous communication to our holy mother? And coming alone on the night train! You possess a noble courage, my child, but the adventure was hazardous to a young and lovely unmarried woman. The Virgin be praised we met you when we did!" said the Sister, devoutly crossing herself.

"Amen, and amen, to that!" sighed Salome.

"Our holy mother will be overjoyed to see you. You are sure she does not expect you, my dear child?"

"No, Sister, she does not expect me, unless she has the gift of second sight. For I did not expect myself to return to St. Rosalie, to-day, or ever. When I took my place in this carriage at midnight, I did not know how far I should go, or where I should stop. I took a through ticket to Paris; but I did not know whether I should stop at Paris, or go on to Marseilles, or Rome, or St. Petersburg, or New York, or where!" moaned the fugitive.

"The holy saints protect us, my child! What wild thing is this you are saying?" exclaimed Sister Josephine, making the sign of the cross.

"No matter what I say now, good Sister, I will tell our holy mother all. Is la Mere Genevieve now your lady superior?" softly inquired the fugitive.

"Yes, surely, my child. And she will be transported to behold her best beloved pupil again. You are sure that she will be taken by surprise?" said the good, simple minded Sister, still innocently angling for a farther explanation.

"Yes, I feel sure that I shall surprise our good mother if I do *not* delight her; for, as I told you before, I gave her no intimation of any intended visit. I repeat that when I set foot upon this train, I had no fixed plan in my mind. I did not know where I should go. My meeting with you is providential. It decides me, nay, rather let me say, it directs me to seek rest and peace and safety there where my happy childhood and early youth were passed, and where I once desired to spend my whole life in the service of Heaven. I, too, fervently praise the Virgin for this blessed meeting. I too thank the Mother of Sorrows for being near me in my sorrow and in my madness!" murmured Salome, in a low, earnest tone.

"Holy saints, my child! What can have happened to you to inspire such words as these?" exclaimed Sister Josephine in alarm.

"Never mind what, good Sister. You shall hear all in time. I am forced by fate to keep a promise that I made and might have broken. That is all."

"Ah, my dear child, I comprehend sorrow and despair in your words; but I do not comprehend your words!" sighed Sister Josephine.

"When I left your convent three years ago, I promised did I not, that after I should have become of age and be mistress of my fate, I would return, dedicate my life to the service of Heaven, and spend the remainder of it here? Did I not?" inquired Salome, in a low voice.

"You did, you did, my child. And for a long time we looked for you in vain.

And when you did not come, or even write to us, we thought the world had won you, and made you forget your promise," sighed Sister Josephine crossing herself.

The two youthful Sisters followed her example, sighed and crossed themselves.

There was a grave pause of a few minutes, and then the voice of Salome was heard in solemn tones:

"The world won me. The world broke me and flung me back upon the convent, and forced me to remember and keep my promise. I return now to dedicate myself to the service of Heaven, at the altar of your convent, if indeed Heaven will take a heart that earth has crushed!"

She sighed.

"It is the world-crushed, bleeding heart that is the sweetest offering to all-healing, all-merciful Heaven," said Sister Josephine, tenderly lifting the hand of Salome and pressing it to her bosom.

Again a solemn silence fell upon the little party.

Salome was the first to break it.

"It seems to me we have come a very long way, since we left the last station. Are we near ours?" she inquired, in a voice sinking with fatigue.

"We will be at our station in a very few minutes. A comfortable close carriage will meet us there to convey us to St. Rosalie," said Sister Josephine, soothingly.

Salome sank wearily back in her corner seat. The short-lived energy that enabled her to talk was dying out. Her hands and feet were cold as ice. Her head was hot as fire. Her frame was faint almost to swooning.

The train sped on. The party in the carriage fell into silence that lasted until the train "slowed," and stopped at a little way station.

"Here we are!" said Sister Josephine, rising to leave the carriage with her companions.

The guard opened the door.

Sister Josephine led the way out, and then took the hand of the half fainting Salome, to help her on.

The two other sisters followed. A close carriage, with an aged coachman on the box, awaited them. The old man did not leave his seat; but Sister Josephine opened the door and helped Salome into the carriage, and placed her comfortably on the cushions in a corner of the back seat, and then sat down beside her.

The two younger sisters followed and placed themselves on the front seat.

The aged coachman, who knew his duty, did not wait for orders, but turned immediately away from the station, and drove off just as the train started again on its way to Paris.

They entered a country road running through a wood--a pleasant ride, if Salome could have enjoyed it--but she leaned back on her cushions, with closed eyes, fever-flushed cheeks, and fainting frame. The sisters, seeing her condition, refrained from disturbing her by any conversation.

They rode on in perfect silence for about a mile, when they came to a high stone wall, which ran along on the left-hand side of their road, while the thick wood continued on their right-hand side. The road here ran between the wood and the wall of the convent grounds.

CHAPTER XX.
SALOME'S PROTECTRESS.

"We have arrived. Welcome home, my dear child," said Sister Josephine, as the carriage drew up before the strong and solid, iron-bound, oaken gates of the convent.

The aged coachman blew a shrill summons upon a little silver whistle that he carried in his pocket for the purpose.

The gates were thrown wide open and the carriage rolled into an extensive court-yard, enclosed in a high stone wall, and having in its centre the massive building of the convent proper, with its chapel and offices.

A straight, broad, hard, rolled, gravelled carriage-way led from the gates through the court-yard and up to the main entrance of the building. This road was bordered on each side by grass-plots, now sear in the late October frosts, and flower-beds, from which the flowers had been removed to their winter quarters in the conservatories. Groups of shade trees, statues of saints, and fountains of crystal-clear water adorned the grounds at regular intervals. In the rear of the convent building was a thicket of trees reaching quite down to the back wall.

The carriage rolled along the gravelled road, crossing the court-yard, and drew up before the door of the convent.

Sister Josephine got out and helped Salome to alight.

The sun was just rising in cloudless glory.

"See, my child," said Sister Josephine, cheerily pointing to the eastern horizon; "see, a happy omen; the sun himself arises and smiles on your re-entrance into St. Rosalie."

Salome smiled faintly, and leaned heavily upon the arm of her companion as they went slowly up the steps, passed through the front doors, and found themselves in a little square entrance hall, surrounded on three sides by a bronze grating, and having immediately before them a grated door, with a little wicket near the centre.

Behind this wicket sat the portress, a venerable nun, whom age and obesity had consigned to this sedentary occupation.

"***Benedicite***, good Mother Veronique! How are all within the house?" inquired Sister Josephine, going up to the wicket.

"The saints be praised, all are well! They are just going in to matins. You come in good time, my sisters! But who is she whom you bring with you?" inquired the old nun, nodding toward Salome, even while she detached a great key from her girdle, and unlocked the door, to admit the party.

"Why, then, Mother Veronique, don't you see? An old, well-beloved pupil come back to see our holy mother? Don't you recognize her? Have you already forgotten Mademoiselle Laiveesong, who left us only three years ago?" inquired Sister Josephine, as she led Salome into the portress' parlor, followed by the two younger sisters, Francoise and Felecitie.

"Ah! ah! so it is! Mademoiselle Salome come back to us!" joyfully exclaimed the old nun, seizing and fondling the hands of the visitor, and gazing wistfully into her flushed and feverish face. "Yes, yes, I remember you! Mademoiselle Laiveesong! Mademoiselle, the rich banker's heiress! I am very happy to see you, my dear child! And our holy mother will be filled with joy! She has gone to matins now, but will soon return to give you her blessing. Ah! ah! Mademoiselle Salome! ***Mais Helas!*** How ill she looks! Her hands are ice! Her head is fire! Her limbs are withes! She is about to faint!" added Mother Veronique, aside to Sister Josephine.

"She is just off a long and fatiguing journey. She is tired and hungry, and needs rest and refreshment. That is all," answered the sister, drawing the arm of the fainting girl through her own, and supporting her as she led her from the portress' parlor.

"Ah! ah! is this so? The dear child! Take her in and rest and feed her, my sisters! And when matins are over, bring her to our venerable mother, whose soul will be filled with rapture to see her," twaddled the old nun, until the party passed in from her sight.

Sister Josephine led Salome to her own cell, and made her loosen her clothes and lie down on the cot-bed, while Sister Francoise and Sister Felecitie went to the refectory and brought her a plate of biscuit and a glass of wine and water.

Wine was not the proper drink for Salome, in her flushed and feverish condition. But she was both faint and thirsty, and the wine, mixed with water, seemed cool and refreshing, and she quaffed it eagerly.

But she refused the biscuits, declaring that she could not swallow. And so she thanked her kind friends for their attention, and sank back on her pillow and closed her eyes, as if she would go to sleep.

The sisters promised to bring the mother abbess to her bedside as soon as the matins should be over. And so they left her to repose, and went silently away to the chapel to take their accustomed places, and join, even at the "eleventh hour," in the morning worship.

But did Salome sleep?

Ah! no. She lay upon that cot-bed with her hands covering her eyes, as if to shut out all the earth. She might shut out all the visible creation, but she could not exclude the haunting images that filled her mind. She could not banish the forms and faces that floated before her inner vision--the most venerable face of her dear, lost father, the noble face of her once beloved--ah! still too well beloved Arondelle!

The music of the matin hymns softened by distance, floated into her room, but failed to soothe her to repose.

At length the sweet sounds ceased.

And then--

The abbess entered the cell so softly that Salome, lying with closed eyes on the cot, remained unconscious of the presence standing beside her, looking down upon her form.

The abbess was a tall, fair, blue-eyed woman, upon whose serene brow the seal of eternal peace seemed set. She was about fifty years of age, but her clear eyes and smooth skin showed how tranquilly these years had passed. She was clothed in the well-known garb of her order--in a black dress, with long, hanging sleeves, and a long, black vail. Her face was framed in with the usual white linen bands, her robe confined at the waist by a girdle, from which hung her rosary of agates; and her silver cross hung from her neck.

The abbess was a lady of the most noble birth, connected with the royal house of Orleans.

In the revolution which had driven Louis Philippe from the throne, her father and her brother had perished. Her mother had passed away long before. She remained in the convent of St. Rosalie, where she was being educated.

And when, early in the days of the Second Empire, her fortune was restored to her, instead of leaving the cloister, where she had found peace, for the world, where she had found only tribulation, she took the vail and the vows that bound her to the convent forever, and devoted her means to enriching and enlarging the house. The convent had always supported itself by its celebrated academy for young ladies. It had also maintained a free school for poor children. But now the heiress of the noble house of de Crespignie added a Home for Aged Women, an asylum for Orphan Girls and Nursery for Deserted Infants. And all these were placed under the charge of the Sisters of Mercy.

Of the fifty years of this lady's life, forty had been spent in the convent where she had lived as pupil, novice, nun and abbess. Her cloistered life had been passed in active good works, if nurturing infancy, educating orphans, cheering age, and ordering and governing an excellent academy for young ladies, can be called so.

And whatever such a life may have brought to others, it brought to this princess of the banished Orleans family perfect peace.

She stood now looking down with infinite pity on the stricken form and face of her late pupil. She saw that some heavy blow from sorrow had crushed her. And she did not wonder at this.

For to the apprehension of the abbess, the world from which her late pupil had returned was full of tribulation, as the convent was full of peace.

She stood looking down on her a moment, and then murmured, in tones of ineffable tenderness:

"My child!"

"Mother Genevieve! My dear mother!" answered Salome, clasping her hands and looking up.

The abbess drew a chair to the side of the cot, sat down, and took the hand of her pupil, saying:

"You have come back to us, my child. I thought you would. You are most welcome."

"Oh, mother! mother! I am *driven* back to you for shelter from a storm of trouble!" exclaimed Salome, in great excitement, her cheeks burning, and her eyes blazing with the fires of fever.

"We will receive you with love and cherish you in our hearts--*unquestioned*--for, my child, you are too ill to give us any explanation now," said the abbess, gently, laying her soft, cool hand upon the burning brow of the girl.

"Oh! mother, mother, let me talk now and unburden my heavy heart! You know not how it will relieve me to do so to *you*. I could not do so to any other. Let me tell you, dear mother, while I may, before it shall be too late. For I am going to be very ill, mother; and perhaps I may die! Oh Heaven grant I may be permitted to die!" fervently prayed Salome, clasping her hands.

"Hush, hush, my poor, unhappy child. I know not what your sorrow has been, but it cannot possibly justify you in your sinful petition. Life, my child, is the greatest of boons, since it contains within it the possibility of eternal bliss. We should be deeply thankful for simple *life*, whatever may be its present trials, since it holds the promise of future happiness," said the gentle abbess.

"Oh, mother, my life is wrecked--is hopelessly wrecked!" groaned Salome.

"Nay, nay, only storm-tossed on the treacherous seas of the world. Here is your harbor, my child. Come into port, little, weary one!" said the abbess, with a tender, cheerful smile.

"Oh, mother, your wayward pupil has wandered far, far from your teachings! She has become a heathen--an idolator! Yes, she set up unto herself an idol, and she worshiped it as a god, until at last, IT FELL!--IT FELL! AND CRUSHED HER UN-

DER ITS RUINS!" said Salome, growing more and more excited and feverish.

"It is well for us, my child, when our earthly idols do fall and crush us, else we might go on to perdition in our fatal idolatry. Yes, my child, it is well that your idol has fallen, even though you lie buried and bleeding under its ruins; for our fraternity, like the good Samaritan of the parable, will raise you up and dress your wounds, and set you on your feet again, and lead you in the right path--the path of peace and safety."

"Mother, mother, will you now hear my story, my confession?" said Salome, earnestly.

"My child, I would rather you would defer it until you are better able to talk."

"Mother, mother, I have the strength of fever on me now; but my mind is growing confused. Let me speak while I may!"

"Speak on, then, my dear child, but don't exhaust yourself."

"Mother, though I have failed, through very shame of broken promises, to write to you lately, yet you must have heard from other sources of my father's tragic death?"

"I heard of it, my child. And I have daily remembered his soul in my prayers."

"And you heard, good mother, of how I forgot all my promises to devote myself to a religious life, and how I betrothed myself to the Marquis of Arondelle, who is now the Duke of Hereward?"

"You yielded to the expressed wishes of your father, my child, as it was natural you should do."

"I yielded to the inordinate and sinful affections of my own heart, and I have been punished for it."

"My poor child!"

"Listen, mother! Yesterday morning, at St. George's church, Hanover Square, in London, I was married by the Bishop of London to the Duke of Hereward. Yesterday afternoon I received secret but unquestionable proof that the duke was an already married man when he met me first, and that his wife was living in London!"

"Holy saints, Mademoiselle! What is this that you are telling me?" exclaimed the astonished abbess. "Surely, surely she is growing delirious with fever," she muttered to herself.

"I am telling you a terrible truth, my mother! Listen, and I will tell you everything, even as I know it myself!" said Salome, earnestly.

The abbess no longer opposed her speaking, although it was evident that her illness was hourly increasing.

And Salome told the terrible story of her sorrows, commencing with the first appointed wedding-day at Castle Lone, and ending with the second wedding-day at Elmhurst House, and her own secret flight from her false bridegroom, just as it is known to our readers.

The deeply shocked abbess heard and believed, and frequently crossed herself during the recital.

As Salome proceeded with what she called her confession, her fever and excitement increased rapidly. Toward the end of her recital her thoughts grew confused and wandered into the ravings of a brain fever.

CHAPTER XXI.
THE BRIDEGROOM.

According to his promise given to Lady Belgrade, the Duke of Hereward returned to Elmthorpe House to make his report.

He found the dowager waiting for him where he had left her, in the back drawing-room.

He greeted her only by a silent bow, and she questioned him only by a mute look.

"I have placed the case in the hands of Setter, confidentially, of course. He will commence secret investigations to-night," he said.

"This morning, you mean, Duke. It is now two o'clock," remarked the dowager.

"Is it, indeed, so late?"

"So early you should say. Yes, it is. But what thinks the detective of this affair?"

"He is inclined to think as we do, that our dear Salome has been decoyed away by some tale of extreme distress, and for purposes of robbery," answered the young duke, pressing his white lips firmly together in his effort to control all expression of the anguish that was secretly wringing his heart.

"And what does he think of the chances of finding her soon and finding her safe?" inquired the dowager.

The duke slowly shook his head.

"Well, and what does that mean?" asked the lady.

"It means that Detective Setter cannot form an opinion, or will not commit himself to the expression of one at present. And now, dear Lady Belgrade, as it is after two o'clock, I must bid you good-night--"

"Good-morning, rather," interrupted the dowager.

"And return to my lodgings," continued the duke, passing his hand across his forehead, like one "dazed" with trouble.

"I beg you will do nothing of the sort, Duke," said Lady Belgrade, hastily interposing. "You have left your lodgings for a wedding tour. You are not expected back there. Your people think that you are far from London with your bride. In the name of propriety, let them think so still. Do not go back there to-night, and wake them all up, and start a nine days' wonder of scandal. Stay where you are, Duke, quietly, until we recover our Salome. When we do, you can both leave for Paris. All the world will know nothing of this distressing affair, which, if it were to come to their knowledge, would be exaggerated, perverted, turned and twisted out of all its original shape, into some horrid story of scandal. Remember now, how few people know anything about it--only you, I, the detective necessarily taken into your confidence, and the servants, for whose discretion I can answer. Remain quietly here, therefore, that all gossip may be stopped."

The duke resumed his seat, but did not immediately answer.

"Do you not think my counsel good?" inquired the lady.

"Very good. Thanks, Lady Belgrade. I will follow your advice. There is another reason why I should do so, but with which you are not acquainted. In the absorption of my thoughts with the subject of our Salome, I totally forgot to tell you that I have just been subpoenaed as a witness for the crown, in the approaching trial of John Potts and Rose Cameron for the murder of Sir Lemuel Levison. The case will come on at the Assizes at Banff on Thursday next. I must leave for Scotland to-morrow," said the young duke.

"Why--you surprise me very much! When was the subpoena served upon you?"

inquired the dowager.

"In a chance recounter at the police-office, where I went to find the detective, and where I also found a sheriff's officer holding a subpoena for me, which he was about to send across the channel by a special messenger--supposing me to be in Paris. So you see, my dear Lady Belgrade, my wedding tour would have been stopped at Paris, if not nearer."

"That is well; for now, if the wedding tour is delayed, it will be known to be a legal necessity, which in no way reflects upon the wedding party. And now, my dear Duke, since you consent to stay all night, let me advise you to retire to rest. You will find your valet waiting your orders in the cedar suite of rooms, to which I had your dressing case and boxes taken."

"Thanks, Lady Belgrade. Your ladyship anticipates everything."

"I certainly anticipated the necessity of your remaining here all night, as soon as I found that you could not leave London. And now, Duke, I must really send you to bed. I am exhausted. I must lie down, even if I do not sleep," said the dowager, as she arose and touched the bell.

The Duke of Hereward raised her hand to his lips, bowed, and left the room.

Lady Belgrade followed his example.

And the weary groom of the chambers entered, in answer to the bell, to turn off the gas and fasten up the rooms.

The young duke knew where to find the cedar suite--a sumptuous set of apartments finished and fitted up in the costly and fragrant wood which gave them their name.

He found his servant waiting in the dressing-room.

His grace's valet was no fine gentleman from Paris, as full of accomplishments as of vices; but a simple and honest young man from the estate. The extra gravity which young James Kerr put into his manner of waiting, alone testified of the reverential sympathy he felt for his beloved master.

The duke threw off the travelling coat that he had assumed for his journey and had worn up to this moment; and he took the wadded silk dressing gown, handed him by his valet, and having put it on, he dropped into an easy resting-chair, and ordered Kerr to lower the gas and then leave the room for the night.

The young Duke of Hereward did not retire to bed that night. As soon as he found himself alone in the half-darkened rooms, he arose from his chair and began to walk restlessly up and down the floor, relieving the pent-up anguish of his bosom by such deep groans as had required all his self-control to suppress while he was in the presence of others.

Thus walking and groaning in great agony of mind, he passed the few remaining dark hours of the morning.

At daylight he sank exhausted into his easy-chair. But even then he neither "slumbered nor slept," but passed the time in waiting and longing for the rising sun, that he might go out and renew his search for his lost bride.

The sun had scarcely risen when he rang for his valet.

The young man appeared promptly.

The duke made a hasty toilet, and then called his servant to attend him down stairs.

None of the household were yet astir.

But, by the direction of the duke, Kerr unlocked, unbolted and unbarred the street door to let his master out.

"Close and secure the house after me, James, for it will be hours yet before the household will be up," said the duke, as he passed out.

It was a clear October day for London. The sun was not more than twenty minutes high, and it shone redly and dully through a morning fog. The streets were still deserted, except by milkmen, bakers, costermongers, and other "early birds."

He walked rapidly to the Church Court police station.

Detective Setter was not there. But the Duke left word for him to call at Elmthorpe as soon as he should return.

He left the police station and went on toward Elmthrope. But he did not enter the house. He could not rest. He walked up and down the sidewalk in front of the iron railings until he thought Lady Belgrade might have risen.

Then he went up the steps and rang the bell.

The hall porter opened the door and admitted him.

"Has Lady Belgrade come down yet?" was his first question.

"My lady has, your grace. My lady is waiting breakfast for your grace," respectfully answered the footman.

He longed to ask if any news had been heard of the missing one, but he forbore to do so, and hurried away up-stairs to the breakfast parlor.

There he found Lady Belgrade, dressed in a purple cashmere robe, and wrapped in a rich India shawl, reclining in a rocking-chair beside a breakfast-table laid for two.

"Good morning, madam. I fear I have kept your ladyship waiting," said the duke, as he entered the room.

"Not a second, my dear duke. I have but just this instant come down," answered the dowager, politely, and unhesitatingly telling the conventional lie, as she put out her hand and touched the bell.

"I fear that it is useless to ask you if there is any news of our missing girl," said the duke, in a low tone.

"I have heard nothing. And you? Of course, you have not, or you would not have asked me the question. But, good Heaven, Duke, you are as pale as a ghost! You look as if you had just risen from a sick bed! You look full twenty years older than you did yesterday. What have you been doing with yourself? Where have you been?" inquired the dowager.

The duke answered her last question only.

"I have been to Church Court to look up Detective Setter. I left orders for him to report here this morning. I expect him here very soon. I must do all that I can do in London to-day, as it is absolutely necessary for me to leave town by the night express of the Great Northern Railroad, in order to attend the trial for which I am subpoenaed as a witness, to-morrow."

"I see! Of course, you must go. There is no resisting a subpoena. But who is to co-operate with Setter in the search for Salome?"

"*You* must do so, if you please, Lady Belgrade, until my return. Of course, I will hurry back with all dispatch."

"No fear of that. The only fear is that you will hurry into your grave. But here is breakfast," said her ladyship, as a footman entered with a tray.

Mocha coffee, orange pekoe tea, Westphalia ham, poached eggs, dry toast, muffins, rolls, and so forth, were arranged upon the table to tempt the appetite of the two who sat at meat.

Lady Belgrade made a good meal. She was at the age of which physicians say, "the constitution takes on a conservative tone," and which poets call "the time of peace." In a word, she was middle-aged, fat, and comfort-loving; and so she was not disposed to lose her rest, or food, or peace of mind for any trouble not personally her own.

She was vexed at the unconventionality of Salome's disappearance, fearful of what the world would say, and anxious to keep the matter as close as possible. That was all, and it did not take away her appetite.

But the anxious young husband could not eat. A feverish and burning thirst, such as frequently attends excessive grief or anxiety, consumed him. He drank cup after cup of tea almost unconsciously, until at length Lady Belgrade said:

"This makes four! I am your hostess, duke; but I am also your aunt by marriage, and upon my word I cannot let you go on ruining your health in this way! You shall not have another cup of tea, unless you consent to eat something with it."

The young duke smiled wanly, and submitted so far as to take a piece of dry toast on his plate and crumble it into bits.

Meanwhile, the dowager, having finished her breakfast, took up the *Times* to look over.

Presently she startled the duke by exclaiming:

"Thank Heaven!"

"What is it?" hastily inquired the duke, setting down his cup and gazing at the silent reader. "Any news of Salome?" he added, and then nearly lost his breath while waiting for the answer.

"Oh, yes, news of Salome! But scarcely authentic news. Listen! Here is a full account of the wedding--with a description of the bride and bridesmaids, and their dresses and attendants, and of the ceremony and the officiating clergy, and the attending crowd, and the wedding-breakfast, speeches, presents, and so on, all tolerably correct for a newspaper report. But now listen to this--"

Her ladyship here read aloud:

"Immediately after the wedding-breakfast, the happy pair left town, by the London and South Coast Railway, *en route* for Dover, Paris and the Continent."

"There! what do you think of that?" inquired Lady Belgrade, looking up.

"I think it is not the first occasion upon which a paper has anticipated and described an expected event that some unforeseen accident prevented from coming off," answered the duke, with a sigh.

"I thank fortune for this! Now you have really started on your wedding tour in the belief of all London, and all outside of London who take the *Times*; and all *our* world *do* take it. And now, if any rumor of this most inopportune disappearance of our bride *should* get out, why, it will never be believed! That is all! For has not the departure of the 'happy pair' been published in the *Times*? Yes, I am very glad of the news reporter's indiscreet precipitancy on this occasion, at least," concluded Lady Belgrade, as she turned to other "fashionable intelligence."

At that moment a footman entered the breakfast parlor and handed a business-looking card to the duke, saying, with a bow:

"If you please, your grace, the person is waiting in the hall."

"By your leave, Lady Belgrade?--Sims! show the man into the library, and tell him I will be with him in a few moments.--It is Detective Setter," said the duke, as he arose and left the breakfast parlor.

He found that officer awaiting him in the library.

"Any news?" inquired the duke, as he sank into a chair and signed to the visitor to follow his example.

"None, your grace. I have made diligent and careful investigations, in the neighborhoods mentioned by the lady's maid, but have found no trace of any Mrs. White or Brown that answered the rather vague description given. I shall, however, resume my search there," answered the man.

"There must be no cessation of the search until that woman is found. I need not caution you to use great discretion," said the duke, earnestly, but wearily, like a man breaking down under an intolerable burden of mental anxiety.

"Discretion is the very spirit of my business, your grace."

"What is to be your next step?"

"If your grace will permit me, I should like to examine the rooms of the lost lady, and I should like to question, singly and privately, the servants of the house."

"A thorough search has been made of the premises, including the apartments of the duchess. And every domestic on the premises has been examined and cross-examined."

"I do not doubt, your grace, that all this has been done as effectually as it could be done by any one, except a skillful and experienced detective; but if you will pardon me, I should like to make an examination and investigation in person."

"Certainly, Mr. Setter. Every facility shall be afforded you," said the duke, touching the bell.

A footman entered.

The duke drew a card from his pocket and wrote upon it:

"Detective Setter wishes to search the premises and cross-examine the servants. What does your ladyship say?"

The duke then placed the card in the hand of the footman, saying:

"Be so good as to take this to Lady Belgrade, and wait an answer."

The servant bowed and left the room.

"You are aware, Mr. Setter, that I am under the necessity of leaving London to-night, to attend the trial of Potts and Cameron to-morrow."

"As a witness for the Crown. I am, your grace."

"I shall get back to London as soon as possible. In the meantime, I wish you to pursue your investigations with the utmost diligence, sparing no expense. Report in person every morning and evening to Lady Belgrade in this house, and by telegraph to me at Lone, in Scotland. Use great discretion in wording your telegrams. Avoid the use of names, or titles, or, in fact, any terms, in referring to the duchess, that may identify her. I hope you understand me?"

"Perfectly, your grace. I also understand how to speak and write in enigmas. It is a part of my profession to do so," answered Mr. Setter.

The duke then drew out his portmonaie, opened it, selected two notes of fifty pounds each and put them in the hands of Setter, saying:

"Here are one hundred pounds. Spare no expense in prosecuting this search. Draw on me if you have occasion."

The detective bowed.

At the same moment the footman re-entered the room, bringing a card on a silver waiter, which he handed to the duke.

The duke took it and read:

"Your grace surely forgets that, as the husband of the heiress, you are the absolute master of the house, and your will is law here. Do as you think proper."

"You may go," said the duke to the messenger, who immediately retired.

"Now, Mr. Setter, do you wish to search the premises, or examine the servants first?" inquired the duke.

"Examine the servants first, your grace; as I may thereby gain some clew to follow in my search."

"Very well," said the duke, again touching the bell.

The prompt footman re-appeared.

"Whom do you wish called first?" inquired the duke.

"The lady's maid," answered the detective.

"Go and tell the duchess's maid that she is wanted here immediately," said the duke.

The footman bowed and went away on his errand.

A few minutes passed, and the lady's maid entered.

"This is--I really forget your name, my good girl," said the duke, apologetically.

"Margaret, sir; Margaret Watson," said the lady's maid, with a courtesy.

"Ay. This is Margaret Watson, the confidential maid of her grace, Mr. Setter. Margaret, my good girl, Mr. Setter wishes to put some questions to you, relating to the disappearance of your mistress. I hope you will answer his inquiries as frankly and fearlessly as you have answered ours," said the duke, as he took up a paper for a pretext and walked to the other end of the library, leaving the detective officer at liberty to pursue his investigations alone.

It is needless for us to go over the ground again. It is sufficient to say that Detective Setter questioned and cross-questioned the girl with all the skill of an old and experienced hand, and at the end of half an hour's sharp and close examination, he had obtained no new information.

The girl was dismissed, with a warning not to talk of the affair. And she was followed by the housekeeper, with no better result.

Thus all the domestics of the establishment were called and examined singly; but without success.

When the last servant was done with, and sent out of the room, the detective walked up to the duke.

"Well, Mr. Setter?" inquired the latter.

"Your grace, I have learned nothing from the servants but what you have already told me."

"Do you still wish to search the premises?"

"If your grace pleases. And I wish to begin with the apartments of the duch-ess."

"Then follow me. I myself will be your guide," said the duke, leading the way from the library.

It would be useless to accompany the detective in this third search. Let it be sufficient to say that this search was thorough, complete, exhaustive, and--unsuc-cessful.

It was late in the day when it was finished, and the duke and the detective re-turned to the library.

"You now perceive Mr. Setter, that a day has been lost in these repeated search-ings and questionings, and no new information, no sign of a clew to the fate of the duchess has been gained. In an hour I must leave the house to catch the Great Northern Night Express. I leave--I am *forced* for the present, to leave the fate of my beloved wife in your hands. In saying that, I say that I leave more than my own life in your keeping. Use every means, employ every agency, spend money freely, the day you bring her safely to me, I will deposit ten thousand pounds in the Bank of England to your account."

"Your grace is munificent. If the duchess is on earth, I will find her;--not for the reward only, though it is certainly a very great inducement to a poor man with a large family; but for the love and honor I bear your grace and the late Sir Lemuel Levison," said the detective, earnestly, as he bowed and took leave.

The first dinner-bell rang.

The duke hastened to his own room, not to dress for dinner, but to prepare for his night journey to Scotland.

He ordered his valet to pack a valise with all that would be necessary for a few days' absence, and then sent him to call a close cab.

By this time the second dinner-bell rang, and the duke went down, not to dine, but to take leave of Lady Belgrade.

He found her ladyship in the drawing-room.

"Give me your arm to dinner, if you please, Duke," she said, rising.

"I hope you will excuse me; but I have only come to say good-by. I have but time to catch the train. Kerr has already put my luggage in the cab, which is waiting for me at the door. Good-by, dear Lady Belgrade. You will co-operate with Setter in all things necessary to a successful search, I know. Setter has my orders to report to you--"

"You take my breath away!" gasped the dowager.

"Write to me by every mail. Keep me informed of events--"

"You will kill yourself, Duke! flying off without your dinner, and looking fitter for going to bed than on a journey!" panted the dowager.

"Now then, good-by in earnest, dear Lady Belgrade, and God bless you," concluded the duke, raising her hand to his lips and bowing.

And before the dowager could say another word he was gone.

"Well, if he lives to be as old as I am, he will take things easier. Though, if he goes on at this rate, he won't live to be old," mused the old lady, as she slowly waddled into the dining-room, and took her seat at the table to enjoy her solitary green turtle soup.

CHAPTER XXII.
AT LONE.

The Duke of Hereward went out to the close cab that was waiting for him before the door.

He found his valet standing by it, with a pair of railroad rugs over his arm.

He directed the man to mount to a seat beside the cabman, and gave the latter orders where to drive.

Then he entered the cab and closed all the doors and windows, that he might not be seen by any chance acquaintance.

He was supposed by all the world of London to be away on his wedding tour, and he was willing to let them continue to believe so, until they should be enlightened by a report of the great trial, when they would learn the fact and the explanation at once, and thus be prevented from making undesirable conjectures and speculations concerning his presence at such a time in England.

He leaned back on his seat, and the cabman, having received directions from the valet, drove rapidly off toward the Great Northern Railway Station at Kings Cross.

An hour's fast drive brought them to their destination.

The duke dispatched his valet to the ticket office to engage a coupe on the express train, so that he might be entirely private.

And he remained in the cab with closed doors and windows until the servant had secured the coupe, and conveyed all the light luggage into it.

Then he left the cab, and passed at once into the coupe, leaving his servant to pay and discharge the cab, and to follow him on the train.

James Kerr, after performing these duties, went to the door of his master's little compartment to ask if he had any further orders, before going to take his place in the second-class carriages.

"No, Kerr, but come in here with me. I want you at hand during the journey," replied the duke, who, much as he confided in the young man's devotion and loyalty, could not quite trust his discretion, and therefore desired to keep him from talking.

The valet bowed and entered the coupe, taking the seat that his master pointed out.

The train moved slowly out of the station, but gaining speed as it left the town, soon began to fly swiftly on its northern course.

The October sun was setting as the train flew along the margin of the "New River," as Sir Hugh Myddellen's celebrated piece of water-engineering is called.

The October evening was chill, and the swift flight of the train drawing a strong draught that could not be kept out, increased the chilliness.

The duke leaned back in his seat and closed his eyes.

The valet attentively tucked the railway rug around his master's knees.

The sun had set. The long twilight of northern latitudes came on.

At the first station where the express stopped, the guard opened the door and offered to light the lamps, but the duke forbade him, saying that he preferred the darkness.

The guard closed the door and retired, and the train started again, and flew on northward through the deepening night.

It stopped only at the largest towns and cities on its route--at Peterboro', at York, at Newcastle, and Edinboro'.

It was sunrise when the train reached Lone, the only small station at which it stopped on the route.

The guard opened the door of the coupe, and the young duke got out, attended by his valet.

The train stopped but one minute, and then shot out of the station and flew on toward Aberdeen.

The distance between the railway station and the "Hereward Arms," was very short, so the duke preferred to walk it, followed by his valet and a railway porter carrying his light luggage.

The sun had risen indeed, although it was nowhere visible.

A Scotch mist had risen from the lake, and settled over the mountains, vailing all the grand features of the landscape.

Early as the hour was, the hamlet, as they passed through it, seemed deserted by all its male inhabitants. None but women and children were to be seen, and even they, instead of being at work, were loitering about their own doors or gossiping with each other.

Though the duke and his servant were the only passengers that got off the train at Lone, the whole force of the "Hereward Arms,"--landlord, head-waiter, hostler, boots and stable boys--turned out to meet them.

"Your grace is unco welcome to the 'Hereward Arms,'" said Donald Duncan, the worthy host, bowing low before his distinguished guest.

And all his underlings followed his example by pulling their red forelocks and scraping their right feet backwards.

"Your hamlet seems to be deserted to-day, landlord. What fair or what else is going on?" inquired the young duke, as he followed the bowing host to the neat little parlor of the inn.

"Ah! wae's the day! Dinna your grace ken! It will be the trial at Banff--the trial of yon grand villain, Johnnie Potts, for the murder of his master."

"Oh, yes, I know the trial will be commenced to-day; but I did not think that the people here would take so much interest in it as to leave their work and go such a distance to see it," remarked the duke.

"Would they nae? They'd gae to the North Pole to see it, if necessary, and they'd gae farrer still to see the murtherer weel hanggit! Ay, your grace, and what will make it a' the mair exciting, is the rumor whilk goes round to the effect that the ne'er-do-well, hizzie, Rose Cameron, hae turnit Crown's evidence to save her ain life, and will gie up all her accomplices. Sae we are a' fain to hear the mystery of the murther cleared up."

"Indeed! Is that so? The girl has turned Crown's witness? Then, we *shall* get at the truth!" exclaimed the duke, with more interest than he had hitherto shown.

"It is a' true, your grace! And your grace may weel ken how the report drawed the heart of the hamlet out to gae to Banff, and hear a' aboot the murther."

"Yes, yes," murmured the duke to himself.

"And now, will your grace please to have a room? And what will your grace please to have for breakfast?" inquired the landlord, remembering his duty, and again bowing to the ground.

"You may show me to a bed-room, where I may get rid of this railway dust, and--for breakfast, anything you please, so that it is quickly prepared. Also, landlord, have a chaise at the door, with a good pair of horses. I must start for Banff within half an hour," said the traveller.

"Save us and sain us! Your grace, also! A' the warld seem ganging to Banff!" cried honest Donald Duncan.

"I am summoned there as a witness on the trial, landlord."

"Ay, to be sure. Sae your grace maun be. For it is weel kenned that your grace was amung the first to discover the dead body of the murthered man, Heaven rest him! And noo, your grace, I will show ye till your room," said the landlord, leading the way to a neat bedchamber on the same floor.

"Be good enough to send my servant here with my luggage," said the duke.

The landlord bowed and went out to deliver the message.

And in another minute the valet entered the room with the valise, dressing-case, and so forth.

The duke made a rapid morning toilet, and then returned to the parlor, where the little breakfast table was already laid--coffee, rolls, oat-meal cake, broiled haddock, broiled black cock, and Dundee marmalade, formed the bill of fare.

The duke forced himself to partake of some solid food in addition to the two cups of coffee he hastily swallowed.

And then, as the chaise was announced, he arose to depart.

"I desire to keep these rooms until further notice, landlord. I shall return here this evening, and stop here during my attendance upon the trial at Banff," said the duke, as he got into the chaise, followed by the valet.

The driver cracked his whip and the horses started.

"Aweel," said the landlord to himself, as he watched the chaise winding its way up the mountain-pass. "Aweel, I waur e'en just confounded to see the dook here away without the doochess; and I just after reading in the *Times* how they were married o' the day before yesterday, and gane for their wedding trip to Paris! Aweel, I suppose, it will be this witness business as hae broughten him back. But where's the young doochess? Ay, to be sure, he hae left her in her grand toon house in London. He wad na be bringing her here at siccan a painfu' time and occasion as the trial of her ain father's murtherer. Nae, indeed! that is nae likely," concluded honest Donald Duncan, as he returned into his house.

Banff was but ten miles north-east of Lone. But the mountain road was difficult; and now that the morning mist lay heavy on the landscape, it was necessary for our travelers to drive slowly and carefully to avoid precipitating themselves over some rocky steep, into some deep pool or stony chasm.

They were, thus, an hour in getting safely through the mountain-pass.

At the end of that time, they came out upon a good road, through a forest of firs, covering a hilly country.

Then the mist began to roll away before the bright beams of the advancing sun.

And another hour of fast driving brought them into the town of Banff.

The duke directed the driver to turn into the street where was situated the town-hall, where the court was being held.

The very looks of the street must have informed any stranger that some event of unusual interest was then transpiring. The sidewalks were filled with pedestrians, whose steps were all bent in one direction--toward the town hall.

As our travellers drew up before the front of the building, the duke alighted and beckoned to a bailiff to come and clear the way for his passage into the court-room.

The officer hurried to the duke, and using his official authority, soon made a narrow path through the dense crowd that choked up every avenue into the edifice.

So, elbowing, pushing and wedging his way, the bailiff led the duke into the court-room, which was even more closely packed than the ante-rooms. Pressing through this solid mass of human beings, the bailiff led him to a seat directly in front of the bench of judges, and there left him.

The duke bowed to the Bench, sat down and looked around upon the strange and painful scene.

The famous Scotch judge, Baron Stairs, presided. On his right and left sat Mr. Justice Kinloch and Mr. Justice Guthrie.

Quite a large number of lawyers, law officers, and writers to the seal were present.

Mr. James Stuart, Q.C., was the prosecutor on the part of the crown. He was assisted by Messrs. Roy and McIntosh.

Mr. Keir and Mr. Gordon, two rising young barristers from Aberdeen, were counsel for the prisoner.

John Potts, alias Peters, the accused man, stood alone in the prisoner's dock.

He was a tall, gaunt, dark man, whose pallid face looked ghastly in contrast with his damp, lank, black hair, that seemed pasted to his cheeks by the thick perspiration, and with his black coat and pantaloons that hung loosely on his emaciated form.

The young duke thought he had never seen a man so much broken down in so short a time.

While the duke was looking at him, the poor wretch turned caught his eye and bowed. And then he quickly grasped the front railing of the dock with both his hands, as if to keep himself from falling.

The young duke turned away his eyes. The sight was too painful. He looked around him over the densely packed crowd, in which he recognized many of his old friends and neighbors, a great number of his clansmen and nearly all the old servants of his family.

Although the month was October, and the weather cool in that northern climate, the atmosphere of such a packed crowd would have been unbearable but for the fact that the six tall windows that flanked the court-room on each side were let down from the top for ventilation.

The duke turned his attention to the Bench.

There seemed to be some pause in the proceedings. The judges were sitting in perfect silence. The prosecuting counsel were arranging papers and occasionally speaking to each other in low tones.

The duke turned to a gentleman, a stranger, who was sitting on his left, and inquired:

"I have heard that the girl Cameron is not to be arraigned. I have also heard that she is held as a witness for the crown. Can you inform me whether it is so?"

"Yes, sir, it is so. You perceive that she is not in the dock with the other prisoner. She is in custody, however, in the sheriff's room. The prosecution cannot afford to arraign her, because they cannot do without her testimony," answered the stranger.

A buzz of conversation passed like a breeze through the impatient crowd.

"Silence in the court!" called out the crier.

And all became as still as death.

Mr. Roy, assistant counsel for the crown, arose and read the indictment, charging the prisoner at the bar with the willful murder of Sir Lemuel Levison, at Castle Lone, on the twenty-first day of June, Anno Domini, so and so. Without making any comment, the prosecutor sat down.

The Clerk of Arraigns then arose, and demanded of the accused--

"Prisoner at the bar, are you guilty or not guilty of the crimes with which you stand indicted?"

Potts, who stood pale and trembling and clutching the rails in front of the dock, replied earnestly though informally:

"Not guilty, upon my soul, my lords and gentlemen, before Heaven, and as I hope for salvation."

And overpowered by fear, he sank down on the narrow bench at the back of the dock.

The trial proceeded.

Queen's Counsel, Mr. James Stuart, took the indictment from the hands of his assistant, and proceeded to open it with a short, pithy address to the judges and the jury, and closed by requesting that Alexander McRath, house-steward of Castle Lone, in the service of the deceased, should be called.

The venerable, gray-haired old Scot, being duly called, came forward and took the stand.

Mr. McIntosh, assistant Queen's Counsel, conducted his examination.

Being duly sworn, Alexander McRath testified as to the facts within his own knowledge relating to the case, and which have already been laid before our readers--briefly, they referred to the finding of the dead body of the late Sir Lemuel Levison in his bed-chamber, to which no one except his confidential valet, the prisoner at the bar, had a pass-key, or could have gained admittance during the night.

The witness was cross-examined by Mr. Keir of the counsel for the prisoner, but without having his testimony weakened.

Other domestic servants were called, who corroborated the evidence given by the last one as to the finding of the dead body, and the intimate and confidential relations which had subsisted between the deceased and the prisoner at the bar, who always carried a pass-key to his master's private apartments.

Then the boy, Ferguson, a saddler's apprentice from the village of Lone, was called to the stand; and being sworn and examined, testified to the meeting and the conspiracy at midnight before the murder, under the balcony, near Malcolm's Tower, at Castle Lone, to which he had been an eye and ear-witness.

This witness was subjected to a very severe cross-examination, which rather developed and strengthened his testimony than otherwise.

McNeil, the ticket agent of the railway station at Lone, was next called, sworn, and examined. He testified to having sold a ticket just after midnight on the night of the murder to a vailed woman, who carried a small but very heavy leathern bag, which she guarded with jealous care. His description corresponded with that given by young Ferguson of the vailed woman, and the bag he had seen given to her by the balcony at Castle Lone on the same night.

This witness, also, was sharply cross-examined without effect.

"Now, my lords and gentlemen of the jury," began Queen's Counsel Stuart, speaking more gravely than he had ever done before, "I shall proceed to call a witness whose testimony will assuredly fix the deep guilt in the case we are trying where it justly belongs. Let Rose Cameron be placed upon the stand."

There was a great sensation in the court-room. The dense crowd was stirred with emotion as thick forest leaves are stirred with the wind.

"Silence in the court!" called out the crier.

And silence fell like a pall upon the crowd.

A door was opened on the left of the Judge's Bench, and the handsome Highland girl was led in by a sheriff's officer. She was dressed in a dark-blue merino suit, with a black felt hat and blue feather to match, and dark-blue gloves. Her long light hair flowed down her shoulders, a cataract of gold. She stepped with an elastic and imperial step as natural to her as to the reindeer. A very Juno of stately beauty she seemed as she rolled her large, fearless eyes over the crowded court-room, until, at length, they fell on the form of the young Duke of Hereward, seated on a front seat.

She started and flushed. Then recovered herself, caught his eyes, and fixed them with her bold, steady gaze, smiled a vindictive, deadly smile, and so passed with stately steps to her place on the witness stand.

CHAPTER XXIII.
A STARTLING CHARGE.

The Duke of Hereward was quite unable to account for the look of vindictive and deadly hatred and malice cast on him by Rose Cameron. He could only suppose that she mistook him for some one else, or that she unreasonably resented his active share in the prosecution of the search for the murderers of Sir Lemuel Levison.

He sat back in his seat and watched her while she stepped upon the witness-stand and turned to face the jury.

Every pair of eyes in the court-room were also fixed upon her. For it was believed that she had been an accomplice in the murder, as well as in the robbery, at Castle Lone, and that she had turned Queen's evidence in order to escape the extreme penalty of the law. And all there who looked upon her were as much dazzled by her wondrous beauty, as appalled by her awful guilt.

The Clerk of the Court administered the oath. The assistant Queen's Counsel proceeded to examine her.

"Your name is Rose Cameron?"

"Na! I'm nae Rose Cameron. I'm Rose Scott, and an honest, married woman," said the witness, turning a baleful look upon the Duke of Hereward, and letting her large, bold, blue eyes rove defiantly, triumphantly over the sea of human faces turned toward her. She never blenched a bit under the fire of glances fixed upon her. These glances would have pierced like spears any finer and more sensitive spirit. They never seemed to touch hers.

"What a handsome quean it is!" said some.

"What a diabolical malignity there is in her looks. Eh, sirs! The vera cut of her 'ee wad convict her, handsome as she is!" whispered another.

"Ay, she looks as if she could ha ta'en a hand in the murther as well as in the robbery," muttered a third. And so on.

These comments were made in so low a tone that they did not in the least disturb the decorum of the court.

"Your name is Rose Scott, then?" proceeded Counsellor Keir.

"Ay, it is."

"What is your age?"

"Twenty-six come next Michael-mas."

"Your residence?"

"Are ye meaning my hame?"

"Yes, your home."

"I dinna just ken. It used to be Ben Lone on the Duk' o Harewood's estate, when I waur a lass. Sin I hae been a guid wife I hae bided in Westminster Road, Lunnun."

At the mention of Westminster Road, the Duke of Hereward started slightly, and bent forward to give closer attention to the words of the witness.

"With whom did you live in Westminster Road?" proceeded the examiner.

"Wi' my ain guid man, ye daft fule!" exclaimed Rose Cameron, in a rage. "Wha else suld I bide wi'? And noo, ye'll speer nae mair questions anent my ain preevit life, for I'll nae answer any sic. A woman maunna gie testimony in open coort against her ain husband, I'm thinking."

"Certainly not."

"Sae I thocht!" said Rose Cameron, cunningly. "And sae ye'll speer nae mair questions anent my ain preevit affair; but just keep ye to the point, and it please ye! I am here to tell all I ken anent the murther and robbery at Castle Lone! Ay! and I will tell a' hang wha' it may!" she added, with a most vindictive glare at the Duke of Hereward.

"The witness is right so far. We have nothing whatever to do with her domestic status. Proceed with the examination, and keep to the point," interposed the judge.

"We will, my lord. We only wished to prove the fact that the witness was living on the most intimate terms with one of the parties suspected of the murder."

"I waur living wi' my ain husband, as I telt ye before, ye born idiwat! An' I'm no ca'd upon to witness for or against him. Sae I'll tell ye a' I ked anent the murther and the robbery at Castle Lone; but de'il hae me gin I tell ye onything else!" exclaimed Rose Cameron.

"The witness is quite right in her premises, though censurable in her manner of expressing them. Proceed with the examination," said the judge.

The assistant Q.C. bowed to the Bench and turned to the witness.

"Tell us, then, where you were on the night of the murder."

"I waur in the grounds o' Castle Lone."

"At what time were you there?"

"Frae ten till twal o' the clock."

"Were you alone?"

"For a guid part of the time I waur my lane i' the castle court."

"What took you out on the castle grounds alone at so late an hour?"

"I went there to keep my tryste with the Markis of Arondelle," answered the witness, with a sly, malignant glance at the young nobleman whose name she thus publicly profaned!

The Duke of Hereward started, and fixed his eyes sternly and inquiringly upon the bold, handsome face of the witness.

Her eyes did not for an instant quail before his gaze. On the contrary, they opened wide in a bold, derisive stare, until she was recalled by the questions of the examiner.

"Witness! Do you mean to say, upon your oath, that you went to Castle Lone at midnight to meet the Marquis of Arondelle?"

"Aye, that I do. I went to the castle to keep tryste wi' his lairdship, the Marquis of Arondelle. He wha was troth-plighted to the heiress o' Lone. Ae wha is noo ca'd his grace the Duk' o' Harewood!" said the witness, emphatically, triumphantly.

The statement fell like a thunderbolt on the whole assembly.

When Rose Cameron first said that she went to the castle to keep tryste with the Marquis of Arondelle, those who heard her distrusted the evidence of their own ears, and turned to each other, inquiring in whispers:

"What did she say?"

Or answering in like whispers:

"I don't know."

But now that she had reiterated her statement with emphasis and with triumph, they asked no more questions, but gazed in each other's faces in awe-struck silence.

And as for the Duke of Hereward! What on earth could a gentleman have to say to a charge as absurd as it was infamous, thus made upon him by a disreputable person in open court?

Why, to notice it even by denial would seem to be an infringement of his dignity and self-respect.

The Duke of Hereward, after his first involuntary start and stare of amazement, controlled himself absolutely, and sat back in his chair, perfectly silent and self-possessed under this ordeal.

Not so the senior counsel for the defence.

Rising in his place, he addressed the bench:

"My lord, we object to the question put to the witness, which, while it tends to compromise a lofty personage of this realm, can, in no manner, concern the case in hand. My lord, we are not trying his grace the Duke of Hereward."

"The bench has already instructed the counsel for the Crown to keep to the point at issue while examining the witness," said the presiding judge.

"Ou, ay! Ye are nae trying the Duk' o' Harewood, are ye nae? Aweel, then, I'm thinking ye'll be trying him before a's ower!" put in Rose Cameron, spitefully.

"Witness, tell the jury what occurred, within your own knowledge, while you were in the grounds of Castle Lone," said Mr. Keir.

"And how will I tell onything right gin I am forbid to name the name o' him wha wur maistly concernit?" demanded Rose Cameron.

"You are to give your own testimony in your own way, unless otherwise instructed by the bench," said Mr. Keir.

"Aweel, then, first of a', I went to the castle by appointment to meet Laird Arondelle, as he was then ca'd. I walked about and waited fu' an hour before his lairdship cam' till me."

"At what hour was that?"

"I heard the castle clock aboon Auld Malcom's Tower strike eleven when I cam' under the balcony o' the bride's chamber, whilk is nigh it. I waited fu' half an hour there before his lairdship cam' stealing through the shrubbery--De'il hae him, wha ha brocht a' this trouble on me!" exclaimed the witness, vehemently, as her eyes, fairly blazing with blue fire, fixed themselves on the face of the young duke.

The Duke of Hereward bore the searching glare quite calmly. He simply leaned back in his chair, with folded arms and attentive face, on which curiosity was the only expression.

"Mr. Keir," said the venerable Counsellor Guthrie, of the defence, "is all this supposed to concern the case before the jury?"

"Ay, does it!" cried Rose Cameron, before the lawyer addressed could reply. "Ay, does it, as ye will sune see, gin ye will gie me leave to speak."

Meanwhile the Duke of Hereward took out his note-book and wrote these lines:

"*Pray let the witness proceed without regard to her use of my name. I think the ends of justice require that she be suffered to give her testimony in her own way*. HEREWARD."

He tore this leaf out and passed it on to Mr. Guthrie, who read it with some surprise, and then waved his hand to Mr. Keir, and sat down with the air of a man who had complied with an indiscreet request, and washed his hands of the consequences.

"The time of the court is being unnecessarily wasted. Let the examination of the witness go on," said the presiding judge.

"It shall, my lord," answered the Queen's Counsel, with an inclination of his white-wigged head. Then turning to the bold blonde on the stand, he proceeded:

"Witness, tell the jury what occurred that night under the balcony of Miss Levison's apartments at Castle Lone."

Rose Cameron threw another vindictive glance at the Duke of Hereward, and commenced her narrative.

Now, as her story was substantially the same that has been already given to the reader, it is not necessary to recapitulate it here. Only in one respect it differed from the stories she had hitherto told to her landlady or housekeeper, Mrs. Brown, of Westminster Road; as on this occasion she reserved all allusion to any real or fancied marriage between herself and the nobleman she claimed as her lover, and then accused as the accomplice of thieves and assassins, in the murder and robbery at Castle Lone, on the night preceding the day appointed for his own marriage with its heiress!

It would be impossible to describe the effect of this terrible testimony on the minds of all who heard it.

The Bench, the Bar, and the Jury, whom, it would seem, nothing in this world had power to startle, astonish, or discompose, sat like statues.

Scarcely less immovable was the young Duke of Hereward, the subject of this awful charge, who sat back in his seat with an air of grave curiosity, and with the composure of a man who was master of the situation.

But the crowd which filled the court-room seemed utterly confounded by what they heard. Upon the whole, they either disbelieved this witness, or distrusted their own ears. Their young laird, as she called the present duke, was their model of all wisdom, goodness, magnanimity. Truly, they had heard a rumor of some little love-making between the young laird and a handsome shepherdess at Ben Lone, probably this same Rose Cameron; even these rumors they did not fully credit; but that the noble young Duke of Hereward should be the accomplice of thieves and murderers in the robbery at Castle Lone, and the assassination of Sir Lemuel Levison, on the very night preceding the morning appointed for his marriage with Sir Lemuel's daughter!

Oh! the charge was too preposterous, as well as too horrible, to be entertained for an instant.

Finally the prevailing opinion settled into this: that the young laird had probably admired the handsome shepherdess a little, and had left her for the heiress; and that, from jealousy and for revenge, the girl was now perjuring herself to ruin her late lover.

Would her testimony be believed? Would it have weight enough to cause the arrest of the young duke?

"Eh, sirs! what an awfu' event the like o' that wad be!" whispered one gray-haired clansman to another.

And all bent eager ears to hear the remainder of the testimony which was still going on.

After relating the history of her journey to London, with the stolen treasure in charge, she proceeded to tell of the abrupt flight of "the duke," with the bulk of the treasure in his possession, and of her own subsequent arrest with the stolen jewels found in her apartments.

She was cross-examined by the defence, but without effect.

Her testimony, if it could be established, would ruin the Duke of Hereward, but could in no way affect the prisoner at the bar.

When the prosecution perceived this, they realized that they had been, in common parlance, "sold."

They were to be sold again.

"You may stand down," said Mr. Keir, sharply.

"Na, I hanna dune yet. I hae mair to say," persisted the witness.

"Say it, then."

"I ken it is nae lawfu' for a wife to gie testimony against her ain husband," said Rose Cameron, with a cunning leer that marred the beauty of her fine blue eyes.

"Certainly not. What has that to do with this case?"

"It hae a' things to do with it."

"Explain yourself, witness; and remember that you are on your oath."

"Ay, I weel ken the solemnity of an aith. And I hae telt the truth under aith; nathless, maybe my teestimony suld na be received."

"Why not?"

"Why no'? Why, gin a wife maunna teestify agin her ain husband, I suld na hae teestified agin the Duk' o' Harewood, who is my ain lawfu' husband!" said Rose Cameron, purposely raising her voice to a clear, ringing tone that was distinctly heard all over the court-room.

Had a shell fallen and exploded in their midst, it could scarcely have caused greater consternation.

"What said the lass?" questioned many.

"I dinna just ken," answered many others.

They certainly did not believe the report of their own ears on this occasion.

As for the Duke of Hereward, who was then engaged in writing a few lines on the fly-leaf of his note-book, he just looked up for a moment and was surprised into the first smile that had lighted his grave face since the opening of the trial.

The cool counsel who was conducting the examination of the witness, and whom nothing on earth could throw off his track, now proceeded to inquire:

"Witness! Do we understand you to say that you are the wife of his grace the Duke of Hereward?"

"Ay, just!" replied Rose Cameron, pertly. "Gin ye hae ony understanding at a', and gin ye are na the auld daft idiwat ye luke, ye'll understand me to say I am the lawfu' wedded wife o' the Duk' o' Harewood. Him as was marrit o' Tuesday last to the heiress o' Lone! Gin ye dinna believe me, I hae my marriage lines, gie me by the minister o' St. Margaret's Kirk, Weestminster, where he marrit me! Ou, ay! and I wad hae tell ye a' this in the beginning, only I kenned weel, if I **did**, ye wad na hae let me gae on gie' ony teestimony agin me ain husband. De'il hae him! But noo, as ye hae heerd the truth anent the grand villainy up in Castle Lone, I dinna mind telling ye wha I am. Ay, and ye may set aside my witness, gin ye like! But the whole coort hae noo heard it. Ay, and the whole warld s'all hear it, or a' be dune! And noo I am thinking ye'll een let the puir mon in the dock just gae free; and pit my laird, his greece, the nubble duk', intil the prisoner's place. Ye'll no hae to seek him far," added the woman, suddenly whisking around and facing the young Duke of Hereward, with a perfectly fiendish look of malice distorting her handsome face. "There he sits noo! he wha marrit me and afterwards marrit the heiress o' Lone! he wha betrayed me intil a prison, and wad hae betrayed me to the gallows, gin I had na been to canny for him! There he is noo, and he can na face me and deny it!"

The Duke of Hereward did not deign to deny anything. He passed the fly leaf, upon which he had written some lines, on to the old lawyer, Guthrie, who looked over it, nodded, and then rising in his place, addressed the Bench:

"My lord, we desire that the witness, who is now transcending the duties and privileges of the stand, be ordered to sit down."

"Oh! I'll sit down!" pertly interrupted Rose Cameron. "I hae had my ain way, and I hae said my ain say, and now I'll e'en gae--gin this auld fule be done wi' me."

"We have done with you; you can stand down," replied Mr. Keir, in mortification and disgust.

Rose Cameron stepped down from the stand with the air of a queen descending from her throne. In look and motion she was graceful and majestic as the antelope. You had to hear her speak to learn how really low and vulgar she was.

She darted one baleful blast of hatred from her blue eyes, as she passed the Duke of Hereward, and was then conducted back to the sheriff's room, where she was to be detained in custody until the conclusion of the trial.

CHAPTER XXIV.
THE VINDICATION.

Mr. Guthrie now requested that the witness Ferguson might be recalled.

The order was given. And the Lone saddler's red-headed apprentice took the stand.

Mr. Guthrie referred to the notes that had been passed to him by the Duke of Hereward, and then said:

"Witness, you told the jury that on the night before the murder of Sir Lemuel Levison, you were employed in your master's service up to a late hour."

"Ay, your honor; but I waur fain to see the wedding decorations, for a' that," said the boy.

"Precisely. But now tell the jury what was the service upon which you were employed to so late an hour that night."

"It wad be a bit wedding offering to our laird, wha hae always favored his ain folks wi' his custom. It waur a Russia leather traveling dressing-bag for his laird-ship, the whilk the master had ta'en unco guid care suld be as brawa bag as ony to be boughten in Lunnen town itsel', whilk mysel' was commissioned, and proud I waur, to tak', wi' my master's duty, to his lairdship."

"Doubtless. Now tell the jury at what hour you took this wedding offering to Lord Arondelle."

"Aweel, it wad be about half-past nine o'clock. I went wi' the dressing-case to the Arondelle Arms, where his lairdship and his lairdship's feyther, the auld duk' were biding. The hostler telt me that his lairdship had gane for a walk o'er the brig to Castle Lone. Sae I were fain to wait there for him."

"How long did you wait?"

"Na lang. I was na mair than five minutes before I saw his lairdship coming o'er the brig toward the house. And sune his lairdship came into the inn, and I made my bow, and offered his lairdship the wedding-gift, wi' my maister's respectful guid wishes. His lairdship smiled pleasantly, and tauld me to fetch it after him up to his chamber. I followed my laird up-stairs to his ain room, where his lairdship's valet, Mr. Kerr, was waiting on him. His lairdship wrote a braw note of acknowledgements to my maister, and gie it me to take away. My laird also gie me a half-sovereign, for mysel'. I dinna tak' the note just then to my maister. I saw by the clock on the mantel that it only lacked a quarter to ten o'clock, sae I e'en made my duty to his lairdship and run down stairs, ran a' the way o'er to Castle Lone, for I war fain to see the decorations. I got to Malcolm's Tower just in time to hear the auld clock in the turret strike eleven, and to see the mon and the woman meet thegither in the shadows."

"Are you sure that you could not identify that man or woman?"

"Anan?"

"Would you know either of them again?" inquired Mr. Guthrie, changing the manner of his question.

"Na! I tauld ye sae before. They were half hidden i' the bushes."

"You say it was a quarter to ten when you left Lord Arondelle in his room at the inn?"

"Ay, war it."

"And that it was eleven o'clock when you witnessed the meeting between the man and the woman at Castle Lone!"

"Ay, war it. And I had to run a' the way to do it in that time. It waur guid rinning."

"You left his lordship's valet with him, do you say?"

"Ay, I did. And the head waiter o' the Arondelle Arms, too, wha was just gaeing in wi' his lairdship's supper."

"That will do. You may now stand down," said Mr. Guthrie.

The shock-headed apprentice, who had done such good service to his Grace the

Duke of Hereward, and such damage to the false witness against him, now left the stand and made his way through the crowd to his distant seat.

Mr. Guthrie once more got upon his feet to address the Bench, and said:

"May it please the Court, I move that the testimony of the Crown's witness, Rose Cameron, alias Rose Scott, be set aside as totally unreliable; and, further, that she be indicted for perjury."

Upon this motion of Mr. Guthrie there followed some discussion among the lawyers.

Finally it was decided to put the duke's valet, the hotel waiter, and other witnesses, on the stand, who would be able to corroborate or rebut the evidence given by the lad Ferguson, and thereby break down or establish the testimony offered by Rose Cameron.

James Kerr was, therefore, called to the witness-stand, sworn and examined.

He said that he had been in the service of the duke's family ever since he was nine years of age, first as page to the late duchess, but for the last three years as valet to the present duke; that he was with his master at the "Arondelle Arms" on the night of the murder; that the duke, who was then the Marquis of Arondelle, left the inn at half-past eight o'clock, to walk over the bridge to Castle Lone; that he returned at half-past nine, accompanied to his room by the boy Ferguson, who brought a handsome Russia leather travelling-case; that the marquis sat down to his writing-table, wrote a note and gave it to the boy, who immediately left the house.

"At what hour was this?" inquired Mr. Guthrie.

"It was a few minutes before ten. The clock struck very soon after the boy left. I remember it well, because his lordship's supper had been ordered for ten, and the waiter just entered to lay the cloth when the lad left, and his lordship sat down to supper at ten precisely. After the supper-service had been removed, his lordship went to his writing-desk and wrote for an hour, and then sealed and dispatched a packet directed to the *Liberal Statesman*. I took it myself to the Post-Office, to ensure its being in time for the midnight mail. It was then about half-past eleven o'clock. I was gone on my message for about five minutes. On my return I found my master where I had left him, sitting at his writing-desk, arranging his papers. But when I entered he locked his desk and said he would go to bed. I waited on him at his night toilet. And then, as the inn was very much crowded, I slept on a lounge in my master's bed-room. The house was full of noise; so many of the Scots were present, making merry over the approaching marriage of their chieftain's son. Neither my master nor myself rested well that night. I arose early to see my master's bath. The marquis arose at eight o'clock."

Such was the substance of James Kerr's testimony, which perfectly corroborated that of the lad Ferguson, and greatly damaged that of Rose Cameron.

The hotel waiter happened to be among those who had cast all their worldly interests to the winds, abandoned their callings of whatever sort, and come at all risk of consequences to be present at the trial. He was found in the court-room, called to the witness-stand, sworn and examined.

His testimony corroborated that of the two last witnesses, and utterly broke down that of Rose Cameron.

There was further consultation between the Bar and the Bench. Finally the testimony of the Crown's witness was set aside, and a warrant was made out for the arrest of Rose Cameron, otherwise Rose Scott, upon the charge of perjury.

The warrant was sent out to the sheriff's room, to which, after leaving the witness-stand, Rose Cameron had been conducted.

And now the crowd in the court-room, composed chiefly of neighbors, friends, kinsmen, and clansmen of the young Duke of Hereward, breathed freely.

The thunder-cloud had passed.

Their hero was vindicated. Truly they had never for an instant doubted his integrity, much less had they suspected him of a heinous, an atrocious crime. Still, it was an immense relief to have the black shadow of that bloody charge withdrawn.

There was but one more witness for the prosecution to be examined; that witness was no less a person than the young Duke of Hereward himself.

He was called to the stand, and sworn.

Every pair of eyes in the court-room availed themselves of the opportunity afforded by the elevated position of the witness-stand, to gaze on the man who had so recently been the subject of such a terrible accusation; and all admired the calmness, self-possession, and forbearance of his conduct during the fearful ordeal through which he had just passed.

He simply testified as to the finding of the dead body, the position of the corpse, the condition of the room, and so forth. He was not subjected to a cross-examination, but was courteously notified that he was at liberty to retire.

He resumed his former seat.

The case for the prosecution was closed.

Mr. Kinlock, junior counsel for the prisoner, arose for the defence. He made a short address to the jury, in which he spoke of the slight grounds upon which his unhappy client had been charged with an atrocious crime, and brought to trial for his life. The law demanded a victim for that heinous crime, which had shocked the whole community from its centre to its circumference, and his unfortunate client had been selected as a sin offering. He reminded the jury how the very esteem and confidence of the master and the fidelity and obedience of the servant had been most ingeniously turned into strong circumstantial evidence, to fix the assassination of the master upon the servant. The deceased, had entirely trusted the prisoner; had given him a pass-key with which he might enter his chambers at any hour of the day or night; and hence it was argued that the prisoner, being the only one who had the entree to the deceased's apartments, must have been the person who admitted the murderer to his victim. The prisoner had faithfully obeyed his master's orders for the day, in declining to enter his rooms before his bell should ring; and thence it was argued that he only delayed to call his master because he knew that master lay murdered in his room, and he wished to give the murderers, with whom he was said to be confederated, time to make good their escape. He was sure, he said, that a just and intelligent jury must at once perceive the cruel injustice of such far-fetched inferences. In addition he would call witnesses who would testify to the good character of the accused, and prove that the great esteem and confidence in which he had been held by his late master was abundantly justified by the excellent character and blameless conduct of the servant.

Mr. Kinlock then proceeded to call his witnesses.

They were the fellow-servants of the accused. Some of them were the very same witnesses that had been called by the prosecution, and were now re-called for the defence. One and all, in turn, testified to the uniform good behavior of the valet while in the service of Sir Lemuel Levison, deceased.

The presiding judge, Baron Stairs, summed up the evidence in a very few words.

The evidence against the prisoner at the bar was circumstantial only. It had appeared in evidence that some servant of the family had admitted the assassin to the house. It did not appear who that servant was. The valet John Potts, was the only one who had the pass-key to the apartments of the deceased. That circumstance had fixed suspicion upon him; had brought him to trial; the trial had brought out no new facts; the witness principally relied on by the prosecution had not only failed to give any testimony to convict the prisoner, but had certainly perjured herself to shield the real criminal, whoever he was, and to accuse a noble personage, whose high character and lofty station alike placed him infinitely above suspicion. On the other hand, many witnesses had testified to the good character and conduct of the prisoner, and the estimation in which he had been held by his late master. Such was the evidence, pro and con.

His lordship concluded by saying that the jury might now retire and deliberate upon their verdict, remembering that in all cases of uncertainty they should lean to the side of mercy.

The jury arose from their seats, and, conducted by a bailiff, retired to the room provided for them.

Many of the people now left the court-room to get refreshments.

But as the judges remained upon the bench, the Duke of Hereward kept his seat. He felt sure that the jury would not long deliberate before bringing in their verdict.

Meanwhile he turned to glance at the prisoner.

John Potts looked like a man without a hope in the world. We have already seen that an awful change had come over him since the day of his arrest, three months before. Now, as he leaned forward where he sat, and rested his head upon his skeleton hands, that clasped the top of the railing of the dock, his face, or what could be seen of it, was ghastly pale with agony, while his emaciated frame trembled from head to foot. ***He looked like a guilty man.*** And his looks were now, as they had been from the moment in which the dead body of his master had been discovered, the strongest testimony against him.

For all that, you know, they cannot hang a man merely because he looks as if he ought to be hung.

After an absence of about fifteen minutes, the jury, led by a bailiff, returned to the court-room.

The prisoner looked up, shivered, and dropped his head upon his clasped hands again.

The dead silence of breathless expectation in the court-room was now broken by the solemn voice of the Clerk of Arraigns, inquiring, in measured tones:

"Gentlemen of the jury, have you agreed upon your verdict?"

"We have," answered the foreman, a jolly, red-headed, round bodied Banff baker.

"Prisoner at the bar, stand up and look upon the jury," ordered the clerk.

The poor, abject, and terrified wretch tottered to his feet and stood, pallid, shaking, and grasping the front rails of the dock for support.

"Gentlemen of the jury, look upon the prisoner. How say you, is the prisoner at the bar guilty or not guilty of the felony herewith he stands charged?" demanded the clerk.

"We find the charge against the prisoner to be--NOT PROVEN,"[A] answered the foreman, speaking for the whole in a strong, distinct voice, that was heard all over the court-room.

[Footnote A: "Not Proven"--a Scotch verdict in uncertain cases.]

On hearing the verdict which saved him from death, even if it did not vindicate him, John Potts let go the rails of the dock and fell back in his chair in a half-fainting condition.

"The prisoner is discharged from custody. The Court is adjourned," said the presiding baron, rising and leaving his seat.

While one of the bailiffs was kindly supporting the faltering steps of the released prisoner, in taking him from the dock, and while the crowd in the court-room were pouring out of the front doors, the presiding judge, Baron Stairs, came down to the place where the young Duke of Hereward still sat. He had known the duke's father, and had also known the duke himself from boyhood. He now held out his hand cordially, saying:

"I am very glad to see your grace, though the occasion is a painful one. Let me congratulate you on your marriage, I wish you every good thing in life. You have already got the *best* thing--a good wife. I knew Miss Levison. A finer young woman never lived. I congratulate you with all my heart, Duke!"

"I thank you very much, Lord Stairs," said the bridegroom, warmly returning the greeting of the judge.

"But I fear I must condole with you also. It was really too bad to have your honeymoon eclipsed at its rising, by a summons to attend as a witness on a criminal trial!--too bad! However, fortunately, the trial was a short one. And you are now at liberty to fly to your bride! I hope the duchess is well," added his lordship.

"She has never been quite well, I grieve to say, since the catastrophe at Lone," answered the duke, evasively.

"Ah, no! ah no! It cannot be expected that she should be so yet. It will take time! It will take time! By the way, where are you stopping, my dear Duke? I am at the 'Prince Consort!' Will you come home with me and dine?" heartily inquired the baron.

"Many thanks, my lord. But I am not staying in town. I must hurry back to Lone this evening in order to secure the midnight express to London. The most important business demands my immediate presence there," gravely replied the young duke.

"Ah, of course! of course! the bride! the duchess! Certainly, my dear duke. I will not press you further," said the baron, laughing cordially.

Neither of the gentlemen made the slightest allusion to the testimony given by the crown's evidence which had cast so foul and false an aspersion on the character of the duke.

By this time the court-room was nearly emptied.

The duke and the baron walked out together.

The crowd had dispersed from before the court-house.

The duke and the baron shook hands and parted on the sidewalk.

"Give my warm respects to the duchess. Tell her grace that I shall hope to meet her and present my congratulations in person, on her return from the Continent. That will be in time for the meeting of Parliament, I presume," said his lordship, as he was about to step into his carriage.

"Thanks, my lord. Yes, I hope so," answered his grace, as he lifted his hat and turned away.

The baron's carriage drove off to his hotel.

The duke walked rapidly to the inn, where he had ordered his post-chaise to be put up.

He partook of a light luncheon while his horses were being harnessed, and then entered the chaise, attended by his valet, and ordered the coachman to drive as fast as possible, without hurting the horses, to Lone.

He was most anxious to reach the "Arondelle Arms," to see if any telegram from Detective Setter had reached the office for him.

So long as the road ran through the Firwood, and was comparatively smooth and level, the coachman kept his horses at their best speed; but when it entered the mountain pass of the chain running around Loch Lone, he was compelled to drive slowly and carefully.

The sun set before they emerged from the pass, and it was nearly dark when the chaise drew up before the Arondelle Arms.

The duke got out of the chaise, and passed through the little assemblage of villagers who were standing there discussing the verdict of the jury. He hurried at once to the bar-room to inquire if any letter or telegram had come for him.

"Na, naething o' the sort," replied the landlord, who, seeing the disappointment expressed upon the duke's face, added: "But, under favor, your grace, there's time eneuch yet. Your grace hae na been twenty-four hours awa' fra Lunnun."

Without waiting to answer the host, the young duke hurried out, and walked rapidly off to the telegraph office, which was at the railway station.

"Ye see yon lad?" said the landlord to his wife. "He hanna been a day fra his bride, and yet he expects to hae a letter or a message frae her every minute. Aweel we hae a' been fules in our time!"

So saying the philosophical host of the Arondelle Arms gave his mind to the service of his numerous customers, who had come from the trial at Banff very hungry and thirsty, and now filled the bar-room with their persons, and all the air with their complaints.

They were not at all satisfied with the verdict. They had had a murder, and they had a right to have a hanging. They had been defrauded of their prospect of this second entertainment, and they were not well pleased.

Meanwhile, the duke hurried off to the telegraph office, to see if by any chance a telegram had been received there for him and detained.

When he entered the little den, he found the operator at work. He forebore to interrupt the man until the clicking of the wires ceased. Then he asked:

"Can you tell if there is any message here for me?--the Duke of Hereward," added his grace, seeing the puzzled look of the operator, who was a stranger in the country.

"Yes, your grace. It has only just now come," respectfully answered the young man, as he drew out a long, narrow strip of thick, white paper, upon which the message had been stamped by the instrument, and proceeded to select an official envelope in which to inclose it.

"Never mind that. Give it to me at once," said the duke, taking the strip from the hand of the operator and hastily perusing it.

The message ran thus:

"OLD CHURCH COURT, KENSINGTON, LONDON,

"October 31st, 3 P.M.

"To HIS GRACE THE DUKE OF HEREWARD, Arondelle Arms, Lone, N.B. She is found. Pray come to London immediately. It is important.

"J.A. SETTER."

CHAPTER XXV.
WHO WAS FOUND!

"She is found."

"Who is found? The lost bride, or that mysterious messenger who was with the fugitive an hour before her flight, who was suspected to have lured her away, and who might be able to give a clew to her whereabouts? Good Heaven! why could not the detective have sent a definite message?" thought the duke, as he studied the telegram.

Suddenly his face lighted up as he said to himself. "It is Salome who is found! Of course it must be Salome, since no one else was really lost. It is Salome, and that is the very reason why Setter spoke so indefinitely; for I remember now that I instructed him to avoid using the name of the duchess in any telegram. Salome is found! Ah! I thank Heaven! She is found! But--" he reflected with a sudden re-action of feeling--"how, where, when, by whom, under what circumstances was my bride found? Is she well or ill? Can she give any satisfactory explanation of her absence?" were the next anxious, soul-racking questions that chased each other through his mind.

"Oh, for the strong pinions of the eagle, that I might fly to her at once and satisfy all these anxious doubts," he breathed.

It was now but six o'clock in the afternoon. The first train for London would not stop at Lone until midnight, and would not reach London until eight o'clock the next morning--fourteen hours of suspense!

He could not bear that.

The telegraph operator was about to close the office.

The duke stopped him by saying:

"I wish to send a telegram to London."

"It is after hours, your grace," answered the operator, very deferentially.

"I will pay you whatever you may demand for your extra services, over and above your usual fee," said the duke.

The operator hesitated.

"That is to say, if there is no rule in your office to forbid it," added the duke.

"There is no rule to prevent it, your grace. My time is up, and I was about to go home to supper, that was all. I will send your grace's message, if you please," the operator explained, as he took his seat again.

The duke hastily dashed off the following message:

"LONE, N.B., October 31st, 6 P.M.

"To J.A. SETTER, Police Station, Old Church Court, Kensington, London: Shall leave for London by this midnight express-train. Is she quite well? Answer immediately. HEREWARD."

The operator took the message with a bow. The click of the instrument was soon heard, as the message, with the speed of light, flew on its errand.

"Will you remain here until I can receive an answer?" inquired the duke, as soon as the sound ceased.

"I should be happy to accommodate your grace; but if there should be no answer, say up to twelve o'clock?" suggested the young man.

"In that case I should not ask you to remain; as you must know by my telegram that I am to take the train for London at that hour."

"Certainly, your grace; but I thought it possible that you might wish the message taken to some other person in the event of your absence."

"Not at all. I want it for myself alone. If it does not come before twelve I shall have no use for it."

"Then I will remain here until midnight, if necessary; but it may not be necessary."

"And you shall set your own price upon your time," said the duke.

"Thanks, your grace; I am happy to be able to accommodate you; and would prefer to leave all other considerations to yourself," said the young man, very politely and--politicly.

Even while they spoke, a warning vibration of the wires was perceived, followed by the ***click, click, click***, of the instrument.

"There is a message coming--most probably an answer to yours, though it is very soon to get one," said the operator, as he turned to give his whole attention to his work.

The duke looked on with breathless eagerness.

As soon as the sound ceased, the operator drew off the message and handed it to the duke, who seized it and hastily read;

"LONDON, October, 31st, 7 P.M.

"TO THE DUKE OF HEREWARD, LONE, N.B.: She is perfectly well.

"J.A. SETTER."

"Thank Heaven! I breathe freely now!" said the young duke to himself, as he arose from his seat.

He liberally rewarded the telegraph operator, and then left the office and walked back to the inn.

The Arondelle Arms was all alive with excitement. More travellers had come down from Banff, and the inn was crowded, principally by men of the Clan Scott. Every room was filled, every window lighted up. The bar and the tap room reeked.

The duke was making his way through the crowd as best he might, when he was met by the landlord, who bowed, and apologized, and finally offered to conduct his grace by a private entrance to the parlor connected with the duke's own reserved suit of apartments.

"An' noo, what will your grace hae to your supper?" hospitably inquired the host, as soon as his guest was comfortably seated in his arm-chair before the fire.

"Anything at all, so that it is cleanly served, for which I can, of course, trust the Arondelle Arms," said the duke, smiling.

The landlord bowed and went out.

The duke leaned back in his chair, and stretched his feet to the genial warmth of the fire.

He was feeling very happy. An immense load of anxiety was lifted from his heart. She was found! She was perfectly well! In twelve hours he would see her, and hear her own explanation of her very strange conduct. Her explanation would be perfectly satisfactory. So great was his confidence in her that he felt sure of this.

She was found. She was perfectly well. There was nothing to prevent them from starting on their wedding tour as soon as they might wish to do so. They would, therefore, leave London by the tidal train for Dover on the next afternoon. The world would take it for granted that the wedding tour had been interrupted and delayed only by the trial. The world would never suspect Salome's strange escapade.

While these thoughts were passing through the mind of the duke, the waiter came in and laid the cloth for supper.

And soon the landlord himself entered, bearing a tray on which was arranged a choice bill of fare, the principal item of which was a roasted pheasant.

The duke who had scarcely tasted food during the twenty-four hours of his terrible anxiety, now that his anxiety was relieved, felt his appetite return, demanding refreshment at the rate of compound interest.

He sat down to the table. The landlord waited on him.

The honest host of the Arondelle Arms was "dying," so to speak, for a confidential conversation with his noble guest. For some little time his respect for the Duke of Hereward held his curiosity in check; but at length curiosity conquered respect, and he burst forth with:

"That wad be an unco impudent claim, the hizzie Rose Cameron tried to set up agin your grace, as I hear all the folk say out by--the jaud maunn be clear daft."

"It would be charitable to suppose that she is 'daft,' as you call it, landlord. It would be well if a jury could be persuaded to think so, as, in that case, it would save her from the penalty of perjury. But we will speak no more of the poor girl. Take away the service, if you please," said the duke, quietly.

The landlord, balked of his desire to gossip, bowed, and cleared the table.

It was not yet nine o'clock. There were more than three hours to be passed before the express-train for London would reach Lone.

The duke, refreshed by his supper, felt no sense of weariness, no disposition to lie down and sleep away the three remaining hours of his stay. His mind was in too excited a condition to think of sleep. Neither could he read.

So, soon after he was left alone by the landlord, he arose and sauntered out through the private entrance into the night air.

The streets of the village were very quiet, for the reason that on this night the men were all collected at the Arondelle Arms, discussing the events of the day; and at this hour the women were all sure to be in their houses, putting their children to bed, setting bread to rise, or "garring th' auld claithes luke amaist as guid as the new."

The hamlet was very still under the starlit sky.

The Arondelle Arms, lighted up and musical, was the only noisy spot about it.

The mountains stood, grand and silent, like gigantic sentinels around it.

The lake, the island, and the castle of Lone lay beneath it.

A sudden impulse seized the duke to cross the bridge, and re-visit once more the home of his youth, the scene of his family's disaster, the stage of that frightful tragedy which had shocked the civilized world.

He went down to the beach, and stepped upon the bridge. Now, no floral wedding decorations wreathed the arches. All was bare and bleak beneath the last October sky.

He crossed the bridge and entered on the grounds of the castle. All here was sear under the late autumnal frosts. He did not approach the castle walls. He would not disturb the servants at this hour. He walked about the grounds until he heard the clock in Malcolm's Old Tower strike ten. Then he turned his steps toward the hamlet.

Just before he reached the bridge, he overtook the tall, dark figure of a man, clothed in a long, close overcoat, in shape not unlike a priest's walking habit. The man tottered and stumbled as he walked, so that the duke was soon abreast to him. And then he discovered the wanderer to be John Potts, valet to the late Sir Lemuel

Levison.

The young Duke of Hereward shrunk from this man. He could not bring himself to speak with one whom he could not, in his own mind, clear from suspicion.

He passed the valet, walking quickly, and gaining the bridge.

Then he heard footsteps rapidly following him, and the voice of the ex-valet excitedly calling after him:

"My Lord Arondelle! oh! I beg pardon! Your grace! Your grace! For the love of Heaven, let me speak to you!"

Thus adjured, the Duke of Hereward paused, and permitted the ex-valet to come up beside him.

The wretched man was out of breath, pale, panting, trembling, ready to faint. He tottered toward the bulwarks of the bridge, grasped them, and leaned on them for support.

"What do you want of me, Potts?" inquired the duke.

"Oh, your grace! only to speak to you!" gasped the man.

"What can you have to say to me?" sternly demanded the duke.

"*This*, your grace!" said the man, suddenly springing forward and falling on his knees at the feet of the duke. "*This* I have to say, your grace! Although the Court has not cleared me, I am innocent of my master's blood! I am! I am! I am! as the Heaven above us hears and knows! Oh! say you believe me, my lord duke!" cried the poor wretch, wringing his hands.

"Your words and manner are very impressive; nevertheless, I cannot place confidence in them," said the duke, coldly.

"Oh, my lord! my lord! Oh, my lord! my lord!" groaned the valet, lifting both his hands to heaven, as if in appeal from a great injustice.

The duke was moved.

"If you *are* guiltless, why should you care whether I, or any other fallible mortal, should consider you guilty?" he inquired.

"Oh," cried the man, clasping his hands with the energy of despair--"because *every* body thinks me guilty! *No* one believes me innocent, though I am guiltless of my master's blood, so help me Heaven!"

"The circumstances, though not enough to convict you in a court of law, where every doubt must go in favor of the accused, were still strong enough to lay you under suspicion, and open to a second arrest and trial for your life, should new evidence turn up," quietly replied the duke.

"I know it! I know it, your grace. But no new evidence against me can turn up! Lord grant that evidence in my favor might do so! But that cannot happen either. The circumstances that accused, but could not convict, nor acquit me, leave me still under the ban! Yes! under the ban I must remain! But do not *you*, my lord duke, believe me guilty of my master's death! Guilty of much I am! Guilty of neglect of duty, but not of my master's death! The Heavens that hear me know it! Oh, pray, pray try to believe it, my lord duke!" pleaded the wretch, still kneeling, still lifting his clasped hands in an agony of appeal.

"Get upon your feet, Potts. Never kneel to any man. To do so is to degrade yourself and the man to whom you kneel. Get up, before I speak another word to you," said the duke.

The miserable creature struggled to his feet and stood leaning against the bulwarks of the bridge, for support.

"Now, then, if you are not guilty, if your conscience acquits you in the sight of Heaven of all complicity in your late master's death, why should you feel and show such extreme distress--distress that has worn your frame to a skeleton, and stricken your life with old age?" gravely demanded the duke.

"Why?--oh, your grace! I loved my master as a son his father! He was more like a father than a master to me. And he was cut off suddenly by a bloody death! In the midst of my grief for his loss I was arrested and accused of murdering him--my beloved master. I have seen the gallows looming before me for the last three months. I have been shut in prison, with no companions but my own awful thoughts. I have been put on trial for my life. And though the jury could not convict me, it would not acquit me! though I am set at large for the present, I am subject to re-arrest and trial for death, if new evidence, however false, should arise against me. Meanwhile, no one believes me innocent. All believe me guilty. No one will ever speak to me. They made the inn too hot to hold me. My life is ruined--my heart is broken! Is not all that enough, lord duke, to have worn my body to a skeleton and turned my hair gray, without remorse of conscience?" impetuously demanded the man.

"No, Potts, it is not. Nothing but remorse, it seems to me, could so reduce a man," gravely replied the duke.

"Oh, your grace! you still believe me guilty of my good master's murder!" passionately exclaimed the man. "Ah, Heaven! what will become of me? I shall die unless I can have the stay of *some* one's faith in me!"

"Potts," said the duke, in a softened tone, "I do not now think that you had any active or conscious share in the foul murder of Sir Lemuel Levison. But not the less do I see that you are suffering from remorse. ***You are still keeping something back from me!*** he added, very solemnly.

The valet groaned, but made no answer.

"That is the reason why I have no confidence in you," said his grace.

The valet wrung his gaunt hands, but continued silent.

"Now I do not ask you to confide in me; but I will give you this warning--so long as you hold in your bosom a secret which, if revealed, would bring the real criminal to justice, so long you will yourself remain the object of suspicion from others and the victim of remorse in yourself. Now, Potts, I must leave you; for I must get to Lone in time to catch the London express. Good-night," said the duke, as he moved away.

"One moment more, oh, my lord duke! for the love of Heaven! One moment to do a piece of justice," pleaded the ex-valet, tottering after the young nobleman.

"Well, well, what is it now?" inquired the latter, pausing and turning back.

"That poor, misguided girl, Rose Cameron," said the valet.

"Well, what of *her*, man?" impatiently demanded the young nobleman.

"Listen, my lord duke! You saw her committed to prison on the charge of perjury."

"A charge that she was self-convicted of."

"My lord duke, she was not guilty of perjury!" sighed the valet.

"What! What is that you say?" quickly demanded the duke.

"I say, Rose Cameron, poor misguided girl that she was, did not, however, perjure herself--*intentionally* I mean," repeated John Potts.

"Is she *mad*, then? The victim of a monomania?" gravely inquired the duke, fixing his eyes upon the troubled face of the valet.

"No, your grace, she was never more in her right senses."

"What do you mean? Do you *dare*--"

"My lord duke, I dare nothing. I never was a daring man; if I had been, the daring would have been taken out of me by the troubles of this last quarter of a year! But, my lord duke, I am right. Rose Cameron did not intentionally perjure herself, neither is she mad. Rose Cameron believes in her heart every word of the statement she made under oath in the open court this morning."

While the man thus spoke, the duke looked fixedly at him in perfect silence, in the forlorn hope of hearing some solution to the enigma.

"Rose Cameron was deceived, my lord duke--grossly, cruelly, basely deceived--not in one respect only, but in many. She was, first of all, deceived into the idea of being the wife of a gentleman of high rank, when, in fact she is nobody's wife at all. Next she was deceived into becoming an accomplice in a robbery and murder, of which she was as ignorant and as innocent as--as *myself.* She could not have been more so!"

"Who was her deceiver?" sternly demanded the duke.

"I beg pardon. I know no more than your grace! I only presumed to speak about it, so as to explain the strange conduct of that poor girl, and clear her of intentional penury in your sight," said the valet, meekly.

"Potts, you know much more than you are willing to divulge. You have, however, unwittingly given me a clew that I shall take care to follow up. Once more let me warn you to get rid of sinful secrets, and amend your life, if you wish to be at peace. Good-night."

So saying, the duke walked rapidly away to make up for the time lost in talking with the ex-valet.

It was after eleven o'clock when he reached the Arondelle Arms, yet the little hostel gave no signs of closing. The windows were all still ablaze with light, and the bar and the tap-room were uproarious with fun. Evidently the Clan Scott had been drinking the health of the duke and duchess until they had become--

"Glorious! O'er all the ills of life victorious!"

The duke slipped in at the private entrance and gained his own apartment, where he found his valet engaged in packing his valise.

He sent the man out to pay the tavern bill.

In a few minutes Kerr returned, accompanied by the landlord, who brought the receipt, and inquired if his grace would have a carriage.

"No," the duke said; as the distance was short, he preferred to walk to the station.

In a few moments he left the inn, followed by his valet carrying his valise.

They caught the train in good time, having just secured their tickets when the warning shriek of the engine was heard, and it thundered up to the station and stopped.

The duke, followed by his servant, entered the coupe he had secured for the journey.

Three nights of sleeplessness, anxiety and fatigue had prostrated the vital forces of the young nobleman, and so, no sooner had the train started, than he sat himself comfortably back among his cushions, and, being now in a great measure relieved from suspense, he fell into a deep and dreamless sleep. This sleep continued almost unbroken through the night, and was only slightly disturbed by the bustle of arrival when the train reached a large city on its route. He awoke when it arrived at Peterborough; but fell asleep again, and slept through the long twilight of that first day of November.

CHAPTER XXVI.
OFF THE TRACK.

It was eight o'clock in the morning of a dark and cloudy day, when the duke was finally aroused by the noise and confusion attending the arrival of the Great Northern Express train at King's Cross Station, London.

He shook himself wide awake, adjusted his wrap, and sprang out of his coupe, while yet his servant was but just bestirring himself.

The first man he met in the station was Detective Setter.

"*How* is she?" eagerly inquired the traveller, hastening to meet the officer.

"She is perfectly well, and expresses herself as not only willing, but anxious to see your grace," replied the detective.

"*Not only willing!* that is a strange phrase, too! But I presume I shall understand it all when I see her. *Where* is she?" demanded the duke.

"At the house on Westminster Road. The address *was* Westminster, and not

Blackfriars Road."

"At the house on Westminster Road! Did you find her there?"

"I did your grace."

"But why, in the name of propriety, and good sense, does she not return home?"

"Your grace, she is at home," said the perplexed detective.

"Just now you told me that she was at the house on Westminster Road!" said the bewildered duke.

"Beg pardon, your grace, but the house on Westminster Road *is* her home. She has no other that I know of."

The duke stared at the detective a moment, and then hastily demanded:

"Who *are* you talking of?"

"Beg pardon again, your grace, but I am afraid there is some misunderstanding."

"*Who* are you talking about?"

"I am talking of the woman who came to the duchess just before she disappeared," answered the detective.

"Good Heaven!" exclaimed the duke, with such a look of deep disappointment that the detective hastened to deprecate his displeasure by saying:

"I am very sorry, your grace, that there should have been any misapprehension."

"You idiot!" were the words that arose spontaneously to the duke's lips; but they were not uttered. The "princely Hereward" habitually governed himself.

"Why did you not tell me in your telegram *who* was found?" he demanded.

"I certainly thought that your grace would have understood. In the telegram dispatched at nine o'clock yesterday morning, I told your grace that I had a clew to the woman who had called at Elmthorpe House on Tuesday. In the telegram sent at three in the afternoon, I said--'She is found.' I certainly thought your grace would understand that the woman to whom I had gained the clew was found. I grieve to know how much mistaken I was," sighed Mr. Setter.

"Ah! that accounts for everything. I never received that first telegram."

"Your grace never received it?"

"Certainly not."

"Then my messenger was false to his trust. I was so indiscreet as to send it to the office by a ticket porter, believing the fellow would do his duty faithfully, after having been paid in advance. The more fool I. I am certainly old enough to have known better!" said the detective, with a mortified air.

"Well Mr. Setter, it is useless to regret that mistake now. Be so good as to call a cab. We will go at once to Westminster Road and see this Mrs. Brown. What information has she given you?"

"None whatever, except this, which we knew before--that she visited the bride on the afternoon of the wedding day. She declines to tell *me* the nature of her business with the duchess; but says that she will explain it to you; she further denies all knowledge of the present abode of the duchess."

"Then we must lose no time in going to the woman," said the duke.

As he spoke, the cab which had been signalled by the detective drove up, and the cabman jumped down and opened the door.

The duke entered it and sat down on the back cushions.

His grace's servant, Kerr, came up to the window for orders.

"Take my luggage home to Elmthorpe House. Give my respects to Lady Belgrade, and say that I will join her ladyship this afternoon," said the duke.

The servant touched his hat and withdrew.

"To Number ----, Westminster Road," ordered Mr. Setter, as he mounted to the box-seat beside the cabman.

The latter started his horses at a good rate of speed, so that a drive of about forty minutes brought them to their destination.

The detective jumped down and opened the door, saying,

"Excuse me, your grace; but, I think, perhaps I ought to go in first to ensure you an interview with the woman?"

"By all means go in first, officer. I will remain here in the cab until you return to summon me," answered the duke.

Detective Setter went up to the door and knocked, and then waited a few seconds until the door was opened, and he was admitted by an unseen hand.

A few minutes elapsed, and then detective Setter reappeared, and came up to the cab and said:

"She will see you at once, early as it is, your grace, I do not know what in the world possesses the old woman; but she is chuckling in the most insane manner in the anticipation of meeting you 'face to face,' as she calls it."

"Well, we shall soon see," said the duke, as, with a resigned air, he followed Mr. Setter into the house.

The detective led him up stairs to the gaudy parlor which had once been Rose Cameron's sitting-room.

There was no one present; but the detective handed a chair to the duke, and begged him to sit down and wait for Mrs. Brown's appearance.

The duke threw himself into the chair, and gazed around him upon the garish scene, until a chamber door opened, and Mrs. Brown, in her Sunday's best suit, sailed in. The duke arose.

Mrs. Brown came on toward him, courtesying stiffly, and saying:

"Good morning to you, Mr. Scott! It is a many months since I have had the pleasure of seeing you in this house."

The duke was not so much amazed at this greeting as he might have been, had he not heard the astounding testimony of Rose Cameron. So he answered quietly:

"I do not think, madam, that you ever 'had the pleasure' of seeing me 'in this house' or, in fact, anywhere else. I have never seen *you* in my life before."

"Oh! oh! oh! here to the man! He would brazen it out to my very face!" exclaimed Mrs. Brown.

The duke started and flushed crimson as he stared at the woman.

"Oh, I am not afeard of you! Deuce a bit am I afeard of you! You may glare till your eyes drop out, but you'll not scare me! And you may be the Markiss of Arondelle and the Duke of Hereward, too, for aught I know, or care either! But you were just plain Mr. John Scott to me, and also to that poor, wronged lass whom you have betrayed into prison, if not unto death! And now, Mr. John Scott, as you wished to see me (and I can guess why you wished to see me,) and as I have no objection to see you, besides having something of importance to tell you, perhaps you will send that man off," said Mrs. Brown pointing to the detective.

"No. I prefer that Mr. Setter should stay here, and be a witness to all that passes between us," answered the duke.

"All right. It is no business of mine, and no *shame* of mine. Only I thought as you mightn't like a stranger to hear all your secrets, and I wish to spare your feelings," said the woman.

"I beg you will not consider my feelings in the least, madam," answered the duke, with a slight smile of amusement; "and I hope you will allow Mr. Setter to remain," he added.

"Oh, in course! *I* have no objection, if *you* have none."

"Pray go on and say what you have to say," urged the duke.

"Then, first of all, I have to tell you that I know why you have come here. You have come to inquire about Miss Salome Levison, the great banker's heiress."

"You are speaking of the Duchess of Hereward, madam," interrupted the duke, in a stern voice.

"No, I'm not. I am speaking of Miss Salome Levison. She is not the Duchess of Hereward. I don't know but one Duchess of Hereward, and *her you are ashamed to own*," spitefully added Mrs. Brown.

"You are a woman, aged and insane, and therefore entitled to our utmost indulgence," said the duke, putting the strongest control upon himself. "But tell me now, what was your business with the Lady of Lone, upon whom you called at Elmthorpe House on Tuesday afternoon?"

"I went from your true wife, whom you had betrayed into prison, to your false wife, to let her know what you were, and to tell her that there was but one step between herself and ruin!"

"Good Heaven! you did that!" exclaimed the duke, utterly thrown off his guard.

"Yes, I did! And I showed the young lady your real wife's marriage lines, all regularly signed and witnessed by the rector of St. Margaret's and the sexton, and the pew-opener! I did! And there were letters in your own handwriting, and photographs, the very print of you, which I took along with the marriage lines, to prove my words when I told her that you had been married for over a year, and had lived in my house with your wife all that time!"

"Heaven may forgive you for that great wrong, woman; but I never can! And-the lady believed you?"

"Of course she did! How could she help it, when she saw all the proofs? It almost killed her. Indeed, and I think it *did* quite craze her! But she saw her duty, and she had the courage to do it! She knew as she ought to leave you, before the false marriage could go any further. So she left you. I do really respect her for it!"

"In the name of Heaven, *where* did she go? Tell me that! Tell me where to find her, and I may be able to pardon the great wrong you have done us under some insane error," said the husband of the lost wife, striving to control his indignation.

"Indeed, then," exclaimed Mrs. Brown, defiantly, "I am not asking any pardon at all from you, Mr. Scott. It ain't likely as I'll want pardon from Heaven for doing my duty, much less from *you*, Mr. John Scott. Oh, yes! I know you are called the Duke of Hereward; and no doubt you are the Duke of Hereward; but I knew you as Mr. John Scott, and nobody else; and I knew a deal too much of you as *him*. But as to wanting your pardon--that's a good one!"

"Will you be good enough to tell me where my wife, the Duchess of Hereward, has gone?" demanded the duke, putting a strong curb upon his anger.

"*You* know where *she* is well enough. *She* is in the *trap* you set for her!" spitefully answered the woman.

In truth, the duke needed all his powers of self-control to enable him to reply calmly:

"I ask you to tell me where is the Lady of Lone, to whom you went on Tuesday afternoon, with a story which has driven her from her home, and driven her, perhaps, to madness, or to death. I charge you to tell me, where is she?"

"Ah! where is Miss Salome Levison, the heiress of Lone, you ask! Exactly! That is what you would give a great deal to know, wouldn't you! You want to follow and join her, and live with her abroad, because you have got a wife living in England. You're a noble duke, so you are! Well, if *this* is what the nobility are a coming to, the sooner them Republicans have it all their own way the better, I say!" exclaimed Mrs. Brown, throwing herself back in her chair and folding her arms.

Detective Setter here joined the Duke of Hereward, and deferentially drew him away to the other end of the room, and whispered:

"I beg your grace not to remain here, subjected to the insolence of this mad woman, whose every second word is treason or blasphemy, or worse, if anything can be worse. Leave me to deal with her. A very little more, and I shall arrest her on the grave charge of conspiracy."

"No, Setter, do nothing of the sort. Use no violence; utter no threats. *Now*, if ever--here, if anywhere--is a crisis, at which we must be not only 'wise as serpents, but **harmless** as doves,' if we would gain any information from this woman," answered Salome's husband, as he walked back and rejoined Mrs. Brown.

"Will you tell me, **on any terms**, where the Lady of Lone is to be found?" he inquired.

"Humph! I like that! Aren't you a sharp? You **can't** call her the duchess, and you **won't** call her Miss Levison, so you call her the Lady of Lone, anyway!" exclaimed Mrs. Brown, with a chuckling laugh.

"But, will you, **for any price**, tell me where she has gone?" repeated the duke.

"As to where Miss Salome Levison has gone, I would not tell you to save your life, even if I could. I could not tell you, even if I would. I left her sitting in her bed-chamber at Elmthorpe House, on that Tuesday afternoon after her false marriage. She was sitting clothed in her deep mourning travelling suit, as she had put on again for her father directly the wedding breakfast was over. She looked the very image of sorrow and despair. She did not tell me where she was going. I don't believe she even knew herself. There, that's all that I have got to tell you, even if you had the power to put me on the rack, as you used to have in the bad old times!" exclaimed Mrs. Brown, once more folding her arms and settling herself in her chair.

The Duke of Hereward walked toward the detective officer.

"There is nothing more to be learned from the woman, at present, Setter. We have already gained much, however, in the knowledge of the base calumny that drove the duchess from her home. It is a relief to be assured that she has not fallen among London thieves. She has probably gone abroad. You must inquire, discreetly, at the London Bridge Railway Stations, for a young lady, in deep mourning, travelling alone, who bought a first-class ticket, on Tuesday evening. There, Setter! There is a mere outline of instructions. You will fill it up as your discretion and experience may suggest," concluded the duke, as he drew on his gloves.

"I would suggest, your grace, that we go to St. Margaret's Old Church, where this strange marriage, in which they try to compromise you, is said to have taken place, and which is close by," said the detective.

"By all means, let us go there and look at the register," assented the duke.

They took leave of Mrs. Brown, and left the house.

Five minutes drive took them to Old St. Margaret's.

They were fortunate as to the time. The daily morning service was just over, and the curate who had officiated was still in the chancel.

The Duke of Hereward went in, and requested the young clergyman to favor him with a sight of the parish register.

The curate complied by inviting the two visitors to walk into the vestry.

He then placed two chairs at the green table, requested them to be seated, and laid before them the brass-bound volume recording the births, marriages and deaths of this populous, old parish.

The Duke of Hereward turned over the ponderous leaves until he came to the page he sought.

And there he found, duly registered, signed and witnessed, the marriage, by special license, of Archibald-Alexander-John Scott and Rose Cameron, both of Lone, Scotland.

"The mystery deepens," said the duke as he pointed to the register.

"It is incomprehensible," answered the detective.

"That is my name," added the duke.

"Some imposter must have assumed it," suggested the officer.

"Then the imposter, in taking my name, must have also taken my face and form, voice and manner, for though, upon my soul, I never married Rose Cameron, there are two honest women who are ready to swear that I did!" whispered the duke, with a humorous twinkle in his eyes; for there were moments when the absurdity of the situation overcame its gravity.

The duke then thanked the curate for his courtesy and left the church, attended by the detective.

"Where shall I tell the cabman to drive?" inquired Setter, as he held the door open after his employer had entered the cab.

"To Elmthorpe House, Kensington. And then, get in here, with me, if you please, Mr. Setter. I have something to say to you," answered his grace.

The detective gave the order and entered the cab.

The duke then made many suggestions, drawn from his own intimate knowledge of the tastes and habits of the duchess, to assist the detective in his search.

"You may safely leave the whole affair in my hands, sir. I will act with so much discretion that no one in London shall suspect that the Duchess of Hereward is missing. For the rest, I have no doubt that we shall soon find out the retreat of her grace. A young lady, dressed in elegant deep mourning, and travelling unattended, would be sure to have attracted attention and aroused curiosity, even in the confusion of a crowded railway station. We are safe to trace her, your grace," said Detective Setter, confidently.

CHAPTER XXVII.
IN THE CONVENT.

Salome was tenderly nursed by the nuns during the nine days in which her fever raged with unabated violence.

At the end of that time, having spent all its force, the fever went off, leaving her weak as a child, in mind as well as in body.

As soon as she was convalescent the abbess had her carefully removed from the infirmary in which she had lain ill, to a spacious chamber, with windows overlooking the convent garden--a gloomy outlook now, however, with its seared grass and withered foliage, shivering under the dreary November sky.

The room was very clean and very scantily furnished; the walls were whitewashed and the floor was painted gray. The two windows were shaded with plain white linen; the cot bedstead, which stood against the wall opposite the windows, was covered with a coarse, white, dimity spread.

Between the windows stood a small table, covered with a white cloth, and furnished with a white, earthen-ware basin and ewer. On each side of this table sat two wooden chairs, painted gray.

In one corner of the room stood a little altar, draped with white linen, and adorned with a crucifix, surrounded with small pictures of saints and angels.

In the opposite corner stood a small, porcelain stove, which barely served to temper the coldness of the air.

There were few articles of comfort, and none of luxury, in the room--a strip of gray carpet, laid down beside the bed, an easy-chair with soft, padded back, arms, and seat, covered with white dimity, drawn up to the window nearest the stove, and a footstool of gray tapestry on the floor before it. These comforts were allowed to none but invalids.

The abbess came in to see her every day.

One morning Salome said to her visitor:

"Mother, I have left this affair with the Duke of Hereward incomplete. I must complete it, that I may have peace."

"I do not understand you, my child," said the abbess, in some uneasiness.

"I have left him as in duty bound. I must write to him to let him know **why** I left him; but I must not let him know the place of my retreat. I think I heard you say that our father-director was going to Rome this week?"

"Yes, my child."

"Then I will write to the Duke of Hereward for the last time, and bid him an eternal farewell. I will not date my letter from any place; but I will give it to the father-director that he may post it from Rome. You shall read my letter before I close it, dear mother. And now, on these terms, will you let me have writing materials?"

"Certainly, my child. I will send them to you; or rather I will bring them," answered the meek lady-superior, as she arose and left the room.

In a very few minutes she returned with the required articles.

Salome wrote her letter, and then submitted it to the perusal of the abbess, who accorded it her full approval.

"Now, dear mother, if the father-director will take that with him and post it from Rome, all will be over between the Duke of Hereward and myself! We shall be dead to each other," said Salome, as the abbess took the letter and left the room.

Then the invalid sank back, exhausted, in her easy-chair.

In this easy-chair by the window, with her feet upon the footstool, Salome sat day after day of her convalescence; sometimes for hours together, with her hands clasped upon her lap, and her eyes fixed upon the floor, in a sort of stupor; sometimes with her sad gaze turned upon the sear garden, as she murmured to herself:

"Withered like my life!"

Some one among the nuns was always with her; but she took no notice of her companion, seeming quite unconscious of the sister's presence.

The abbess had taken care to have books of devotion laid upon her little table, but Salome never opened one of them.

Apathy, lethargy, like a moral death, had fallen upon her.

The story of her sorrows, known only to the abbess, to whom she had confided it on the eve of her illness, was never alluded to.

Salome seemed to have buried it in silence. The abbess feared to raise it from the dead.

Not one in the convent suspected the real circumstances of the case.

All the sisterhood knew Miss Salome Levison, the young English heiress, who had been educated within their walls; all knew that in leaving the convent, three years before she had declared her intention to return at the end of three years and take the vail. She had returned, according to her word, and no one was surprised. Her sickness they considered purely accidental. They had no knowledge of her marriage. She was to them still Miss Salome Levison, who had once been their pupil, and was now soon to be their sister.

No newspapers were taken in at the convent, or the nuns might have seen repeated notices of her approaching marriage before it took place, as well as a long account of the ceremony and the breakfast, after they had come off.

The abbess tried many gentle expedients to arouse Salome from her moral torpor, but all her efforts were fruitless.

Salome had once been an enthusiast in music, and a very accomplished performer on several instruments. Her favorite had always been the harp, and next to that the guitar.

She was not yet strong enough to play on the former, but she might very well manage the latter.

So the abbess caused a light and elegant little guitar to be placed in her room.

Salome never even noticed it; but sat with her eyes fixed on her clasped hands that lay on her lap.

So November and a good part of December passed, with very little change.

The abbess, whose rule was absolute in her own house, had most solemnly warned the whole sisterhood that they were not to speak of "Miss Levison's" presence in the convent to any visitor, or pupil, or any other person whatever, or to write of it to any correspondent. The nuns had obeyed their abbess so well, that not a whisper of Salome's presence in the house had been heard outside its walls.

At length Christmas drew near.

The academy was closed for the season, and the pupils all went home to spend their holidays.

After the departure of their young charges, the sisterhood were very busy in making preparations to celebrate the joyous anniversary of our Lord's birth.

There were so many delightful little duties to be done; the chapel to be decorated with evergreens and exotics; the shrines of the saints to be decked; extra dainties to be made for the sick in the Infirmary; presents to be got up for the aged men and women of the "Home" attached to the convent; entertaining books to be selected and inscribed with the names of the boys and girls of their Orphan Asylum; doll-babies to be dressed and toys to be chosen for the infants of their Foundling; and, finally, a great Christmas-tree to be mounted and decorated for the delight of the whole community within their walls.

The sisterhood took so much pleasure in all these preparations for Christmas, that it occurred to the abbess she might be able so far to interest her unhappy guest in the work as to arouse her from that fearful lethargy which seemed to be destroying both her mind and body.

Salome Levison, while she had been a pupil in the convent, had never performed any services for the charities of the community except by giving liberally from her ample means.

Gladly would she have ministered in person to the needs of old age, illness, or infancy; but for her to have done so would have been against the rules of the establishment. The pupils of the academy were not permitted to hold any intercourse whatever with the inmates of the charitable institutions of the convent. This was a concession to the prudence of parents, who feared all manner of contaminations from any communication between their children and such *miserables*.

The convent was so planned as to effect a complete separation between the academy and the asylums.

The buildings were erected around a hollow square. They measured a hundred feet on each side, and arose to a height of four stories.

In the centre of the front, or northern, face, stood the chapel, a beautiful little Gothic temple, surmounted by a steeple and a gilded cross; on each hand, in a line with the chapel, stood the buildings containing the cloisters, dormitories, and refectories of the nuns and novices.

On the east front stood the Foundling for abandoned infants; the Asylum for orphan boys and girls, and the Home for aged men and women.

On the south end were the offices, kitchens, laundries, store-houses, gas-house, and so forth, for the whole establishment.

Finally, on the west front, farthest removed from the asylums, were the academy buildings, containing school and class-rooms, dormitories and refectory for the accommodation of pupils.

It was in these west buildings that Salome had lived and learned during the years she had spent at the Convent of St. Rosalie. She had never entered any other part of the establishment except the chapel, and on the north front, which was reached by a long passage running with an angle from the school-hall to the chapel aisle.

The square courtyard within the enclosure of these buildings was paved with gray flag-stones, and adorned in the centre by a marble fountain. But no footstep ever crossed it except that of some lay sister occasionally sent from the cloisters to the office, on some household errand. So no opportunity was afforded of making the courtyard a place of meeting between the "young ladies" of the academy and the poor little children of the asylums.

The academy opened from its front upon its own gardens, lawns, shrubberies, and other pleasure-grounds, the resort of its pupils during their hours of recreation.

Thus Salome Levison, with all her school-mates, had been completely cut off from all intercourse with the objects of the convent's charity during the whole period of her residence at the academy, which, indeed, covered the greater portion of her young life.

Now, however, since her return to the convent, she had been domiciliated in the nun's house on the right of the chapel, and possessed, if she pleased to exercise it, the freedom of the establishment.

On the Saturday before Christmas (which would also come on Saturday that year) the abbess went into the room occupied by her invalid guest.

Salome was seated in the white easy-chair beside the window, and near the porcelain stove. She was dressed in a deep mourning wrapper of black bombazine, and an inside handkerchief and undersleeves of white linen. Her pallid face and plain hair, and the severe, funereal black and white of her surroundings, made a very ghastly picture altogether.

The Sister Francoise sat there in attendance on her.

The mother-superior dismissed the nun, took her vacated seat, and looked in the face of her guest.

Salome seemed utterly unconscious of the superior's presence. She sat with her hands clasped upon her lap and her eyes fixed upon the floor.

"Salome, my daughter, how is it with you?" softly inquired the abbess, taking one of the limp, thin hands within her own, and tenderly pressing it.

"I am the queen of sorrow, crowned and frozen on my desert throne," murmured the girl, in a trance-like abstraction.

"Salome, my child!" said the mother-superior, gazing anxiously into her stony face, whose eyes had never moved from their fixed stare; "Salome, my dear daughter, look at me."

"'I am the star of sorrow, pale and lonely in the wintry sky.'"

"My poor girl, what do you mean?"

"I read that somewhere, long ago,--oh, so long ago, when I was a happy child, and yet I wept then for that solitary mourner as I am not able to weep now for myself, though it suits me just as much," murmured Salome, in the same trance-like manner, still staring on the floor, as she continued:

"Yes, just as much, just as much, for--

"Never was lament begun By any mourner under sun That e'en it ended fit but one!"

"Salome, look at me, speak to me, my dear daughter," said the abbess, tenderly pressing her hand, and seeking to catch her fixed and staring eyes.

Salome slowly raised those woeful eyes to the lady's face, and asked:

"Mother, good mother, did you ever know any one in all your life so heavily stricken as I am?"

The abbess put her arms around the young girl and drew her head down upon her own pitying bosom, as she replied:

"Have I ever known one so heavily stricken as you? My child, I cannot tell. 'The heart knoweth its **own** bitterness,' and one cannot weigh the grief of another. Salome, you have been heavily smitten; but so have many others. Daughter! I never do speak of my own sorrows. They are past, and 'they come not back again.' But I think it might do you good to hear of them now. Child! like **you**, I never knew a mother's love; but there were three beings in the world whom I loved, as **you** love, with inordinate and idolatrous affection. They were my noble father, my only brother, and my affianced husband. Salome, in the Revolution of '48, my father was assassinated in the streets of Paris, as yours was in his chamber at Lone. My brother, true as steel to his sovereign, was guillotined as a traitor to the Republican party. Last, and hardest to bear, my affianced lover--he on whom my soul was stayed in all my troubles, as if any one weak mortal could be a lasting stay to another in her utmost need--my affianced lover, false to me as yours to you, was shot and killed in a duel by the lover, or husband, of a woman, for whom he had left his promised bride! Daughter, did I ever know any one who was so heavily stricken as yourself?" gravely inquired the abbess, laying her hand upon the bowed head of her guest.

"Oh, yes, good mother, you have," murmured the weeping girl, in a voice full of tears. "Your fate has been very like my own--you, like me, were motherless from your infancy; you, like me, spent your childhood and youth in this very convent school. Your father, like mine, met his death at the hands of an assassin; your lover, false as mine, abandoned you for a guilty love. Ah! your sorrows have been very like mine, only much heavier and harder to bear." And Salome drew the caressing hands of the abbess to her lips and kissed them over and over again, as she repeated, "Oh, yes, good mother, much heavier and harder to bear than mine."

"I do not know that, my daughter; but I do know, if I had set myself down a grieving egotist, to brood over my own individual troubles, in a world full of troubles, needing ministrations, I should have lost my reason, if not my soul."

"But you came back to your convent, as I have come, for refuge," said Salome.

"Yes, I came here to give my life to the Lord; not in idle, selfish prayers and meditations for my own soul's sake; no, but in an active, useful life of work. And I have found deep peace, deep joy. So will you, my beloved child, if you take the same way. But you must begin by shutting the doors of your soul against the thoughts of your sorrow, and especially by banishing the image of your false and guilty lover every time it presents itself to your mind."

"Oh, mother! mother! I loved him so! I loved him so!" cried Salome, bursting into a paroxysm of sobs and tears, the first tears she had been able to shed over her awful sorrows.

The abbess was glad to see them; they broke up the fatal apathy as a storm disperses malaria. She gathered the weeping girl to her bosom, and let her sob and cry there to her heart's content.

When the gust of grief had spent itself, Salome lifted her head and dried her eyes, murmuring:

"Yes, I loved him! I loved him! but it is past! it is past! I must forget him, henceforth and forever!"

"Yes, daughter, you must forget him, for to remember him would be a grievous sin. And you must forgive him, though he meditated against you the deepest wrong," said the abbess, solemnly.

"I will try to forgive the wrong-doer and forget the wrong, but oh! mother, mother, it will be very hard to overlive it! Oh, I hope, I hope, if it be Heaven's will, that I shall not have to live very long," said Salome, with a heavy sigh.

"That is the way I felt in the first bitterness of my sorrow: but the feeling passed away in duty-doing. And now, although I know that in the next life every need and aspiration of the soul will be fulfilled, yet I find such peace and joy here, that I am willing, yes and glad, to live in this world as long as my Lord has any work for me to do in his vineyard."

"Tell me what I ought to do, and I will try to do it," said Salome, with another deep sigh; for her very breathing was sighing now.

"You know that this is Saturday, the last Saturday before Christmas," said the abbess.

"Is it? I did not know, I have taken no note of time."

"And to-morrow is Sunday, the last Sunday before Christmas."

"Yes, of course."

"Daughter, you have not been to chapel once since your arrival among us."

"Ah, no! I came from the infirmary here, and I have not left this room to go anywhere since!" sighed Salome.

"That is not because you are not able to do so, but because you are not willing. You have allowed yourself to sink into a sinful and dangerous lethargy of mind and body in which you have brooded morbidly over your afflictions. You must do so no longer. You must rouse yourself from this moment. You must go with us to-night to vespers. To-morrow morning you will attend high mass. A fellow-countryman of yours, Father F----, an Oratorian priest from Norwood, England, will preach. He will do you good. Since the days of St. John, the beloved disciple, no wiser, more loving, or more eloquent soul ever spoke to sinners," said the abbess.

"But--coming from England!--If he should recognize me!" exclaimed Salome.

"Why, do you know him?"

"Oh, no, not at all; but then there are sometimes people with whom we have no sort of acquaintance, who yet know us by sight from seeing us in public places, or meeting us on public occasions."

"That is very true, my child; but you need have no fear of being recognized by the officiating priest to-morrow, whoever he may be, for you will sit with us behind the screen."

"Thanks, dear mother; I will go with you this very evening."

"You are a good and obedient child. Receive my benediction," said the mother-superior, rising.

Salome bent her head, and the abbess solemnly blessed her, and then withdrew from the room.

CHAPTER XXVIII.
THE SOUL'S STRUGGLE.

That same evening, while the vesper bells were ringing, Salome dressed herself, and, leaning on the arm of the mother-superior headed the procession of the sisterhood as they marched to the chapel and took their seats in the recess behind the screen, which was so cunningly devised, that, while it afforded the nuns a full view of the altar, the priests, the interior of the pews and the whole congregation, it effectually concealed the forms and faces of the sisterhood seated within it.

Father Francois, the confessor of the convent, officiated at the altar.

A rustic congregation of the faithful filled the pews in the body of the church. They came from farm-houses and villages in the immediate neighborhood of the convent.

The vesper hymn was raised by the nuns.

Salome joined in singing it. She had a rich, sweet, clear soprano voice.

Many were the heads in the rustic assemblage that turned to listen to the new singer in the nuns' choir.

Salome saw them, and shrank back as if she herself could have been seen, though she was quite invisible to them, for the screen, which was transparent to her eyes, was impenetrable to theirs. She remembered this, at length, and recovered her composure.

The sweet vesper service soothed her soul, and when it was over, and the benediction was given, the "peace that passeth all understanding" descended upon her troubled spirit.

She left the chapel, leaning on the mother-superior's arm.

When she reached her room door she kissed the lady's hand in bidding her good-night.

"This has done you good, my daughter," said the abbess, gently.

"It has done me good. Thanks for your wise counsel, holy mother. I will follow it still. I will go again tomorrow. Bless me, my mother," said Salome, bowing her head before the abbess, who blessed her again, and then softly withdrew.

Salome entered her room and retired to rest, and slept more calmly than she had done for many days and nights.

She arose on Sunday morning refreshed; but it seemed as if her stony apathy had passed off, only to leave her more keenly sensitive to her cause of grief; for as she dressed herself, a flood of tender memories overflowed her soul, and she threw herself, weeping freely, on her cot.

In this condition she was found by the abbess, who was pleased to see her weep, knowing that the keenness of sorrow is much softened by tears.

She sat down in silence by the cot, and waited until the paroxysm was past.

"Good mother, I could not help it," said Salome, with a last convulsive sob, as she wiped her eyes, and arose.

"Nor did I wish you to do so. Thank the Lord for the gift of tears. Have you had breakfast, my daughter?"

"Yes, dear mother. Sister Francoise brought it to me before I was up. This is the last time I will allow myself such an indulgence. To-morrow morning, if you will permit me, I will join you in the refectory."

"I am rejoiced to hear you say so my child. Your recovery depends much upon yourself. Every exertion that you make helps it forward. And now I came to tell you that in ten minutes we shall go on to the chapel. Will you be ready to accompany us?"

"Yes, dear mother, I will come on and join you almost immediately," said Salome standing up and shaking down her black robe into shape.

The abbess softly slipped out of the room and left the guest to complete her toilet.

In a few minutes Salome passed out and joined the procession of nuns to the chapel.

As soon as they were seated in the screened choir, Salome looked through the screen, to see if the English priest was at the altar. He was not there yet; but the body of the little chapel was filled with an expectant crowd of small country gentry, farmers and laborers with their families, all drawn together by the fame of the great Oratorian.

Presently the procession entered--six boys, in white surplices, preceding a pale, thin, intellectual-looking young man in priestly robes.

The priest took his place before the altar, the boys kneeling on his right and left, and the solemn celebration of the high mass was begun.

The nuns sang well within their screened choir; but the new soprano voice that sang the solos, and rose elastic, sweet and clear, soaring to the heavens in the *Gloria in Excelsis*, seemed to carry all the worshipers with it.

"Who is she?" inquired one of another, in hushed whispers, when the divine anthem had sunk into silence.

"Who is she?"

No one in the congregation could tell; but many surmised that she must be some young postulant of St. Rosalie, just beginning, or about to begin, her novitiate.

At length the pale priest passed into the pulpit, and, amid a breathless silence of expectancy, gave out his text:

"GOD IS LOVE."

A truth revealed to us by the Divine Saviour, and confirmed to our hearts by the teachings of His Holy Spirit.

The preacher spoke of the divine love, "never enough believed, or known, or asked," yet the source of all our life, light and joy; he spoke of human love, a derivative from the divine, in all its manifestations of family affection, social friendship, charity to the needy, forgiveness of enemies.

And while he spoke of love, "the greatest good in the world," his tones were full, sweet, deep and tender, his pale face radiant, his manner affectionate, persuasive, winning.

He was listened to with rapt attention, and even when he had brought his sermon to a close, and his eloquent voice had ceased, his hearers still, for a few moments, sat motionless under the spell he had wrought upon them.

As soon as the benediction had been pronounced, the abbess arose from her seat in the choir, drew the arm of her still feeble guest within her own, and, followed by her nuns, walking slowly in pairs, left the choir.

She took Salome to the door of her room in perfect silence, and would have left her there but that the girl stopped her by saying:

"Holy mother, I wish to speak to you, if you can give me a few minutes, before we go to the refectory."

"Surely, my daughter," answered the abbess, kindly, as she followed her guest into the chamber.

"Sit down in the easy-chair, good mother," said Salome, drawing the soft, white-cushioned seat toward her.

"No, sit you there, poor child," answered the abbess, taking her guest kindly and seating her in the easy-chair. "I shall be well enough here," she added, as she sat down on one of the painted, wooden seats. "Now, tell me what you wish to say, daughter," she concluded.

"Dear mother, I have been very deeply interested in Father F. this morning."

"You should be interested in the message only, not in the messenger, my child," gravely replied the elder lady.

"In the message alone I believe I was most concerned; but the message was most eloquently delivered by the messenger," said Salome, as her pale cheeks flushed.

"Well, my daughter, go on in what you were about to say."

"Holy mother, that message, so earnestly spoken, has moved me to greater diligence in what I have purposed to do. You know that I have intended to take the vail in this convent, and devote my life and my fortune to good works."

"Yes, my child, I know that such has been your pious purpose. What then?"

"I wish to use all diligence in carrying out that purpose. I wish to enter upon my novitiate immediately."

"My good daughter, far be it from me to throw any stumbling-block in the way of such praise-worthy intentions; but the strict rules of our order require that a postulant should remain in the convent twelve calendar months, to test her vocation, before she is suffered to bind herself by any vows," said the abbess, very gravely.

"As if *my* vocation had not been sufficiently tested," sighed Salome.

"It may have been so, my daughter. This probation may not be necessary in your case, yet we can make no exception to our rules even in your favor. You will, therefore, if you wish, remain with us for one year, unfettered by any vows. At the end of this year of probation, if you shall still desire to do so, you may be permitted to take the white vail and commence your novitiate. In the meantime you need not, and ought not, to be idle. You may be as zealous and diligent in good works while a postulant as you possibly could be as a white-vailed novice or a black-vailed nun."

"Show me how I may be so, holy mother, and I will bless you," exclaimed Salome.

"I will very gladly be your guide, my child. Listen, Salome. Hitherto, you have been very charitable in giving alms. You have given liberally of your means; but you have never yet given your personal services to the poor and needy. That was not our Lord's way, whose servants we are. He gave alms, indeed, and he performed miracles to supply them, as in the case of the loaves and fishes; but most of all, better than all, He gave His personal ministrations; He taught the ignorant; He anointed the eyes of the blind; ***He laid His hands on the leper***; He shrank from no personal contact with disease, however loathsome; distress, however ignominious; nor must we, His children, do so. We must give our personal services to the poor."

"Tell me what to do, and how to do it, good mother, and I will gladly obey your instructions. Tell me, for I am so very ignorant."

"To-morrow, the Monday before Christmas, you may go with me the rounds of our asylums and schools, and see for yourself destitute old age, destitute childhood and abandoned infancy; and you may choose your work among these poor, needy, helpless ones," said the abbess, gravely.

"And are laborers wanted in that vineyard, mother?"

"Always."

"Then here am I, for one, poor one. I am longing to go to work."

"At first your work shall be a very bright and pleasant labor, dear child. This is the joyous week of preparation for the glad, Christmas festival. This week we are all, young and old, engaged in the delightful recreations of charity. Our Lord Himself, who, in His Divine benignity, blessed the marriage feast of Cana with a miracle, smiles on our recreations of charity, which with us just now consist in the preparation of Christmas gifts to gladden the hearts of our poor these Christmas times. To-morrow, if you please, I will take you to our work-rooms, where you may choose your own task."

"Oh, how willingly I will do that!" said Salome, earnestly.

A bell had been ringing for a few moments; and so the abbess arose and said:

"That is the dinner-bell. You promised to join us in the refectory, and I think it is best you should do so, my daughter."

"I will follow your counsels in everything, holy mother," answered Salome, sweetly, as she arose and put her hand on the offered arm of her friend.

The abbess led her protegee down a long passage and deep flights of stairs to the refectory, where, at each side of a very long table, running down the length of the room, stood about fifty nuns waiting for their mother-superior.

The abbess gave her guest a seat next to her own, then crossed herself and sat down.

The nuns all made the sign of the cross upon their breasts, and seated themselves at the table.

This was the first occasion upon which Salome sat down at the nuns' table; but it was not the last, for from this day she regularly appeared there, and, though she was given to frequent and violent fits of weeping, her health and spirits steadily improved under the regimen of the abbess.

On Monday morning the lady-superior took Salome through all the asylums on the east side of the convent.

They went first into the aged men's home, where, in a large, clean, well-warmed and well-lighted hall, furnished with arm-chairs, tables, and many plain and cheap conveniences, were gathered about thirty gray-haired or bald-headed patriarchs, whose ages ranged from seventy to a hundred years. Yet not one of them was idle. They were all engaged in plaiting chip-mats, baskets, hampers and other useful articles that could be made out of reeds or cane. The oldest man among them, a centenarian, was employed in plaiting straw for hats.

"They look very happy and busy," said Salome, after she had responded to their respectful nods and smiles of welcome.

"Yes, and they nearly half pay expenses by their handicrafts. Even they, aged and infirm as they are, can half support themselves if they have only shelter, protection and guidance."

"And there seems to be no sick among them," said Salome.

"Ah, yes," answered the abbess, gravely, "there are five in the infirmary connected with this home; but we will not go there now. Let us pass on to the aged women's home."

They entered the next house, where, in a large, warm, light room, plainly furnished, about twenty old women, from sixty to ninety years of age, were collected. They were neatly dressed in gray stuff gowns, white aprons, white kerchiefs, and white Normandy caps. And all were busy--some knitting, some sewing, some tatting.

They bowed and smiled a welcome to the visitor, who responded in the same manner.

"These, also, half support themselves by their work," said the abbess; "but the proportion of sick among them is greater than among the men. There are ten in the infirmary."

They went next to the orphan boys' asylum, where fifty male children of ages from three to twelve years were lodged, fed, clothed, and educated.

"What becomes of these when they leave here?" inquired Salome.

"We send them out as apprentices to learn trades; and we find homes for them," answered the abbess.

"Can you always find good homes and masters for them?"

"Yes, always. We do it through the secular clergy. Now let us go into the girls' asylum," said the abbess, leading the way to the next institution.

The orphan girls' asylum was, in many respects, similar to the boys' home.

"Do you wish to know what becomes of these, when they leave here?" inquired the abbess, anticipating the question of her companion. "I will tell you. The greater number of them are sent out to service as cooks, chambermaids, seamstresses, or nursery governesses. Some few, who show unusual intelligence, are educated for teachers. If any one among their number evinces talent for any particular art, she is trained in that art. My child, we have sent out more than one artist from our orphan girls' asylum," said the abbess.

"How much good you do!" exclaimed Salome.

"Let us go into the Foundling," said the mother-superior, leading the way to the last house of the eastern row of buildings.

Ah! here was a sight sorrowful enough to make the "angels weep!"

The abbess led her companion into a long room, clean, warm, light and airy, with about thirty narrow little cots, arranged in two rows against the walls, fifteen on each side, with a long passage between them. About half a dozen of these cots were empty. On the others lay about twenty-four of the most pitiable of all our Lord's poor--young infants abandoned by their unnatural parents. All these were under twelve months old, and were pale, thin, and famished-looking. Some were sleeping, and seemingly, ah! so aged and care-worn in their sleep; some were clasping nursery-bottles in their skeleton hands, and sucking away for dear life; one little miserable was wailing in restless pain, and sending its anguished eyes around in appealing looks for relief.

Four women of the sisterhood were on duty here, and each one sat with a pining infant on her lap, while there was no one to attend to the wants of that wailing little sufferer on the bed.

"Oh, merciful Father in Heaven! what a sight!" cried Salome, overcome with compassionate sorrow.

"Yes, it is piteous! most piteous!" said the mother-superior, in a mournful tone. "We do the very best we can for these poor, deserted babes; but young infants, bereft of their mother's milk, which is their life, and of their mother's tender love and intuitive care, suffer more than any of us can estimate, and are almost sure to perish, out of *this* life, at least. With all our care and pains, more than two-thirds of them die."

"Is there no help for this?" sadly inquired the visitor.

"No help within ourselves. But the peasant women in our neighborhood have Christian spirits and tender hearts. When any one among them loses her sucking child, she comes to us and asks for one of our motherless babes. We select the most needing of them and give it to her, and the nurse child has then a chance for its life;

but even then, if it lives, it is because some other child has died and made room for it."

"Oh, it is piteous! it is piteous, beyond all words to express! Destitute child-hood, destitute old age, are both sorrowful enough, Heaven knows! But they have power to make their sufferings known, and to ask for help! ***But destitute infancy!*** Oh! look here! look here! Can anything on earth be so pathetic as this?

"They are so innocent; they have not brought their evils on themselves. They are so helpless! They have not even words to tell their pain, or ask for relief! Mother! You said that I might choose my work! I have chosen it. It is here. And I begin it from this moment," said Salome.

And she threw off her hat and cloak, and drew her gloves and cast them all on a chair, and went and took up the wailing infant from the cot.

The abbess sat down and watched her.

She soothed the baby's plaints upon her bosom as she walked it, up and down the floor, singing a sweet, nursery song in a low and tender voice, until it fell asleep. Then she came and laid it sleeping on its cot.

"My dear daughter," said the abbess, gravely, "before you select this field of duty, I must warn you that it is, and it ***must needs*** be, of all charitable administrations, the most laborious and trying."

"It may be so; but it is also the most divine," said Salome, with a grave, sweet smile. "Listen, dear mother. I know not how it is, but--with all its pathos--the sphere of this room is heavenly. And while I held that baby to my bosom and soothed it to sleep, its little, soft form seemed to draw all the fever and soreness from my own aching heart as well. Here is my earthly work, dear mother! Nay, rather, here is my heavenly mission and consolation. Leave me here."

The mother-superior took the votaress at her word, and left her then and there.

In the course of the same day a small closet, communicating with the infants' dormitory, was fitted up as a sleeping berth for Salome, and her few personal effects were conveyed from the convent and arranged within her new dwelling.

Salome had not mistaken her vocation. To serve these forsaken and suffering children was to her a labor of love; to relieve them, a work of joy.

She never left her charge, except to go to chapel, or to her meals, which she took at the nuns' table, in their refectory.

On Christmas Eve, as she returned from dinner, Sister Francoise invited her to look into the work-room and see the Christmas presents in process of preparation.

To please the kind sister, she followed her into a long hall, furnished with little tables, at each of which sat two or three of the nuns at work.

As Salome, with her conductor, walked down the room, she saw that on one table was a pile of children's illustrated books of great variety to suit little ones, from three years old to thirteen. The two nuns seated at the table were busy writing in the books the names of those for whom they were intended.

Another table was piled with woolen scarfs, socks, gloves, and night-caps for the aged men and women, which the two nuns seated there were employed in rolling up into separate little parcels, and labeling with the names of the intended recipients.

Still another, and a longer table, was bright and gay with party-colored scraps of silk, satin, velvet, ribbon, muslin, lace and linen, with which half a dozen young nuns seated there were cheerfully engaged in making dresses for a basket full of dolls, for the Christmas gifts to the infants.

The blooming young nun Felecitie presided at this table. Seeing Salome approach with Sister Francoise, she accosted her:

"Our holy mother told us that you would come in and help us dress these dolls."

"And so I would have done, only I found some living and suffering dolls to dress and feed," said Salome, smiling.

"Yes, I know, the babies of the Foundling. Well, we are dressing these dolls for your babies," said the smiling sister.

"But do you suppose my tiny little ones will care for dolls?" inquired Salome.

"Be sure they will; from six months old, up, boys or girls, sick or well, babies will love dolls. I have seen a sick baby hug her doll, just as I have seen a sick mother clasp her child," answered the sister.

"These are the recreations of charity the holy mother told me of," said Salome, as she passed out of the work-room and went back to her own sphere of duty.

On Christmas morning after matins, the Christmas gifts were distributed in every one of the asylums, and every inmate was made happy by an appropriate present.

At ten o'clock high mass was celebrated in the chapel of the convent, and all the sisterhood assembled in their screened choir.

Three priests in their sacerdotal robes, and a dozen boys in white surplices, were expected to serve at the altar. The chapel was profusely decorated with holly, and the shrines were dressed with flowers. The pews were filled with a congregation of a rather better social position than usually assembled there in the convent chapel.

The services had not yet commenced. Salome bent forward with all the interest and curiosity of a recluse, to look, for a moment, upon the strangers.

She gave but one glance through the screen, and then suddenly, with a low cry, she sank back upon her seat.

"What is the matter, my daughter? Are you ill?" inquired the mother-superior, in a whisper.

Salome lifted up a face ashen pale with dismay, and gasped:

"I have seen him! I have seen him! He is there--there in the congregation below!"

"Who?" inquired the abbess, in vague alarm.

"My husband?--yet, no; oh, Heaven! not my husband, but the Duke of Hereward!"

CHAPTER XXIX.
THE STRANGER IN THE CHAPEL.

"The Duke of Hereward in the congregation?" echoed the abbess, with a troubled look.

"Yes, there in the middle aisle, in the third pew from the altar," replied Salome, in trembling tones.

"No matter. *You* have nothing to fear, my daughter; you will be protected. *He* has everything to fear; he is a felon before the law, and he may be prosecuted. Compose yourself, my child, and give your mind to heavenly subjects. See, the priest is coming in," murmured the abbess, who immediately crossed herself, and lowered her eyes in devotion.

Salome, though trembling in every limb, and feeling faint, almost to falling, followed the mother-superior's example, and tried to concentrate her mind in worship.

The solemn procession of the service entered the chancel--the priests in their sacerdotal vestments, the boys in their white robes. The officiating priest took his station before the altar, with his assistants on each side. And the impressive celebration of the high mass commenced.

But, ah! Salome could not confine her attention to the service! Her eyes, guard them carefully as she might, would wander from her missal toward the stalwart form and stately head of the stranger in that third pew front; her thoughts would wander back to the past, forth to the future, or, if they stayed upon the present at all, it was but in connection with that stranger.

Father F----, the great English priest, preached the sermon, from the text: "Glory to God in the highest, and on earth peace, good will to men." He preached with all the force, fervor and eloquence inspired by the Divine words, and he was heard with rapt attention by all the cloistered nuns and all the common congregation--by all within the sound of his voice, perhaps, except one--the most sorrowful one on that glad day. Salome tried in vain to follow the golden thread of his discourse.

But how little she was able to do, may be known from the deep sigh of relief she heaved when it was all over.

As soon as the benediction was pronounced, the nuns arose to leave their screened choir, and the congregation got up to go out from the chapel.

Salome lingered behind the sisterhood, and watched the handsome stranger in the third pew front--a stranger to every one present except herself.

He also lingered behind all his companions, and turned and looked intently up into the screened choir.

Salome saw his full face for the first time since his appearance there--and she saw that it was deadly, ghastly pale, with white lips and glassy eyes. He gazed into the screened choir as into vacancy.

Salome knew that he could see nothing there, yet she shrank back and stood in the deepest shadow, until she saw him pick up his hat and glide from the chapel, the last man that went out.

"Ah, what could have changed him so?" she thought--"love, fear, remorse--what?"

He had nothing to fear from her. If no one should take vengeance on him until she should do so, then would he go unpunished to his grave, and his sin would never have found him out in this world. Nay, sooner than to have hurt him in life, liberty, honor, or estate, she, herself, would have borne the penalty of all his crimes. Yet of those crimes what an unspeakable horror she had, though for the criminal what an unutterable pity--what an undying love.

While she stood there, gazing through the choir-screen upon the spot whence the stranger had disappeared, her bosom, torn by these conflicting passions of horror, pity, love, she felt a soft touch on her shoulder, and turning, saw the mother-superior at her side.

"My daughter, why do you loiter here?" she tenderly inquired.

Salome's pale face flushed, as she replied:

"Oh, mother, I was watching him until he left the church."

"My daughter, it was a deadly sin to do so!" gravely replied the abbess.

"He could not see me, mother," sighed Salome, in a tremulous voice.

"That was well. Come now to your own room, daughter, and do not tremble so. You have nothing to fear, except from your own weak and sinful nature," said the abbess, as she drew the girl's arm within her own and led her from the choir.

"Am I so weak and sinful, mother?" inquired Salome, after a silence which had lasted until the two had reached the door of the Infants' Asylum, where Salome now lodged.

"As every human being is! and especially as every woman is in all affairs of the heart," gravely returned the abbess.

"Can you spare me a few minutes, mother? Will you come in and let me talk to you a little while? Have you time? I want to talk to you. Oh! I wish we had mother-confessors for women--for girls, I mean, instead of father-confessors. Can you come in and let me talk to you, mother, for a little while?"

"Surely, daughter," said the abbess, gently as with her own hand she opened the door and led her votaress into the room.

Salome offered the one chair to the lady-superior, and then took the foot-stool at her feet, and laid her head upon her knees.

"Now speak to me freely, child. Tell me what you wish and how I can help you," said the abbess, kindly.

"Oh, mother! mother! I wish to be rid of the sin of loving him, for I love him still. In spite of all, I love him still!" exclaimed Salome, breaking down in a passion of tears and sobs.

The abbess laid her hands upon the bowed young head, and kept them so in silence until the storm of grief had passed. Then she said:

"Child you must fast and pray, and so combat the 'inordinate and sinful affections of the flesh.' Bethink you what you do in suffering them. You make an idol of that monster of iniquity who was an accomplice in the murder of your father--"

Salome uttered a low cry, and hid her face in her hands. The abbess went on steadily, almost pitilessly:

"A man who, having already a living wife, of whom he had grown tired and ashamed, married you, and so would have ruined you in soul and body."

Salome groaned deeply, and then suddenly broke forth in passionate exclamations:

"I know it! I know it? I know it from the evidence of my own senses, no less than from the testimony of others! I *know* it, but I cannot *feel it*, mother! I cannot feel it? My *mind* adjudges him *guilty*; my *mind condemns* him upon unquestionable proof; but my *heart* holds him *guiltless*; in the face of all the proofs, my *heart acquits* him! I *know* him to be a criminal; but I *feel* him to be one of the greatest, best and noblest of mankind! In spite of all I have heard and seen with my own ears and eyes, corroborated by the testimony of others--in spite of everything past, I *feel*, I *feel* that if he should now come and take my hand in his, and whisper to me, I should believe all that he might tell me, and go with him whithersoever he might choose to lead me! Mother, *save me from myself*!"

The abbess laid her hands again upon the throbbing head that lay on her lap, as she answered, mournfully:

"Said I not that you have nothing to fear except from your weak and sinful self. Child, you have nothing else on earth to dread. You are to be protected from yourself alone."

"And from *him*! Oh, mother, keep the great temptation from me!"

"He shall be kept from you, if, indeed, he should presume to seek you here," said the abbess.

"He will seek me, mother! He came to seek me, and for nothing else. He has by some means found out my retreat, and he has come to seek me! Be sure that he will present himself here to-morrow, if not to-day."

"In that case, we shall know how to deal with him, even though he is the Duke of Hereward; for he has, and can have, no lawful claim on you. So far from that, he is in deadly danger from you. He is liable to prosecution by you; for you are not his wife; you are only a lady whom he entrapped by a felonious marriage ceremony, and sought to ruin. It is amazing," added the abbess, reflectively, "that a nobleman of his exalted rank and illustrious fame should have stooped *so* low as to stain his honor with so deep a crime, and to risk the infamy and destruction its discovery must have brought upon him."

"It is amazing and incredible! That is why, in the face of the evidence of my own eyes and ears, the testimony of other eye and ear witnesses, and of my own certain knowledge, based upon proof as sure as ever formed the foundation of any knowledge, I still feel in my heart of heart that he is guiltless, stainless, noble, pure and true as the prince of noblemen should be," sighed Salome, adding word upon word of eulogy, as if she could not say enough.

"In the face of all positive proof, and of the convictions of your judgment, your *heart* tells you that this criminal is innocent," said the abbess, incisively.

"In the face of all, my heart assures me that he is pure, true, and noble!" exclaimed Salome.

"Do you believe your heart?" gravely inquired the elder lady.

"No; for is it not written: 'The heart is deceitful, and desperately wicked.' No, I do not believe my weak and sinful heart, which I know would betray me into the hands of my lover, if I should be so unfortunate as to meet him."

"You shall not meet him; you shall be saved from him," answered the abbess.

At that moment a bell was heard to ring throughout the building.

"That calls us to the refectory--to our happy Christmas festival. Come, my daughter," said the lady, rising.

"I cannot go! Oh, indeed I cannot go, mother. I am utterly unnerved by what has happened. I hope you will pardon and excuse me," pleaded Salome.

"What! Will you not join us at our Christmas feast?" kindly persisted the abbess.

"Indeed, it is impossible! I will rest on my cot for a few minutes, and then I will go and take my poor little Marie Perdue on my bosom and rock her to sleep. I hear her fretting now; and when I hush her cries, she also soothes my heartache."

"I will send you something; and I will come to you, before vespers," said the abbess, kindly, as she glided away from the room.

Salome lay alone on the cot, with closed eyes and folded hands, praying for light to see her duty and strength to do it.

She expected, in answer to her earnest prayers, that scales should fall from her eyes, and impressions pass from her heart, and that she should see her love in monstrous shape and colors, and be able to thrust him from her heart. Instead of which, she saw him purer, truer, nobler, than ever before. With this perception came a sweet, strange peace and trust which she could not comprehend, and did not wish to cast off.

She arose and went into the infants' dormitory, and took up the youngest and feeblest of the babes--the one which, on her very first visit, had so appealed to her sympathies, and which she had adopted as her own.

This child, like many others in the asylum, had no known story.

A few days before Christmas, late in the evening, a bell had been rung at the main door of the Infants' Asylum.

The portress who answered it found there a basket containing an infant a few weeks old. It was cleanly dressed and warmly wrapped up in flannel; but it had no scrap of writing, no name, nor mark upon its clothing by which it might ever be identified.

The portress took it into the dormitory, where it was tenderly received and cared for by the sisters on duty there.

The case was too common a one to excite more than a passing interest.

On the next day after the arrival of the infant, it happened that the mother-superior brought Salome there on her first visit, when the misery of the motherless and forsaken infant so moved the sympathies of the young lady that she immediately took it to her own bosom.

Subsequently, since she had devoted herself to the care of these deserted babies, she took an especial interest in this youngest and most helpless of their number.

She named it Marie Perdue, and stood godmother at its baptism.

It lay in her arms often during the day, and slept at her bosom during the night. It had grown to know its nurse, and to recognize her presence and caresses by those soft, low sounds, half cooing and half complaining, with which very young babes first try to utter their emotions or their wants.

Now, as she took little Marie Perdue from the cot, the child greeted her with sweet smiles and soft coos, and nestled lovingly to her bosom. And peace deepened in Salome's heart.

She sat down in a low nursing-chair, fed the child with warm milk and water until it was satisfied, and then rocked it and sang to it in a low, melodious voice, until it fell asleep.

She was still rocking and singing when the rosy-cheeked and cheery young Sister Felecitie came in.

"Our holy mother was going to send your dinner in here, Miss Levison; but I think it must be so dismal to eat one's dinner alone on Christmas day, so I pleaded to be allowed to plead with *you* that you will come and dine with us young sisters at the second table, which is just as good as the first, I assure you, only it is served an hour later. Will you come? Say yes!" urged the merry and kind-hearted girl.

"I will come, thank you; though I did too moodily decline the invitation of the abbess," said Salome, rising and placing her sleeping charge upon its little cot.

"Now! what did I tell you about the children and the dolls! Look there!" gleefully exclaimed Sister Felecitie, pointing to a row of cots where about a dozen infants lay asleep, clasping their dolls tightly.

"Yes, the tiny mimic mothers really do love their doll babies," Salome confessed with a smile.

As they went out of the dormitory they passed into the children's day-room, where about twenty infants, from one to two years old, were at play--some sitting on mats or creeping on all fours, because they could not yet stand; some walking around chairs and holding on to support themselves; and some running here and there, in full possession of the use of their limbs.

All rejoiced in the possession of little dolls.

"Look at them!" exclaimed Sister Felecitie, gleefully.

"We tried the least little ones with other toys: but, bless you, nothing else pleases them so well as dolls. We once tried the little yearlings with rattles, which we thought, it being noisy nuisances, would please them better; but save us! If any one doubts the doctrine of original sin and total depravity, they should have seen the three year-old babies fling down their rattles in a passion and go for the other babies' dolls, to seize and take them by force and violence; and the corresponding rage and resistance of the latter."

"All that was very natural," said Salome, with a smile.

"Oh, yes, natural, and perhaps something else too, beginning with a 'd.' They call children 'little angels.' Yes. I know they are, when they are sound asleep," exclaimed the sister, laughing.

"If they are not angels, they have angels with them. I feel they have, for when I am in their sphere, I possess my soul in peace."

As the young lady said this, the children noticed her presence for the first time, and all who could walk ran to her, clustered around her and thrust their dolls upon her, for inspection and approval.

All this Salome bestowed freely with many caresses and gentle, playful words.

Then the children sitting on the mats reached out their dolls at arm's-length, and screamed to have them noticed.

Salome made her way to these little sitters, while all the other children, clinging to her skirt, attended her, impeding her progress.

It was a great confusion.

The merry little sister laughed aloud.

"Now!" she said, gayly. "You are in their sphere, do you possess your soul in peace?"

"Something even better. My soul goes out to them, delighting in their innocent delight!" answered Salome.

And after she had patted their heads and praised their dolls, and pleased them all with loving notice, she followed her conductress from the children's play-room through the long rectangular passage that led to the nun's refectory.

The sisterhood, abstemious nearly all the days of the year, feasted on certain high holidays.

The Christmas dinner, laid for the young nuns in the refectory, would have satisfied the most fastidious epicure. But I doubt if any epicure could have enjoyed it half as well as did these abstemious young women, whose appetites were only let loose on certain high days and holidays.

Salome wondered at herself, who but two hours before had given way to a storm of passionate sobs and tears, yet now felt a strange peace of mind that enabled her to enter sincerely into the happiness of those around her.

In the afternoon, the convent was visited by a large number of benevolent people in the neighborhood, who brought their Christmas offerings to the poor and needy of the house.

These visitors were shown through all the various departments of charity, and left their offerings in each before they went away.

"I do wish **one** thing," said little Sister Felecitie, as she lingered near Salome, after the departure of the visitors.

"What do you wish, dear?" inquired the latter.

"Why, then, that the good people who give to our poor, whatever else they give, would **always** give the children dolls and the old people tobacco. The children **never** can have **too many** dolls, nor the old people **enough** tobacco."

"But is not the use of tobacco a vicious habit?"

"I **hope** not. It makes the poor old souls so happy."

CHAPTER XXX.
THE HAUNTER.

The vesper bell called them to the chapel, and the conversation ceased.

Salome joined the procession and entered the choir.

As soon as she had taken her seat she looked through the screen upon the congregation assembled in the public part of the church. A great dread seized her that she should see again the man whose presence had so disturbed her in the morning.

Heaven! he was there!--not where he sat before, but in one of the end pews, facing the choir, so that she had a full view of his ghastly face and glassy eyes.

A sudden superstitious fear fell upon her. She almost thought the figure was his ghost, or was some optical illusion conjured up by her own imagination.

She wished to test its reality by the eyes of another. She wished to whisper to the abbess, and point him out, and ask her if she, too, saw him; but she dared not do this. The vesper hymn was pealing forth from the choir, and all the sisterhood, except herself, were singing.

She was their soprano, and she had to join them. She began first in a tremulous voice, but soon the spell of the music took hold of her, and carried her away, far, far above all earthly thoughts and cares, and she sang, as her hearers afterward declared, "like a seraph."

At the end of the service she whispered to the abbess, calling her attention to the pallid stranger in the end pew; but when both turned to look, the man had vanished!

"Mother, I do not know whether that ghostly figure was a real man, after all!" whispered Salome, in an awe-stricken tone.

"My good child, what do you mean?" inquired the abbess, uneasily.

"Mother, I feel as if I were haunted!" said Salome, with a shudder.

"Come! your nerves have been overtasked. You must have a composing draught, and go to bed," said the superior, decisively.

"It may be that I am nervous and excitable, and that I have conjured up this image in my brain--such a ghastly, ghostly image, mother! It could not have been real, though I thought nothing else this morning than that it was real. But this evening-- oh! madam, if you had seen it, with its blanched face and glazed eyes, like a sceptre risen from the grave!"

"I have not seen the man yet, either this morning or this evening," said the elder lady, as she drew the younger's arm within her own.

"No, you have never seen him. I have no one's eyes but my own to test the matter. You have never seen him, and that is another reason why I think of the man as ghostly or unreal," whispered Salome.

They were now in the long passage leading from the chapel to the cells.

"I will take you again to your own little room in the Infants' Asylum," murmured the lady, as she turned with her protegee into the rectangular passage leading to the asylums.

She took Salome to the door of the house, gave her a benediction, and left her.

"Out there I have trouble, here I shall have peace," muttered the young woman, as she entered the children's dormitory, where every tiny cot was now occupied by a little, sleeping child.

Salome prepared to retire, and in a few moments she also was at rest, with her little Marie Perdue in her arms.

Christmas had come on Saturday that year. The next day being Sunday, there was another high mass to be celebrated in the chapel.

Salome, as usual, joined the nuns' procession to the choir, where the sisterhood, as was their custom, took their seats some few minutes before the entrance of the priest and his attendants.

With a heart almost pausing in its pulsations, Salome bent forward to peer through the screen upon the congregation, to see if by any chance the Duke of Hereward (or his ghost) sat among them.

With a half-suppressed cry, she recognized his form, seated in the opposite corner of the church, from the spot he had last occupied.

"He shifts his place every time he appears," she said to herself.

And now, being determined that other eyes should see him as well as her own, she touched the abbess' arm and whispered:

"Pray look before the priest enters. There is the Duke of Hereward (or his ghost) sitting quite alone in the corner pew, on the left hand side of the altar. Do you see him now?"

The abbess followed the direction with her eyes, and answered:

"No, I do not see any one there."

"Why, he is sitting alone in the left hand corner pew. Surely, you must see him now?" said Salome, bending forward to look again at the stranger.

The next instant she sank back in her seat, nearly fainting.

The pew was empty!

"There is really no one there, my child. Your eyes have deceived you," murmured the abbess, gently.

"He was there a moment since, but he has vanished! Oh! mother, what is the meaning of this?" gasped the girl, turning pale as death.

"The meaning is that your nervous system is shattered, and you are the victim of optical illusions. Or else--if there was a man really in that pew--he may have passed out through that little corner door leading to the vestry. But hush! here comes the priest," said the abbess, as the procession entered the chancel, preceded by the solemn notes of the organ.

Since "Miss Levison" was obliged to keep her place in the choir, it was well that she was an enthusiast in music, and thus able to lose all sense of care and trouble in the exercise of her divine art.

But for the music she would scarcely have got through the morning service.

And very much relieved she felt when the benediction was at length pronounced, and she was at liberty to leave the chapel.

"Oh, madam, this mystery is killing me! I have seen, or fancied I have seen, the Duke of Hereward in the church three times; yet no one else has been able to see him! If it was the duke, he has come here for some fixed purpose. He has, probably, by means of those expert London detectives, traced me out, and discovered my residence under this sacred roof. He has followed me here to give me trouble!" said Salome, as soon she found herself alone with the superior.

"My child," said the lady, "I must reiterate that *you* have nothing--*he* has everything to fear! I do not know, of course, for even you are not sure that you have really seen him. If you have, he is in this immediate neighborhood. If he is, why, then, the fact must be known to nearly every one outside the convent walls. The Duke of Hereward is not a man whose presence could be ignored. To-morrow, therefore, I will cause inquiries to be made, and we shall be sure to find out whether he is really here or not."

"Thanks, good mother, thanks. It will be a great relief to have this question decided in any way," said Salome, gratefully.

The mother-superior smiled, gave the benediction, and retired.

At vespers that evening, Salome looked all over the church in anxious fear of seeing the form that haunted her imagination; but her "ghost" did not appear, and, after all, she scarcely knew whether she was relieved or disturbed by his absence.

The next day, Monday, the abbess set diligent inquiries on foot to discover whether the Duke of Hereward, or any other stranger of any name or title whatever, had been seen in the neighborhood of St. Rosalie's for many days. Winter was not the season for strangers there.

After this, the Duke of Hereward (or his ghost) was seen no more in the chapel.

Every time Salome accompanied the sisterhood to the chapel, she peered through the choir-screen, in much anxiety as to whether she should see the duke, or his apparition, among the congregation below; but she never saw him there again, nor could she decide, in the conflict between her love and her sense of duty, whether she most desired or deplored his absence.

So the days passed into weeks, and nothing more was heard or seen of the Duke of Hereward.

The Christmas holidays came to an end after Twelth-Day; the pupils returned to the school, and the academy buildings grew gay with the exuberance of young life.

Salome, who, during many years of her childhood and youth, had shared this bright and cheery school-life, now saw nothing of it.

The academy buildings, as has been explained before this, were situated on the opposite side of the court-yard from the asylums and entirely cut off from communication with them.

Salome, devoted to her duties in the Infants' Asylum, was more completely secluded from the world than even the cloistered nuns themselves; for the nuns were the teachers of the academy, and in daily communication with their pupils and frequent correspondence with their patrons, saw and heard much of the busy life without.

So the weeks passed slowly into months, and the winter into spring, yet nothing more was seen or heard of the Duke of Hereward.

Salome lost the habit of looking for him, and gradually recovered her tranquility. In the work to which she had consecrated herself--the care of helpless and destitute infancy--she grew almost happy.

Already she seemed as dead to the world as though the "black vail" had fallen like a pall over her head. No newspapers ever drifted into the asylum, nor did any visitor come to bring intelligence of the good or evil of the life beyond the convent walls.

Her year of probation was passing away. At its close she would take the white vail and enter upon the second stage of her chosen vocation--her year of novitiate--at the end of which she would assume the black vail of the cloistered nun, which would seal her fate.

She knew that before taking that final step she must make some disposition of that vast inheritance which, in her flight from her home, she had left without one word of explanation or instruction. She was assured that her fortune was in the hands of honest men, and there she was content to leave it for the present. She had in her possession about a thousand pounds in money and several thousand pounds in diamonds--ample means for self-support and alms-giving.

And so she was satisfied for the present to leave her financial affairs as they were, until the time should come when it would be absolutely necessary for her to give attention to them.

Meanwhile, had she forgotten him who had once been the idol of her worship?

Ah, no! however diligently her eyes, her hands, her feet were employed in the service of the little children she loved so tenderly, her thoughts were with him. She loved him still! It seemed to her at once the sin and the curse of her life that she loved him still. She prayed daily to be delivered from "inordinate and sinful affections," but in this case prayer seemed of little use; for the more she prayed the more she loved and trusted him. It was a mystery she could not make out.

So the spring bloomed into summer, and the world outside became so disturbed and turbulent with "wars and rumors of wars," that its tumult was heard even within the peaceful convent sanctuary.

The news of the abdication of Her Most Catholic Majesty, Isabella II of Spain, fell like a thunderbolt upon the little community of the faithful in the convent; and nowhere, in the political conclaves of Prussia or of France, was the Spanish succession discussed with more intensity of interest than among the simple sisterhood of St. Rosalie.

Who would now fill the throne of the Western Caesars, left vacant by the abdication of their daughter, the Queen Isabella?

These were the topics which filled the minds and employed the tongues of the quiet nuns, whenever and wherever their rules permitted them to indulge in conversation.

No sound of this disturbance however penetrated the peaceful sphere of the Infants' Asylum, which, indeed, seemed to be the innermost retreat, or the holy of holies in the sanctuary.

Salome lived within it, the chief ministering angel, dispensing blessings all around her, and growing daily into deeper peace, until one fatal morning, when a great shock fell upon her.

It was a beautiful, bright morning near the end of June, and the day in regular rotation on which the mother-superior of the convent made her official rounds of inspection in the Infants' Asylum.

She arrived early, and, accompanied by Salome, went over every department of the asylum, from attic to cellar, from dormitory to recreation grounds, and found all well, and approved and delighted in the well-being.

After her long walk she sat down to rest in the children's play-room, and directed Salome to take a seat by her side.

The room was full of little children. Not seated in orderly rows, as we have too often seen in Infant Asylums on exhibition days; but moving about everywhere as freely as their little limbs would carry them, and making quite as much noise as their health and well-being certainly required.

Among them was little Marie Perdue, now a bright, fair, blue-eyed cherub of seven months old, seated on a mat, and tossing about with screams of delight a number of small, gay-hued India-rubber balls.

The abbess was watching the children with pleased attention, when one of the lay sisters entered and put a card in her hands, saying that the gentleman and lady were waiting at the porter's wicket, and desired permission to see the interior of the Infant Asylum.

"Certainly, they are welcome," said the abbess. "Go and tell Sister Francoise to be their guide."

The lay sister left the room, and the abbess gave her attention again to the children, making occasional remarks on their health, beauty, playfulness, and so forth, which were all sympathetically responded to by Salome, until they heard the sounds of approaching voices and footsteps, and the visiting party, escorted by Sister Francoise.

Then the abbess and her companion ceased speaking, and lowered their eyes to the floor until the strangers should pass them.

But the strangers lingered on their way, noticing individual children for beauty, or brightness, or some other trait which seemed to attract.

The gentleman, speaking French with an English accent, asked questions in too low a tone to reach the ears of the abbess and her companion; but the lady kept silence.

At length, as the visitors drew nearer, they came upon little Marie Perdue, sitting on her mat, engaged in tossing about her gay-colored balls, and laughing with delight.

"Whose child is that?" asked the gentleman, in a voice that thrilled to the heart of Salome.

She forgot herself, and looked up quickly, but the form of Sister Francoise, standing, concealed the figure of the speaker, who seemed to be stooping over the child.

"Ay! wha's bairn is it?" inquired another voice, that fell with ominous familiarity on her ear, as she turned her head a little and saw the female visitor, a tall, handsome blonde, with bold, blue eyes and a cataraet of golden hair falling on her shoulders.

Sister Francoise did not understand the language of the woman, and turned with a helpless and appealing look to the gentleman, who still speaking French with the slightly defective English accent, replied:

"Madame asks whose child is that?"

"Oh, pardon! We do not know, Monsieur. It was left at our doors on the eighteenth of December last," replied Sister Francoise.

"A very fine child! Its name?"

"Marie Perdue."

"'Marie Perdue?' What? 'Marie Perdue?' What's 'Perdue?'" querulously inquired the tall, blonde beauty.

"'Thrown away,' 'lost,' 'abandoned,'" answered the gentleman, in a low voice.

As he spoke he stood up and turned around.

Salome uttered a low, half-suppressed cry, and covered her face with both hands.

The abbess impulsively looked up to see what was the matter, and--echoed the cry!

There was dead silence in the room for a minute, and then Salome lifted up her head and cautiously looked around.

The visitors had gone, and the children, who with child-like curiosity had suspended their play to gaze upon the strangers, were now re-commencing their noise with renewed vehemence.

Salome still trembling in every limb, turned toward her companion.

The abbess sat with clasped hands, lowered eyelids, and face as pale as death.

Salome, too much absorbed in her own emotion to notice the strange condition of the abbess, touched her on the shoulder and eagerly whispered:

"Mother, did you observe the visitors?"

"Yes," breathed the lady, in a very low tone, without lifting her eyelids.

"Did you notice--*the man*?" Salome continued.

"I did," murmured the abbess, in an almost inaudible voice, as she devoutly made the sign of the cross.

"Do you know who he was?"

"*I do.*"

"He was like our Christmas visitor in the chapel! He was the Duke of Hereward!"

"Nay," said the abbess, in a stern solemn voice. "He was not the Duke of Hereward. He was one whom I had reckoned as numbered with the dead full twenty years ago!"

CHAPTER XXXI.
THE ABBESS' STORY.

"'Not the Duke of Hereward!'" echoed Salome, astonishment now overcoming every other emotion in her bosom.

The abbess bowed her head in grave assent.

"'One whom you thought numbered with the dead, full twenty years ago?'" continued Salome, quoting the lady's own words, and gazing on her face.

"Full twenty-five years ago, my daughter, or longer still," murmured the abbess.

"This man is young. He could not have been grown up to manhood twenty-five years ago."

"He is well preserved, as the selfish and heartless are too apt to be; but he is not young."

"And he is not the Duke of Hereward?"

"Most certainly not the Duke of Hereward."

"Then in the name of all the holy saints, madam, *who* is he?" demanded Salome, in ever increasing amazement.

"He is the Count Waldemar de Volaski, once my betrothed husband, but who forsook me, as I have told you, for another and a fairer woman," gravely replied the abbess.

"Once your betrothed husband, madam! Great Heaven! are you sure of this?" exclaimed Salome, in consternation.

"Yes, sure of it," answered the abbess, slowly bending her head.

"But--pardon me--I thought that *he* had been killed in a duel by the lover of the woman whom he had won."

"Even so thought I. The news of his falsehood and of his death at the hands of the wronged lover, came to me in my convent retreat at the same time, and I heard no more of him from that day to this, when I have again seen him in the flesh. The saints defend us!"

"And you are absolutely certain that he was Count Waldemar?"

"I am absolutely certain."

"Mother Genevieve, did you know the woman who was with him?"

"No, not at all. I never saw or heard of her before. She seems to belong to the *demi-monde*, for she dresses like a princess, and talks like a peasant. Let us not speak of her," said the lady, coldly.

"We *must* speak of her, for I think I know who she is."

"You recognize her, then?"

"I cannot say that I do; at least, not by her person. I never saw her face before; but I have heard her voice under circumstances that rendered it impossible for me ever to forget its tones; and from her voice I believe her to be Rose Cameron, a Highland peasant girl of Ben Lone."

"Stop!" exclaimed the mother-superior, suddenly raising her hand. "You do not mean to intimate that *she* is the girl whom you overheard talking with the young

Duke of Hereward at midnight, under your balcony, on the night before the murder of Sir Lemuel Levison?"

"She is the very same woman, as he is the very same man, who **planned**, if they did not perpetrate the robbery--who **caused**, if they did not commit, the murder; and their names are John Scott, Duke of Hereward, and Rose Cameron."

"My daughter, in regard to the girl you may be quite right; but in respect to the man you are utterly wrong."

"Should I not know my own betrothed husband?" demanded Salome, impatiently.

"Should *I* not know *mine*?" inquired the abbess, very patiently.

Salome made a gesture of desperate perplexity, and then there was a silent pause, during which the two women sat gazing in each other's faces in silent wonder.

Suddenly Salome started up in wild excitement and began pacing the narrow cell with rapid steps, exclaiming:

"There have been strange cases of counterparts in persons of this world so exact as to have deceived the eyes of their most intimate friends. If this should be a case in point! Great Heaven, if it should! If this Count Waldemar de Volaski should be such a perfect counterpart of the Duke of Hereward as to have deceived even my eyes and ears! Oh, what joy! Oh, what rapture! What ecstacy to find 'the princely Hereward' as stainless in honor as he is noble in name; and this most unprincipled Volaski the real guilty party! But--the marriage certificate in Hereward's own name! The letters to his so-called 'wife,' Rose Cameron, in Hereward's own handwriting! Ah, no! there is no hope! not the faintest beam of hope! And yet--"

She suddenly paused in her wild walk, and looked toward the abbess.

That lady was still sitting on the stool, at the foot of the cot, with her hands folded on her lap, and her eyes cast down upon them as in deep thought or prayer.

Salome sat down beside her, and inquired in a low tone:

"Mother Genevieve, was the Count Waldemar de Volaski ever in Scotland? Has he been there within the last twelve months?"

The lady lifted her eyes to the face of the inquirer, and slowly replied:

"My daughter, how should I know? Have I not said that, until this day, when I have seen him in the flesh standing in this room, I had believed him to have been in purgatory for twenty-five years or more?"

"True! true!" sighed Salome.

The abbess folded her hands, cast down her eyes, and resumed her meditations or prayers.

"You heard that he was killed in a duel, you say?" persevered Salome.

"Yes; the news of his treachery, and the news of his death at the hands of the Duke of Hereward reached me at the same moment in this convent, where I was then passing the first year of mourning for my parents. It was that news which decided me to take the vail and devote my life and fortune to the service of the Lord," said the lady, reverently bending her head.

Salome sat staring stonily as one petrified. She was absolutely speechless and motionless from amazement for the space of a minute or more. Then suddenly recovering her powers, she exclaimed:

"Mother! Mother Genevieve! For Heaven's sake! Did I understand you? From *whose* hand did you hear Count Waldemar received his death in a duel?"

"From the hand of the deeply injured husband, of course."

"But--who was he? Who? You mentioned a name!" wildly exclaimed Salome.

"Did I mention a name? Ah! what inadvertence! I never intended to let that name slip out. I am very sorry to have done so. *Mea Culpa! Mea Culpa! Mea maxima culpa!*" muttered the abbess, bending her head and smiting her bosom.

"Mother Genevieve! Oh, do not trifle with me! *do* not torture me! I heard a name! Did I hear aright? Oh, I hope I did not! What name did you murmur? Tell me! tell me! WHO met Count Waldemar in a duel?" demanded Salome.

"I have no choice but to tell you now, though I would willingly have kept the fact from you. It *was* the Duke of Hereward, the late duke of course, the deeply-wronged lover of that fair woman, who met, and, as I heard, killed Count Waldemar de Volaski. But there were wrongs on both sides, deep, deadly wrongs on every side!" moaned the lady, clasping her hands convulsively and lowering her eyes.

"The Duke of Hereward! Heaven of heavens! the Duke of Hereward! Yes! I heard aright the first time; but I could not believe my own ears! The father of my betrothed!" murmured Salome, sinking back in her seat.

The abbess gravely bent her head.

"What of the frail woman? She was not--oh! no, she *could not* have been the mother of the present duke?"

"No," murmured the abbess, in a low voice.

"Mother Genevieve!" exclaimed Salome, suddenly, "will you tell me all you know of this terrible story?"

"My daughter, my past is dead and buried these many years; so I would leave it until the last great day of the Resurrection. Nevertheless, as the story of my life is interwoven with that of the princely line in whom you feel so deep an interest, I will relate it."

"Thanks, good mother," said Salome, nestling to her side and preparing to listen.

"Not here, and not now, my child, can I enter upon the long, sorrowful, shameful story--a story of pride, despotism and cruelty on one side; of passion, wilfulness and recklessness on the other; of selfishness, sin and ruin on all sides! Daughter, in almost every tale of sin and suffering you will find that there has always been sin on *one* side and suffering on the *other*; but in this story *all* sinned deeply, all suffered fearfully!"

"Except yourself, sweet mother. You never sinned," said Salome, taking the thin, pale hand of the lady and pressing it to her lips.

"*Mea culpa!* I sin every hour of my life!" cried the abbess, crossing herself.

"We all do; but you did not sin *there*," said the girl.

"I had no part--no active part, I mean--in that tale of guilt and woe. I was a pupil here in this convent then, waiting to be brought out and married to my betrothed. No, I had no part in that tragedy."

"Except the passive part of suffering."

"Ay, except the passive part of suffering; but hark, my child! the vesper bell is ringing; it calls us to our evening worship: let us go to the choir, and there forget all our earthly cares and seek the peace of Heaven," said the pale lady, slowly rising from her seat.

"When will you tell me the story, good mother?" pleaded Salome, in a low and deprecating tone.

"The vesper bell is ringing. The rules of the house must not be disturbed by your individual necessities. After the evening service comes the evening meal. Then, for me, my hour of rest in my cell; and for you, the duty of seeing your infant charge put to bed. When all these matters have been properly attended to, come to me in my cell. You will find me there. We shall be uninterrupted until the midnight mass; and in the interim I will tell you the story of a life that 'was lost, but is found, was dead, but is alive'--***Benedicite***, my daughter!" said the abbess, spreading her hands upon the bowed head of the girl, and solemnly blessing her.

Then she glided away.

Salome soon followed her, and joined the procession of nuns to the chapel.

As soon as she took her seat in the choir, she looked through the screen over the congregation below, to see if the strangers were in the chapel; but she saw them not.

When the vesper service was over, she took her tea with the nuns in their refectory; and then returned to the play-room in the Infants' Asylum.

The nurses were engaged in giving the little ones their supper, and putting them to bed.

Salome took up her own little Marie Perdue, to undress her.

As she divested the child of her little slip, something rolled out of its bosom and dropped upon the floor.

One of the nurses picked it up and handed it to Salome.

It was a small, hard substance, wrapped in tissue paper.

Salome unrolled it and found a ring, set with a large solitaire diamond. With a cry of surprise and pain, she recognized the jewel. It was her late father's ring! While she gazed upon it in a trance of wonder, the paper in which it had been wrapped, caught by a breeze from the open window, fluttered under her eyes. She saw that there was writing on the paper, and she took it up and read it.

"The ring must be sold for the benefit of the child and of the house that has protected her. She must be educated to become a nun."

There was no signature to this paper.

Salome rolled it around the ring again, and put it in her bosom, then she sent one of the nurses to call Sister Francoise.

When the old nun came into her presence, she inquired:

"Sister Francoise, you showed a lady and gentleman through the asylum, this afternoon; they came into this room; they stopped and noticed little Marie Perdue particularly. Did they ask any questions or make any remarks concerning her? I have an especial reason for asking."

"Oh, yes, sister! they did ask many questions--when she came, how long she had been, who took care of her, what was her name, and many more; and as I answered them to the best of my knowledge, I could not help seeing that they knew more about the child than I did," answered the nun, nodding her head.

"Did the gentleman or lady give anything to the child?"

"Not that *I* saw, which I thought unkind of them, considering all the interest they showed in **words**; for, as I say of all the fine ladies who come here and fondle the infants, what's the use of all the fondling if they never put a sou out, or a stitch in?"

"That will do, sister; I only wanted to know," answered the young lady, as she determined to keep her own counsel, and confide the news of the surreptitiously offered ring to the abbess only.

When she had rocked her child to sleep, laid it on its little cot, and placed two novices on duty to watch over the slumbers of the children, she left the dormitory by the rectangular passage that led to the nuns' house, and repaired at once to the cell occupied by the abbess.

It was a plain little den, in no respect better than those tenanted by her humble nuns, twelve feet long, by nine broad, with bare walls, and bare floor, and a small grated window at the farther end, opposite the narrow, grated door by which the cell was entered. It was furnished poorly with a narrow cot bed, a wooden stool, and a small stand, upon which lay the office-book of the abbess, and above which hung the crucifix.

As Salome entered the cell, the abbess arose from her knees and signed for her visitor to be seated.

Salome sat down on the foot of the cot, and the abbess drew the stool and placed herself near.

Then Salome saw the lady-superior was even paler and graver than usual; and anxious as the young lady felt to hear the abbess' story, she thought she would give her more time to recover, and even assist her in doing so, by diverting her thoughts to the new incident of the ring, which she produced and laid upon the mother's lap, saying:

"That was found by me in the bosom of little Marie Perdue's dress. It was donated to the house, for the benefit of the child. Here is the scrap of writing in which it was rolled."

The abbess silently took up the ring and the paper, and examined the first and read the last, saying:

"Such mysterious donations to the children are not uncommon, and are generally supposed to be offered by the unknown parents. This, however, is by far the most valuable present that has ever been made by any one to the institution, and must be worth at least a thousand Napoleons. It was made by the visitors of this morning, I suppose?"

"Yes, madam, it was."

"I see, I understand. Take charge of it, my daughter, until we can deliver it to the sister-treasurer," directed the lady-superior, as she replaced the ring in its wrapper and returned both to Salome.

"But, mother, I wish myself to become the purchaser of this ring. I have a thousand pounds with me. I will give them for the ring."

"My daughter!" exclaimed the abbess in surprise. "Why should you wish to possess this bauble? It can be of no use to you in the life you are about to enter, even if the rules of our order would permit you to retain it, which you know they would not."

"Mother! it was my father's ring! It was a part of the property stolen from him on the night of his murder," solemnly answered Salome.

"Holy saints! can that be true?" exclaimed the abbess.

"As true as truth. I know the ring well. He always wore it on his finger. Inside the setting is his monogram, 'L.L.,' and his crest, a falcon," answered Salome, once more unwrapping the ring and offering it to the inspection of the lady-superior.

"I see! I see! It is so. Ah, Holy Virgin! that it should have been offered by Count Waldemar, or by him whom you overheard conspiring with his female companion under the windows on the night of your father's murder!" cried the abbess, covering her face with a fold of her black vail.

"Count Waldemar, or the duke of Hereward, I know not which, I know not whom. Oh! mother, this mystery grows deeper, this confusion more confounded."

"Take back your ring, my child, and keep it without price. It was your father's, and it is yours. We cannot receive stolen goods even as alms offered to our orphans," said the abbess, dropping her vail and returning the jewel.

"I will take it and keep it because it was my dear father's; but I will give a full equivalent for its value. No one could object to that," said Salome, as she replaced the ring in her bosom. "And now, Mother Genevieve, will you tell me the promised story? It may possibly throw some light even upon this dark mystery."

The pale abbess bowed assent, and immediately began the narrative, which, for the Sake of convenience, we prefer to render in our own words.

CHAPTER XXXII.
THE DUKE'S DOUBLE.

First it is necessary to revert to the history of the Scotts of Lone, Dukes of Hereward.

He who married Salome Levison was the eighth of his princely line. Any one turning to Burke's Peerage of the preceding year, might have read this record of the late duke:

"Hereward, Duke of, (Archibald-Alexander-John Scott) Marquis of Arondelle and Avondale in the Peerage of England, Earl of Lone and Baron Scott in the Peerage of Scotland; born, 1st of Jan., 1800; succeeded his father as seventh duke, 1st Feb., 1840; married, first, March 15th, 1843, Valerie, only daughter of Constantine, Baron de la Motte; divorced, Nov, 1st, 1844; married, secondly, July 15th, 1845, Lady Katherine-Augusta, eldest daughter of the Earl of Banff, and has a son--Archibald-Alexander-John, Marquis of Arondelle, born 1st of May, 1846."

A whole domestic tragedy is comprised in one line of this record:

"Married, first, March 15th, 1843, Valerie, only daughter of Constantine, Baron de la Motte; divorced, Nov. 1st, 1844."

Now as to this poor, unhappy first wife:

Some few years before this first fatal marriage, the Baron de la Motte, one of the most illustrious French statesmen, was dispatched by his sovereign as Envoy Extraordinary and Minister Plenipotentiary from the Court of France to the Court of Russia.

The baron, with his suite, proceeding to St. Petersburg, accompanied by the baroness, a handsome Italian woman, and by their only child, Valerie, a beautiful brunette of only seventeen summers.

Valerie de la Motte was first introduced to the world of fashion at a great court ball, given by the Czar, in honor of the French Ambassador, in the Imperial Palace of Annitchkoff.

On this occasion the dark, brilliant beauty of Mademoiselle de la Motte, inherited from her Italian mother, was the more admired from its rarity and its perfect contrast to the radiant fairness of the Russian blondes. Here Valerie de la Motte met, for the first time, Waldemar de Volaski, the second son of the Polish Count de Volaski, and a captain of the Royal Guards, stationed at the palace. He was but twenty years of age, yet a model of fair, manly beauty. He was even then called "the handsomest man in all the Russias."

There was a Romeo and Juliet case of love at first sight between the young Russian officer and the youthful French heiress.

During the first season, the beauty's hand was sought by some among the most princely of the nobles that surrounded the throne of the Czar; but, to the disappointment of her ambitious parents, she refused them every one.

Certainly the French father might have followed the custom of his class and country, and coerced his young daughter into the acceptance of any husband he might have chosen for her; but he did not feel disposed to use harsh measures with his only and idolized child; he rather preferred to exercise patience and forbearance toward her, until she should have outlived what he called her childish caprices.

It was, however, no childish caprice that governed the conduct of Valerie de la Motte, but the unfortunate and fatal passion, inspired by the handsome young captain of the Royal Guards, whom she had waltzed with about a half a dozen times at the court balls.

Waldemar de Volaski was indeed as beautiful as the youthful god, Apollo Belvidere, and in his radiant blonde complexion a perfect contrast to the dark, splendid style of the lovely brunette, Valerie de la Motte; but he was only a younger son, with no hope or prospect of succession to his father's title or estates.

He did not dare openly to seek the hand of Mademoiselle de la Motte, for he knew that to do so would only be to have himself banished forever from her presence, by her ambitious father; but, loving her with all the passion of his heart, he sought secretly to win her love, and he succeeded.

It would seem strange that the carefully shielded daughter of the French minister should have been exposed to courtship by the young captain of the Royal Guards; but love is fertile in devices, and full of expedients, and "laughs," not only "at locksmiths," but at all other obstacles to its success.

The willful young pair loved each other ardently from the first evening of their meeting, and they could not endure to think of such a possibility as their separation. They found many opportunities, even in public, of carrying on their secret courtship. In the swimming turn of the waltz, hands clasped hands with more impassioned earnestness than the formula of the round dance required: in the casual meetings in the fashionable promenades of the beautiful summer gardens in Aptekarskoi Island--

"Eyes looked love to eyes that spake again. And all went merry as a marriage bell,"

so long as they could see each other every day.

As the summer passed, the young captain, grown more confident, wrote ardent love letters to his lady, which were surreptitiously slipped into her hands at casual meetings, or conveyed to her by means of bribed domestics; and these the willful beauty answered in the same spirit, as opportunity was offered her by the same means. But--

"A change came o'er the spirit of their dream."

The French minister was recalled home by his sovereign, and only awaited the arrival of his successor to take an official leave of the Czar.

About this time a letter from Volaski to Valerie was sent by the captain's faithful valet, and put in the hands of the lady's confidential maid, who secretly conveyed it to her mistress. This letter, which was fiery enough to have set any ordinary postbag in a blaze, declared, among other matters, that the lady's answer would decide the writer's fate, for life or for death.

Mademoiselle de la Motte sat down and wrote a reply which she sent by her confidential maid, who placed it in the hands of the captain's faithful valet, to be secretly carried to his master.

Whether the answer decided the fate of the lover for life or for death, it certainly controlled his action in an important matter. Immediately on its receipt he hastened to the Hotel de l'Etat Major, the headquarters of the army department, and solicited a month's leave of absence to visit his father's family.

As it was the very first occasion upon which the young officer had asked such a favor, it was promptly granted him.

Of course no one suspected that the cause of the young captain's action had been the announcement that the French minister had been recalled by his government, and was about to return to Paris.

The next day Waldemar de Volaski left St. Petersburg, ostensibly to visit his father's estates in Poland.

And the next week the French minister, having presented his successor to the Czar, and received his own conge, left the court and the city, and set out for France.

The ministerial party travelled by the new railway from St. Petersburg to Warsaw, a distance of nearly seven hundred miles.

At the capital of Poland they designed to stop a few days to rest the baroness, whose health was suffering.

One day while in that city the baroness, her daughter, and the lady's maid, went out together, shopping for curiosities in the Marieville Bazaar, a square in the midst of the city, surrounded by many gay arcades.

The square was full of visitors, and every arcade was crowded with customers.

The baroness became somewhat interested in her purchases, and from moment to moment turned to consult her daughter, who seemed ever ready so assist her choice.

At length, however, in speaking to Mademoiselle de la Motte, her mother failed to receive an answer.

Turning to rebuke the inattention of her daughter, the baroness discovered that Valerie was missing.

Thinking only that she had got mixed up with the crowd, yet feeling very much annoyed thereat, Madam de la Motte called her maid and instituted a search, only to find, with dismay, that Mademoiselle was nowhere in the square.

Believing then that the young girl must have taken the extraordinary and very reprehensible proceeding of returning to the hotel alone and resolving to give her daughter a severe reprimand for her imprudence, the baroness returned to their temporary home, only to learn that Mademoiselle de la Motte had not been seen there by any one since she had left the house in company with her mother, attended by her maid.

Fearing then that her daughter, in rashly attempting to return home alone, had lost herself in the streets of Warsaw, the baroness sent messengers in every direction to seek for her and guide her back.

Meanwhile the Baron de la Motte, who had been to inspect the fine gallery of paintings preserved in the old villa of Stanislaus Augustus, returned to his hotel, and was informed by the now half distracted baroness of the disappearance of their daughter.

The Baron, struck with dismay, inquired into the circumstances of the case, and was told of the shopping expedition to the Marieville Bazaar, where Valerie was first missed.

"It was at her own earnest solicitation that I took her there, to pick up some of the curiously carved jewelry and trinkets. First, she wished, in consideration of my health, to go there attended only by her maid; but I would not allow any such indiscretion. I took her there myself, and even while I was talking with her before one of the arcades, she vanished like a spirit! One moment she was there, the next moment she was gone! We looked for her immediately, but found no trace of her."

The baron replied not one word to this explanation, but took his hat and walked out to join the search for the missing girl, while the baroness remained in her rooms, a prey to the most poignant anxiety.

It was near midnight when the baron returned, looking full ten years older than he did when he went forth.

No trace of the missing girl had been found, and whether her disappearance was a flight or an abduction no one could even conjecture.

The condition of the agonized mother became critical; she could not be persuaded to lie down, or to cease from her restless walking to and fro in her chamber.

At length, a physician was summoned, who administered a potent sedative, which conquered her nervous excitement, and laid her in a blessed sleep upon her bed.

The next morning the search, which had not been quite abandoned even during the night, was renewed with great vigor, stimulated by the large rewards offered by the afflicted father for the recovery of his lost child; but still no trace of Valerie de la Motte could be found, no news of her be heard.

And so, without any change a week passed away, and then, while the baroness lay in extreme nervous prostration, hovering between life and death, and the baron crept about her bed like a man bowed down by the infirmities of age, and all hope seemed gone, a letter arrived from Mademoiselle de la Motte to her parents.

It was written from San Vito, a small mountain hamlet in the northern part of Italy. By this letter she informed them that she was safe and happy as the wife of Captain Waldemar de Volaski, who had long possessed her heart, and to whom she had just given her hand. She begged her father and mother to pardon her for having sought her happiness in her own way, and assured them, notwithstanding her seemingly unfilial conduct, she still cherished the strongest sentiments of love and honor toward them both, and ever remained their dutiful and affectionate daughter--VALERIE DE LA MOTTE DE VOLASKI.

The mother, who under any other circumstances, would have been overwhelmed with mortification and sorrow at this *mesalliance* of her daughter, was now so glad to know that Valerie was alive in health, even though as the bride of a poor young captain of the Guards, that she thanked Heaven earnestly, and rejoiced exceedingly.

But the baron who would as willingly have never heard of his lost daughter, as that she had so degraded herself, left his wife's bed-chamber abruptly, and went off to his smoking-room, where he could vent his feelings by cursing and swearing to his heart's content.

The next day the Baron de la Motte, breathing maledictions, set out for Italy, accompanied by the baroness, who had wonderfully rallied in health and strength since she had received news of her missing daughter.

The proud baroness was, in one respect, like the poor Hebrew mother of the Bible story. She preferred to give up her child to another claimant rather than lose that beloved child by death.

The baron's party traveled day and night, without pause or rest, until they crossed the northern frontier of Italy, and halted at the little hamlet of San Vito, at the foot of the Apennines.

Here they found the fugitive pair living a sort of Arcadian life: and here they learned the facts which they had not hitherto even suspected.

Captain Waldemar de Volaski and Mademoiselle Valerie de la Motte had loved each other from the first moment of their meeting at the ball given in honor of the French minister, at the Imperial Palace of Annitchkoff, and had betrothed themselves to each other during the first month of their acquaintance. They had kept their betrothal a secret, only because they felt assured it would meet with the most violent opposition from the young lady's haughty parents; but they had carried on a constant epistolary correspondence through the instrumentality of the lover's valet and the lady's maid; but they had not intended to take any decisive step, until, at length, they were both startled by the recall home of the French minister.

When the announcement of this event reached the ears of Waldemar de Volaski, he was filled with despair at the prospect of parting from his betrothed.

He instantly dashed off a hasty letter to Valerie de la Motte, earnestly entreating her to save his life, and his reason, and secure their happiness, by consenting to an immediate marriage.

Mademoiselle de la Motte, closing her ears to the voice of conscience and discretion, and listening only to the pleadings of a reckless and fatal passion, wrote a favorable answer.

They knew that their plan would be exceedingly difficult of execution; but this did not deter them.

They made their arrangements with more tact than could have been expected of so youthful a pair of lovers.

He obtained leave of absence and left St. Petersburg, as has been stated, upon the pretext of visiting his father's estate in Poland; but really with the intention of preceding the minister's party to Warsaw, where, he had learned, they would break their journey and remain for a few days to recruit the strength of the baroness.

There, disguised as a peasant, and concealed in the suburban cottage of a faithful retainer of his family, Waldemar de Volaski waited for the arrival of the baron's party.

Then, through the instrumentality of the lover's valet and the lady's maid, a meeting was arranged between the imprudent young pair, at the Marieville Bazaar.

There Mademoiselle de la Motte found her lover watching for her.

Taking advantage of a few minutes during which her mother was engaged in the examination of some curious malachite ornaments, Valerie de la Motte slipped into the thickest of the crowd, joined her lover, and escaped with him to the suburban hut of the old retainer, where she changed her clothes, and from whence, in the disguise of a page, and carrying her female apparel in a small valise, she finally fled with him to Italy.

They stopped at the little mountain hamlet of San Vito, where she resumed her proper dress, and where, by a lavish expenditure of money, and a liberal disbursement of fair words, Waldemar de Volaski prevailed on a priest to perform the marriage ceremony between himself and Valerie de la Motte.

When this was done, the reckless pair took lodgings at a vine-dresser's cottage in the neighborhood of the hamlet, to spend their honeymoon, and wait for "coming events."

The coming events came. The parents arrived, and found the lovers living carelessly and happily in their Arcadian home. Here the outraged and infuriated father thundered into the ears of the newly-married pair the terrible truth that their marriage was no marriage at all without his consent, but was utterly null and void in the law.

At this astounding revelation, Valerie, overwhelmed with humiliation, fainted and fell, and was tenderly cared for by her mother; but the gallant captain very coolly replied that he knew the fact perfectly well, and had always known it, although Mademoiselle de la Motte had not even suspected it; and he ventured to represent to the haughty baron, that their illegal marriage only required the sanction of his silent recognition to render it perfectly legal, and that for his daughter's own sake he was bound to give it such recognition.

This aroused the baron to a perfect frenzy of rage. He charged Volaski with having traded in Mademoiselle de la Motte's affections and honor, from selfish and mercenary motives alone, and swore that such deep, calculating villainy should avail the villain nothing. He would not ratify his daughter's marriage with such a caitiff, but would use his parental power to tear her from her unlawful husband's arms, and immure her in the living tomb of an Italian convent.

He finished by dashing his open hand with all his strength full into the mouth of the bridegroom, inflicting a severe blow, and covering the handsome face with blood.

Valerie de la Motte, in a fainting condition, was placed in the cart of a vine-dresser, the only conveyance to be found, and carried to a neighboring nunnery, where she lay ill for several weeks, tenderly nursed by her sorrowful mother and by the compassionate nuns.

The Baron de la Motte remained in the village, awaiting a challenge from Waldemar de Volaski; but when a week had passed away without such an event, the furious old Frenchman, bent upon his enemy's destruction, dispatched a defiance to Captain Volaski, couched in such insulting and exasperating language as compelled the young officer, much against his will, to accept it.

They met to fight their duel in a secluded glade of the forest, lying between the hamlet and the foot of the mountains.

At the first fire, Volaski, who was resolved not to wound the father of his beloved Valerie, discharged his pistol in the air, but instantly fell, shot through the lungs by the Baron de la Motte!

CHAPTER XXXIII.
AFTER THE EARTHQUAKE.

The Baron de la Motte, leaving Captain de Volaski stretched on the ground, to be cared for by the seconds and the surgeon in attendance, went back to the hotel and made preparations to leave San Vito.

Mademoiselle de la Motte, still very weak from recent illness, was placed in a carriage at the risk of her life, and compelled to commence the journey back to France.

Madame de la Motte, grieved with the grief and anxious for the health of her daughter, dared not show the sufferer any pity or kindness.

Monsieur de la Motte was no longer the tender and affectionate father he had hitherto shown himself: for, in his bitter mortification and fierce resentment, his love seemed turned to hatred, his sympathy to antipathy.

The attenuated form, the pale face, and the sunken eyes of his once beautiful child, failed to move his compassion for her. He told her with brutal cruelty that he had slain her lover in the duel, and left him dead upon the ground; and that she must think no more of the villain who had dishonored her family.

On arriving in Paris, the baron established his household in the magnificent Hotel de la Motte, in the most aristocratic quarter of the city; and here began for Valerie a life that was a very purgatory on earth.

At home, if her purgatory could be called her home, she was studiously and habitually treated with scorn and contempt, as a creature unworthy to bear the family name, or share the family honors; until at length the child herself began to look upon her fault in the light her father wished her to see it, and with such exaggerating eyes, withal, that she came to think of herself as a dishonored criminal, unworthy even to live. Her grief sank to horror, and her depression to despair.

She was treated as an outcast in all respects but one, and this exception was an additional cruelty; for she was introduced into the gay world of fashion, and compelled to mix in all its festivities, at the same time being sternly warned that if this same world should suspect her fault, she would not be received in any drawing-room in Paris.

Valerie was too broken-spirited to answer by telling the truth, that the world and the world's favor had lost all attraction for her, who would willingly have retired from it forever.

Valerie was presented to society as Mademoiselle de la Motte, and nothing was said of her stolen marriage with the young Russian officer.

That season was perhaps the gayest Paris had ever known during the quiet reign of the citizen king and queen. Brilliant festivities in honor of the Spanish marriages were the order of the days and nights. Representatives from every court in Europe were present, as special messengers of congratulation--or expostulation; for it will be remembered the Spanish marriages were not universally popular with the sovereigns of Europe.

Among the representatives of the English Court, present at the Tuileries, was the seventh Duke of Hereward, recently come into his titles and estates.

It was at a ball at the Tuileries that Valerie de la Motte first met the Duke of Hereward, then a very handsome man of middle age, of accomplished mind and courtly address. The beautiful, pale, grave brunette at once interested the English duke more than all the blooming and vivacious beauties at the French capital could do. At every ball, dinner, concert, play, or other place of amusement where Mademoiselle de la Motte appeared with her parents, the Duke of Hereward sought her out; and the more he saw of her, the more interested he became in her; and it must be confessed that the conversation of this handsome and accomplished man of middle age pleased the grave, sedate girl more than that of younger and gayer men could have done.

The duke, on his part, was not slow to perceive his advantage, and he would willingly have paid his addresses to Mademoiselle de la Motte in person, and won her heart and hand for himself, before speaking to her father on the subject; but as such a proceeding would not have been in accordance with the customs of the country, no opportunity was allowed him to do so; for whereas in England, or America, a suitor must win the favor of his lady before he asks that of her parents, in France the process is precisely the reverse of all this, and the lover must have the sanction of the father or mother, or both, before he may dare to woo the daughter; and this rule of etiquette holds good in all cases except in those of stolen marriages, which are illegal and disreputable.

It was not long, therefore, before the Duke or Hereward called at the Hotel de la Motte, and requested a private interview with the baron, which was promptly and politely accorded.

The duke then and there made known to the baron the state of his affections, and formally solicited the hand of Mademoiselle Valerie de la Motte in marriage.

The "mad duke" was not then mad; he had not squandered his princely fortune; his dukedom was one of the wealthiest as well as one of the oldest in the United Kingdom; the marriage he offered the baron's daughter was one of the most brilliant (under royalty) in Europe.

The baron did not hesitate a moment, but promptly accepted the proposals of the duke in behalf of his daughter.

The Duke of Hereward hurried away, the happiest man in Europe.

The Baron de la Motte went and informed his daughter that she must prepare to receive the middle-aged suitor as her future husband.

Now, Valerie, in a languid way, liked the Duke of Hereward better than any one else in the whole world except her mother, but she did not like him in the character of a husband. The idea of marriage even with him was abhorrent to her. In her first surprise and dismay at the announcement of the duke's proposal for her hand, and her father's acceptance of that proposal, she betrayed all the unconquerable antipathy she felt to the contemplated marriage; but in vain she wept and pleaded to be left in peace; to be left to die; to be sent to a convent; to be disposed of in any way rather than in marriage!

The baron was no longer a tender and compassionate father, but a ruthless and implacable tyrant.

Valerie's life had been a purgatory before, it was a hell now. She was covered with reproach, contumely and threats by her father; she was lectured and mourned over by her mother; and when her mother at length took sides with her father, in urging her to this marriage, the very ground seemed to have slidden from beneath her feet; she had not a friend in the world to whom to turn in her distress.

Meanwhile the Duke of Hereward was impatiently awaiting the promised summons to the Hotel de la Motte to meet Mademoiselle Valerie as his future wife.

Valerie believed that her young lover-husband had been slain in the duel with her father; and that she was free to bestow her hand, if she could not give her broken heart; she was worn out with the ignominious reproaches heaped upon her by her father; by the tears and sighs lavished upon her by her mother; by all the humiliation and degradations of her daily life, and by the dreariness and desolation of her home. She longed for peace and rest; she would gladly have sought them in a convent had she been permitted to do so, or in the grave, had she dared.

I repeat that she did not dislike the Duke of Hereward; but on the contrary, she liked him better than any one else in the world except her mother, and so it followed that at length she began to look upon a marriage with him as the only possible refuge from the horrors of her home.

What wonder, then, that, goaded and taunted by her father, implored by her mother, solicited by the handsome duke, believing her young lover to be dead, slain by the hands of her father, longing to escape from the persecutions of her family, prostrated in body and mind, broken in heart and in spirit, Valerie at last succumbed to the pressure brought to bear upon her, and accepted the refuge of the Duke of Hereward's love, although the very next moment, in honor of herself and him, she would willingly have recalled her decision, if she could have done so.

From the moment that her acceptance of the duke's proposal was announced to her parents, the domestic sky cleared; her ruthless tyrant became again her tender father; her weeping mother brightened into smiles; she herself was once more the petted daughter of the house, and her lover showed himself the proudest and happiest of men; and Valerie de la Motte would have been at peace but for her consciousness of the secret that they were all keeping from the duke.

"Mamma, he ought to be told, he is so good, so noble, so confiding. I feel like a wretch in deceiving him; he ought to be told of my fault before he commits himself by marrying me," she pleaded with her mother.

"Valerie, you frighten me half to death! Do not dream of such a folly as telling the duke anything about your mad imprudence in running away with the young Russian! It would make a great and terrible scandal! Your father would kill you, I do believe! Besides, for that fault, committed while you were in our keeping and under our authority, you are accountable only to me and to your father. Your betrothed husband has nothing to do with it. No good would come of your telling it; no harm can come of your keeping it. The wild partner of your imprudence is dead and buried, the saints be praised! and so he can never rise up to trouble your peace. While you are here with us, and under our authority, you must obey us, and hold your peace, and keep your secret," said the baroness.

"Come weal, come woe, my honor requires that this secret should be told to the noble and confiding gentleman who is about to make me his wife," murmured Valerie.

"Your honor, Mademoiselle, is in the keeping of your father, until, by giving you in marriage, he passes it into the keeping of your husband. You are not to concern yourself about it. If your father should deem that your 'honor' demands your secret to be confided to your betrothed husband, he will divulge it to him: if he does not divulge it, then rest assured honor does not require him to do so. Now let us hear no more about it."

Valerie sighed and yielded, but she was not satisfied.

The betrothal was immediately announced to the world, and the marriage, which soon followed, was celebrated in the church of Notre Dame with the greatest *eclat*.

Directly after the wedding the duke took his bride on a long tour, extending over Europe and into Asia; and after an absence of several months, carried her to England, and settled down for the autumn on his English patrimonial estate, Hereward Hold, (for Castle Lone was then a ruin and Inch Lone a wilderness, which no one had yet dreamed of rebuilding and restoring.)

The youthful duchess, in her quiet English home, was like Louise la Valliere in the Convent of St. Cyr, "not joyous, but content."

She tried to make her noble husband happy, by fulfilling all the duties of a wife--*except one*. She knew a wife should have no secrets from her husband, yet, in her fear of disturbing the sweet domestic peace, in which her wearied spirit rested, she kept from him the secret of her first wild marriage.

At the meeting of Parliament in February, the Duke of Hereward took his beautiful young wife to London, and established her in their magnificent townhouse--Hereward House, Kensington.

At the first Royal drawing-room at Buckingham Palace, the young duchess was presented to the queen, and soon after she commenced her career as a woman of fashion by giving a grand ball at Hereward House.

The Duke of Hereward was very fond and very proud of his lovely young bride, whose beauty soon became the theme of London clubs--though invidious critics insisted that she was much too pale and grave ever to become a reigning belle.

Yes, she was very pale and grave; peaceful, not happy.

Scarcely twelve months had passed since she had been cruelly torn from the idolized young husband of her youth and thrown into a convent, where the only news that she heard of him was, that he had been killed in a duel with her ruthless father. She had mourned for him in secret, without hope and without sympathy, and before the first year of her widowhood had passed--a widowhood she had been sternly forbidden by her father either to bewail or even to acknowledge--she had been driven by a series of unprecedented persecutions to give her hand where she could not give her broken heart, and to go to the altar with a deadly secret on her conscience, if not with a lie on her lips!

Now her persecutions had ceased, indeed; but not her sorrows. Her home was quiet and honored, her middle-aged husband was kind and considerate, and she loved him with filial affection and reverence; but she could not forget the husband of her youth, slain by her father; his memory was a tender sorrow cherished in the depths of her heart, the only living sentiment there, for it seemed dead to all else.

"If he were a living lover," she whispered to herself, "I should be bound by every consideration of honor and duty to cast him out of my heart--if I could! But for my dead boy, my husband, slain in the flower of his youth for my sake, I may cherish remembrance and sorrow."

Thus, it is no wonder that she moved through the splendor of her first London season, a beautiful, pale, grave Melpomene.

But the splendor of that season was soon to be dimmed.

News came by telegraph to the Duke of Hereward, announcing the sudden death of the Baron de la Motte, of apoplexy, in Paris.

Now much has been said and written about the ingratitude of children; but quite as much might be said of their indestructible affection. The Baron de la Motte had shown himself a very cruel father to his only child; he had shot down her young husband in a duel; yet, notwithstanding all that, Valerie was wild with grief at the news of his sudden death. She wondered, poor child, if she herself had not had some hand in bringing it on by all the trouble she had given him, although that trouble had passed away now more than twelve months since; and the late baron was known to have been a man of full habit and excitable temperament, and, withal, a heavy feeder and hard drinker--a very fit subject for apoplexy to strike down at any moment.

The Duke and Duchess of Hereward hastened to Paris, where they found the remains of the baron laid in state in the great saloon of the Hotel de la Motte, and the widowed baroness prostrated by grief, and confined to her bed.

The duke and duchess remained until after the funeral, when the will of the late baron was read. It was then discovered for the first time that his daughter, Valerie, was not nearly the wealthy heiress she was supposed to be.

All the late baron's landed estates went to the male heir-at-law, a young officer in the Chasseurs d' Afrique, then in Algiers. All his personal property, consisting of bank and railroad stocks, after a deduction as a provision for his widow, was bequeathed to his only daughter Valerie, Duchess of Hereward. But this property was so inconsiderable, that, without other means, it would scarcely have sufficed for the respectable support of the mother and daughter.

After the settlement of the late baron's affairs, the duke and duchess would have returned immediately to London but for the condition of the widowed baroness' health.

Madame de la Motte had for years been a delicate invalid, and she had experienced, in the sudden death of her husband, a severe shock, from which she could not rally; so that, within a few weeks after the baron's remains had been laid in the family vault, she passed away, and hers were laid by his side.

Valerie was even more prostrated with sorrow by the loss of her mother than she had been by that of her father.

The duke, to distract her grief, telegraphed to New Haven, where his yacht, the **Sea-Bird**, was lying to have her brought over to meet him at Dieppe, took his duchess down to that little seaport and embarked with her for a voyage to Norway.

The season was most favorable for such a northerly voyage. They sailed on the first of July, and spent three months cruising about the coasts of Norway, Iceland, and down to the Western Isles. They returned about the first of October.

The duke left his yacht at Dieppe, and, accompanied by the duchess, went up to Paris, to attend to some business connected with the estate of the late baron.

As but a third of a year had passed since the death of her parents, and the duchess had scarcely passed out of her first deep crape mourning, she went very little into society. Nevertheless, she was constrained, at the duke's request, to accept one invitation.

There was to be a diplomatic dinner given at the British Legation, at which the Prussian, Austrian and Russian ministers, with the higher officers of their suites, were to be present.

Valerie, living her recluse life in the city, did not know the names of one of these ministers, nor, in the apathy of her grief, did she care to inquire.

On the evening appointed for the entertainment, she went to the hotel of the British Legation, escorted by her husband.

Dressed in her rich and elegant mourning of jet on crape, glimmering light on blackest darkness, and looking herself paler and fairer by its contrast, she entered the grand drawing-room, leaning on the arm of her husband. She heard their names announced:

"The Duke and Duchess of Hereward."

Then she found herself in a room sparsely occupied by a very brilliant company, and stood--not, as she had expected to stand, among strangers--but in the midst of her own familiar friends, whom she had known in her girlhood at the court of St. Petersburg, or met, in her womanhood, in the drawing-rooms of London.

It was while she was still leaning on her husband's arm and receiving the courteous salutations of her old friends, that their host, Lord C--n, approached with a gentleman.

Valerie looked up and saw standing before her the young husband of her girlish love!

CHAPTER XXXIV.
RISEN FROM THE GRAVE.

Waldemar de Volaski, left as dead upon the duelling ground by his antagonist, the Baron de la Motte, was tenderly lifted by his second and the surgeon in attendance, laid upon a stretcher, and conveyed to the infirmary of a neighboring monastery, where he was charitably received by the brethren.

When he was laid upon a bed, undressed, and examined, it was discovered that he was not dead, but only swooning from the loss of blood.

When his wound was probed, it was found that the bullet had passed the right lobe of the lungs, and lodged in the flesh below the right shoulder blade. To extract it, under the circumstances, or to leave it there, seemed equally dangerous, threatening, on the one hand, inflammation and mortification, and, on the other, fatal hemorrhage. Therefore, the surgeon in charge of the case sent off to the nearest town to summon other medical aid, and meanwhile kept up the strength of the patient by stimulants. In the consultation that ensued on the arrival of the other surgeons, it was decided that the extraction of the bullet would be difficult and dangerous; but that in it lay the only chance of the patient's life.

On the next morning, therefore, Waldemar de Volaski was put under the influence of chloroform, and the operation was performed. His youth and vigorous constitution bore him safely through the trying ordeal, but could not save him from the terrible irritative fever that set in and held him in its fiery grasp for many days there after.

He was well tended by the holy brotherhood, who sent to the vine-dresser's cottage for information concerning him, that they might find out who and where were his friends, and write and apprise them of his condition.

But the vine-dresser could tell the monks no more than this--that the young man and young woman had come as strangers to the village, were married by the good Father Pietro in the church of San Vito, and had come to lodge in his cottage. The young pair had lived as merrily as two birds in a bush until the sudden arrival of an illustrious and furious signore, who tore the bride from the arms of her husband, and carried her off to the convent of Santa Madelena. That was all the vine-dresser knew.

The surgeon supplemented the vine-dresser's story with an account of the duel between the enraged baron and the young captain.

The good Father Pietro was next interviewed, and gave the names of the imprudent young pair whom he had tied together, as Waldemar Peter de Volaski and Valerie Aimee de la Motte; but besides this, who they were, or whence they came, he could not tell.

Inquiries were made in the village of San Vito, which only resulted in the information that the "illustrious" strangers had departed with their daughter no one knew whither.

Meanwhile the unfortunate victim of the duel tossed and tumbled, fumed and raved in fever and delirium, that raged like fire for nine days, and then left him utterly prostrated in mind and body. Many more days passed before he was able to answer questions, and weeks crept by before he could give any coherent account of himself.

His first sensible inquiry related to his bride.

"Where is she? What have they done with her?" he demanded to know.

"The illustrious signore has taken the signorita away with him, no one knows whither," answered the monk who was minding him.

"I know--so he has taken her away?--I know where he has taken her,--to Paris," faltered the victim, and immediately fainted dead away, exhausted by the effort of speaking these words.

His next question, asked after the interval of a week, related to the length of time he had been ill.

"How long have I lain stretched upon this bed?" he asked.

"The Signore Captain has been here four weeks," answered his nurse.

"Great Heaven! then I have exceeded my month's leave by two weeks! I shall be court-martialed and degraded!" cried the patient, starting up in great excitement, and instantly swooning away from the reaction.

In this manner the recovery of the wounded man became a matter of difficulty and delay; for as often as he rallied sufficiently to look into his affairs, their threatening aspect threw him back prostrated.

He recovered, however, by slow degrees.

As soon as he was able to sustain the continued exertion of talking, he requested one of the brothers on duty in the infirmary to write two letters at his dictation. The first was addressed to the colonel of his regiment, informing that officer of the long and severe illness of Captain de Volaski, and petitioning for the invalid an extended leave of absence. The other was to the Count de Volaski, apprising that nobleman of the condition of his son, and imploring him to hasten at once to the bedside of the patient.

The next morning Waldemar de Volaski sat up in bed and asked for stationery, and wrote with his own weak and trembling hand a short letter to his youthful bride--telling her that he had been very ill, but was now convalescent, and that as soon as he should be able to travel he would hasten to Paris and claim his wife in the face of all the fathers, priests and judges in Paris, or in the world. He addressed her as his well beloved wife, signed himself her ever-devoted husband, and had the temerity to direct his letter to Madame Waldemar de Volaski, Hotel de la Motte, Rue Faubourg St. Honore, Paris.

The mail left St. Vito only twice a week, so that the three letters left the post office on the same day to their respective destinations; one went to St. Petersburg, to the Colonel of the Royal Guards; one to Warsaw, to the Count de Volaski; and one to Paris, to Madame de Volaski.

In the course of the next week the writer received answers from all three letters. The first came from the colonel of his regiment, enclosing an extension of his leave of absence to three months; the second was answered in person by the Count de Volaski; the third was only an envelope, enclosing his letter to Valerie, crossed with this line:

"No such person to be found."

The meeting between the Count de Volaski and his reckless son was not in all respects a pleasant one. There was an explanation to be demanded by the father a confession to be made by the son. The count was divided between his anxiety for his son and indignation at that son's conduct.

"You exposed more than your own life by the escapade, sir!" said the elder Volaski, "You abducted a minor, sir; for doing which you might have been prosecuted for felony, and sent to the gaol!--a fate so much worse than your death in the duel would have been for the honor of your family, that, had you been consigned to it, I should have cursed the hour you were born and blown my own brains out, in expiation of my share in your existence!"

The yet nervous invalid shuddered, and covered his face with his hands.

"But even that was not the greatest calamity your rashness provoked! You presumed to carry off the French minister's daughter while they were yet in the dominions of the Czar! by doing which you might have caused a war between two great nations, and the sacrifice of a million of lives!"

"Sir, forbear! I have not yet recovered from the severe illness consequent upon my wound. Surely, I have suffered enough at the hands of the ruthless Baron de la Motte!" said Waldemar de Volaski.

"The Baron de la Motte, being your enemy, is mine also; yet I cannot but admit that he has dealt very leniently with the abductor of his daughter by merely shooting him through the lungs, and laying him on a bed of repentance, when he might have prosecuted him as a felon, and sent him to penal servitude!" said the count, severely. "But there," he exclaimed, "I will say no more on that subject. As you say, you have suffered enough already to expiate your fault. You have nearly lost your life, and you have quite lost your love; for, of course, you know that your fooling marriage with a minor was no marriage at all, unless her father had chosen to make it so by his recognition. And if you ever had a chance of winning the girl, you have lost it by your imprudence. You must try to get up your strength now, so as to go with me back to Warsaw."

So saying, the count left the bedside of his son, and went into the refectory of the monastery, where a substantial repast had been prepared to regale the traveler.

The young man wrote yet another letter to his love, enclosing it on this occasion in an envelope directed to the lady's maid, who had once assisted the lovers in
carrying on their correspondence; but as the maid had been long discharged from
the service of her mistress, it was impossible that the letter should have reached
her. The lover wrote again and again without receiving an answer to letters which
it is certain his lost bride never received.

Captain de Volaski's three months' extended leave of absence had nearly ex-
pired before he was in a condition to travel; and even then he had to go by slow
stages, riding only during the day and resting at night, until they reached Warsaw.

He spent a week at his father's castle, watched and wept over by his mother,
who had not a reproach for her son, nor anything to offer him but her sympathy
and her services. Six months had now passed away since his parting with his stolen
bride; and it was the day before his expected return to his regiment that a packet of
newspapers arrived for him, forwarded from St. Petersburg.

He tore the envelopes off them. They were English, French and German papers. He threw all away except the French papers. He eagerly examined them, in
the hope of seeing the name of the Baron de la Motte, and forming thereby some
idea of the movements of the family, and the whereabouts of Valerie.

The first paper he took up was *Le Courier de Paris*, and the first item that
caught his eye was this--

"MARRIED.--At the Church of Notre Dame, on Tuesday, March 1st, by the
Most Venerable, the Archbishop of Paris, the Duke of Hereward, to Valerie, only
daughter of the Baron de la Motte."

With the cry and spring of a panther robbed of its young, Volaski bounded
to his feet. His rage and anguish were equal, and beyond all power of articulate
or rational utterance. He strode up and down the floor like a maniac; he raved; he
beat his breast, and tore his hair and beard; and finally, he rushed into the parlor
where his father and mother were seated together over a quiet game of chess, and
he dashed the paper down on the table before them, smote his hand upon the fatal
marriage notice, and exclaimed in a voice of indescribable anguish:

"See! see! see! see!"

"It is just as I thought it would be," said the count, as he calmly read over the
item, and passed it to his amazed wife. "The baron has wisely taken the first oppor-

tunity of marrying off his wilful girl--the best thing he could have done for her. I am sure I am glad she is no daughter-in-law of mine! She who could so lightly elope from her father might as lightly elope from her husband also."

Waldemar made no reply, but stood looking the image of desolation, until his mother having read through the notice, and grasped the situation, arose and threw her arms around his neck, exclaiming in a burst of sympathy:

"Oh, my son! my son! my son! my son! forget her! forget the heartless jilt! she was unworthy of you!"

A burst of wild and bitter laughter answered this appeal and frightened the good lady half out of her wits.

"Let him go back to his regiment and be a man among men, and not lose his time whimpering after a silly girl, who has not sense enough even to take care of herself. The man to be most pitied is that husband of hers! Upon my word and honor, I am sorry for that English duke! Yes, *that* I am!" said the count, heartily.

The next day Waldemar de Volaski returned to his regiment at St. Petersburg.

As his brother officers happily knew nothing of his elopement with the minister's daughter, and the duel that followed it; but supposed that his long absence had been occasioned by a long illness, he escaped all that exasperating chaff that might, under the circumstances, have half maddened him.

He threw himself, for distraction, into all the wildest gayeties of the Russian capital, and led the life of a reckless young sinner, until he was suddenly brought to his senses by a domestic calamity. He received a telegram announcing the sudden death of his father and his elder brother, both of whom were instantly killed by an accident on the St. Petersburg and Warsaw Railroad, while on their way to the Russian capital.

Stricken with grief, and with the remorse which grief is sure to awaken in the heart of a wrong-doer not altogether hardened, Waldemar de Volaski hastened down to Warsaw to support his almost inconsolable mother through the horrors of that sudden bereavement and that double funeral.

By the death of his father and elder brother, he became the Count Volaski, and the heir of all the family estates; and there were left dependent on him his widowed mother and several younger brothers and sisters.

At the earnest request of his mother he resigned his commission in the Royal

Guards, and went down to reside with the family on the estate, during their retirement for the year of mourning.

Before that year was half over, however, the young Count de Volaski received a summons to the court of his sovereign.

He obeyed it immediately by hurrying up to St. Petersburg.

On his arrival, he presented himself at the Annitchkoff Palace to receive the commands of the Czar, and he was appointed Secretary of Legation to the new Russian Embassy about to proceed to Paris.

To Paris! to the home of Valerie de la Motte! The order agitated him to the profoundest depths of his being. He would have declined the honor about to be thrust upon him, could he have done so with propriety; but he could not, so there was no alternative but to kiss his sovereign's hand, express his sense of gratitude, and obey.

The embassy left St. Petersburg for the French capital almost immediately.

On the arrival at Paris they were established in the splendid Maison Francoise in the Champs Elysees.

As soon as he was at leisure, the Count de Volaski drove to the Rue Faubourg St. Honore, and to the Hotel de la Motte. He found the house shut up, and upon inquiry of a gend'arme, learned, with more surprise than regret, that the Baron and Baroness de la Motte had both been dead for some months; the baron, who was a free liver, had been suddenly stricken down by apoplexy, and the baroness, whose health had long been feeble, could not rally from the shock, but soon followed her husband.

"And,--where is their daughter, Madame la Duchesse d'Hereward?" hesitatingly inquired the Count de Volaski.

The gend'arme could not tell; he did not know; but supposed that she was living with her husband, Monsieur le Duc, on his estates in England.

No, clearly the gend'arme did not know; for, in fact, the Duke and the Duchess of Hereward were at that time living very quietly in the closed-up house at which the count and the gend'arme stood gazing while they talked.

Count de Volaski re-entered his carriage and returned to the Maison Francoise in time to attend the official reception of the embassy by the citizen-king at the Tuileries.

After the act of national and official etiquette, the embassy were free to enter into the social festivities of the gayest capital in the world.

Among other entertainments, a great diplomatic dinner was given at the English Legation, then the magnificent Hotel Borghese, once the residence of the beautiful Princess Pauline Bonaparte, but now the seat of the British Embassy. Among the invited guests were the Russian minister and his Secretary of Legation, Count de Volaski.

The count came late and found the splendid drawing-room honored with a small, but brilliant, company of ladies and gentlemen, the former among the most celebrated beauties, the latter the most distinguished statesmen of Europe.

Nearly every one in the room were strangers to the Russian count; but his English host, with sincere kindness and courtesy, took care to present him to all the most agreeable persons present.

"And now," whispered Lord C--n, in conclusion, "I have reserved the best for the last. Come and let me introduce you to the most interesting woman in Paris."

Count de Volaski suffered himself to be conducted to the upper end of the room, where a tall and elegant-looking woman, dressed in rich mourning, stood, leaning on the arm of a stately, middle-aged man.

Her face was averted as they approached; but she turned her head and he recognized the beautiful, pale face and lovely dark eyes of his lost bride.

And while the floor of the drawing-room seemed rocking with him, like the deck of a tempest-tossed ship, he heard the words of his host whirling through his brain:

"Madame, permit me to present to you Count de Volaski of St. Petersburg; Count, the Duchess of Hereward."

CHAPTER XXXV.
FACE TO FACE.

"Madame, permit me to present to you Count de Volaski, of St. Petersburg-- Count, the Duchess of Hereward," said Lord C., with old-time courtesy and formality.

The gentleman bowed low; the lady courtesied; nothing but the close compression of his lips beneath the golden mustache, and the paler shade on her pale cheeks, betrayed the "whirlwind of emotion" which swept through both their hearts; and these indications of disturbance were too slight to attract any attention.

Neither spoke, neither dared to speak. It was as much as each could do to maintain a conventional calmness through the terrible ordeal of such an introduction.

Lord C., happily unconscious of anything wrong, did the very best thing he could have done under the circumstances. Scarcely allowing the count and the duchess time to exchange their bow and courtesy, he turned to her companion and said:

"Duke, the Count de Volaski. Count, the Duke of Hereward."

Both gentlemen bowed; but *one*, the count, quivered from head to foot in the presence of his unconscious but successful rival.

"By the way, Count," said the duke, pleasantly, "the duchess, when Mademoiselle de la Motte, passed a year at the court of St. Petersburg with her parents. It is a wonder that you have not met before. Although, indeed, you may have done so," he added, as with an after-thought.

"We have met before," replied the Count de Volaski, in a low and measured tone.

"Of course! Of course! You are quite old friends," said the duke, gayly.

Fortunately, then a diversion was made. The heavy, purple satin curtains vailing the arch between the drawing-rooms and dining saloon were drawn aside by invisible hands, and a very dignified and officer-looking personage, in a powdered wig, clerical black suit, and gold chain, appeared, and with a low bow and with low tones, said:

"My lord and lady are served."

"Count, will you take the duchess in to dinner?--Duke, Lady C. will thank you for your arm," said the host, as, with a nod and a smile, he moved off in search of that particular ambassadress whom custom, or etiquette, or policy, required him to escort to the dining-room.

The Duke of Hereward with a polite wave of the hand, left his duchess in the charge of her appointed attendant, and went to meet Lady C., who was advancing toward him.

Count Volaski bowed, and silently offered his arm to the young duchess.

She did not take it; she could not; she stood as one paralyzed.

He was stronger, firmer, calmer; perhaps because he really felt less than she did. He took her hand and drew it within his own, and led her to her place in the little procession that was going to the dining-room.

He placed her in her chair at the table, and took his seat at her side.

Then the self-control of their order, the self-control instilled as a virtue by their education, and standing now in the place of all virtues, enabled them to maintain a superficial calmness that conducted them safely through the trying ordeal of this dinner-table.

Count de Volaski entered freely into the conversation of the guests. The Duchess of Hereward spoke but little; hers was a passive self-control, not an active one; she could force herself to be, or seem, composed; she could not force herself to talk; but her deep mourning dress was a good excuse for her extreme quietness, which was naturally ascribed to her recent and double bereavement.

The dinner was a long, long agony to her; the courses seemed almost endless in duration and numberless in succession; but at length the hostess arose and gave the signal for the ladies to retire and leave the gentlemen to their wine and politics.

The gentlemen all stood up while the ladies passed out to the drawing-room.

Valerie would willingly have gone off to hide herself in some bay-window or other nook or corner of the vast drawing-room, and taken up a book or a piece of music as an excuse for her reserve; but as they passed through the curtained archway leading from the dining-saloon to the drawing-room, Lady C., with the kindest intentions toward the supposed mourner, and with the motherly grace for which her ladyship was noted, drew Valerie's arm within her own and began a conversation, to draw her mind from the contemplation of her bereavements.

"What do you think of the young Russian count who brought you in to dinner, my dear?" inquired Lady C.

"I--he is a Pole," answered Valerie, in a low voice.

"Yes, I am aware that he is a Pole by birth; but he is a thorough Russian in politics and principles; has been in the service of the Czar since the age of fifteen.-- Here, my love, sit beside me," added her ladyship, as she sank gracefully down upon a sofa and drew her young guest to her side.

Valerie submitted in silence.

"Oh, by the way, however, I think I heard some one say that you had met the count at the court of St. Petersburg?" pursued Lady C.

"I--have met him," answered Valerie, in the same level tone.

"I am boring you, I fear, with this young Russian, my dear, but--"

"Oh no," softly interrupted Valerie.

"I was about to explain that I feel some interest in him from the fact that he is betrothed to my niece--"

"Betrothed! Your niece!" exclaimed Valerie, surprised out of the apathy of her despair.

"Yes, my love. Is there anything wonderful in that? It is a way these continental people have of doing things, you see. The Count Waldemar and my niece were betrothed to each other in their childhood. There is a very great attachment between them--at least on her part. The child seems to think that there is but one man in the world and his name is Waldemar de Volaski."

"But--I did not know--I thought--I did not think--the count had ever been in England," incoherently murmured Valerie.

"Nor has he; but what has that to do with it?" smiled her ladyship.

"Your niece--"

"Oh, I see! Because I am an Englishwoman my niece must be one, you think. You are mistaken, dear; she is French. My sister Anne married a Frenchman, the Marquis de St. Cyr. They had two children--Alphouse, a colonel in the Chasseurs d'Afrique, now in Algiers; and Aimee, now in the Convent of St. Rosalie. It was when the late Count de Volaski was here as the minister from Russia, that the acquaintance between the two families commenced and ripened into intimacy and the intimacy into friendship. Then Waldemar and Aimee were betrothed."

"How many years ago was that?" faintly inquired Valerie.

"Oh, about six--the young man was then about fifteen; the girl not more than twelve."

"They could not have known their own minds at that age," murmured Valerie.

"Oh, that was not at all necessary in a French betrothal," laughed the lady; "but, however, Aimee, child as she was, certainly knew her mind. The love of her betrothed husband was, and is, the religion of her life. I presume that Count Waldemar is equally constant; and that he will now press for a speedy marriage. My brother-in-law is down on his estates in Provence, just now; but I shall write and ask his permission to withdraw Aimee from her convent, in anticipation of her marriage, for of course she will be married from this house."

"But--her mother?"

"Oh! I should have told you; her mother, my dear sister Anne, passed away about a year after the betrothal of her daughter. The marquis took her loss very much to heart, and has never married again. The motherless girl has passed her life in a convent; but I hope to have her out soon. Here, my love, is an album containing portraits of my sister and brother-in-law and their children, taken at various times. You cannot mistake them, and they may interest you," said Lady C., taking a photographic volume from a gilded stand near, and laying it upon her guest's lap.

Valerie received it with a nod of thanks, and the lady glided away to give some of her attention to her other guests.

"The young English duchess is lovely, but too sad," said an embassadress, as the hostess joined her.

"Ah! yes, poor child! lost her father and mother within a few weeks of each other," answered Lady C.

"But that was six months ago; she ought to have recovered some cheerfulness by this time," remarked old Madame Bamboullet, who was a walking register of all the births, deaths and marriages of high life in Paris for the last half century.

"Well, you see she has not done so; but here come the gentlemen," observed Lady C., as a rather straggling procession from the dining-room entered.

The host, Lord C., went up to the embassadress to whom it was his cue to be most attentive.

The Duke of Hereward sought out his hostess, and entered into a bantering conversation with her.

Count Waldemar de Volaski came directly up to Valerie where she sat alone on the sofa in a distant corner of the room. The little gilded stand stood before her, and the photographic album lay open upon it. Her eyes were fixed upon the album, and were not raised to see the new-comer; but the sudden accession of pallor on her pale face betrayed her recognition of him.

He drew a chair so close to her sofa that only the little gilded stand stood between them. His back was toward the company; his face toward her; his elbows, with unpardonable rudeness, were placed upon the stand, and his hands supported his chin, as he stared into her pale face with its downcast eyes.

"Valerie," he said.

She did not look up.

"Valerie de Volaski!" he muttered.

"My wife!"

She shuddered, but did not lift her eyes.

She shrank into herself, as it were, and her eyes fell lower than before.

"Is it thus we two meet at last?" he demanded, in low, stern, measured tones, pitched to meet her ear alone. "Is it thus I find you, after all that has passed between us, bearing the name and title of another man who calls himself your husband, oh! shame of womanhood!"

"They told me our marriage was not legal, was not binding!" she panted under her breath.

"It should have been religiously, sacredly binding up on you as it was upon me, until we could have made it legal. It is amazing that you could have dreamed of marriage with another man!" muttered Volaski.

"But they told me you were dead. They told me you were dead!" she gasped, as if she were in her own death throes.

"Even if they had told you truly--even if I had been dead--dead by the hand of your father--could that circumstance have excused you for rushing with such indecent haste to the altar with another man? It was but a poor tribute to the memory of the husband of your choice (if he had been dead) to marry again within six months."

"Oh, mercy! Oh, my heart! my heart! They forced me into that marriage, Waldemar! They forced me into that marriage! I was as helpless as an infant in the hands of my father and my mother!" she panted, in a voice that was the more heart-rending from half suppression.

"Valerie! love! wife!" murmured Volaski, in low and tender tones, as he essayed to take her hand.

But she snatched it from him hastily, gasping:

"Do not speak to me in that way! Do not call me love or wife!"

"No man on earth has a better right to speak to you in this way than I have. No **other** man in the world has the right to call you love or wife but me! You **are** my wife!" grimly answered the young count.

"I am the wife of the Duke of Hereward. Oh, Heaven, that I were a corpse instead!" gasped Valerie.

"'The wife of the Duke of Hereward!' Have you then forgotten our betrothal at St. Petersburg? Our flight from Warsaw to St. Vito? Our marriage at the little chapel of Santa Maria? Our short, blissful honeymoon in the vine-dresser's cottage under the Apennines?" he inquired, bitterly.

"I have forgotten nothing! Oh, Heaven! Oh, earth! Oh, Waldemar! that I could die! that I could die!" she wailed in low, heartbroken tones.

It was well for her that the corner sofa stood in the shade, far removed from the seats of the other guests in that long drawing-room.

"Valerie! love! wife!" he murmured again.

"Oh, Waldemar, if I were your wife, as I truly believed myself then to have been, oh, why did you not defend and protect me from all the world, even from my father--even from myself? Oh, why did you suffer me to be torn from your protection, to be deceived with a false story of your death, and forced into this marriage? Oh, Waldemar! if I were indeed and in truth your lawful wife, as I believed myself to be, why, oh why did you permit all these evils to happen to me? Ah, what a position is mine! What a position! I cannot bear it! I will not bear it! I will not live! I will kill myself! I **ought** to kill myself! It is the only way out of this!" she wailed, wringing her hands.

"I will kill that Duke of Hereward!" hissed Volaski, through his clenched teeth.

"Hush! For mercy's sake, hush! Put away such thoughts from your heart! I, the only wrong-doer, should be the only victim! Whatever wrong has been done, the Duke of Hereward has been blameless. He knew nothing of my former marriage; if he had, I do not believe he would have married me, even if I had been a princess."

"He was deceived, then?" coldly inquired the count.

"He was; but not willingly by me. I was forced to be silent about my marriage."

"You were 'forced' from my protection! 'forced' to conceal the fact of your marriage with me! and 'forced' to marry the Duke of Hereward under false colors. Could force on one side, and feebleness on the other, be carried any further than this?" muttered Volaski, between his teeth.

"I knew how helpless, in the hands of my parents, I was," wailed Valerie.

"Well, you are a duchess! Do you love the Duke of Hereward?"

"Oh, mercy! what shall I say? He deserves all my love, honor, and duty!"

"Does he **get** his deserts?" mockingly inquired Volaski.

"Ah! wretch that I am, why do I live?--I give him honor and duty; but love! **love is not mine to give!**" she murmured, in almost inaudible tones.

Their conversation--if an interview so emotional, so full of "starts and flaws" could be called so--had been carried on in a very low tone, while the count turned over the leaves of the photographic album, as if examining the portraits, but really without seeing one.

They were, however, so absorbed that neither perceived the approach of a footman until the man actually set down a small golden tray with two little porcelain cups of tea on the stand between them, and retired.

Valerie looked up with a sudden shudder of terror. Had the company, or any one of their number, overheard any part of the fatal interview? No, the company were drinking tea, at the other end of the room.

And now the Duke of Hereward, with a tea-cup in his hand, sauntered toward them, saying, as he reached the stand:

"Lady C. has just been telling me that you are showing the duchess some interesting family pictures there--among the rest, those of your **belle fiancee**. When shall I congratulate you, Count?"

"Not yet; I will advise your grace of my marriage," answered the count, gravely.

"Something gone wrong in that direction," thought the duke, but his good humor was invincible.

"If you have no engagement for to-morrow evening, I hope you will come and dine with us **en famille**, for we do not see much company, the duchess and myself."

Valerie cast an imploring look on the count, silently praying him to decline the invitation; but Volaski did not understand the meaning of the look, or did not care to do so, for he immediately accepted the invitation in the following unequivocal terms:

"I have no engagement for to-morrow; and I shall be very happy to come and dine with you."

"So be it then," said the duke, frankly. "Now, Valerie, my love, bid the count good-evening. It is time to go."

The young duchess arose wearily from the sofa, and slightly courtesied her adieux.

The count stood up and bowed with a profound reverence that seemed ironical to her sensitive mind.

The guests were now all taking leave of their host and hostess.

The Duke and Duchess of Hereward were among the last to go.

"I am very sorry that I brought you out this evening, love. I saw--indeed, every one saw, and could not help seeing--that this dinner-party has been a great trial to you. It will not bear an encore. You must have time to recover your cheerfulness, dearest, before you are again brought into a large company," said the duke, kindly, as soon as they were seated together in their carriage.

"Did people attribute my dullness to--to--to--," began Valerie, by way of saying something, but her voice faltered and broke down.

"To your recent double bereavement?--certainly they did, my love. They knew

   'No crowds Make up for parents in their shrouds,'
and were not cruel enough to criticise your filial grief, my Valerie."

"I am glad of that; but I am very sorry you have invited the Count de Volaski to dinner to-morrow."

"Oh, why?"

"Because I do not like company."

"He is only one guest and will dine with us quietly. He will amuse you."

"No, he will not; he will bore me. I wish you would write and put him off."

"Impossible, my dear Valerie! What earthly excuse could I make for such an unpardonable piece of rudeness?"

"Tell him that I am ill, out of spirits, anything you like so that you tell him not to come."

"My dearest one, you certainly are ill and out of spirits, and very morbid besides. So much the more reason why you should be gently aroused and amused. Dinner parties weary and distress you; but the count's visit will relieve and amuse you."

"Oh! I *do* think I *ought* to know what is good for me and what I want better than any one else," exclaimed Valerie, speaking impatiently to the duke for the first time during their married life.

"But you don't, love; that is all. The count is coming to dine with us to-morrow. That is settled. Now, here we are at home," said the duke, as the carriage rolled through the massive archway and entered the court-yard of the magnificent Hotel de la Motte.

CHAPTER XXXVI.
A GATHERING STORM.

After a night of sleeplessness and anguish, Valerie arose to a day of duplicity and terror.

The anticipation of the evening was intolerable to her; the prospect of sitting down at her own table between the Duke of Hereward and the Count de Volaski overwhelmed her with a sense of horror and loathing.

Faint, pale, and trembling, she descended to the breakfast-room, where she found the duke already awaiting her.

Shocked at her aspect, he hastened to meet her and lead her to an easy-chair on the right of the breakfast-table.

"You are not able to be out of your bed, Valerie. You should not have attempted to rise," he said, as he carefully seated her.

"I told you last night that I was very ill," she answered coldly, as she sank wearily back on the cushion.

"That infernal dinner party! It has prostrated you quite. I am so grieved; I will not suffer you to be so severely tried again!" said the duke, vehemently.

"And you will write this morning and put off the count's visit," pleaded Valerie.

"No, my dear, I cannot," answered the duke, regretfully.

"Then I cannot come down to dinner. That is all," she said, sullenly closing her eyes.

"I shall be sorry for that; but we must do the best we can without you for the count, having been invited, must be permitted to come."

She languidly drew up to the table, and touched the bell that summoned the footman with the breakfast-tray.

When it was placed upon the table, she poured out two cups of coffee, handed one to the duke, and took the other herself.

When she had drained it, she arose, excused herself, and went back to her own room.

She closed and locked the door, and threw herself upon the bed, groaning:

"Oh! how could Waldemar accept that invitation? How can he bear to sit down with me at the Duke of Hereward's table? Has he no delicacy? No pity? Ah, mercy, what a state is mine! And yet I was not to blame for *this*! I have not deserved it! I have not deserved it! One of us three must die; I, or Waldemar, or the Duke of Hereward; and I am the one; for, *I hate myself* for the position I am in! I *hate,* LOATHE and utterly ABHOR myself! I do. I do. I wish the lightning would strike me dead! dead, before I have to meet one of them again!" she moaned, rolling and grovelling on the bed.

There came a soft rap at the door, followed by the kind voice of the duke, saying:

"Valerie, Valerie, my love! How are you? Do you want anything? May I come in?"

"No! I want rest! I do not want you!" she answered, so sharply as to astonish the duke, who spoke again however, deprecatingly and soothingly.

"Is there anything that I can do for you outside, then, my dear?"

"You can go away and let me alone, or you can stand there chattering until you drive me crazy!" she answered, ungratefully.

"Good morning, my love; I will not trouble you again soon," muttered the duke, as he walked away from the duchess' door.

"I never knew such a change as this that has come over her. She is as cross as a catamount! There may be a cause for it. There may--I will send for a physician," he added, as he went down stairs.

Valerie kept her room all day.

Count de Volaski came to dinner at eight o'clock and was received by the duke alone.

He smiled grimly when his host apologized for the absence of the duchess, by explaining the delicate condition of her health since the death of her parents, and the injury she had received from the fatigue and excitement of the dinner-party on the preceding evening.

The duke and the count dined *tete-a-tete*, and sat long over their wine, although they drank but little. After dinner they played chess together all the evening, and then parted, apparently the best of friends on both sides, really good friends on the duke's.

The next morning a letter was handed Valerie, while she sat at breakfast with the duke.

She recognized the handwriting of Count de Volaski, and put it in her pocket to read when she was alone.

The duke was not suspicious or inquisitive. He asked no questions.

As soon as the duchess found herself alone in her chamber, she locked the door to keep out intruders, and sat down and opened the letter.

Its contents were sufficiently startling. They were as follows:

"RUSSIAN LEGATION, RUE ST. HONORE.

"VALERIE: You avoid me in vain! You cannot shake me off. I accepted the duke's invitation to dinner last evening for the sake of seeing you again, and for the chance of having a final explanation with you; but you kept away from the dinner. Such expedients will not avail you.

"I write now to assure you that I must and will see you, to make an arrangement with you. I write openly, at the risk of having this letter fall into the hands of the duke; for I do not care if it does so fall. I would just as willingly say to him what I now say to you. I am quite willing to provoke a crisis. The present state of things maddens me. I wonder it does not *kill* you! When you married the Duke of Hereward within six months after my supposed death by the hands of your father, you acted cruelly, but not criminally; now that you know I am living, you must also know that every hour you continue to live under the roof of the Duke of Hereward you are a criminal. I do not require you to come to *me*. I do not wish to live with you again, although I love you; but I *do* require you to leave the Duke of Hereward and go away by yourself. I know you now, Valerie. You are as weak as water. You cannot go to the noble gentleman who has been so deeply deceived by you and your parents and tell him the secret that you have kept from him so long. You have not the moral courage to do so. But you can leave him. It is to arrange for your flight and for your future safety that I now demand and *insist* upon a private interview with you.

"Write to me at the *poste-restante*, and tell me when and where I can see you alone. Should you refuse to grant me this interview, I will myself go to the Duke of Hereward and tell him the whole story. He may not resent your former marriage; but he will never forgive you, living, or your parents in their graves, for the deception that has been practiced upon him. I will wait twenty-four hours for your answer, and then if I fail to receive it, or fail to get a favorable one, I shall come immediately to the Hotel de la Motte and seek an explanation with the duke. I shall direct this letter by the name and title you now bear, so as to prevent mistakes; but it is the last time I shall so address you. And I sign myself, for all eternity,

"Your true husband, WALDEMAR DE VOLASKI."

Valerie read the cruel letter to its close, then dropped it on her lap, and sank back in her chair, helpless, breathless, almost lifeless. Minutes crept into hours, and still she sat there in the same position, without motion, thought, or feeling-- stricken, spell-bound, entranced.

She was aroused at length by a rap at her chamber-door.

She started, shuddering, to her feet, and spasm after spasm shook her galvanized frame, as she picked up her letter, found a match, drew it, set fire to the paper, threw it, blazing, down upon the marble hearth, and watched it until it was consumed to a little heap of light ashes.

"There! That can never fall into the Duke of Hereward's hands *now*!" she said with a bitter laugh.

Meanwhile the rapping continued.

"Well! well! well! well! Can't you be patient!" she exclaimed, very *im*patiently, as she tottered tremblingly across the room and opened the door.

Her dressing-maid, Mademoiselle Desiree, was there.

"*Pardonnez moi, madame*; but you ordered me to come to dress you for a drive at twelve. The clock has just struck, madame," said the girl deprecatingly.

Valerie put her hand to her head in a bewildered way, and stared at the speaker a full minute before she could recollect herself sufficiently to reply.

"Yes--yes--yes--yes--I believe so. You can come in."

The girl entered and stood waiting for orders. Receiving none, she ventured to inquire:

"What dress shall madame wear?"

"My--my writing desk! Bring it here to me," answered the lady, as she sank into a chair, and drew a little ivory stand before her.

"I wonder if madame indulges in absinthe in the morning?" was the secret thought of the discreet Mademoiselle Desiree, as she brought the elegant little malachite writing-desk, and placed it before her mistress.

Valerie opened it, took out a piece of note-paper and wrote:

"I cannot write much. I am stricken. I am dying. I hope you are right in what you say. Come here tomorrow at twelve, noon. I will give you the interview you seek."

*   *   *   *   *

This note was without date, address or signature, or any word to guide a strange reader to its true meaning. She put it into a sealed envelope, and directed it to ***Count de Volaski, Poste Restante***.

Then she sat back in her chair, exhausted from the slight exertion.

The maid watched her mistress for a little while, and then said:

"Pardon, madame; but it is half-past twelve."

"Yes! I must dress," said Valerie rising.

"What costume will madame wear?"

"Any. It does not signify."

The maid indulged in an imperceptible shrug of her shoulders, and laid out an elegant black rep silk, heavily trimmed with black crape and jet, with mantle, bonnet and vail to match.

"White or black gloves, madame?"

"Black, of course. It is not a wedding reception."

"Pardon, madame," said the girl; and she added the black gloves to the costume.

Valerie was soon dressed, and then the maid said:

"The carriage waits, madame."

Valerie took the note she had prepared and went down stairs, entered her barouche, and ordered the coachman to drive to the British Legation, Hotel Borghese, Rue Faubourg St. Honore.

When the carriage rolled through the archway into the courtyard, and drew up before the magnificent palace, interesting from having been built for and occupied by the beautiful Princess Pauline Bonaparte, Valerie alighted and handed her letter to the footman, with directions to go and post it while she was making her call.

The man knocked at the door for his mistress, and then hurried away to do her errand.

It was the conventional "dinner call" that brought Valerie to the Hotel Borghese.

An English footman admitted the visitor, conducted her to the private drawing-room of Lady C., and announced her.

Several other ladies, whom Valerie had met at the dinner party, were there on the same duty as herself.

Lady C. advanced from among them to receive the new comer, kissed her on both cheeks, inquired affectionately after her health and then made her sit down in the most comfortable of the easy-chairs at hand.

After courteously saluting the ladies present, Valerie subsided into a dull silence, from which she could not arouse herself; but her voice was not missed, since every visitor seemed anxious to talk rather than listen, and therefore kept up a chattering that would have carried off the palm in a contest with a village sewing-circle or aviary full of excited magpies.

Valerie, the last to enter, was also the first to rise, but Lady C. detained her by a slight signal, and she sat down again, and relapsed into dullness and silence.

One by one the visitors arose and took leave, chattering to the very last.

As soon as the two ladies were left alone together, Lady C. took Valerie's hand, and gazing earnestly in her face, said:

"What is the matter with you, my child? You look pale and ill. Although I am so glad to see you, under any circumstances, I am half inclined to scold you for coming out at all."

For a moment Valerie felt inclined to open her oppressed and suffering heart to this sweet, matronly friend, and tell her the whole, bitter truth, and seek her wise counsel; but again the want of moral courage, which had always been so fatal to her welfare, sealed her lips.

"Well," said Lady C., after a short pause for that answer that never came, "I will not press the question. 'The heart knoweth its own bitterness.'"

"Yes," murmured Valerie, in a very low voice. Then, not to seem indifferent or unsocial, and also, if the truth must be told of her, to gratify a gnawing curiosity, she inquired:

"How goes the expected marriage of your niece, madame?"

"I cannot tell you dear. I have been daily expecting some communication on the subject from de Volaski: but as yet he has made none. After coming to Paris for the purpose, (for of course his office in the embassy is a mere sinecure and a plausible excuse,) he betrays the bashfulness of a girl in pressing his suit; but some men, some of the best and purest of men, are just that way--in love affairs as shy women," said her ladyship.

Valerie smiled bitterly. She thought she understood the reason why the Count de Volaski was in no hurry to press the suit for marriage with a dreaming girl, to whom he had been arbitrarily contracted when he was a boy of fifteen, and she a child of twelve.

"I shall, however, write again to her father. I will not have my sister's daughter wasting her youth in a convent, while waiting for a tardy suitor."

Valerie smiled again, and then arose to take her leave.

Lady C. kissed her affectionately, and promised soon to visit her at the Hotel de la Motte.

"But--how long will you remain there?" inquired her ladyship.

"I do not know. Until some business connected with my father's will shall be arranged, I think. We are there on sufferance only. My cousin, Louis, the present baron, wrote from Algiers, very kindly asking us to occupy the Hotel de la Motte at any time when business or pleasure should call us to Paris. The house was the home of my childhood, and I prefer to live in it as long as I may. The duke, though he would rather live at the '*Trois Freres*,' yields to my whim, and so we occupy the Hotel de la Motte, but I do not know for how long a time."

"Until you leave Paris, I presume?"

"Yes, probably," answered Valerie, as with another kiss, she took leave of her kind friend.

"Shall I ever see her sweet face, hear her sweet voice again?" murmured the young duchess, as she passed out to her carriage.

"You posted my letter?" she inquired of the footman who opened the carriage-door.

"Yes, your grace."

"That will do. Home."

The footman repeated the order to the coachman, who drove back to the Hotel de la Motte.

As Valerie entered her morning-room after laying off her bonnet and wrappings, she found the Duke of Hereward there, reading the papers.

He arose and placed a chair for her, saying kindly:

"I hope your drive has done you good, dear; if it has not been so long as to fatigue you."

"I have only been to the Hotel Borghese to call on Lady C.," replied Valerie, sinking into the chair and leaning back.

"Now that I look well at you, I see that you are tired. A very little exertion seems to fatigue you now, Valerie. I do not understand your condition. It makes me anxious. I have asked Velpeau to call and see you. He will look in this afternoon."

"Thanks, you are very kind--too kind to me, as fretful and miserable as I am," replied Valerie, with a momentary compunction--only a momentary one, for the deep fear, horror and despair which had seized her soul left her little sensibility to comparative trifles.

"My poor child," said the duke, looking compassionately on her pale, worn face, "do you not know that I can make all allowance for you? You are suffering very much. I hope Velpeau will be able to do something for you. You know he stands at the head of the medical profession in Paris, which is as much as to say, in the world."

"Yes, I know," said Valerie, indifferently. Then, with sudden earnestness, she exclaimed: "I wish *you* would do something for me."

"Why, my poor girl, I would do anything in the world for you. Tell me what you want me to do."

"I know you cannot leave Paris now, and so you cannot, yourself, take me to England; but I wish to go there; I wish you to send me there to Hereward Hold, where we passed so many peaceful months."

"To send you there *alone*, Valerie?" inquired the duke, in surprise.

"No, but with my personal attendants, and with any discreet old lady you may choose to appoint as my companion, if, like an old Spanish husband, you think your young wife may require watching when she is out of your sight," she added, with a relapse into her irritable mood.

"Valerie! you wrong me and yourself by such a thought," said the duke, gravely.

"I know I do, and I know I am a wretch! but I want to go to England. I want to get away from everybody, and be by myself. You promised to do what I wanted done. That is what I want done."

"Do you wish 'to get away' from *me*, Valerie?"

"Yes, from you and from *everybody*, except from my servants, who are not my companions, and therefore don't bore me."

"It must be as I thought," said the duke to himself; "all this eccentricity, this nervous irritability has a natural cause, and not an alarming one, and it must be humored."

"Will you keep your promise?" she testily inquired.

"Certainly, my dear child. Anything to please you. You will see Velpeau this afternoon. If after consulting him you still think it necessary to leave Paris for Hereward Hold, I will send you there under proper protection. By the by, you succeed very well in getting away from your friends I think. The Count de Volaski called here while you were away this forenoon. He seemed disappointed in not seeing you. He looks ill. I never saw a man change so within the last few days. I should not wonder if he were on the very verge of a bad fever. I wish you had seen him. He was quite a friend of yours in St. Petersburg, I believe."

"I used to see him every day in the public assemblies to which we were always going. I wish you wouldn't talk about him," gasped Valerie, with a nervous shudder, as she arose and left the room.

"What a little misanthrope she has grown to be; but it is only a temporary affliction. She will get over it in a few weeks," said the duke to himself, as he resumed the reading of his newspaper.

The next day Valerie arose at her usual hour, and breakfasted *tete-a-tete* with the duke. She knew that this day must decide her fate, and she tried to nerve herself to bear all that it might bring her, even as the frailest women sometimes brace themselves to bear torture and death.

At eleven in the forenoon, the duke left the house to go to the Hotel de Ville to keep an appointment that would detain him until three in the afternoon.

Valerie knew all about this appointment, and had therefore fixed the hour of noon as the safest time for her interview with the count.

Twelve o'clock, therefore, found her dressed in her deepest mourning, and seated in her private drawing-room, awaiting the advent of her most dreaded visitor, Waldemar de Volaski.

CHAPTER XXXVII.
A SENTENCE OF BANISHMENT.

Valerie, in an agony of terror, waited for her expected visitor.

Did she love him, then?

Ah, no! Horror at the position in which she found herself so filled her soul as to leave no room for any softer emotion. She loved no one in the world, not even herself; she wished for nothing on earth but death, and only her religious faith, or her superstitious fears, restrained her from laying sacrilegious hands upon her own life.

While watching for her dreaded guest she bitterly communed with herself.

"No one ever really loved me," she moaned. "Every one connected with me loved only himself, or herself, and sacrificed me. My father and my mother cared only for themselves and their own ambitions, and so they immolated me, their only child, to their gratification; my suitors loved only themselves and their passions, and immolated me! And I--I love no one and hate myself! hate the creature they have all combined to make me! If it were not for that which comes after death I would not exist an hour longer--I would die!"

As she muttered this the little ormolu clock on the mantlepiece struck twelve.

"The hour has come. He will be here in another moment! Oh, why could he not leave me in peace? Oh, what shall I do?" she exclaimed, in her excitement rising from her seat and beginning to pace up and down the room with wild, disordered steps.

Sometimes she stopped to listen, but without hearing any sound that might herald the approach of a visitor; then resumed her wild and purposeless walk, until the clock struck the quarter, when she suddenly threw herself down in the chair, muttering:

"Fifteen minutes late! I do not want to see him! But since he is to come, I wish he had come, and this was all over."

Another quarter of an hour passed, and her visitor had not arrived.

Again in her anxiety she arose and began to walk the floor and to look out occasionally at a window which commanded the approach to the house.

No one, however, was in sight.

She sat down again, muttering:

"This seems an intentional affront, an insult. He treats me with no consideration. Well, perhaps I deserve none. Oh! I wish I knew to whom my duty is due! I wish I had some one of whom I dared to ask counsel! I certainly did wed Waldemar. I certainly did believe him to be my lawful husband, and **then** my duty was clearly due to him. But my parents came and tore me away from him, and told me that my marriage was not lawful, and that Waldemar de Volaski was not my husband. Then they took me to Paris, and told me that I must forget the very existence of my lover. Still, I should never have dreamed of another marriage while I thought Waldemar lived; for I loved him with all my heart, and only wished to live until I should be of an age to contract a legal marriage with him, with whom I had already made a sacramental one. But they told me that Waldemar was **dead**, slain by the hand of my father! and they bade me keep the secret of my first marriage, and to contract a second one with the Duke of Hereward! Oh, if I had but known that Waldemar still lived, the tortures of the Inquisition should not have forced me into this second marriage! But believing Waldemar to be dead, I suffered myself to be persecuted, worried and ***weakened*** into this marriage! Oh! that I had been strong enough to bear the miseries of my home; to resist the forces brought to bear against me! Oh, that I had been brave enough to tell the whole truth of my marriage with Waldemar de Volaski to the Duke of Hereward before he had committed his honor to my keeping by making me his wife! That course would have saved me then with less of suffering than I have to bear now. But I weakly permitted myself to be forced, with this secret on my conscience, into a marriage with the Duke of Hereward. And now I dare not tell him the truth! And now my first husband has come back and hates me for my inconstancy, and my second husband knows nothing about it! Now to whom do I rightly belong! To whom do I owe duty? To Waldemar? To the duke? Who knows? Not I! One thing only is clear to me, that I must not live with either of them as a wife, henceforth! Heaven forgive those who forced me into this position, for I fear that I never can do so!"

While these wild and bitter thoughts were passing through her tortured mind the clock struck one and startled her from her reverie.

"Ah! something has prevented his coming," she said to herself, as she once more looked out of the window. Then she relapsed into her sad reverie.

"I can never, never be happy in this world again--never! But if I only knew my duty I would do it. I don't know it. I only know that I must go clear away from both these--" She shuddered and left the sentence incomplete even in her thoughts.

Just then a footman entered with a note upon a little silver tray.

She took it languidly, but all her languor vanished as she recognized the handwriting of Waldemar de Volaski.

"Who brought this?" she inquired of the servant.

"Un garcon from the Hotel de Russe, madame."

"Is he waiting for an answer?"

"Oui, madame."

She had asked these questions partly to procrastinate the opening of the note she dreaded to read. Now slowly and sadly she drew it from its envelope, unfolded and read:

"HOTEL DE RUSSE, Tuesday Morning.

"UNFAITHFUL WIFE--An engagement at the Tuileries, for the very hour you named, prevents me from meeting you at your appointed time. Write by the messenger who brings this, and tell me when you can see me.

"Your wronged husband, VOLASKI."

While reading this, she shivered as with an ague. When she had finished she crushed it up in her hand and put it in her pocket with the intention of destroying it on the first opportunity.

Then she went to a little ornamental writing-desk that stood in the corner of the room, and took a pencil and a sheet of note paper and wrote these words, without date or signature:

"I was ready to see you this noon. I cannot at this instant tell at what hour I can be certain to be alone; but will find out and let you know in the course of this day."

She placed this note in an envelope, sealed it with a plain seal, and sent it down by the footman to Count Waldemar's messenger.

Then she hurried up to her own bedchamber, rang for her maid, changed her dress for a white wrapper, and threw herself down, exhausted, upon a lounge.

She was almost fainting.

"This must be something like death! Oh, if it were only death!" she sighed, as she closed her eyes.

An hour later she was found here by the Duke of Hereward, who showed no surprise at finding her reclining there, but only said that Doctor Velpeau was below stairs and would like to see her.

"Let him come up, then," coldly answered Valerie.

And the duke himself went to conduct the physician to his patient.

He left them together for an hour, at the end of which Doctor Velpeau came down and reported to the anxious husband that his wife was not seriously out of health that her malady was more of the mind than the body, and that amusement and society would be her best medicines.

"Just what I cannot prevail on her to take," said the duke, with an impatient shrug. "She will go nowhere, will see nobody; but shuts herself up and mopes. Now, to-day, I have received intelligence concerning the rather intricately embarrassed affairs of the late Baron de la Motte, which will oblige me to start for Algiers, for a personal interview with his heir-at-law, an officer in the Chasseurs d'Afrique, who cannot get leave of absence to come to me. Now the question is, Doctor, shall I take the duchess with me, or leave her here? Is she well enough to be left, or strong enough to travel?"

"Both! She is both. I assure you she is not at all ill in body. Put the question to herself. If she should be willing to go, take her. The trip will do her good. If she prefers to stay, leave her. She is in no danger of illness or death."

"But I should be gone, probably, a fortnight. Could I, with safety to herself, take her so far away, for so long a time, from the best medical advice? or could I, on the other hand, leave her here for so distant a bourne and so long an absence?"

"With perfect safety; barring, of course, the human possibilities to which even the most fortunate, the most healthful and the best-guarded among us are more or less subject. But again I counsel you to leave it to the duchess, whether she shall remain here or accompany you to Algiers. She is equally fit for either plan," said the great physician, as he drew on his gloves.

"I will take the duchess with me, if she will go. If not, I will leave here under your charge, Doctor," said the duke.

"Much honored, I am sure, in attending her grace," replied the French physician, with the extravagant politeness of his countrymen.

As soon as Doctor Velpeau had gone, the Duke of Hereward went up stairs to see his wife, and, sitting by the lounge on which she still reclined, he told her of the urgent business that required his immediate departure for Algiers.

"Algiers! Why, that is in Africa! another quarter of the globe! a long, long way off!" she exclaimed, starting up with an eagerness that the duke mistook for alarm and distress.

"Oh, no, dear, it is not. It only *sounds* so. It is about eight hundred miles nearly due south of Paris. We go by train to Marseilles in a few hours, and by steamer to Algiers in a couple of days. You will go with me, dear. The change will do you good," said the duke, gayly.

"I! Oh, no, I could not think of such a thing! Pray, pray, do not ask me to do so!" exclaimed Valerie, in a tone of such genuine terror that the duke hastened to say:

"Certainly not, if you do not wish it, my love. I should be happier to have you with me, and I think the trip would benefit your health, but--"

"Did that horrid doctor advise you to take me to Algiers?" testily interrupted the young duchess.

"He said the change would do you good if you should like to go; but not other-wise. He said that you should be left to decide for yourself."

"Then he has quite as much judgment as the world gives him credit for, and that is not the case with every one."

"Now you are left to your own choice, to go or not to go."

"Then I choose not to go, most decidedly."

"Very well," said the duke, with a disappointed air; "then there is no need that I should delay my departure for another day. I shall leave for Marseilles by the night's express, Valerie."

"As you please," she wearily replied.

"I may be gone a fortnight, Valerie, and I may not be gone more than ten days; the length of my absence will depend upon contingencies; but I shall hurry back with all possible dispatch."

"Yes, I am sure you will," she answered, because she did not know what else to say.

"And I will write to you every day."

"Thank you."

"Will you write to me every day?"

"Certainly, if you wish me to do so."

"Of course I wish you to do so, my love," said the duke, as he stooped and pressed his lips on the pale cheek of his "wayward child," as he sometimes called her.

He then left the room to give orders to his valet and groom to pack up and be ready to attend him on his journey.

As soon as she found herself alone, Valerie arose, slipped on a dressing-gown, sat down to her writing-desk, and wrote the following note, as usual, without name, date, or signature:

"Come to me at noon to-morrow; or, if you cannot do so, write and fix your own hour, any time will suit me equally well, or rather, *ill*."

She put this note in an envelope, sealed it, and directed it to Monsieur Le Count de Volaski, Russian Embassy.

Then she rang for her maid, and sent her out to post the letter.

Valerie made an effort to dress for dinner that evening, and dined with the duke for the last time--yes, for the very last time in this world.

After the Duke had risen from the table and pressed a parting kiss upon her lips before leaving her to enter the carriage that was to take him to the railway station, she never saw his face again--nay more--though she honored and revered him, she never even wished or intended to see him again.

She witnessed his departure with tearful eyes, yet with a sense of infinite relief. ***One of them was gone!*** Oh, how she wished that the other would go also!

She loved neither of them. She had lost the power of loving. Her love, by her awful position, was frightened into its death-throes. All she desired to do, was to get away from them both, and like a haunted hare, or wounded bird, creep into some safe hiding-place to die in peace.

She retired early that evening, and, for the first time for several days, slept in peace.

The next day she arose, and, contrary to her custom in the morning, dressed herself to receive company.

She waited all the forenoon in expectation of receiving a note from the Count de Volaski, either accepting her appointment or arranging another one; but when the clock struck the hour of noon without her having heard from him, she naturally concluded that he meant to answer her note in person, by coming at the hour named. So she went down into the small drawing-room to be ready to receive him.

She was right in her conclusions; for she had scarcely been seated five minutes when a footman entered and presented the count's card.

"Show the gentleman up," she said in a voice that she vainly tried to render steady.

A few minutes passed, the door opened, and Count de Volaski entered the room.

She arose to receive him, but did not advance a single step to meet him.

He came on, and bowed low--much lower than any ceremony required.

She bent her head, and silently pointed to a chair at a short distance.

He sat down.

Up to this time not a word had passed between them.

A monk and a nun, who keep their vows, could not have met more coldly than this pair who had once plighted their hands and hearts in marriage before the altar of the Church of St. Marie.

Valerie was the first to speak.

"Well, you insisted upon this interview. Now you have it. What do you want of me?"

"I want you to leave the Duke of Hereward," he answered, sternly.

"You are right, so far. But the Duke of Hereward has saved me the trouble of taking the initiative step. He has left me. I shall never see him, more."

"How! What!" exclaimed de Volaski, starting up.

"The Duke of Hereward left for Algiers last night. I shall not remain here to receive him when he returns."

"You told him, then, and he has left you? Good!"

"No, I have not told him; he knows nothing--not even that he has left me forever. Business of a financial nature connected with his duties as executor of my father's estates, takes him to Algiers for a few weeks. During his absence I shall make arrangements for leaving this house forever."

"Valerie, where will you go?" he inquired, in a more softened tone.

"I do not know--*not with you that is certain*. You were quite right when you said that I could not live with either--that a single life was the only possible one for me. I feel that it is so, and I hope that it will be a short one."

"Valerie, do not say so. You are very young yet. The duke is an elderly man; he will die and leave you free."

"I shall not be free *while* EITHER of *you live*! nor can I build any hope in life *on death*! Oh! I have been cruelly wronged, and I am very miserable, but I am not selfish or wicked, Waldemar."

"How soon do you propose to leave this house?"

"I do not know. I only know that I must go before the duke's return."

"What should hinder your going at once?"

"I must make some provision for the miserable remnant of life left me. I must collect and sell my jewels and my shawls and laces, and invest the money in some safe place, where it will bring me interest enough to live cheaply in some remote country neighborhood. Wretched as I am, soon as I hope to die, I do not wish to be dependant on *you*, Waldemar."

"No, nor do I wish anything but independence and honor for *you*, Valerie. But you must let me assist you in realizing capital from your personal property, and in making other necessary arrangements for your removal. You cannot do this for yourself. You are more ignorant of the world than a child. So you must let me see you safely through this trial. You have no alternative, Valerie. You have no one else to consult with but me, and you may confide in me, for I will endeavor to forget that I ever called you wife, and will treat you with the reverential tenderness due to a dear sister. When I once have seen you safely lodged in a secure retreat, I will leave you there, never to intrude upon you again."

"Thanks! thanks! that is the kindest course you could pursue toward me."

"You accept all my service then?"

"Yes, on the condition that I shall seem to you only as a sister. But, oh! Waldemar! you, who are so kind and considerate *now*, how could you have *ever* written to me so cruelly--calling me an unfaithful wife--calling yourself a wronged husband? I never was consciously unfaithful to any one in my life. I never voluntarily wronged any creature since I was born. How could you have written so cruelly, Waldemar?"

"Forgive me, Valerie! I was crazed with the contemplation of you,--*you* whom I considered as my own wife, living here as the Duchess of Hereward. Only since I have learned that the duke is gone--and gone forever from you, have I come to my senses. Do you understand me, and do you forgive me?"

"Yes, both; but now, do not think me rude or unkind; but you must go. It is not well that you should stay too long."

"Good-morning, Valerie," he said immediately preparing to obey her.

She held out her hand. He took it, pressed it lightly, dropped it, turned and left the room.

After this day the Count de Volaski came daily to the Hotel de la Motte on some errand connected with the duchess' financial business. These interviews were as coldly formal as the most severe etiquette would have required.

Valerie received frequent letters from the Duke of Hereward, in which he spoke of the protracted business that still kept him an unwilling absentee from her side; promised as speedy a return as possible; expressed great anxiety concerning her health, and besought her to write often.

She complied with his request: she wrote daily as she had promised to do, but she could not write deceitfully; she told him of her health, which she described as no better and no worse than it had been when he left Paris; she told him any little political news or rumor that happened to be stirring, and any social gossip that she thought might interest or amuse him; but she deluded him by no expressions of affection or devotion.

The duke's absence, that was expected to last but two weeks, was prolonged to six.

Still Valerie delayed leaving the Hotel de la Motte. She shrank from taking the final step, until it should seem absolutely necessary.

At length, after an absence of nearly seven weeks, the Duke of Hereward wrote to his young wife that he was about to return home, and would follow his letter in twenty-four hours.

This letter threw her into a state of excessive nervous excitement, and when her daily visitor entered her room a few hours after its reception, he found her in this condition.

"Why, what is the matter, Valerie? What on earth has happened?" he inquired, in much anxiety.

"The hour has come! I must go!" she answered, trembling.

"Well, so much the better. You are ready to go. You have been ready for weeks past! Do not falter now that the time is at hand."

"I do not falter in resolution, only in strength."

"The sooner it is over the better. I will take you away this afternoon, if you wish."

"Yes, yes, take me away as soon as possible!"

"Have you thought of where you would like to go first?"

"Yes! I have thought and decided! I want you to take me to Italy--to St. Vito, where we were married, and to the vine-dresser's cottage, in the Apennines, where we passed the first days of our marriage, and the happiest days of our lives."

"It will be very sad for you there," said Waldemar, compassionately.

"Yes! I know it will be so without you! for of course I must live without you! and though I do not love you as I used to do, because love has perished out of my soul, still, I know, there in that place where we were so happy in our honeymoon, I shall be always comparing the happy days that *were* with the sorrowful days that *are*!"

"But still, if that is so, why do you go there?"

"Oh, Waldemar, it is the only place for me! I cannot go among entire strangers. I am such a coward. I am afraid in my loneliness: I should be driven to despair or to insanity, or worse than all, to the unpardonable sin of suicide! I dare not go among strangers, nor dare I go among people who know me as the Duchess of Hereward, or knew me as Valerie de la Motte, for they would scorn and abhor me, and their company would be far worse than the very worst solitude. No! I must go to the vine-dresser's cottage in the Apennines. Good Beppo and Lena knew me only as your wife and loved me dearly, and wept bitter tears when my father tore me away from you. They will be glad to see poor Valerie again! And the good Father Antonio, who married us! He loved us both! He will comfort and counsel me. Yes, Waldemar! St. Vito is my City of Refuge, and the vinedresser's cottage my only possible home. Take me there and leave me in peace."

"I believe you are right, Valerie. By what train would you like to leave Paris? There is an express that starts at seven. Could you be ready for that?"

"Yes! yes! thanks! I can be ready for that!"

"Shall you take your maid with you?"

"No. I shall pay her and discharge her with a present."

"Then I shall have to secure only two seats. I will get a coupe, if it be possible."

"Anything you like! Go now, Waldemar!"

Count de Volaski pressed her hand and withdrew; but before leaving the room he turned back and inquired:

"Shall I come here for you, or shall I meet you at the station?"

"Meet me at the station, of course! Spare my poor name as long as it can be spared! In twenty-four hours it will be in everybody's mouth, and the worst that can be said of it will seem too good! And yet they will all be wrong, and I shall not deserve their condemnation."

Count de Volaski waved his hand, and hurried from the room and the house, for he had many hasty preparations to make for the sudden journey.

As soon as he had gone Valerie set about making her final arrangements. She paid off her maid and discharged her with a handsome present, but without a word of explanation. She sent off her luggage to the railway-station, and ordered the carriage to take her to the same point. She took in her hand a small bag containing her money, jewels, and other small valuables, when she seated herself in her carriage and gave the order to her coachman. And so she left her own magnificent home forever.

The wondering servants, who had been too well trained even to look any comment in their mistress' hearing, let loose their tongues as they watched the carriage roll away.

CHAPTER XXXVIII.
THE STORM BURSTS.

The Duke of Hereward arrived at home the next morning. When the fiacre that brought him from the railway station rolled through the porte-cochere into the court yard and drew up before the main entrance of the Hotel de la Motte, he sprang out with almost boyish eagerness, and ran up the stairs, and rang and knocked with vehemence and impatience.

The gray-haired porter opened the door.

"How is the duchess, Leblanc? Has she risen? Send some one to let her know that I have arrived," he exclaimed, hurriedly.

"*Helas!* Monseigneur!" answered the venerable old servant, in a distressed tone.

"What do you mean? Is the duchess ill? I got a letter from her yesterday, in which she said she was quite well. It met me at Marseilles. She continues well. I hope? Why don't you speak?" impatiently demanded the duke.

"*Mille pardons*. Monseigneur; but madame has gone," sadly replied Leblanc.

"What do you say?" exclaimed the duke, discrediting the evidence of his own ears.

"*Mille pardons*, Monsieur le Duc, Madame la Duchesse has gone."

"Gone! the duchess gone!" exclaimed the duke, in amazement, not unmixed with incredulity.

"Oui; Monseigneur."

"Gone! the duchess gone! Where?"

"*Miserable* that I am, Monseigneur, I do not know. I cannot tell. Will Monsieur le Duc design to consult the coachman who drove Madame la Duchesse in the carriage when she left the house last night, not to return. He can probably give Monseigneur some information," respectfully suggested the old porter.

"Send Dubourg to me in the library, then," said the duke, as he strode down the hall, full of vague alarm, but far from suspecting the fatal truth.

Soon the coachman came to him in the library, and in answer to his questions told how he had driven the duchess alone to the railway station to catch the night express for Marseilles.

"The night express for Marseilles! Then the foolish child was going to meet me, and must have passed me on the road!" said the duke to himself, with a strange blending of flattered affection and anxious fears.

"That will do, Dubourg. The duchess went down to the seaport to meet me on the steamer, and we have missed each other on the road. It is a pity, but it cannot be helped!" said the duke dismissing his coachman by a wave of his hand.

The man bowed and retired.

"Silly child, to go and do such an absurd and indiscreet thing as that! I would go down after her by the next train only I should be sure to pass her on the road again; for she will hasten immediately back when she finds that I have arrived at Marseilles and left for Paris," said the duke to himself, as he rang for his valet and retired to his own room to dress for breakfast.

But there, on the bureau, he found a letter addressed to him in the handwriting of Valerie.

At the moment he picked it up his valet entered the room in answer to his ring.

Some intuition warned the duke to send the man away while he should read his letter.

"Have a warm bath ready for me at nine o'clock, Dubois, and order breakfast at half-past," he said.

The man bowed and left the room.

The duke dropped into a chair, and with a strange, vague foreboding of evil, opened the letter.

Well might he shrink from the dread perusal of the story--the story of her cowardice and folly, and of his own humiliation and despair.

It was Valerie's full confession, the revelation of her woeful history as it is known to the reader, with one single reservation--the name of her lover.

The Duke of Hereward had wonderful powers of self-control. He read the fatal letter through to the bitter end. Then he folded it up carefully, and locked it up in a cabinet for safe-keeping.

And when, fifteen minutes later, his valet came to tell him that it was nine o'clock, and his bath was ready, no one could have guessed from his looks that a storm had passed through his soul.

He was rather pale, certainly; but that might well be explained by the fatigue of a long night's journey, and his gray mustache and beard concealed the close compression of his lips. He went through his morning toilet and his breakfast with apparently his usual composure.

After breakfast, however, he instituted a cautious but close investigation of the circumstances attending the flight of the duchess.

The servants, having nothing to gain from concealment and nothing to fear from communication, spoke freely of the daily visits of the Count de Volaski, continued through the seven weeks of the duke's absence.

Then the dreadful light of conviction burst full upon his startled intelligence. Count Waldemar de Volaski had been her acquaintance at the Court of St. Petersburg! He it was, then, who had been the hero of her foolish love story and mad marriage, before the duke had ever seen her. He it was who had been her constant visitor during the duke's absence. He it was who was the companion of her flight!

The duke did not believe Valerie's solemn declaration, that she left Paris only to isolate herself from every one and live a single, lonely life. Valerie had deceived him once, by keeping a fatal secret from him, and he would not trust her now. He believed that she had gone away with the Russian count to remain with him. The duke's rage and jealousy were roused and burning against them both.

He was determined to find out the place of their retreat, and to take immediate and signal vengeance.

He put the case in the hands of the most expert detectives, with instructions to use the utmost caution and secrecy in their investigations.

He permitted his first theory of the duchess' absence, made in good faith at the time it was first stated--that she had gone down to Marseilles to meet him, and had missed him on the way--to prevail in the household, and penetrate through that medium to the world of Paris.

He left the Hotel de la Motte, which he had only occupied in right of his wife's family, and saying that he should not return until the arrival of the duchess, he took up his residence at "*Meurice's*."

He shut himself up in his apartments, and never left them. He refused to see all visitors except the detectives in his employment. Thus he escaped the annoyance of having to answer questions and to make explanations.

He had remained at "*Meurice's*" about five days, when Villeponte, the chief detective, came to him and told him that they had succeeded in making out the facts connected with the flight of the duchess.

The duke, controlling all manifestations of excitement, directed the officer to proceed with the story at once.

Villeponte then related that on the Wednesday of the preceding week, madame, the Duchess of Hereward, had left Paris in company with Monsieur the Count de Volaski; that they took a coupe on the evening express for Marseilles, traveling alone together without servants or attendants; that they were now domiciliated at a vine-dresser's cottage in the little village of San Vito, at the foot of the Appenines.

Having concluded his information, Monsieur Villeponte asked for further instructions.

The duke told the detective that he had no further orders to give; but thanked him for his zeal, congratulated him on his success, paid him liberally, and bowed him out.

That evening the Duke of Hereward, unattended by groom or valet, took a coupe on the night express train for the south of France, and started for Marseilles, en route for Italy.

On the evening of the third day after leaving Paris he reached his destination--the little hamlet of San Vito at the foot of the Appenines.

He stopped at the small hotel.

Coming alone and unattended, carrying a small valise in his hand, and looking weary, dusty, and travel-stained, the Duke of Hereward was not intuitively recognized as a person of distinction, and therefore escaped the overwhelming amount of attention usually lavished upon English tourists of rank and wealth by continental hosts.

He was shown to a little room blinded by clustering vines, and there left to his own devices.

He ordered a bottle of the native wine, and sent for the landlord.

The latter came promptly--a thin, little, old man, with a skin like parchment, hair and beard like a black horse's mane, and eyes like glowworms.

He saluted the shabby stranger with courtesy, but without obsequiousness; for how should he know that the traveler was a duke?

"Pray sit down. I wish to ask you some questions," said the Duke of Hereward, with a natural, courteous dignity that immediately modified the landlord's estimate of his value.

"Non, signor; but I will answer questions," he declared, as he bowed deferentially, and remained standing.

"Did a gentleman and lady arrive here about ten days ago!"

"Si, signor--a grand milord, and a beautiful miladi. But they have been here before, signor, about two years ago."

"Ah! Where are they now?"

"At their old lodgings, signor--at the cottage of Beppo, the vine-dresser. The signor is a good friend of the young milord and miladi?" questioned the landlord, deferentially, but very anxiously; for just then it flashed upon his memory that two years previous another grand "signor," of reverend age like this one, had come inquiring about the young pair, and had ended in breaking up their union for the time.

"I have known the lady for about a year, or a little longer; the gentleman only a few months; but I can scarcely lay claim to so an intimate a relation to them as 'friendship' would imply," answered the duke, evasively, and putting a severe constraint upon himself.

The landlord was completely deceived and thrown off his guard.

"How far from the village does this vine-dresser live?" inquired the duke.

"Just on the outside, signor--just at the foot of the mountain--about three miles from this house."

"Can I have a carriage to take me there this evening."

"Si, signor, assuredly; but will not the signor refresh himself before he leaves?" inquired the host.

"No; I will refresh myself after I come back. Let me have the carriage as soon as possible."

"Si, signor," said the landlord, bowing himself out.

The duke, unable to rest, even after a long and fatiguing journey, walked up and down the floor of his little room, until the landlord re-appeared and announced the carriage.

The duke caught up his rough traveling-cap, clapped it on his head, hurried out and entered the rustic vehicle, dignified with the name of a carriage.

And in another moment he was rolling off in the direction of the Vine-dresser's cottage at the foot of the mountain.

CHAPTER XXXIX.
THE RIVALS.

The sun was setting behind the western ridge, and throwing a deep shadow over the valley, as the rustic vehicle conveying the Duke of Hereward drew up before the vinedresser's cottage, nestled almost out of sight amid thick foliage and deep shade.

It was the hour of rest, and Beppo, the vine-dresser, sat at the gate, strumming an old, dilapidated lute; his red jacket and white shirt making the only bits of bright color in the sombre picture.

As the rude carriage stopped before the gate, Beppo arose and put aside his lute, and stood with a look of expectancy on his dark face.

The duke did not alight, but put his head out of the carriage window and beckoned the man to approach him.

Beppo came up, curiosity expressing itself in every feature of his speaking countenance.

"You have a young gentleman and lady--a young married couple--staying with you?" said the duke, but speaking in the Italian language.

"No, Excellenzo. The signora is here. The signor went away on the same day on which he brought the signora," deferentially answered the peasant, with a profound bow.

"The man has gone!" exclaimed the duke, losing his caution and his politeness in the phrenzy of baffled vengeance.

"Si, signer, the man has gone!" with another deep bow.

"Where, then, has he gone?"

"To Paris, signor; but the signora is still here. Will the signor deign to come into my poor house and see the signora, then?"

"See *her*! No!" vehemently exclaimed the duke. Then recollecting himself, he inquired:

"Are you sure the man has gone to Paris?"

"Si, signor; I drove him myself, in my little cart, to San Stephano, where he took the train."

"You say that he left on the same day in which he brought the lady here?" inquired the duke, with more interest.

"Si, signor. They arrived in the afternoon, and he went away again in the evening."

"Hum. Why did he go so soon?"

"Affairs, signor. It is not to be thought he would have left the signora so sick if it had not been for affairs."

"The lady is sick, then?"

"Very sick, signor."

"What is the matter with her?"

"We do not know, signor. She will not have a doctor, but sits and pines."

"Ah! no doubt," said the duke to himself.

"Will the signor condescend to honor our poor shed by coming under its roof, where he may for himself see the signora?" said the vine-dresser, with much courtesy.

"Thanks, no. Back to the hotel!" he added, to the driver, who immediately turned his horse's head to the village.

With a parting nod to the courteous vine-dresser, the duke sank back on his seat, closed his eyes, and gave his mind up to thought.

Volaski had gone back to Paris. Why had he left Valerie and gone there? To resign his position in the embassy? To settle up business previous to taking up his permanent abode in Italy? Or had he returned so quickly to Paris only to conceal his crime and deceive the world into the opinion that he had not been out of Paris.

The duke did not know what his motive for so sudden a return could be; but judged the last-mentioned theory of causes to be the most probable.

"I do not know what *else* the caitiff has gone back for; but I know one thing-- he has gone there to give me satisfaction," said the duke, grimly, to himself.

The horse, with the prospect of stall and fodder before him, made much better time in going home than in coming away, and so, in less than half an hour, the rumbling vehicle drew up before the little hotel.

The landlord himself came out to meet the returning traveler.

"I hope the illustrious signor found the excellent signor and the beautiful signora in good health," said the polite host, as he opened the carriage-door for his guest.

"The beautiful signora is sick and the excellent signor is gone," said the duke, grimly, as he got out.

"*Misericordia!*" cried the host, with a look of unutterable woe.

"That will do. Now let me have some supper as soon as you can get it, and when it is ready to be served, come yourself and tell me why I was not informed of the young man's departure before taking that useless drive to the vine-dresser's," said the duke, gravely.

"Pardon, illustrissimo, if I tell you now. We did not know the young signor had gone. He did not come this way. He must have taken another route and got his train at San Stephano," humbly replied the host.

"Ah! yes! the vine-dresser did tell me he had driven the man over to San Stephano. Well, then, hurry up my supper," said the duke, passing on to his room.

The landlord looked after him, muttering to himself:

"Ah! so not finding the excellent young signor, he has turned his back on the beautiful young signora. I know it! The *other* ancient and illustrious signor, who raised the devil in Beppo's cottage last year, and carried off the bride, was her father; but this illustrissimo is **his** father, wherefore he cares not to bring away the lovely signora."

The host then gave the necessary orders for the duke's supper to be prepared, and when it was ready he took it up to his guest.

The duke had no more questions to ask, and only two orders to give--breakfast at seven o'clock on the next morning, and a conveyance to take him to the railway station at half-past seven.

The next day the duke set out on his return to Paris, and on the fourth evening thereafter found himself re-established at his comfortable quarters at Meurice's.

He changed his dress, dined, and ordered the files of English and French newspapers for the past week to be brought to him.

He was interested only in political affairs when asking for the papers, and so he was quite as much astonished as grieved when his eyes fell upon this paragraph in the **Times**:

"A painful rumor reaches us from Paris. It is to the effect that a certain young and lovely duchess, who made her **debut** in English society as a bride only twelve months since, has left her home under the protection of a certain Polish count, attached to the Russian Embassy."

Stricken to the soul with shame, the unhappy duke sank back in his chair and remained as one paralyzed for several minutes; then slowly recovering himself he took up other papers, one by one, to see if they too recorded his dishonor.

Yes! each paper had its paragraph devoted to the one grand sensation of the day--the flight of the beautiful Duchess of Hereward with the young Russian count; and very few dealt with the deplorable case as delicately as the **Times** had done.

"So my dishonor is the talk of all Paris and London!" groaned the duke, dropping his head upon his chest. "If all the civilization of the nineteenth century had power to stay my arm in its vengeance, it has lost it now! And nothing is left for me to do but to kill the man and divorce the woman."

There was a certain Colonel Morris, of the Tenth Hussars, staying at Paris on leave.

The duke sat down at his writing-table and dashed off a hasty note to this compatriot, asking him to come to him immediately.

Then he rang the bell and gave the note to his own groom, saying:

"Take this to Colonel Morris, at the *Trois Freres*, and wait an answer."

The man took the message, bowed and hurried away.

The duke sank back in his chair with a deep sigh, and covered his face with his hands, and so awaited the return of his messenger.

Half an hour crept slowly by, and then the groom came back, opened the door, and announced:

"Colonel Morris."

The gallant colonel entered the room, looking as little like the dead shot and notorious duellist he was reported to be, as any fine gentleman could.

He was a tall, slight, fair and refined looking young man, exquisite in dress, soft in speech, and suave in manners.

"You have guessed the reason why I have sent for you, Morris?" said the duke, advancing to meet him, and plunging into the middle of his subject.

"Yes," murmured the colonel, sinking into the seat his host silently offered him.

"You can go, Tompkins. I will ring when I want you," said the duke, throwing himself into his own chair.

When the man had bowed himself out, and the duke and his visitor were left alone, the former said:

"You know why I have sent for you here. Now what do you advise?"

"You must blow out the man's brains and break the woman's heart," softly and sweetly replied the dandy duellist.

"The question arises whether the man has any brains to blow out, or the woman any heart to break," grimly commented the duke. "However," he added, "you are right, Morris, I must kill the man--divorce the woman. You are with me?"

"To the death," answered the *elegant*, in the same easy tone in which he ever uttered even the most ferocious words.

"You will take my challenge?"

"With much pleasure."

"I wonder where the fellow is to be found. At the Russian Embassy, I suppose," observed the duke, as he turned to his writing-table.

"No, not there. The Count de Volaski has withdrawn or been dismissed from the Embassy. It is not certainly known which. He is, meanwhile, at the Trois Freres.

He has the honor of being my fellow-lodger," suavely observed the colonel.

"There," said the duke, as he folded and directed his note, "no time should be lost in an affair of this sort. It is not yet ten o'clock. You may even deliver this challenge to-night, if you will be so kind."

"Certainly," murmured the graceful colonel rising.

"I leave everything absolutely in your hands. Make every arrangement you may think proper; I will agree to it all; and many thanks," said the duke, striving to maintain a calm exterior, while his spirit was troubled within him.

"Expect me back to-night. I may be late, but I shall certainly report myself here," were the parting words of Colonel Morris as he left the room.

The duke walked slowly up and down the floor for nearly half an hour, and then he sat down to his desk and employed some hours in writing letters to his family, friends and men of business in England.

When he had completed his task he sealed and directed all these letters and locked them in his desk.

At a quarter past twelve the colonel returned to the hotel, and immediately presented himself at the duke's apartments.

He entered with a soft smile, and gently sank into a seat.

"Well?" inquired the duke.

"Well," cheerfully responded the second; "everything is pleasantly arranged. I had the good fortune of finding the count 'with himself,' as they say here. I explained my errand and delivered your missive. He read it and expressed his gratification at its reception, declaring that you had anticipated him by but a few hours, as he should certainly have called you out immediately upon hearing of your arrival in Paris."

"The diabolical villain!" hotly exclaimed the duke.

"He claimed the first right to the lady in question, and affirmed that it was your grace who had appropriated his wife--"

"*O-h-h-h!* when shall I have the opportunity of shooting him!" cried the duke.

"By and by," soothingly responded the colonel. "He referred me to his friend, Baron Blowmonozoff, then staying at the same house."

"Blowmonozoff! Yes, I know him. A very good fellow."

"A gentleman, I think. Of course I went directly from the presence of the count to that of the baron, who received me with much politeness, and was so kind as to express the pleasure he should feel in negotiating with me the terms of so interesting a meeting."

"And the terms, Colonel! What are they?"

"I am coming to them. The meeting is to take place at sunrise in the wood of Vincennes. We are to leave here an hour before dawn, in order to be on the spot in time. The weapons are to be pistols; the distance ten paces. Other minor details will be arranged on the spot. We shall each take a surgeon. I have engaged Doctor Legare. We will call and pick him up on our way to the ground. And now all we have got to do is to ring for the English waiter here, and get him to send us some coffee before we go out. I will see to that also, as I have taken a room in the house, and intend to stay here to-night, so as to be up in time in the morning."

"Thanks very much. You are really very good to take so much trouble," said the duke, with some emotion.

"No trouble, I assure you, duke; quite a pleasure," serenely answered the colonel.

"My friend, I have left half a dozen letters locked up in my writing-desk. I shall hand the key of that desk to you as we go out. If I should fall, I hope you will take charge of the desk and see to the delivery of the letters at their proper addresses," said the duke, more gravely than he had spoken before.

"Certainly, with much pleasure. Have you also made your will?" cheerfully inquired the colonel.

"No," shortly replied the duke.

"Then permit me to say that I think you should do so, by all means."

"There is no need. My estates are all entailed. My personal property is not worth winning. The--duchess is provided by her own dower, which came out of her own property, I am thankful to say. No, there is no need of a will."

"Then allow me to suggest that we ought to go to bed. It is now two o'clock. We must be up at five. We have just three hours to sleep, and--if you have no other commissions for me--I will retire," said the colonel, smoothly.

"Many thanks. I believe there is nothing more to be said or done to-night," responded the duke, in a desponding tone--for it *cannot* be an exhilarating anticipation to have to get up in the morning and stand up to murder, or be murdered, even where the duellist is the bravest of men, backed by the serenest of seconds.

"Then, since there is no further use for me this evening, I will say good-night and pleasant dreams," said the colonel, suavely, as he slid from the room.

Good-night and pleasant dreams to a duellist on the eve of a duel! Was it a sarcasm on the colonel's part? By no means; it was only the manifestation of his habitual smooth politeness.

The duke, left to himself, walked up and down the floor for a few minutes, and then rang for his valet to attend him, and retired to bed, leaving orders to be called at five o'clock in the morning.

Though left in quietness, he could not compose himself to sleep, but tossed and tumbled from side to side, spending the most wakeful and the most miserable night he had ever known in the whole course of his life. The time seemed stretched out upon a rack of torture, until the four hours extended to forty; for from the moment he had lain down he had not slept an instant, until he was startled by a rap at his bedroom door, and the voice of his valet calling:

"If you please, your grace, the clock has struck five; the coffee is ready, and the cab is at the door."

"Then come in and dress me quickly," answered the duke, rising, as the prompt servant entered and handed a dressing-gown.

The toilet of the duke was quickly made.

When he passed into the next room, he found the breakfast table laid and the colonel waiting for him.

"Good-morning, Duke. I hope you slept well. The day promises to be delightful. We have no time to lose, however, if we are to be on the ground at sunrise. Shall we have our coffee?" serenely inquired the second.

"Certainly--Tompkins, touch the bell," replied the duke.

The obedient valet rang, and a waiter entered with the breakfast-tray, which he set upon the table and proceeded to arrange.

"Take this case of pistols down very carefully, and place it in the cab, and put in a railway rug also," quietly directed the colonel, after the waiter had completed the arrangement of the breakfast table.

"What possible use can we make of a railway rug on such a mild morning as this?" gloomily inquired the duke.

The colonel looked calmly at the questioner, and quietly replied:

"To cover the body of the fallen man, whoever he may happen to be. I am so used to these affairs that I know what will be wanted beforehand. Shall we sit down to breakfast?"

Now the duke was a courageous man, but he shuddered at the coolness of his second, as he assented.

They sat down to the table and drank their coffee in silence.

Then with the assistance of the obsequious Mr. Tompkins, they drew on light overcoats suitable to the autumnal morning, and went down stairs, caps and gloves in hand, and entered the carriage that was to take them to the appointed place.

On their way they stopped at the Rue du Bains and took the surgeon who had been engaged to attend them.

Dr. Legare was a young graduate who had just commenced practice, and was eager for the fray.

He came into the carriage, bringing a rather ostentatious looking case of instruments and roll of bandages.

On being introduced by the second, he bowed to the duke and took his seat.

The carriage started again.

It was yet dark.

After an hour's ride they reached a quiet, solitary glade in the wood of Vincennes.

The carriage drove up under some trees on one side.

It was yet earliest morning, and the glade lay in the darksome, dewy freshness of the dawn. There was no living creature to be seen.

"We are the first on the ground, as I always like to be," remarked Colonel Morris, as he alighted from the carriage, bearing the pistol-case in his hands.

He was followed by the duke, who slowly came out, stood by his side and looked around.

The young surgeon remained in the carriage in charge of his very suggestive and alarming instruments and appliances.

"The sun is just rising," said the duke, as the first rays sparkled up above the rosy line of the eastern horizon.

"And look, with dramatic precision, there are our men," cheerfully remarked the colonel, as a second carriage rolled into the glade and drew up under the trees at a short distance from the first.

The carriage door was thrown open and the Russian Baron Blomonozoff came out--a thin, ferocious-looking little man, with a red face, encircled by a red beard and red hair, of all of which it would be difficult to say which was reddest.

He was followed by the beautiful Adonis, the Count de Volaski, looking very fair and dainty, very languid and melancholy.

The four gentlemen simultaneously raised their hats in courteous greeting; but no words passed between them then.

The seconds advanced toward each other, and went apart to settle the final details of the meeting. They divided their duties equally.

The colonel gave the pistol-case to the baron, who opened it and examined the weapons. The colonel stepped off the ten paces of ground, and the baron marked the positions to be taken by the antagonists.

Then each went after his man and placed him in position. Then the Colonel took the case of pistols and placed it in the hands of the baron, who carried it to his principal, that the latter might take his choice of the pair of revolvers, in accordance with the terms of the meeting.

The count took the first that came to hand. The baron carried back the case to the colonel, who placed the remaining weapon in the hands of the duke.

The antagonists stood opposite each other in a line of ten paces running north and south, so that the sun was equally divided between them. The seconds stood opposite each other, in a line of six paces running east and west, across the line of their principals; so that the positions of the four men, as they stood, formed the four points of a diamond.

They stood prepared for the mortal issue.

A fatal catastrophe is always sudden and soon over.

The final question was asked by the duke's second:

"Gentlemen, are you ready?"

"We are," responded both principals.

"One--two--three--FIRE!" intoned the Russian baron.

Two flashes, a simultaneous report, and the Count de Volaski leaped into the air and fell down, with a heavy thud, upon his face!

The seconds hastened to raise the fallen man. The duke stood panic-stricken for an instant, and then followed them.

The unfortunate count lay in a tumbled, huddled, shapeless heap, with his head bent under him. Not a drop of blood was to be seen on his person or clothing. The Russian baron raised him up. There was a gasp, a momentary flutter of the lips and eyelids, and all was still.

The colonel hurried off to the carriage to call the surgeon.

The duke stood gazing on his murdered foe, aghast at his own deed and feeling the brand of Cain upon his brow, notwithstanding that he had acted in accordance with the "code of honor."

The surgeon came in haste with his box of instruments in his hands, and the roll of linen under his arm.

He put these articles on the ground, and knelt down to examine his subject; for the body of the count was only a subject now, and not a patient.

After a careful investigation, the surgeon arose and pronounced his verdict.

"Shot through the heart: quite dead."

The Duke of Hereward groaned aloud. None of his wrongs could have been such a calamity as this! None of his sufferings could have equalled in intensity of agony this appalling sense of blood-guiltiness!

"Can *nothing* be done?" he inquired, not with the slightest hope that anything could, but rather in the idiocy of utter despair.

"Nothing. No medical skill can raise the dead," solemnly answered the surgeon.

"One of you fellows can bring the railway rug out of our carriage. I knew it would be needed," said the serenely practical colonel.

The count's servant started to obey.

The duke groaned and turned away from the body of his fallen foe, upon which he could not endure longer to gaze.

The Russian baron came up to him, and with the knightly courtesy of his caste and country, said:

"Monseigneur may rest tranquil. Everything has been conducted in accordance with the most rigid rules of honor. The result has been unfortunate for my distinguished principal, but Monseigneur has nothing with which to reproach himself."

"Thanks, Baron. You are kind to say so. Yet I would that I had never lived to see this day; or the worthless woman who has caused this catastrophe!" exclaimed the duke, as he walked hurriedly away and hid himself and his remorse in the inclosure of his own carriage.

There he was soon joined by his serene second, who entered the carriage and gave the order to the coachman;

"Drive to the Depot St. Lazare."

"Why to the depot?" gloomily inquired the duke, as the coachman closed the door and remounted to his box.

"Because we must get out of Paris--yes, and out of France also," calmly replied the colonel, sinking back in his seat as the cab drove off.

"Who is looking after--after--"

"The body? I left Legare to help Blomonozoff and his servant to remove it. We must get away. An arrest would not be pleasant."

"No, no, certainly not; yet not on that account, but for the peace of my own spirit, I would to Heaven this had not happened!" exclaimed the duke.

"Why? Everything went off most agreeably. Indeed, this was one of the most satisfactory meetings at which I ever assisted," said the colonel, comfortably.

"I wish to Heaven it had never taken place! I would give my right hand to undo its own deed to-day--if that were possible!" groaned the homicide.

"Why should you disturb yourself?--but perhaps this is your first affair of the kind?" calmly inquired the colonel.

"My first and last! I do not know how any one can engage in a second one after feeling what it is to kill a man."

"You feel so because it *is* your first affair. You would not mind your second, and you would rather enjoy your third," suavely observed the colonel, who then drew a railway card from his pocket, examined it, looked at his watch, and said:

"We shall be in time to catch the morning's express to Calais, and we may actually eat our dinners in London. When we arrive you can get some of your people to send a telegram to Tompkins, to order him to pay your hotel bill and bring your effects to London, or wherever else you may think of stopping."

"Thanks for your counsel. I leave myself entirely in your hands," said the duke, with a half-suppressed sigh.

They caught the express to Calais, connected with the Dover boat, and crossed the channel the same day. They ran up to London by the afternoon train, and arrived in good time for a dinner at "Morley's."

Two telegrams were dispatched to Paris--one to the respectable Mr. Tompkins, with orders to pay bills and return with his master's effects; the other to the estimable Mr. Joyce, the groom of the colonel, with orders to perform the same services in behalf of his own employer.

Then the principal and his second separated--the duke to go to his town-house in Piccadilly and the colonel to join his regiment, then stationed at Brighton.

And as the extradition treaty had not at that day been thought of, both were perfectly safe.

CHAPTER XL.
AFTER THE STORM.

The Duke of Hereward only remained in town until the arrival of his servants with his effects from Paris.

He avoided looking at the newspapers, which, he knew, must contain exaggerated statements of the duel and its causes, if, indeed, any statement of such horrors could be exaggerated.

On the third day after his arrival in London, he went down to Greencombe, a small family estate in a secluded part of Sussex, near the sea.

Here he hid himself and his humiliations from the world.

The primitive population around Greencombe had never seen the duke, or any of his family, who preferred to reside at Hereward Hold, in Devonshire, or their town-house in Piccadilly, leaving their small Sussex place in charge of a land-steward and a few old servants.

They had never even heard of the marriage of the duke in Paris, much less the flight of the duchess, or the duel with Volaski.

This neglect of his poor people at Greencombe had hitherto been a matter of compunction to the conscientious soul of the duke, but he now was satisfied with the course of conduct which had left them in total ignorance of himself and his unhappy domestic history.

The duke and his fine servants were received with mingled deference, gladness and embarrassment by the aged and rustic couple who acted as land-steward and housekeeper at Greencombe, and who now bestirred themselves to make their unexpected master and his attendants comfortable.

The duke gave orders that he should be denied to all visitors, though there was little likelihood of any calling upon him, except perhaps the vicar of Greencombe church.

Here the duke vegetated until the meeting of Parliament, when he went up to London to institute proceedings for a divorce.

At that time there was no divorce court, and little necessity for one. Divorces were to be obtained by act of Parliament only.

The duke commenced proceedings immediately on his arrival in London. His case was a clear and simple one; there was no opposition; consequently he was soon, matrimonially considered a free man.

The Duke of Hereward was now nearly fifty years of age. Life was uncertain, and the laws of succession very certain.

If the present bearer of the coronet of Hereward should die childless, the title would not descend to the son of his only and beloved sister, but would go to a distant relative whom the duke hated.

A speedy marriage seemed necessary.

The duke looked around the upper circle of London society, and fixed upon the Lady Augusta Victoria McDugald, the eldest daughter of the Earl of Banff, and a woman as little like his unhappy first wife as it was Possible for her to be.

"The daughter of an hundred earls" was tall and stately, cold and proud, embodying the child's or the peasant's very ideal of "a duchess."

"Dukes," like monarchs, "seldom woo in vain."

After a short courtship the duke proposed for the lady, and after a shorter engagement, married her.

The newly-wedded pair went on a very unusually extended tour over Europe, into Asia and Africa, and then across the ocean and over North and South America.

After twelve months spent in travel, they returned to England only that the anticipated heir of the dukedom might be born on the patrimonial estate of Hereward Hold.

There was the utmost fulfillment of hope. The expected child proved to be a fine boy, who was christened for his father, Archibald-Alexander-John, by courtesy styled Marquis of Arondelle.

Had the duke's mind been as free from remorse for his homicide as his heart was free from regret for his first love, he would have been as happy a man as he was a proud father; but ah! the sense of blood-guiltiness, although incurred in the duel, under the so-called "code of honor," weighed heavily upon his conscience, and over-shadowed all his joys.

His duchess was a prolific mother, and brought him other sons and daughters as the years went by; but, as if some spell of fatality hung over the family, these children all passed away in childhood, leaving only the young Marquis of Arondelle as the sole hope of the great ducal house of Hereward.

So the time passed in varied joys and sorrows, without bringing any tidings, good or bad, of the poor, lost girl who had once shared the duke's title and possessed his heart.

He believed her to be as dead to the world as she was to him. And so he gradually forgot even that she had ever lived! She had long been "out of mind" as "out of sight."

Fifteen years of married life had passed over the heads of the Duke and Duchess of Hereward.

The duchess at thirty-five was still a very beautiful woman, a reigning belle, a leader of fashion, a queen of society.

The duke at sixty-five was still a very handsome, stately and commanding old gentleman, with hair and beard as white as snow. He was a great political power in the House of Lords. Their son, the young Marquis of Arondelle, was a fine boy of fourteen.

It was very early summer in London. Parliament was in session, and the season was at its height.

The Duke and Duchess of Hereward were established in their magnificent town-house in Piccadilly.

The Marquis of Arondelle was pursuing his studies at Eton.

A memorable day was at hand for the duke.

It was the morning of the first of June--a rarely brilliant and beautiful day for London.

The duchess had gone down to a garden party at Buckingham Palace.

The duke sat alone in his sumptuous library, whose windows overlooked the luxuriant garden, then in its fullest bloom and fragrance.

The windows were open, admitting the fine, fresh air of summer, perfumed with the aroma of numberless flowers, and musical with the songs of many birds.

The duke sat in a comfortable reading-chair, with an open book on its rotary ledge. He was not reading. The charm of external nature, appealing equally to sense and sentiment, won him from his mental task, and soothed him into a delicious reverie, during which he sat simply resting, breathing, gazing, luxuriating in the lovely life around him.

In the midst of this clear sky a thunderbolt fell.

A discreet footman rapped softly, and being told to enter, glided into the room, bearing a card upon a tiny silver tray, which he brought to his master.

The duke took it, languidly glanced at it, knit his brows, and took up his reading-glass and examined it closely. No! his eyes had not deceived him. The card bore the name: ARCHBALD A. J. SCOTT.

"Who brought this?" inquired the duke.

"A young gentleman, sir," respectfully answered the footman.

"Where is he?"

"I showed him into the blue reception room, your grace."

The duke paused a moment, gazing at the card, and then abruptly demanded:

"What is the young man like?"

"Most genteel, your grace; most like our young lord, and about his age, and dressed in the deepest mourning, your grace; and most particular anxious to see your grace."

"I do not know the boy at all; do not know where he came from, nor what he wants; but he bears the family name, and looks like Arondelle," mused the duke, gazing at the card and knitting his brow.

"I will see the young man. Show him up here," at length he said, abruptly.

The footman bowed and withdrew.

A few moments passed and the footman re-entered and announced:

"Mr. Scott," and withdrew.

The duke wheeled his chair around and looked at the visitor, who stood just within the door, bowing profoundly.

The newcomer was a youth of about fifteen years of age, tall, slight and elegant in form; fair, blue-eyed and light-haired in complexion; refined, graceful and self possessed in manner; and faultlessly dressed in deep mourning; but! how amazingly like the duke's own son, the young Marquis of Arondelle.

The duke's short survey of his visitor seemed so satisfactory that he arose and advanced to meet him, saying kindly:

"You wished particularly to see me, I understand, young gentleman. In what manner can I serve you?"

The youth bowed again with the deepest deference, and said:

"Thanks, your grace. I bring you a letter of introduction."

"Sit down, young sir, sit down, and give me your letter," said the duke, pointing to a chair, and resuming his own seat. "Good Heaven, how like this boy's voice was to the voice of the young Marquis of Arondelle! Who could he be?" mused the duke, as he sat and waited the issue.

The youth seated himself as directed, and seemed to hesitate, as if respectfully referring to his host's convenience.

"Your letter of introduction, now, if you please, young sir," said the duke, at length.

"Thanks; your grace. It's from my mother. She--" Here the boy's voice faltered and broke down; but he soon, recovered it and resumed: "She wrote it on her death-bed--on the very day she died. Here it is, your grace."

The duke took the letter and held it gravely in his fingers while he gazed upon the orphaned boy with sympathy and compassion in every lineament of his fine face, saying, slowly and seriously:

"Ah! that is very, very sad. You have lost your mother, my boy; and if I judge correctly from the circumstance of your coming to me, you have lost your father also. I hope, however, I am wrong."

"Your grace is right. I have lost my father also. I lost him first, so long ago that

I have no memory of him. I have no relatives at all. That is the reason why my dear mother, on her death-bed, gave me that letter of introduction to your grace, who used to know her, so that I might not be without friends as well as without relatives," modestly replied the youth.

"Ah! I see! I see! And she wrote this letter on her death-bed, which gives it a grave importance. I must therefore pay the more respect to it. The wishes of the dying should be considered sacred," said the duke, as he adjusted his glass and looked at the letter, wondering who the writer could be and what claims she could possibly have on him; but feeling too kindly toward the orphan-boy to let such thought betray itself.

He scrutinized the handwriting of the letter. He could not recognize the faint, scratchy, uncertain characters as anything he had ever seen before. After all, the whole thing might be an imposture, and he himself an exceedingly great dupe, to suffer his feelings to be enlisted by a perfect stranger, merely because that stranger happened to be a counterpart of his own idolized boy Arondelle.

Still dallying with the note, he looked again at the youth, and as he looked, his confidence in him revived. No boy of such a noble countenance could possibly be an impostor. He might have satisfied himself at once, by opening the note and reading the signature; but from some occult reason that even he could not have given, he held it in his hands for a few moments longer, as if it contained some oracle he dreaded to discover. At length he broke the seal and looked at the signature. It was a faint maze of scratches, so difficult to decipher that he gave it up in despair, and turning to the boy, said:

"Your name is Scott, young sir?"

"Yes, your grace--a very common name," modestly replied the youth.

"It is ours also" added the duke with a smile.

"I beg your grace's pardon," said the boy, with some embarrassment.

"No offence, young sir. Your mother's name was also Scott, I presume?"

"Yes, your grace; my mother never re-married."

"Ah," said the duke, and he turned the letter for the first page, and commenced its perusal.

And then--

Reader! If the Duke of Hereward's hair had not already been white with age, it must have turned as white as snow with amazement and horror as he read the astounding disclosures of that dying woman's letter!

CHAPTER XLI.
FATHER AND SON.

The first part of the letter was written in a much clearer chirography than the latter, where it grew fainter and more irregular as it proceeded, until at last, in the signature, it was so nearly illegible as to baffle the ingenuity of the reader to decipher it; as if, in the course of her task, the strength of the dying writer had grown weaker and weaker, until at the end the pen must have fallen from her failing hand.

The Duke of Hereward, who could not make out the name at the bottom of the letter, at once recognized the handwriting at the top, and knew that his correspondent from the dead was his lost wife, Valerie de la Motte.

He grew cold with the chill of an anticipated horror; but with that supreme power of self-control which was as much a matter of constitution as of education with him, he suppressed all signs of emotion, and courteously apologized to his visitor, saying:

"Excuse me, young sir; my eyes are not so good as they were some twenty years ago, and I must turn to the light," and he deliberately wheeled his chair around so as to bring his face entirely out of range of his visitor's sharp vision, while he should read the fatal letter, which was as follows:

"SAN VITO, ITALY, MARCH 1st, 18--

"DUKE OF HEREWARD: This paper will be handed you by Archibald-Alexander-John Scott, my son and yours.

"This news will startle you, if you have not already been sufficiently startled by the living likeness of the boy to yourself, and by the electric chain of memory which will bring before you the weeks immediately preceding our separation, when you yourself had suspicions of my condition, and hopes of becoming a father. Those fond hopes were destined to be fulfilled by me, but doomed to be ruined by you.

"Yes, Duke of Hereward, your son stands before you, strong, healthy, beautiful, perfect as ever wife bore to her husband; yet denied, delegalized, and defrauded by you, his father!

"If you are inclined still to deny him, turn and look upon him, as he stands, and you can no longer do so. If you want further proof, find it in these circumstances: That this letter is written, and these statements are made by a dying woman, with the immediate prospect of eternity and its retribution before her.

"But on one point be at ease before you read farther; the boy does not know who his father is, and therefore does not know how grievously, how irretrievably you wronged him by divorcing his mother and delegalizing him before his birth. I would not put enmity between father and son by telling him anything about it. *He* thinks that his father is dead, and I have never undeceived him. He has heard of you only as one who was a friend of his mother, and who, for her sake, may become the friend of her son. It must be for you to decide whether to leave him in this ignorance or to tell him the truth.

"Perhaps you will ask why I have concealed your son's existence from you up to this time. I will tell you; but in order to do so clearly, I must refer to those last few weeks spent with you in Paris before our separation.

"Remember the ball at the British Embassy, to which you persuaded me to go, and where I met, unexpectedly the Count de Volaski, my secretly married husband, supposed to be dead; remember my illness that followed! and how earnestly I tried to avoid him, an effort that was totally useless, because he, considering that he possessed the only rightful claim to my society, constantly sought me, and you, ignorant of all his antecedents, constantly helped him to see me.

"My position was degrading, agonizing, intolerable. I found myself, though guiltless of any intentional wrong-doing, in the horrible dilemma of a wife with two living husbands.

"Yes, by the laws of love and nature, justice and the church, I was the wife of Waldemar de Volaski; by the laws of France and England, I was the wife of the Duke of Hereward.

"The discovery shocked, confused, and, perhaps, unsettled my reason. At first I knew not what to do. I prayed for death. I contemplated suicide. At length, I thought I saw a way out of my dreadful dilemma. It was to escape and to live apart from both forever.

"So also thought the Count de Volaski. I consulted with him. I dared not confess to you the secret that my parents had compelled me to conceal so long. Volaski would have told you, but I would not consent that he should do so, until I should be safe out of the house; for I could not have borne, after such confession, to have met you again; and again, under any circumstances, I preferred that I myself should be your informant. I determined to leave yon, and to live apart from both, as the only life of peace and honor possible for me, and to write you a letter confessing the whole truth, as an explanation of my course of conduct. I thought that you would understand and pity me, and leave me to my fate.

"I did ***not*** think that you would disbelieve my statement, publish my flight, and blast my reputation by a divorce.

"I was never false to you in thought, word or deed.

"Volaski was not my lover; he was my sternest mentor. He came to the house during your absence; not for the pleasure of seeing me, for he took no pleasure in my society; he came to arrange with me the programme of my departure; an angel of purity or a demon of malice might have been present at our interviews, and seen nothing to grieve the first or please the last.

"I was ill and nervous and fearful; I could not travel alone, and therefore Volaski went with me, and took care of me; but it was the care a pitiless gend'arme would have taken of a convicted criminal. It was a care that only hurried me to my destination, my chosen place of exile--San Vito--and which left me on the day of my arrival there. I have never seen him since. And now let me say and swear on the Christian faith and hope of a dying woman--that--from the moment I met Count Waldemar de Volaski at the British embassy, to the moment I parted with him at San Vito, he never once came so near me as even to kiss my hand--a courtesy that any gentleman might have shown without blame. You may not believe me now; that you did not believe me before was your great misfortune, and mine, and our son's.

"A week after Volaski had left me you followed us and traced us to San Vito. I heard of your visit and trembled; for, though really guiltless, I felt that to meet your eye would seem worse than death. Fortunately for us both, perhaps, you declined to see me and went away.

"The next news that I heard was of the duel in which you had killed Volaski. I should scarcely have believed in his death this time, had not a packet been forwarded to me, through his second. This packet contained a letter that he had written to me on the eve of the duel, and with a presentiment of death overshadowing him. In this letter he said that in death he claimed me again as his wife, and bequeathed to me, as to his widow, all that he had the power to leave, his personal property, and he took a last solemn farewell of me.

"In the packet, besides, was his will and other documents necessary to put me in possession of his bequest, and also a great number of valuable jewels.

"These, together with my own small dower, have made me independent for life.

"It will show how perfectly palsied was my heart when I tell you that I could not feel either horror of crime, grief for Volaski's death, or gratitude for his bequest.

"I could feel nothing.

"Days and weeks passed in this apathy of despair, from which I was at length painfully aroused by a most shocking discovery.

"Madelena, my hostess, who tenderly watched over my health had her suspicions aroused, and put some motherly questions to me, and when I had answered them she startled me with the announcement that in a very few months I should become a mother.

"This news, so joyful to most good women, only filled my soul with sorrow and dismay. It seemed to complicate my difficulties beyond all possibility of extrication.

"Lena, poor woman, who had never heard of my marriage with the Duke of Hereward, but had known me as the wife of the Count de Volaski, believed that all my distress was caused by the prospect of becoming the mother of a fatherless child, and bent all her energies to try to comfort me with the assurance that this motherhood would be the greatest blessing of my lonely life.

"Ah! how willing would I have confided the whole truth to this good woman if I had dared to do so! It will show how timid I had grown when I assure you that I, a faithful daughter of the church, had not even ventured to go to confession once since my arrival in Italy.

"Now, Duke of Hereward, attend to my words! Had you been less bitterly incredulous of my statements, less cruel in your judgment of me, less murderous in your vengeance upon one much more sinned against than sinning, I should have ventured to write to you of my condition and my prospect of giving you an heir to your dukedom, in time to prevent your rash and fatal act by which you unconsciously delegalized your own lawful son!

"But your murderous cruelty had left me in a state of stupor from which I could not rally.

"Night after night I resolved to write to you. Day after day I tried to carry my resolution into effect. Time after time I failed through fear of you!

"At length I persuaded myself that there was no immediate necessity for action on my part. I might defer writing to you until the arrival of my child. That child might prove to be a girl, who could not be your heir, and, therefore, could not be an object of momentous importance to you; or it might die. Either of which circumstance would relieve me from the painful duty of opening a correspondence with you; or I myself might perish in the coming trial, when the duty of communicating the facts to you would devolve upon some one whom I would appoint with my dying breath.

"These were the causes of my fatal delay in writing to you.

"At length the time arrived. On the fifth of April, just five months after our separation. I became the mother of a fine, healthy, beautiful boy. He brought with him the mother-love that is Heaven's first gift to the child. I loved my son as I never loved a human being before. I *had* prayed for death; but as I clasped my first-born to my bosom, I asked pardon for that sinful prayer, thanked the Lord that I had lived through my trial, and besought him still to spare my life for my boy's sake. From that day forth I was able to pray and to give thanks. I resolved that my first act of recovery should be to go to the church and make my confession to the good father there, gain my absolution, and then write and inform you of the birth of your heir, the infant Earl of Arondelle, for such I knew was even then the baby boy's title! With these fond hopes I rapidly recovered. "Perfect love casteth out fear." Mother-love had cast out from my soul all fear of you. I thought that you would feel so rejoiced at the news of the birth of your son, your heir, and so fine a boy, that even for his sake you would forgive his mother, supposing that you should still think you had anything to forgive.

"In the midst of my vain dreaming a thunderbolt fell upon me!

"My boy was six weeks old. I had not yet left the house to carry out any of my happy resolutions, when my good Madelena entered my room and brought two large parcels of English papers, such as were sent me monthly by my London correspondent. She told me that the first parcel had arrived during my confinement to my bed, and that she had laid it away and forgotten all about it until this day, when the arrival of the second parcel had reminded her of it, and now she had brought them both, and hoped I would excuse her negligence in not having remembered to bring the first parcel sooner. I readily and even hastily excused her, for I was anxious to get rid of my good hostess and read my files of papers.

"As any one else would have done under the like circumstances, I opened the last parcel first, and selected the latest paper to begin with. It was the London *Times* of April 7th. As I opened it, a short, marked paragraph caught my eyes.

"Judge of my consternation when I read the notice of your marriage with the Lady Augusta McDugald!

"The letters ran together on my vision, the room whirled around with me, all grew dark, and I lost consciousness. When I recovered my senses I found myself in bed, with Madelena and several of her kind neighbors in attendance upon me. Many days passed before I was able to look again at the file of English newspapers.

"You had married again! you had married just one week before the birth of my son! But under what circumstances had you married? Did you suppose me to be dead, and that my death had set you free? Or--oh, horror! had you dragged my name before a public tribunal, and by lying *facts*--for facts do often lie--had you branded me with infidelity, and repudiated me by divorce?

"Such were the questions that tormented me, until I was able to examine the file of English newspapers, and find out from them; for, as before, I would not have taken any one into my confidence by getting another to read the papers for me, even if I could have found any one in that rural Italian neighborhood capable of reading English.

"At length, one morning, I sent for the papers, and began to look them over, and I found--merciful Heaven! what I feared to find--the full report of our divorce trial! found myself held up to public scorn and execration, the reproach of my own sex--the contempt of yours! Found myself, in short, convicted and divorced from you, upon the foulest charge that can be brought upon a woman! Guiltless as I was! wronged as I had been! wishing only to live a pure and blameless life, as I did!

"Oh! the intolerable anguish of the days that followed! But for my baby boy, I think I should have died, or maddened!

"In my worst paroxysms, good Madelena would come and take up my baby and lay him on my bosom, and whisper, that no doubt, though his handsome young father had gone to Heaven, it was all for the best; and we too, if we were good, would one day meet him there, or words to that effect.

"Surely angels are with children, and their presence makes itself felt in the comfort children bring to wounded hearts.

"One day, in a state bordering on idiocy, I think, I examined and compared dates, in the sickening hope that my darling boy might have been born before the decree of divorce had been pronounced, and thus be the heir of his father's dukedom, notwithstanding all that followed.

"But, ah! that faint hope also was destined to die! The dates, compared, stood thus:

"The decree of divorce was pronounced February 13th, 18--.

"The marriage between yourself and Lady Augusta McDugald was solemnized April 1st, 18--.

"My boy was born April 15th, 18--.

"Yes, you divorced the guiltless mother two months, and married another woman two weeks, before the birth of your innocent boy.

"You cruelly and unjustly disowned, disinherited, and even delegalized, and degraded your son before he was born! So that your son was not born in wedlock, could not bear your name, or inherit your title! And this misfortune came upon him by no fault of his, or of his most unhappy mother's but by the jealousy, vengeance, and fatal rashness of his father! And now there was no help, either in law or equity, for the dishonored boy.

"This, Duke of Hereward, is the ruin you have wrought in his life, in mine, and in yours.

"Do you wonder that when I realized it all I fell into a state of despair deeper than any I had ever yet known?--a despair that was characterized by all who saw it as melancholy madness.

"My dear boy, who was at first such a comfort to me, was now only a beloved sorrow! When I held him to my bosom, I thought of nothing but his bitter, irreparable wrongs.

"I do not know how long I had continued to live in this despairing and heathenish condition, when one day, in harvest time, Madelena brought good Father Antonio to see me. This Father Antonio was the priest of the chapel of Santa Maria, who had performed the marriage ceremony between Waldemar de Volaski and myself.

"The father also naturally supposed that all my grief was for the death of my child's father. He began in a gentle, admonitory way to rebuke me for inordinate affection and sinful repining, and to remind me of the comfort and strength to be found in the spirit of religion and the ordinances of the Church.

"My heart opened to the good old priest as it had never opened to a living man or even woman before.

"Then and there I told him the whole secret history of my life, including every detail of my two unhappy marriages, and the fatal divorce preceding the birth of my son. I concealed nothing from him. I told him all, and felt infinitely relieved when I had done so.

"The gentle old man dropped tears of pity over me, and sat in silent sympathy some time before he ventured to give me any words.

"At length he arose and said:

"'Child, I must go home and pray for wisdom before I can venture to counsel you.'

"'Bless me, then, holy father.'

"He laid his venerable hands upon my bowed head, raised his eyes to Heaven, and invoked upon me the divine benediction, of which I stood so much in need.

"Then he silently passed from the room.

"That night I slept in peace.

"The next day the good old man came to me again.

"He told me that my first marriage with Waldemar de Volaski was my only true marriage, indissoluble by anything but death, however invalid in law it might be pronounced by those who were interested in breaking it.

"That my second marriage contracted with the Duke of Hereward during the life of my first husband, was sacrilegious in the eyes of religion and the church, however legal it might be considered by the laws of England or of France, and pardonable in me only on account of my ignorance at the time of the continued existence of my first husband.

"That the desperate step I had taken of leaving the Duke of Hereward, upon the discovery of the existence of Waldemar de Volaski, was the right and proper course for me to pursue; but that he regretted I had not possessed the moral courage to tell the duke the whole story, for he had that much right to my confidence.

"As for the divorce I so much lamented, it was to be regretted only for the sake of the son whom it had outlawed, for he was the son of a lawful marriage in the eyes of the world, if not a sacred one in the eyes of the church.

"For the boy thus cruelly wronged there seemed no opening on earth. He was disowned, disinherited, delegalized, deprived even of a name in this world. All earth was closed against him.

"But all Heaven was open to him. The church, Heaven's servant, would open her arms to receive the child the world had cast out. The church in baptism would give him a name and a surname; would give him an education and a mission. I must, like Hannah of old, devote my son, even from his childhood up, to the service of the altar, and the church would do the rest.

"How comforted I was! I had something still to live for! My outcast son would be saved. He could not inherit his father's titles and estates; he could not be a duke, but he would be a holy minister of the Lord; he might live to be a prince of the church, an archbishop or a cardinal.

"Foolish ambition of a still worldly mother you may think. Yes! but he was her only son, and she was worse than widowed.

"I agreed to all the good priest said. I promised to dedicate my son to the service of the altar.

"The next Sunday I went to the chapel of Santa Maria and had my child christened. I gave him in baptism the full name of his father. Beppo and Madelena stood as his sponsors. They told me St. John would be his patron saint.

"I rallied from my torpor. I built a roomy cottage in a mountain dell near the chapel of Santa Maria, furnished it comfortably, and moved into it, and engaged an Italian nurse and housekeeper, for I had resolved to pass my life among the simple, kindly people who were the only friends misfortune had left me.

"Another trial awaited me--a light one, however, in comparison to those I had suffered and outlived.

"This trial came when my son was but little over a year old, and I had been about six months in the "Hermitage," as I called my new home.

"One morning I received a file of English papers for the month of May just preceding. In the papers of the first week in May I saw announced the birth of your son, called the infant Marquis of Arondelle, and the heir. I read of the great rejoicings in all your various seats throughout the United Kingdom, and the congratulations of royalty itself, upon this auspicious event. I clasped my disinherited son to my bosom and wept the very bitterest tears I had ever shed in my life.

"Later on I read in the papers for the last of May a graphic account of the grand pageantry of the christening, which took place at St. Peter's, Euston Square, where an archbishop performed the sacred rites and a royal duke stood sponsor, and of the great feastings and rejoicings in hall and hut on every estate of yours throughout the kingdom. I thought of my disowned boy's humble baptism in the village church by the country priest, where two kind-hearted peasants stood sponsors for him, and I wept myself nearly blind that night.

"The next day I went to the little church and told the good father there all about it. He understood and sympathized with me, counselled and comforted me as usual.

"He admonished me that to escape from the wounds of the world, I must not only forsake the world, as I had done, but forget the world as I had not done; to forget the world I must cease to search and inquire into its sayings and doings; and he advised me to write and stop all my newspapers, which only brought me news to disturb my peace of mind.

"I followed the direction of my wise guide. I wrote immediately and stopped all my newspapers.

"After that I devoted myself to the nurture of my child, to the care of my little household, to the relief of my poorer neighbors, and to the performance of my religious duties; and time brought me resignation and cheerfullness.

"From that day to this, Duke of Hereward, I have never once seen your name printed or written, and never once heard it breathed. You may have passed away from earth, for aught I know to the contrary; though I hope and believe that you have not.

"My boy throve finely. The good priest of Santa Maria took charge of his education for the first twelve years of the pupil's life, made of him, even at that early age, a good Latin and Greek scholar, and a fair mathematician; and would have prepared him to enter one of the German Universities, had not the summons come that cut short the good father's work on earth, and carried him to his eternal home.

"It was soon after the loss of this kind friend, who had been the strong prop of my weakness, the wise counsellor of my ignorance, that my own health began to fail. The seeds of pulmonary consumption, inherited from my mother, began to develop, and nothing could arrest their progress. For the last three years I have been an invalid, growing worse and worse every year. Perhaps in no other climate, under no other treatment, could I have lived so long as I have been permitted to live here by the help of the pure air and the grape cure.

"My boy, now fifteen years of age, is everything that I could wish him to be, except in one respect. He will not consent to enter the church. He wants to be a soldier, poor lad! Well, we cannot coerce him into a life of sanctity and self-denial. Such a life must always be a voluntary sacrifice. Neither do I wish to cross him, now that I am on my death-bed and doomed so soon to leave him.

"In these last days on earth, lying on my dying bed, travailing for his good, it has come to me like an inspiration that I must send him to his father. I must not leave him friendless in the world. And now that the priest Antonio has long passed away, and I am so soon to follow, he will have no friends except these poor, helpless Italian peasants among whom he has been reared. Therefore I must send him, in the hope that you will recognize him by his exact likeness to yourself, and prove his identity as your son, by all the testimony you can be sure to gather in Paris and at San Vito. I have written this long letter, in the intervals between pain and fever, during the last few weeks.

"Yesterday, my faithful physician warned me that my days on earth had dwindled down to hours; that I might pass away at any moment now, and had therefore best attend to any necessary business that I might wish to settle.

"This warning admonishes me to finish and close my letter. I end as I began, by swearing to you, by all the hopes of salvation in a dying woman, that Archibald

Scott is your own son. You can prove this to your own satisfaction by coming to San Vito and examining the church register as to the dates of his birth, baptism, and so forth; by which you will find that he was born just five months after I left your roof, and just six months after our return from our long yachting cruise, and the renewal of my acquaintance with Count de Volaski, at the British minister's dinner. You see, by these circumstances, there cannot be even the shadow of a doubt as to his true parentage.

"I repeat, that I have not told the boy the secret of his birth; to have done so might have been to have embittered his mind against you, and I would not on my death-bed do anything to sow enmity between father and son.

"I leave to yourself to tell him, if you should ever think proper to do so, and with what explanations you may please to add.

"I have constituted you his sole guardian, and trustee of the moderate property I bequeath him. He wishes to enter the army, and he will have money sufficient to purchase a commission and support himself respectably in some good regiment. I hope that when the proper time comes you will forward his ambition in this direction.

"And so I leave him in your hands, for my feeble strength fails, and I can only add my name.

CHAPTER XLII.
HER SON.

The last lines of this sad letter were almost illegible in their faintness and irregularity; and the tangled skein of light scratches that stood proxy for a signature could never have been deciphered by the skill of man.

The Duke of Hereward had grown ten years older in the half hour he had spent in the perusal of this fatal letter. He was no longer only sixty-five years of age, and a "fine old English gentleman;" he seemed fully seventy-five years old, and a broken, decrepit, ruined man. In fact, the first blow had fallen upon that fine intellect whose subsequent eccentricities gained for him the sobriquet of the mad duke.

The hand that held the fatal letter fell heavily by his side; his head drooped upon his chest; he did not move or speak for many minutes.

His young visitor watched him with curiosity and interest that gradually grew into anxiety. At length he made a motion to attract the duke's attention--dropped a book upon the floor, picked it up, and arose to apologize.

The duke started as from a profound reverie, sighed heavily, passed his handkerchief across his brow, and finally wheeled his chair around, and looked at his visitor.

No! there could be no question about it; the boy was the living image of what he himself had been at that age, as all his portraits could prove! and his eldest son, his rightful heir, stood before him, but forever and irrecoverably disinherited and delegalized by his own rash and cruel act.

The young man stood up as if naturally waiting to hear what the duke might have to say about his mother's letter.

But the duke did not immediately allude to the letter.

"Where are you stopping, my young friend?" he asked, in as calm a voice as he could command.

"At 'Langhams,' your grace," respectfully answered the youth.

"Very well. I will call and see you at your rooms to-morrow at eleven, and we will talk over your mother's plans and see what can be done for you," said the duke, as he touched the bell, and sank back heavily in his chair.

The young man understood that the interview was closed, and he was about to take his leave, when the door opened and a footman appeared.

"Truman, attend this young gentleman to the breakfast-room, and place refreshments before him. I hope that you will take something before you go, sir," said the duke, kindly.

"Thanks. I trust your grace will permit me to decline. It is scarce two hours since I breakfasted," said the boy, with a bow.

"As you please, young sir," answered the duke.

The youth then bowed and withdrew, attended by the footman.

The duke watched them through the door, listened to their retreating steps down the hall, and then threw his clasped hands to his head, groaning:

"Great Heaven! What have I done? What foul injustice to her, what cruel wrong to him. I thank her that she has never told him! I can never do so! Nay, Heaven forbid that he should ever even suspect the truth! Nor must I ever permit him to come here again; or to any house of mine, where the duchess, where *his brother*, where every servant even must see the likeness he bears to the family, and--discover, or, at least, suspect the secret!"

Meanwhile the youth, respectfully attended by the footman, left the house.

As he entered his cab that was waiting at the door, a bitter, bitter change passed over his fine face; the fair brow darkened, the blue eyes contracted and glittered, the lips were firmly compressed for an instant, and then he murmured to himself:

"That they should think a secret like this could be buried, concealed from me, the most interested of all to find it out! Was ever son so accursed as I am? Other sons have been disinherited, outlawed--but I! I have been delegalized and degraded from my birth!"

The fine mouth closed with a spasmodic jerk, the brow grew darker, the eyes glittered with intenser fire. He resumed:

"It will be difficult, if not impossible, but I will be restored to my rights, or I will ruin and exterminate the ducal house of Hereward! I am the eldest son of my father; the only son of his first marriage. I am the heir not only of my father, but of the seven dukes and twenty barons that preceded him, to whom their patent of nobility was granted, to them and *their heirs forever*! 'Their heirs forever!' It was granted, therefore, to *me* and to all of *my* direct line! Each baron and duke had but his life-interest in his barony or dukedom, and could not alienate it from his heirs by will. It was an infamous, a fraudulent subterfuge to divorce my poor mother, and so delegalize me a few months before my birth. But--I will bide my time! This false heir may die. Such things do happen. And then, as there is no other heir to his title and estates, *my father* may acknowledge his eldest son, and try to undo the evil he has done. But if this should not happen, or if my father, who is old, should die, and this false heir inherit, *then* I will spend every shilling I have inherited from my mother to gain my own. I will have my rights, though I convict my father of a fraudulent conspiracy, and it requires an act of Parliament to effect my restoration! And if, after all, this wrong cannot be righted--although it can be abundantly proved that I am the only son of my father's first marriage, and the rightful heir of his dukedom, if, after all, I cannot be restored to my position, I will prove the mortal enemy of the race of Scott, and the destruction of the ducal house of Hereward.

Meanwhile I must watch and wait; use this old man as my friend, who will not acknowledge himself as my father!"

These bitter musings lasted until the cab drew up before Langham's Hotel, and the youth got out and went into the house.

The boy, wrong in many instances, was right in this, that the secret of his birth could not be concealed from him.

His poor mother had never divulged it to him, never meant him to know that, the knowledge of which, she thought, would only make him unhappy; but she had told no falsehoods, put forth no false showing to hide it irrecoverably from him.

She was known among her poor Italian neighbors as Signora Valeria, and supposed by them to be the widow of that handsome young Pole to whom they had seen her married, and from whom they had seen her torn by her father, some years before. Of the Duke of Hereward, her second husband, and of her divorce from him, they knew nothing. But she was known to her father-confessor, to her news-agent, and later to her son, as Valerie de la Motte Scott, for though no longer entitled to bear the latter name, she had tacitly allowed it to cling to her.

Now as to how the boy discovered the secret that was designed to be concealed from him.

When with childish curiosity he had inquired, his mother had told him that he had lost his father in infancy; and the boy understood that the loss was by death: but as time passed, and the lad questioned more particularly concerning his parentage, his mother, in repeating that he had lost his father in infancy, added that the loss had been attended with distressing circumstances, and begged him to desist in his inquiries. This only stimulated the interest and curiosity of the youth, and kept him on the *qui vive* for any word, or look, or circumstance that might give him a clew to the mystery. And thus it followed that with a mother so simple and unguarded as Valerie, and a son so cunning and watchful as Archibald, the secret she wished to keep be soon discovered. But he kept his own counsel for the sake of gaining still more information. And, at length, the full revelation and confirmation of all that he had suspected came to him in a manner and by means his mother had never foreseen or provided against.

Valerie had made a will leaving all her property to her son, and appointing the Duke of Hereward as his guardian. After her death, all her papers and other effects had to be overhauled and examined and her son took care to read every paper that he was free to handle. Among these was a copy of the will of the late Waldemar de Volaski, by which he bequeathed to Valerie de la Motte Scott, Duchess of Hereward, all his personal property.

Here was both a revelation and a mystery! Valerie de la Motte Scott, his most unhappy mother, Duchess of Hereward! and his guardian, appointed by her--the Duke of Hereward!

Who was the Duke of Hereward? That he was a great English nobleman was evident! But aside from that, who and what was he?

The boy was in a fever of excitement. It was of no use to ask any of his poor Italian neighbors, for they knew less than he did. He had heard of a mammoth London annual, called *Burke's Peerage*, which would tell all about the living and dead nobility; but there was no copy of it anywhere in reach.

However, his mother's dying directions had been that he should proceed at once to England, and report himself to his guardian, that very Duke of Hereward so mysteriously connected with his destiny.

Intense curiosity stimulating him, he hurried his departure, and after traveling day and night arrived in London on the evening of the last day of May.

He waited only to engage a room at Langham's and change his dress, and partake of a slight luncheon, before he ordered a cab, drove to the nearest bookstore, and purchased a copy of *Burke's Peerage* for that current year.

As soon as he found himself alone in his cab again, he tore the paper off the book and eagerly turned to the article Hereward, and read:

"Hereward, Duke of--Archibald-Alexander-John Scott, Marquis and Earl of Arondelle in the peerage of England, Viscount Lone and Baron Scott in the peerage of Scotland, and a baronet; born Jan. 1st, 1795; succeeded his father as seventh duke, Feb. 1st, 1840; married, March 15th 1845, Valerie, only daughter of the Baron de la Motte; divorced from her grace Feb. 13, 1846; married secondly, April 1st, 1846, Lady Augusta-Victoria, eldest daughter of the Earl of Banff, by whom he has:

"Archibald-Alexander-John, Marquis of Arondelle."

Then followed a long list of other children, girls and boys, of whom the only record was birth and death. Not one of them, except the young Marquis of Arondelle, had lived to be seven years old.

Then followed the long lineage of the family, going over a glorious history of eight centuries.

The youth glanced over the lineage, but soon recurred to the opening paragraphs.

"'Married, March 15th, 1845, Valerie, only daughter of the Baron de la Motte.' That was my poor, dear mother!

"'Divorced from her grace, Feb, 13th, 1846,' He divorced her, and what for! She was a saint on earth, I know! Perhaps it was for being *that* she was divorced! Let us see. 'Married secondly, April 1st, 1846, Lady Augusta Victoria, eldest daughter of the Earl of Banff.' Ah, ha! that was it! He divorced my beloved mother for the same season that the tryant Henry VIII. divorced Queen Catherine, because he was in love with another woman whom he wished to marry!"

(The study of history teaches as much knowledge of the world as does personal experience.)

"But here again," continued the youth. "He divorced my dear mother on the 13th of February, married his Anne Boylen on the 1st of April--appropriate day-- and I was born on the 15th of the same month! Yes! my angel mother and my infant self branded with infamy two months before my birth, and by the very man whom nature and law should have constrained to be our protector! Will I ever forgive it? No! When I do, may Heaven never forgive me!"

As the boy made this vow he laid down the "Royal and Noble Stud-Book," and took up the bulky letter that his mother had entrusted to him to be delivered to the Duke of Hereward. He studied it a moment, then had a little struggle with his sense of right, and finally murmuring:

"Forgive me, gentle mother; but having discovered so much of your secret, I must know it all, even for *your* sake, and for the love and respect I bear you."

He broke the seal and read the whole of the historical letter from beginning to end.

Then he carefully re-folded and re-sealed the letter, so as to leave no trace of the violence that has been done in opening it.

Then he sat for a long time with his elbows on the table before him, and his head bowed upon his hands while tear after tear rolled slowly down his cheeks for the sad fate of that young, broken hearted mother who had perished in her early prime.

The next day, as we have seen, he went to Hereward House and presented his mother's letter to the duke. He had watched his grace while the latter was reading the letter. He had foolishly expected to see some sign of remorse, some demonstration of affection. But he had been disappointed. He had been received only as the son of some humble deceased friend, consigned to the great duke's care. His tender mood had changed to a vindictive one, and he had sworn to be restored to his rights, or to devote his life to effect the ruin and extermination of the house of Hereward.

CHAPTER XLIII.
THE DUKE'S WARD.

The next morning, at the appointed hour, the Duke of Hereward drove to Langham's, and sent up his card to Mr. John Scott.

The youth himself, to show the greater respect, came down to the public parlor where the duke waited, and after most deferentially welcoming his visitor, conducted him to his own private apartment.

"I see by your mother's letter, as well as by her will, that she has done me the honor to appoint me your guardian," said the elder man, as soon as they were seated alone together, and cautiously eyeing the younger, so as to detect, if possible, how much or how little he knew or suspected of the true relationship between them.

"My mother did *me* the honor to consign me to your grace's guardianship, if you will be so condescending as to accept the charge," replied the youth, with grave courtesy and in his turn eyeing the duke to see, if possible, what might be his feelings and intentions toward himself.

The duke bowed and then said:

"I would like to carry out your mother's views and your own wishes, if possible. She mentioned in her letter the army as a career for you. Do you wish some years hence to take a commission in the army?"

"I *did*, your grace: but now I prefer to leave myself entirely in your grace's hands," cautiously replied the youth.

"But in the matter of choosing a profession you must be left free. No one but yourself can decide upon your own calling with any hope of ultimate success. Much mischief is done by the officiousness of parents and guardians in directing their sons or wards into professions or callings for which they have neither taste nor talent," said the duke.

The youth smiled slightly; he could but see that the duke was utterly perplexed as to his own course of conduct, and to cover his confusion he was only talking for talk's sake.

"You will let me know your own wishes on this subject, I hope, young sir," continued the elder.

"My only wish on the subject is to leave myself in your grace's hands. I feel confident that whatever your grace may think right to do with me, will be the best possible thing for me," replied the boy, with more meaning in his manner, as well as in his words, than he had intended to betray.

The duke looked keenly at him; but his fair impassive face was unreadable.

"Well, at all events, it is, perhaps, time enough for two or three years to come to talk of a profession for you. Would you like to enter one of the universities? Are you prepared to do so?" suddenly inquired the guardian.

"I *would* like to go to Oxford. But whether I am prepared to do so, I do not know. I do not know what is required. I have a fair knowledge of Latin, Greek, and Hebrew, and of the higher mathematics. I was in course of preparation to enter one of the German universities, when my good tutor, Father Antonio, died," replied the youth.

The duke dropped his gray head upon his chest and mused awhile, and then said:

"I think that you had better read with a private tutor for a while; you will then soon recover what you may have lost since the death of your good teacher, and make such further progress as may fit you to go to Oxford at the next term. What do you think? Let me know your views, young sir."

"Thanks, your grace; I will read with any tutor you may be pleased to recommend," respectfully answered the youth.

"You are certainly a most manageable ward," said the guardian, dryly, and with, perhaps, a shade of distrust in his manner.

The boy bowed.

"Well, since you place yourself so implicitly in my hands, I must justify your faith as well as your mother's by doing the very best I can for you. There is a very worthy man, the Vicar of Greencombe, on one of my estates, down in Sussex, near the sea. He is a ripe scholar, a graduate of Trinity College, Oxford, and occasionally augments his moderate salary by preparing youth for college. I will direct my secretary to write to him this morning to know if he can receive you, and I will let you know the result in a day or two."

"Thanks, your grace."

"And now how are you going to employ your time while waiting here?"

"By taking a good guide-book, your grace, and going through London. Your grace will remember that I am a perfect stranger here, and even one of your great historical monuments, such as Westminster Abbey or the Tower, has interest enough in it to occupy a student for a week."

"I commend your taste in the occupation you have sketched out for your time. I must request you, however, to take great care of yourself, and to be *here* every day at this hour, as I shall make it a point to look in upon you."

"Thanks, your grace."

"And now good-day," said the visitor, offering his hand, and then abruptly leaving the room.

The youth, however, with the most deferential manner, attended him down stairs and to his carriage, and only took his leave, with a bow, when the footman closed the door.

Again as soon as his back was turned upon his father, the youth's face changed and darkened, and--

"I bide my time--I bide my time," he muttered to himself as he re-ascended the stairs.

He had not deceived his guardian, however, as to the manner in which he meant to spend his time while in London. At this time of his unfortunate position he had not yet contracted any evil habits, and he had a genuine liking for interesting antiquities. So, after partaking of a light luncheon, he went out, guide-book in hand and spent the whole day in studying the architectural glories and the antique monuments in Westminster Abbey.

The second day he passed among the gloomy dungeons and bloody records of the Tower of London.

On the third day he received another visit from the Duke of Hereward, who came to tell him the Reverend Mr. Simpson, the Vicar of Greencombe, had returned a favorable answer to his letter, and would be happy to receive Mr. Scott in his family.

"Now I do not wish to hurry you my dear boy; but I think the sooner you resume your long-neglected studies, the better it will be for you," said the duke, speaking kindly, but watching cautiously, as was his constant habit when conversing with this unacknowledged son.

"I am ready to go the moment your grace commands," answered the young man.

"I issue no commands to you, my boy. I will give you a letter of introduction to Dr. Simpson, which you may go down and deliver at your own leisure. If you choose to spend a week longer in London to see what is to be seen, why do so, of course. If not, you can run down to Greencombe to-day or to-morrow. It is about two hours' journey by the London and South Coast Railroad from the London Bridge Station."

"I will go down this afternoon."

"That is prompt. That is right. All you do my boy, all I see of you, commends you more and more to my approval and esteem. Go this afternoon, by all means. I will myself meet you at the station, to see you off and leave with you my letter of introduction. Stay; by what train shall you go? Ah! you do not know anything about the trains. Ring the bell."

The youth complied.

A waiter appeared, a Bradshaw was ordered and consulted, and the five P. M. express fixed upon as the train by which the youth should leave London.

The duke then took leave of the boy, with an admonition of punctuality.

"Well," said John Scott to himself, as soon as he was left alone, "if my father gives me nothing else, he is certainly disposed to give me my own way. Perhaps in time he may give me all my rights. If so, well. If not--I *bide my time*," he repeated.

At the appointed hour the guardian and ward met at the depot.

The duke placed the promised letter in the youth's hand, saw him into a first-class carriage, and there bade him good-by.

John Scott sped down into Sussex as fast as the express train could carry him, and the Duke of Hereward went back to Hereward House, much relieved by the departure of the youth, whose presence in London had seemed like an incubus upon him.

The deeply injured boy had departed; but--so also had the father's peace of mind, forever! Certainly he was now relieved of all fear of an unpleasant ecclaircissement; but he was not freed from remorse for the past, or from dread for the future.

He told the duchess that day at dinner that a ward had been left to his guardianship, that this ward was, in fact, the son of a near relation, and bore the family name, which made it the more incumbent upon him to accept the charge; and, finally, that he had sent the boy down to Dr. Simpson, at the Greencombe Vicarage, to read for the university.

The duchess was not in the least degree interested in the duke's ward, and rather wondered that he should have taken the trouble to tell her anything about him; but the duke did so to provide for the future contingency of an accidental meeting between the duchess and the boy, so that she might suppose him to be a blood relation, and thus understand the family likeness without the danger of suspecting a truth that could not be explained to her.

But the duke could not silence the voice of conscience and affection. The deeply-wronged boy whom he had sent away was his own first-born son--the son of his first marriage and of his only love; and he had wronged him beyond the power of man to help! He was the rightful heir of his title and estates, yet he could never inherit them; he had been delegalized by his father's own hasty, reckless and cruel act; and for no fault of the boy's own--before he was capable of committing any fault--before his birth--he was disinherited.

All this so worked upon the duke's conscience that he could not give his mind to his ordinary vocations.

But about this time, the duchess, through the death of a near relative, inherited a very large fortune, principally in money.

With this she wished to purchase an estate in Scotland. And so, when Parliament rose, the duke and duchess went to Scotland, personally to inspect certain estates that were for sale there; for the duchess said that, in the matter of choosing a home to live in, she would trust no eyes but her own.

It seemed, however, that neither of the seats in the market pleased the lady, and she had given up her quest in despair, when the duke suggested that, before leaving Scotland, they should make a visit to the famous historical ruins of Lone Castle, in Lone, on Lone Lake, which had been in the Scott-Hereward family for eight centuries.

It was while they were tarrying at the little hotel of the "Hereward Arms," and making daily excursions in a boat across the lake to the isle and to the ruins, that the stupendous idea of restoring the castle occurred to the duke's mind--and not only restoring it as it had stood centuries before, a great, impregnable Highland fortress, but by bringing all the architectural and engineering art and skill of the nineteenth century to bear upon the subject, transforming the ruined castle and rocky isle and mountain-bound lake into the earthly paradise and century's wonder it afterwards became.

What vast means were used, what fortunes were sacrificed, what treasures were drawn into the maelstrom of this mad enterprise, has already been shown.

It is probable, however, that the duke would not have thrown himself so insanely into this work had it not seemed a means of escaping the torture of his own thoughts.

He could restore the old Highland stronghold, and transform the barren, water-girt rock into a garden of Eden; but he could not restore the rights of his own disinherited son.

He had consulted some among the most eminent lawyers in England, putting the case supposititiously, or as the case of another father and son, and the unanimous opinion given was that there could be no help for such a case as theirs; and even though the father had had no other heir, he could not reclaim this disinherited one.

It was not with unmingled regret that the duke heard this opinion given. It certainly relieved him from the fearful duty of having to oppose the duchess and all her family, as he would have been obliged to do, had it been possible to restore his eldest son to his rights; for the duchess would not have stood by quietly and seen her son set aside in favor of the elder brother.

The duke spoke of his ward from time to time, so that in case the duchess should ever meet him, or hear of him from others, she could not regard him as a mystery that had been concealed from her, or look upon his likeness to the family with suspicion.

But the duchess seemed perfectly indifferent to the duke's ward, or if she did interest herself, it was only slightly or good-naturedly, as when she answered the duke's remarks, one day, by saying:

"If the dear boy is a relative of the family, however distant, and your ward besides, why don't you have him home for the holidays?"

"Oh, schoolboys at home for the holidays are always a nuisance. He will go to Wales with Simpson and his lads, when they go for their short vacation," answered the duke, not unpleased that his wife took kindly to the notion of his ward.

In due time the youth entered Oxford. The duke spoke of the fact to the duchess. Then she answered not so good-humoredly as before; indeed, there was a shade of annoyance and anxiety in her tones, as she said:

"Oxford is very expensive, and a young man may make it quite ruinous. I hope the youth's friends have left him means enough of his own. I would not speak of such a matter," she added apologetically, "only the restoration of Lone seems so to swallow up all our resources as to leave us nothing for charitable objects."

"The youth has ample means for educational purposes, and to establish him in some profession. Of course, he cannot indulge in any of those university extravagances and dissipations that are the destruction of so many fine young men; but, then, he is not that kind of lad; a steady, studious boy, brought up by--a widowed mother and a priest," answered the duke, with just a slight faltering in his voice, in the latter clause of his speech.

"Such boys are more apt than others to develop into the wildest young men," replied the lady; and circumstances proved that she was right.

John Scott, at Trinity College, Oxford, passed as the grand-nephew of the Duke of Hereward, and the next in succession, after the young Earl of Arondelle to the dukedom.

The young Earl of Arondelle was still at Eton. And the duke determined to send him from Eton to Cambridge, instead of Oxford, where John Scott was at college; for the father of these two boys wished them never to meet!

At Oxford, John Scott, as the grand-nephew of the Duke of Hereward, bearing an unmistakable likeness to the family, and being, besides, a young man of pleasing address, soon won his way among the most exclusive of the aristocrats there; and pride and vanity tempted him to vie with them in extravagant and riotous living!

His income *only* was limited, his credit was *un*limited. When his money fell short, he ran into debt; and at the end of the first term his liabilities were alarming, or would have been so to a more sensitive mind.

It is true, the amount was much greater than his inexperience had led him to expect; but he only smiled grimly when he had all his bills before him, and had estimated the sum total, and he said to himself:

"If my allowance will not support me here like a gentleman, my father must make up the deficiency, that is all!"

The Duke of Hereward was indeed confounded when his ward wrote to him and told him boldly that he wanted fifteen hundred pounds for immediate necessities--namely, twelve hundred for the liquidation of debts, and three hundred for traveling expenses.

But could he scold the poor, disinherited boy, who, kept to himself at Oxford, had doubtless fallen among thieves and been mercilessly fleeced.

No; he would pay these debts out of his own pocket, and write the young man a kind letter of warning against the university sharks.

The duke carried out this resolution, and John Scott, freed from debt, and with three hundred pounds in his possession, went on a holiday tour through the country.

He had heard at Oxford of the rising glories of Lone, and determined to take his holiday in that neighborhood.

It happened that the Duke and Duchess of Hereward, with the Marquis of Arondelle, and their attendants, went that summer to Baden-Baden; so when the Oxonion arrived at the "Hereward Arms," in the hamlet of Lone, and, from his age and his exact likeness to the family, was mistaken for the heir, there was no one to set the people right on the subject.

The obsequious host of the Hereward Arms called him "my lord," and inquired after his gracious parents, the duke and the duchess.

John Scott did not actually deceive the people as to his identity, but he tacitly allowed them to deceive themselves. He did not tell them that he was the Marquis of Arondelle; neither did he contradict them when they called him so. Nor did his conscience reproach him for his silent duplicity. He said to himself:

"I **am** the rightful Marquis of Arondelle. They do but give me my own just title! If this comes to the ears of the duke and brings on a crisis, I will tell him so!"

While he was in the neighborhood, he went up to Ben Lone on a fishing excursion, and there, as elsewhere, on the Scottish estate, he was everywhere received as the Marquis of Arondelle. There John Scott first met by accident the handsome shepherdess, Rose Cameron, and fell in love for the first time in his young life.

We have already seen how the Highland maiden, flattered by the notice of the supposed young nobleman, encouraged those attentions without returning that love.

After this, John Scott spent all his holidays at Lone, and much of them in the society of the handsome shepherdess. His attentions in that direction were regarded with strong disapproval by his father's tenantry, but it was not their place to censure their supposed "young lord," and so they only expressed their sentiments with grave shaking of their heads.

During the progress of the work, the ducal family never came to Lone, so that the tenantry there were never set right as to the identity of John Scott.

Only once the duke made a visit, to inspect the progress of the workmen. He stopped at the Hereward Arms, and there heard nothing of the pranks of John Scott, although, upon one occasion, he came very near doing so.

The landlord respectfully inquired if they should have the young marquis up there as usual.

The duke stared for a moment, and then answered:

"You are mistaken. Arondelle does not come up here. Whatever are you thinking of, my man?"

The host said he was mistaken, that was all, and so got himself out of his dilemma the best way he could, and took the first opportunity to warn all his dependents and followers that they were not to "blow" on the young marquis.

"He was an unco wild lad, nae doobt, but his feyther kenned naething about his pranks, and sae the least said, sunest mended," said the landlord.

And thus, by the pranks of his "double," the reputation of the excellent young

Marquis of Arondelle suffered among his own people.

CHAPTER XLIV.
RETRIBUTION.

But a crisis was at hand.

The debts of John Scott increased every year, while the ready means of the Duke of Hereward diminished--everything being engulfed by the Lone restoration maelstrom.

The guardian determined to expostulate with his ward.

He went down to Oxford just before the close of the term. He found his ward established in elegant and luxurious apartments, quite fit for a royal prince, and very much more ostentatious than the unpretending chambers occupied by the young Marquis of Arondelle at Cambridge, and ridiculously extravagant for a young man of limited income and no expectations like John Scott.

The duke was excessively provoked; the forbearance of years gave way; the bottled-up indignation burst forth, and the guardian gave his ward what in boyish parlance is called, "an awful rowing."

"You live, sir, at twenty times the rate, your debts are twenty times as large, you cost me twenty times as much as does Lord Arondelle, my own son and heir!" concluded the duke, in a final burst of anger.

John Scott had listened grimly enough to the opening exordium, but when the last sentence broke from the duke's lips, the young man grew pale as death, while his compressed lips, contracted brow, and gleaming blue eyes alone expressed the fury that raged in his bosom.

He answered very quietly:

"Your grace means that I cost you twenty times as much as does your younger son, Lord Archibald Scott, as it is natural that I should being the elder son and the heir of the dukedom."

To portray the duke's thoughts, feelings or looks during his deliberate speech would be simply impossible. He sat staring at the speaker, with gradually paling cheeks and widening eyes, until the quiet voice ceased, when he faltered forth:

"What in Heaven's name do you mean?"

"I should think your grace should know right well what I have known for years, and can never for a moment forget, though your grace may effect to do so--that I am your eldest son, the son of your first marriage, with the daughter of the Baron de la Motte, and therefore that I, and not my younger half brother, by your second marriage, am the right Marquis of Arondelle, and the heir of the Dukedom of Hereward," calmly replied the young man, with all the confidence an assured conviction gave.

The duke sank back in his seat and covered his face with his hands. However John Scott had made the discovery, it was absolutely certain that he knew the whole secret of his parentage.

"What authority have you for making so strange an assertion?" at length inquired the duke.

"The authority of recorded truth," replied the young man, emphatically. "But does your grace really suppose that such a secret could be kept from me? My dear, lost mother never revealed it to me by her words, but she unconsciously revealed enough to me by her actions to excite my suspicions, and set me on the right track. The records did the rest, and put me in possession of the whole truth."

"What records have you examined?" inquired the duke, in a low voice.

"First and last, in Italy and France, I have examined the registers of your marriage with my mother, and of my own birth and baptism; and in England, Burke's Peerage. All these as well as other well-known facts, As easily proved as if they were recorded, establish my rights as your son--your eldest son and *heir*."

"As my son, but not as my heir, for your most unhappy mother--"

"STOP!!" suddenly exclaimed the young man, while his blue eyes blazed with a dangerous fire. "I warn you, Duke of Hereward, that you must not breathe one word reflecting in the least degree on my dear, injured mother's name. You have wronged her enough, Heaven knows! and I, her son, tell you so. Yes! from the beginning to end, you have wronged her grievously, unpardonably. First of all, in marrying her at all, when you must have seen--you could not have failed to see--that she, gentle and helpless creature that she was, was *forced* by her parents to give you her hand, when her broken heart was not hers to give! And, secondly, when she discovered that the lover (to whom she had been sacredly married by the church, though it seems not lawfully married by the state,) and whom she had supposed to be dead, was really living; and when she took the only course a pure and sensitive woman could take, and withdrew herself from you both, ***writing to you her reasons for doing so***, and expressing her wish to live apart a quiet, single, blameless life, you did not wait, you did not investigate, but, with indecent haste, you so hurried through with your divorce, and hurried into your second marriage, as to brand my mother with undeserved infamy, and delegalized her son and yours before his birth."

"Heaven help me," moaned the Duke of Hereward, covering his face with his hands.

"You have done us both this infinite wrong, and you cannot undo it now. I know that you cannot, for I have taken the pains to seek legal advice, and I have been assured that you cannot rectify this wrong. But--use my injured mother's sacred name with reverence, Duke of Hereward, I warn you!--"

"Heaven knows I would use it in no other way! I loved your mother. She and you were not the only sufferers in my domestic tragedy. Her loss nearly killed me with grief even when I thought her unworthy. The discovery of the great wrong I did her has nearly crazed me with remorse since that."

"Then do not grudge her son the small share you allow him of that vast inheritance which should have been his, had you not unjustly deprived him of it."

"I will not. Your debts shall be paid."

"And do not upbraid me by drawing any more invidious comparisons between me and one who holds my rightful place."

"I will not--I will not. John we understand each other now. Your manner has not been the most filial toward me, but I will not reproach you for that. You say that I have wronged you; and you know that wrong can never be righted in this world. 'If I were to give my body to be burned,' it could not benefit you in the least toward recovering your position; but I will do all I can. I will sell Greencombe, which is my own entailed property, and I will place the money with my banker, Levison, to your account. I have a pleasant little shooting-box at the foot of Ben Lone. We never go to it. You must have the run of it during the vacations. When you are ready for your commission I will find you one in a good regiment. In return I have one request to make you. For Heaven's sake avoid meeting the duchess or her family. Do this for the sake of peace. I hope now that we *do* understand each other?" said the duke with emotion.

"We do," said the young man, his better spirit getting the ascendency for a few moments. "We do; and I beg your pardon, my father, for the hasty, unfilial words I have spoken."

"I can make every allowance, for you, John. I can comprehend how you must often feel that you are only your mother's son," answered the duke, grasping the hand that his son had offered.

So the interview that had threatened to end in a rupture between guardian and ward terminated amicably.

John Scott's debts were once more paid, his pockets were once more filled, and he left for Scotland to spend his vacation at the hunting-box under Ben Lone, in the neighborhood made attractive to him, not by black cock or red deer, but by the presence of his handsome shepherdess.

The duke sold Greencombe, and placed the purchase-money in the hands of Sir Lemuel Levison and Co., Bankers, Lombard Street, London, to be invested for the benefit of his ward, John Scott.

The unhappy duke did this at the very time when he was so pressed for money to carry on the great work at Lone, as to be compelled to borrow from the Jews at an enormous interest, mortgaging his estate, Hereward Hold, in security.

And John Scott, with an ample income, and without any restraint, took leave of his good angel and started on the road to ruin.

Meanwhile, the great works at Lone were completed and the ducal family took possession, and commenced their short and glorious reign there by a series of splendid entertainments given in honor of the coming of age of the heir.

John Scott was not an invited guest, either to the castle or the grounds; but he presented himself there, nevertheless, and caused some confusion by his close resemblance to his brother, and much scandal by his improper conduct among the village girls. And many an honest peasant went home from the feast lamenting the behavior of the young heir, and trying to excuse or palliate his viciousness by the vulgar proverb:

"Boys will be boys."

And so the reputation of the young Marquis of Arondelle suffered and continued to suffer from the evil doings of his double.

John Scott kept one part of his compact with the duke; he avoided the family; even when he could not keep away from Lone, he contrived to keep out of sight of the duke, the duchess, and the marquis.

The young Marquis of Arondelle, indeed, was very little seen at Lone. He was at Cambridge, or on his grand tour, nearly all the time of the family's residence in the Highlands.

John Scott left the university without honors. This was a disappointment to the duke, who did not, however, reproach his wayward son, but only wrote and asked him if he would now take a commission in the army. But the young man, who had lost all his youthful military ardor, and contracted a roving habit that made him averse to all fixed rules and all restraints, replied by saying that his income was sufficient for his wants, and that he preferred the free life of a scholar.

The duke wrote again, and implored him to choose one of the learned professions, saying that it was not yet too late for him to enter upon the study of one.

The hopeful son replied that he was not good enough for divinity, bad enough for law, or wise enough for medicine; that, therefore, he was unsuited to honor either of the learned professions; and begged his guardian to disturb himself no longer on the subject of his ward's future.

Then the duke let him alone, having, in fact, troubles enough of his own to occupy him--a life of superficial splendor, backed by a condition of hopeless indebtedness.

We have already, in the earlier portions of this story, described the short, glorious, delusive reign of the Herewards at Lone, and the culminating glory and ruin of the royal visit, so immediately to be followed by the great crash, when the magnificent estate, with all its splendid appointments, was sold under the hammer, and purchased by the wealthy banker and city knight, Sir Lemuel Levison. We have told how the noble son--the young Marquis of Arondelle--sacrificed all his life-interest in the entailed estate, to save his father, and how vain that sacrifice proved. We have told how the duchess died of humiliation and grief, and how the duke and his son went into social exile, until recalled by the romantic love of Salome Levison, who wished to bestow her hand and her magnificent inheritance upon the disinherited heir of Lone.

We have now brought the story of John Scott up to the night of the banker's murder, and his own unintentional share in the tragedy.

At the time of the projected marriage between the Marquis of Arondelle and the heiress of Lone, John Scott was deeply sunk in debt, and badly in want of money.

The capital given him by his father had been so tied up by the donor that nothing but the interest could be touched by the improvident recipient. It had, in fact, been given to Sir Lemuel Levison in trust for John Scott, with directions to invest it to the best advantage for his benefit.

This duty the banker had most conscientiously performed by investing the money in a mining enterprise, supposed to be perfectly secure and to pay a high interest. This investment continued good for years, affording John Scott a very liberal income; but as John Scott would probably have exceeded any income, however large, that he might have possessed, so of course he exceeded this one and got into debt, which accumulated year after year, until at length he felt himself forced to ask his trustee to sell out a part of his stock in the mining company to liquidate his liabilities.

This the banker politely but firmly refused to do, representing to the young spendthrift that his duties as a trustee forbade him to squander the capital of his client, and that he had been made trustee for the very purpose of preserving it.

The obstinacy of the banker enraged the young man, who protested that it was unbearable to a man of twenty-five years of age to be in leading-strings to a trustee, as if he were an infant of five years old.

The time came, however, when the trustee was compelled by circumstances to sell out.

The rare foresight which had made him the millionaire that he was, warned Sir Lemuel Levison that the mining company in which he had invested his ward's fortune was on the eve of an explosion. As no one else perceived the impending catastrophe, Sir Lemuel Levison was enabled to sell out his ward's stock at a good premium some days before the crash came--not an honest measure by any means, *we* think, but--a perfectly business-like one.

He informed John Scott of the transaction, telling him at the same time that he had the capital of thirty thousand pounds in his possession, ready to be re-invested, and the premium of three hundred pounds, which last was at the orders of Mr. Scott.

Mr. Scott was not contented with the three hundred pounds premium. He wanted a few thousands out of the capital, and he wrote and told his trustee as much.

Sir Lemuel Levison was firm in refusing to diminish the capital that had been placed in his hands for the benefit of the spendthrift.

Then John Scott in a rage, went up to London and called at the banking house of Levison Brothers.

Being admitted to the private office of Sir Lemuel Levison, the young man used some very intemperate language, accusing the great banker of appropriating his own contemptible little fortune for private and unhallowed purposes.

"You are the most unmitigated scamp alive, and I wish I had never had anything to do with you; however, I will convince you that you have wronged me, and then I will wash my hands of you!" exclaimed the banker.

And so saying, he unlocked a great patent safe that stood in his private office, took from it a small iron box, and set it on his desk before him, in full sight of his visitor.

"See here," he continued; "here is this box, read the inscription on it."

The visitor stooped over and read--in brass letters--the following sentence: "John Scott--L30,000."

"Now, sir," continued the banker, opening the box and displaying the treasure, all in crisp, new, Bank of England notes of a thousand pounds each--"here is your money. I cannot betray my trust by giving it into your hands. But I intend, nevertheless, to resign my trust into the hands that gave it me. I am going down to Lone to celebrate the marriage of my daughter with the Marquis of Arondelle, and I shall take this box and its contents down with me. I shall, of course, meet the Duke of Hereward there. As soon as the marriage is over, and the pair gone on their tour, I shall deliver this box with its contents over to the duke, who can then hand over any part or the whole of this money to you, if he pleases to do so."

If any circumstance could have increased the uneasiness of the spendthrift, it would have been this resolution of the banker and trustee.

John Scott begged Sir Lemuel Levison to reconsider his resolution, and not return his capital to the donor, who, in his impoverished condition, might, for all he knew, choose to resume his gift entirely, and appropriate it to his own uses.

But the banker was inflexible, and the next day set out for Lone, carrying John Scott's fortune locked up in the iron box, besides other treasures in money and jewels, secured in other receptacles.

John Scott was in despair.

At length, a daring plan occurred to his mind. His evil life had brought him into communication with some outlaws of society of both sexes, with whom, however, he would not willingly have been seen in daylight, or in public. One of these--a brutal ruffian and thief, with whose haunts and habits he was well acquainted--he sought out. He gave him an outline of his scheme, telling him of the great treasures in jewels and other bridal presents that would be laid out in the drawing-room at Lone on the night of the sixth of June, in readiness for the wedding display on the morning of the seventh.

The man Murdockson listened with greedy ears.

The tempter then told him of the iron box, inscribed with his own name, and containing *important papers* which it was necessary he should recover, and proposed that if Murdockson would promise to purloin the iron box from the chamber of Sir Lemuel Levison, and bring it safely to him, John Scott, *he* would engage to leave the secret passage to the castle open for the free entrance of the adventurers.

Murdockson hesitated a long time before consenting to engage in an enterprise which, if it promised great profit, also threatened great dangers.

At length, however, fired by the prospect of the fabulous wealth said to lie exposed in the form of bridal presents displayed in Castle Lone, Mr. Murdockson promised to form a party and go down to Lone to reconnoitre, and if he should see his way clear, to undertake the job.

The plan was carried out to its full and fatal completion.

Disguised as Highland peasants, Murdockson and two of his pals went down to Lone to inspect the lay.

They mingled with the great crowd of peasantry and tenantry that had collected from far and near to view the grand pageantry prepared for the celebration of the wedding, and their presence in so large an assemblage was scarcely noticed.

They met their principal in the course of the day, and with him arranged the details of the robbery.

One thing John Scott insisted upon--that there was to be no violence, no blood-shed; that if the robbery could not be effected quietly and peaceably, without bodily harm to any inmate, it was not to be done at all, it was to be given up at once.

The men promised all that their principal asked, on condition that he would act his part, and let them into the castle.

That night John Scott did his work, and attained the climax of his evil life.

He tampered with the valet, treated him with drugged whiskey, and while the wretched man was in a stupid sleep, stole from him the pass-key to Sir Lemuel Levison's private apartment.

We know how that terrible night ended. John Scott could not control the devils he had raised.

Only robbery had been intended; but murder was perpetrated.

John Scott, with the curse of Cain upon his soul, and without the spoil for which he had incurred it, fled to London and afterwards to the Continent, where he became a homeless wanderer for years, and where he was subsequently joined by his female companion, Rose.

CHAPTER XLV.
AFTER THE REVELATION.

During the latter portion of the mother-superior's story--the portion that relat-ed to the delegalized elder son of the Duke of Hereward--a light had dawned upon the mind of Salome, but so slowly that no sudden shock of joy had been felt, no wild exclamation of astonishment uttered: yet that light had revealed to the amazed and overjoyed young wife, beyond all possibility of further doubt, the blessed truth of the perfect freedom of her worshiped husband from all participation in the awful crimes of which over-whelming circumstantial evidence had convicted him in her own mind, but of which it was now certain that his miserable brother, his "double" in appearance, was alone guilty.

The dark story had been told in the darkness of the abbess' den, so that not even the varying color that must otherwise have betrayed the deep emotion of the hearer, could be seen by the speaker.

At the conclusion of the story, one irrepressible reproach escaped the lips of the young wife.

"Oh, mother! mother! If you knew all this, why did you not tell me before? For you must also have known, what is now so clear to me, that not the Duke of Hereward, who, after all, is my husband, I thank Heaven--not the noble Duke of Hereward, but his most ignoble brother, his counterpart in person and in name, has married that terrible Scotch woman, and mixed himself up in murder and robbery. Oh, mother! you should have told me before!"

"My daughter be patient! Only this week have I been able to fit in all the links in the chain of evidence to make the story complete. Your mention of the Duke of Hereward as your false husband, my memory of the Duke of Hereward as the wronged husband who had slain my betrothed in a duel, all set me to thinking deeply, very deeply thinking. I did not express my thoughts unnecessarily. Silence is, with our order, a duty--the handmaid of devotion; but I set secret inquiries on foot, through agencies that our orders possess for finding out facts, and means that we can use, superior to those of the most accomplished detectives living. Through such agencies, and by such means, I learned not only external facts--which are often lies, paradoxical as that may seem--but I learned, also, the internal truths without which no history can be really known, no subject really understood."

"But oh! you should not have kept silence. You should not have left me to misjudge my noble husband a day longer than necessary!" burst forth Salome.

"Calm yourself, daughter, and listen to me. I have kept nothing from you a day longer than necessary. The facts that exonerate the Duke of Hereward came to me last of all. Hear me. From Father Garbennetti, the new cure of San Vito, I learned the truth of that miscalled elopement of the late Duchess of Hereward. I learned that--in the words of your own charming poet--

'My rival fair A saint in heaven should be.'

For a most innocent and most deeply wronged and long-suffering martyr on earth she had been. From him I also learned the existence of her boy, and the adoption of the boy, after the mother's death, by the Duke of Hereward. That was all I could learn from the Italian priest, who had lost sight of the lad after the mother's death. Next I pushed inquiries through our agents in England, and through the investigations of Father Fairfield, the eloquent English oratorian, I learned the truth of John Scott's life in England and Scotland, as I have given it to you. I received Father Fairfield's letter only this day; only this day I have learned, Salome, that you are really the Duchess of Hereward; that the Duke of Hereward was, and is, really your husband, and was never the husband of any other woman."

"Oh, how bitterly! how bitterly! how unpardonably I have wronged him! He will pardon me! Yes, he will! for he is all magnanimity, and he loves me! But I can never, never pardon myself!" exclaimed the young wife, her first joy at discovering the absolute integrity of her husband now giving place to the severest self-condemnation.

"You need not reproach yourself so cruelly, so sternly, under circumstances in which you would not reproach another at all. Remember what you told me, you had the evidence of your own eyes and ears, and the testimony of documents, and of individuals against him!" said the abbess, soothingly.

"Yes! the evidence of my own eyes and ears, which mistook the counterfeit for the real! the testimony of documents that were forgeries, and of individuals that were false! And upon these I believed my noble husband guilty of a felony, and without even giving him an opportunity to explain the circumstances, or to defend himself, I left him even on our wedding-day! and have concealed myself from him for many months! exposing him to misconstruction, to dishonor and reproach. Oh, no! I can never, never pardon myself! Nor do I even know how *he* can ever pardon me. But he will! I am sure he will! Even as the Lord pardons all repented sin, however grievous, so will my peerless husband pardon me!" fervently exclaimed Salome.

The abbess reverted to her own troubles.

"I cannot understand," she said, "the mystery of that man's appearance here this morning."

"What man?" inquired Salome, who was so absorbed in thinking of her husband that she had nearly forgotten the existence of other men.

"'What man?' Why, daughter, the Count Waldemar de Volaski--the man who came here with the woman this morning--the man whom you mistook for your own husband, the Duke of Hereward, but whom I knew to be Waldemar de Volaski, once my betrothed, who was said to have been killed in a duel, shot through the heart, a quarter of a century ago!" answered the lady, emphatically.

Salome stared at the abbess for a few moments in amazed silence, and then exclaimed:

"Dear madam, good mother, are you still under that deep delusion?"

"Delusion!" echoed the lady.

"Yes, the deepest delusion. Dear lady, do you not know, can you not comprehend *now* that the man who visited us this morning was no other than John Scott, the counterpart whom even I really did mistake for the Duke of Hereward, as you say; and that the bold, bad beauty who accompanied him was his wife, Rose Cameron?"

"Nay, daughter, he was Count Waldemar de Volaski!" persisted the abbess.

"What an hallucination! Dear lady, do you not see--But what is the use of talking? I cannot convince you of your mistake: but circumstances may; for, of course, sooner or later the unhappy man will be arrested and brought to trial for his share in the robbery and murder at Castle Lone."

"No, you cannot convince me of mistake, because I have not made any; but *I* will convince *you* of *yours*," said the lady, rising and striking a match and lighting a lamp; for they had hitherto sat in darkness.

Salome smiled incredulously.

The abbess went to a little drawer of the stand upon which her crucifix and missal stood, and drew from it a small box, which she opened and exhibited to Salome, saying:

"This, daughter, is the only memento of the world and the world's people that I have retained. I should not have kept even this, but that it is the likeness of my once betrothed, bestowed on me on the occasion of our betrothal, cherished once in loyal love, cherished now in prayerful memory of one whom I supposed had expiated his sins by death, long, long ago. I have kept it, but I have not looked at it for twenty years or more."

Salome took the miniature, and examined it carefully with interest and curiosity.

It was very well painted in water-colors on ivory. It represented a young man of from twenty to twenty-five years of age, with a Roman profile, fair complexion, blue eyes and blonde hair and mustache; and so far as these features and this complexion went, the miniature certainly did bear an external and superficial resemblance to John Scott and to the young Duke of Hereward; but in character and expression the faces were so totally different that Salome could never have mistaken the miniature to be a likeness of the duke or his brother, or either of these men to be the original of the picture.

After gazing intently at the miniature for a few minutes, she turned to the abbess and said:

"You tell me that you have not looked at this for twenty years?"

"I have not," said the lady.

"And you tell me that the man who visited the asylum this morning is the original of this picture?"

"I do."

"Then, dear mother, your memory is at fault and your imagination deceives and misleads you. Both the supposed original and the miniature are thin-faced, with Roman features, fair complexion, blue eyes and blonde hair--points of resemblance which are common to many men who are not at all alike in any other respect. Now look at this miniature again, and you will see that, except in the points I have named, it is in no way like the man you mistook for its original."

"I would rather not look at it. I have not seen it since--Volaski's supposed death," said the abbess, shrinking.

"Oh, but do, for the satisfaction of your own mind. You see so few men, that you may easily mistake one blonde for another after twenty years of absence from them," persisted Salome, pressing the open miniature upon the lady.

So urged, the abbess took it, gazed wistfully at the pictured face, and murmured:

"It is possible. I may be mistaken."

"You are," muttered Salome.

The abbess continued to gaze on the portrait, and whispered:

"I think I am mistaken."

"I am *sure* that you are, good mother," said Salome.

The lady's eyes were still fixed upon the relic, until at length she closed the locket with a click and laid it away in the little drawer, saying, clearly and firmly:

"Yes, I see that I *was* mistaken."

"I am very glad you know it," remarked Salome.

"So am I. It is a relief. And now, dear daughter, I will dismiss you to your rest. To-morrow we will consult concerning your affairs, and see what is best for you to do," said the abbess.

"I know what is best for me to do--*my duty*. And my very first duty is to hasten immediately to England, seek out my dear husband, confess all my cruel misapprehension of his conduct, and implore his pardon. I am sure of his pardon, and of his love! As sure as I am of my Heavenly Lord's pardon and love when I kneel to Him and confess and deplore my sins!" fervently exclaimed the young wife.

"Yes, I suppose you must return to England now. I do suppose that, after what we have discovered, you cannot remain here and become a nun," sighed the abbess, unwilling to resign her favorite.

"No, indeed, I cannot remain here. But I will richly endow the Infants' Asylum, dear mother. And I will visit, it every year of my life. I am going to retire now, good mother. Bless me," murmured Salome, bending her head.

"*Benedicite*, fair daughter," said the abbess, spreading her open palms over the beautiful, bowed head as she invoked the blessing.

Then Salome arose, left the cell, and hurried back through the two long passages at right angles that conducted her from the nursery to the Infants' Asylum.

She passed silently as a spirit through every dormitory where her infant charges lay sleeping, assured herself that they were all safe and well, and then she entered her own little sleeping-closet adjoining the dormitory of the youngest infants, then disrobed and went to bed.

She was much too happy to sleep. She lay counting the hours to calculate in how short a time she could be with her beloved husband!

She had no dread of meeting him, not the least.

"Perfect love casteth out fear."

She arose early the next morning, and, after going through all her duties in the Infants' Asylum, she went to the lady-superior's sitting-room to consult her about making arrangements for an immediate departure for England.

"But shall you not write first to announce your arrival?" inquired the abbess.

"No; because I can go to England just as quickly as a letter can, and I would rather go. There is a train from L'Ange at five P. M. I can go by that and reach Calais in time for the morning boat, and be in London by noon to-morrow--as soon as a letter could go. And I could see my husband, actually see him, before I could possibly get a letter from him," said Salome, brightening.

"If his grace should be in London," put in the abbess.

"I think he will be in London. If he is not there, I can find out where he is, and follow him. Dear madam, *do* not hinder me. I *must* start by the first available train," said Salome, earnestly.

"I do not desire to hinder you," answered the lady-superior.

Their conversation was interrupted by the entrance of Sister Francoise, who pale and agitated, sank upon the nearest seat, and sat trembling and speechless, until the abbess exclaimed:

"For the love of Heaven, Sister Francoise, tell us what has happened. Who is ill? Who is dead?"

"*Helas!* holy mother!" gasped the nun, losing her breath again immediately.

Salome drew a small phial of sal volatile from her pocket and uncorked and applied it to the nose of the fainting nun, saying soothingly:

"Now tell us what has overcome you, good sister."

"Ah, my child! It is dreadful! It is terrible! It is horrible! It is awful! But they are bringing him in!" gasped Sister Francoise, snuffing vigorously at the sal volatile, and still beside herself with excitement.

"What! What! Who are they bringing in?" demanded the abbess, in alarm.

"I'm going to tell you! Oh, give me time! It is stupefying! It is annihilating! The poor gentleman who has just shot himself through the body!" gasped Sister Francoise, losing her breath again after this effort.

"A gentleman shot himself!" echoed Salome, in consternation.

The abbess, pale as death, said not a word, but left the unnerved sister to the care of Salome, and went out to see what had really happened.

She met the little Sister Felecitie in the passage.

"What is all this, my daughter?" she inquired, in a very low voice.

"They have taken him into the refectory, madam. That was the nearest to the gate, where it happened. It happened just outside the south gate, madam. They took off a leaf of the gate, and laid him on it and brought him in," answered the trembling little novice, rather incoherently.

"Daughter, I have often admonished you that you must not address me as 'madam,' but as 'mother.'"

"I beg your pardon, holy mother; but I was so frightened, I forgot."

"Now tell me quickly, and clearly, what happened near the south gate?"

"Oh, madam!--holy mother, I mean!--the suicide! the suicide!"

"The suicide! It was not an accident, then, but a suicide?" exclaimed the abbess, aghast, and pausing in her hurried walk toward the refectory.

"Oh, madam--holy mother!--yes, so they say! It is enough to kill one to see it all!"

"Go into my room, child, and stay there with Sister Francoise until I return. Such sights are too trying for such as you," said the abbess, as she parted from the young novice, and hurried on toward the refectory.

CHAPTER XLVI.
RETRIBUTION.

She entered the long dining-hall, where a terrible sight met her eyes.

Stretched upon the table lay a man in the midst of a pool of his own blood!

In the room were gathered a crowd, consisting of three Englishmen, three gend'armes, several countrymen, several out-door servants of the convent, and half a hundred nuns and novices.

The crowd had parted a little on the side nearest the door by which the abbess entered, so as to permit the approach of an old man who seemed to be a physician, and who proceeded to unbutton the wounded man's coat and vest, and to examine his wound.

"How horrible! Is he quite dead?" inquired the abbess, making her way to the side of the village surgeon, for such the old man was.

"No, madam; he has fainted from loss of blood. The wound has stopped bleeding now, however, and I hope by the use of proper stimulants to recover him sufficiently to permit me to examine and dress his wounds," replied the surgeon, who now drew from his pocket a bottle of spirits of hartshorn, poured some out in his hands, and began to bathe the forehead, mouth and nostrils of the unconscious man.

The abbess drew nearer, stooped over the body, and gazed attentively into the pallid and ghastly face, and then started with a half-suppressed cry as she recognized the features of the man who had visited the Infants' Asylum on the day previous, and whom the abbess now believed to be John Scott, the half brother and the "double" of the Duke of Hereward.

"Will you kindly order some brandy, madam?" courteously requested the surgeon.

"Certainly, monsieur," replied the lady superior, who immediately dispatched a nun to fetch the required restorative.

As soon as it was brought, a few drops were forced down the throat of the fainting man, who soon began to show signs of recovery.

"I should like to put my patient to bed, madam; but the nearest farm-house is still too far off for him to be conveyed thither in safety. The motion would start his wound to bleeding again, and the hemorrhage might prove fatal," said the surgeon suggestively.

The abbess took the hint.

"Of course," she said, "the poor wounded man must remain here. I will have a room prepared for him in our Old Men's Home. It will not take ten minutes to get the room ready, and carry him to it. Can you wait so long, good Doctor?"

"Assuredly, madam," answered the surgeon.

The abbess gave the necessary orders to a couple of young nuns, who hurried off to obey them.

In less time than the abbess required, they came back and reported that the room was ready for the patient.

"Now, then, Monsieur le Docteur, you may remove your patient," said the abbess, courteously.

The surgeon, assisted by two of the countrymen, tenderly lifted the wounded man, and laid him on the leaf of the gate, and, preceded by an aged nun to show the way, bore him off toward the Old Men's Home.

One of the Englishmen and one of the gend'armes followed him.

The remaining two Englishmen and two gend'armes showed no disposition to depart.

The abbess was not two well pleased at this masculine invasion of her sanctuary, and so after waiting for some explanation of their presence from these strange men, she went up to them and inquired, with suggestive politeness:

"May we know, messieurs, how we can further serve you?"

"Your pardon, holy madam, but we are not willing intruders. I am Inspector Setter, of Scotland Yard, London, at your service. The wounded man is one John Scott, charged with complicity in the murder and robbery of the late Sir Lemuel Levison of Lone Castle. I bear a warrant for his arrest, countersigned by your chief of police. But for the prisoner's dying condition, we should convey him back to England immediately. As it is, we must hold him in custody here until the end," said the elder and more respectable-looking of the two Englishmen.

"I am very sorry to hear what you have to tell me; but since it seems your duty to remain here on guard for the security of your prisoner, I think it would be better that you should be nearer to him. The Old Men's Home will afford the most proper lodging for you as well as for him. One of my nuns will show you the way there, when a room near that of your wounded prisoner shall be assigned you," said the abbess, with grave courtesy, as she beckoned a withered old nun to her presence, and silently directed her to lead the way for the strangers to the lodging provided for them.

"John Scott, the half brother of the Duke of Hereward, charged with complicity in the murder and robbery at Castle Lone! Well, I am more grieved than surprised," murmured the abbess to herself.

Then she sent the younger nuns and novices about their several duties, and directed one of the elders to see that the refectory was restored to order.

The abbess was about to return to her own room when she was stayed by the re-entrance of Inspector Setter, the three gend'armes, and the countrymen.

The abbess looked up in a grave inquiry at this second intrusion.

"I beg your pardon, reverend madam; I have come to report to you the condition of your wounded guest, and to relieve you of the presence of these trespassers," said Inspector Setter, indicating his companions.

"Well, monsieur, what of the wounded man?" inquired the lady.

"The surgeon has dressed his wound, but pronounces it mortal. The man, he says, cannot live over a few days, perhaps not over a few hours. The surgeon will not leave him to-day."

"I am very sorry to hear that. Will you be so good as to tell me, monsieur, how the unfortunate man received his fatal injury? I heard--I heard--but I hope it is not true," said the abbess, shrinking from repeating the awful rumor that had reached her ears.

"You heard, holy madam, that he had committed suicide?" suggested the harder-nerved inspector.

The abbess bowed gravely.

"It is unfortunately quite true," said Inspector Setter. "You see, reverend madam, we traced him and his young--woman--I beg your reverend ladyship's pardon, holy madam--to Paris. Afterwards, we tracked them to L'Ange. We reached L'Ange this morning, and learned that our man had walked out toward the convent here. We followed, and came upon him near the south gate. I accosted him, and arrested him. He was as cool as a cucumber, and quick as lightning! Before we could suspect or prevent the action, he whipped a pistol out of his breast-pocket, and presented it at his own head. I seized his arm while his finger was on the trigger; but was too late to save him. He fired! I only changed the direction of the ball, which, instead of blowing off his head, buried itself somewhere in his body. He fell, a crowd gathered, we picked him up, took a leaf of the gate off its hinges, laid him on it, and brought him in here. That is all, your reverend ladyship. The doctor says the wound is mortal; I must remain in charge until all is over; but I don't want a body-guard, and if your ladyship's politeness will permit me. I will dismiss all these men and see them out."

"Do so, if you please, Monsieur l'Inspecteur. Oh, this is too horrible!" said the abbess.

While she was yet speaking, the surgeon also re-entered the refectory.

"How goes it with your patient, Monsieur le Docteur?" inquired the lady.

"He will die, good madam. Velpeau himself could not save him; he knows that he will die as well as we do, for he has recovered consciousness, and desired that a telegram be sent off immediately to summon the Duke of Hereward, whom he seems extremely anxious to see. I have written the message; here it is. I cannot leave my patient, or I would take it myself; but Monsieur l'Inspecteur, perhaps you can provide me with a messenger to carry this to L'Ange," said the surgeon.

"Certainly," agreed Mr. Setter, taking the written message and reading it. "But you have directed this to Hereward House, Piccadilly, London?"

"I wrote it at the dictation of my patient."

"He is mistaken. The Duke of Hereward is living in Paris, at Meurice's. I will make the correction," said Mr. Setter, drawing from his pocket a lead pencil and a blank-book, upon a leaf of which he re-wrote the message. He tore out the leaf, and read what he had written:

"To HIS GRACE THE DUKE OF HEREWARD, MEURICE'S, PARIS: I am dying. Come immediately.

"JOHN SCOTT, Convent of St. Rosalie, L'Ange."

"That will do," said Mr. Setter, inspecting his work. "Now, Smith," he added, handing the paper to one of his officers, "hurry with this message to the telegraph office at the railway station at L'Ange. See that it is sent off promptly, for it is a matter of life and death, as you know. Wait for an answer, and when you get it hasten back with it."

"All right, sir," answered the man, taking the paper, and hurrying away.

The other men, whose services were no longer required, followed him out to go about their business.

The inspector and the surgeon, seeing the lady abbess about to address them, lingered.

"I hope, messieurs, that you will freely call upon us for anything that may be needed for the relief of your patient, or for the convenience of yourselves," she said, with grave courtesy.

"Thanks, madame, we will do so," replied the surgeon, with a deep bow.

"And, above all, the interests of his immortal soul should be taken care of. If he should need spiritual comfort, here is Father Garbennetti, who will wait on him," added the abbess, solemnly.

"Your ladyship's holiness is very good. I happen to know the man is a Romanist, and if he should ask for a priest, I will let your reverend ladyship know," said Mr. Setter.

"Do so. Monsieur l'Inspecteur. And tell him the name of the priest I proposed for him--Father Garbennetti, of San Vito, Italy; for I have reason to believe that this holy father once knew your patient very intimately," added the abbess.

"Stay, now--what was the priest's name again? I never can get the name of these foreigners," muttered Mr. Setter, with a puzzled air.

"Father Garbennetti, of San Vito, Italy. But I will write it for you. Lend me your pencil and tablets, monsieur, if you please."

Mr. Setter placed his pocket writing material in the hands of the lady, with his best bow.

She carefully wrote the name of the Italian priest on a blank leaf and returned the pencil and the book to the inspector, who received them with another bow.

Doctor Dubourg and Inspector Setter then "bowed" themselves out of the lady's presence and returned to the bedside of the wounded man.

The abbess gave a few more directions to the lay sisters who were engaged in restoring the room to order, and then she withdrew from the refectory and returned to her own apartment, where she had left Salome and the little Sister Felecitie.

She found them still waiting there; and both engaged in the little bit of knitting or embroidery that they always carried in their pockets to take up at odd moments that would otherwise be wasted in idleness, which was held to be a grave fault, if not a deadly sin, by the sisterhood, and, besides, from the sale of this work they realized a very considerable income.

"I waited here, good mother, to learn more of the poor wounded man. Sister Felecitie tells me that he is a suicide. I hope that is a mistake," said Salome.

"It is too true, *helas*! But, my daughter," said the abbess, turning to the young nun, "leave us alone for a few minutes."

The little sister retired obediently, but very unwillingly, for she was tormented with unsatisfied curiosity concerning the unfortunate stranger, who had committed suicide at their convent gate.

"Salome! do you know, can you conjecture, who the unhappy man is?" solemnly inquired the abbess, as soon as she was left alone with her young friend.

"I do not know. I--*fear to conjecture*," whispered the young wife; growing pale.

"Yet your very fear proves that you *have* conjectured, and conjectured correctly. Yes! the wretched suicide is no other than John Scott, the 'double' of the Duke of Hereward."

"Heaven of heavens! What drove him to the fatal deed? But why should I ask?

Of course, it was remorse! remorse that was slowly killing him! too slowly for his suffering and his impatience!" exclaimed the young lady, with a shudder.

"Yes, it was remorse, and--*desperation*."

"Desperation!"

"Yes! The English detectives had traced him down to this neighborhood; they followed him down here with a warrant for his arrest, countersigned by our chief of police. They surprised him near the south gate of the convent; but he was too quick for them; and before they could prevent him, driven to desperation, he caught a pistol from his pocket and shot himself through the body, inflicting a mortal wound. They brought him into the convent. I have had him placed in a comfortable room in the Old Men's Home, where he is attended by Doctor Dubourg, of L'Ange, who Providentially happened to be passing the convent at the time of the occurrence."

Salome covered her face with her hands, and sank back in her chair, with a groan.

A few moments elapsed, and then Salome, still vailing her face, murmured a question:

"How long may the dying man last? Surely--surely--" Her voice faltered, and broke down with a sob.

"He *can* not last more than a very few days. He *may* not last more than a few hours," said the abbess, in a low tone.

"Surely--surely, then," resumed Salome, in a broken voice, "he will make a confession before he dies. He will vindicate his brother, and so save his own soul."

"I think that he will do so, Sister Salome. Calm yourself. He has caused a telegram to be sent to the Duke of Hereward, calling him here."

Salome started and trembled violently. She could scarcely gasp forth the words of her broken exclamation:

"The Duke of Hereward! Called! Here!"

"Yes, my daughter. So you perceive that your proposed journey to England is forestalled."

"My husband coming here! Oh! how soon will he come? He cannot be here in less than twenty-four hours, can he?" eagerly demanded Salome.

"He may be here in less than six hours. The Duke of Hereward does not have to come from London; he is not there, but in Paris; so you perceive, also, that if you

404 *The Lost Lady of Lone*

had gone to England, as you proposed to do, you would have missed seeing him there," added the lady, smiling.

"My husband in Paris--so near. My husband to be here this evening--so soon. Oh, this is too much, too much happiness!" exclaimed the young wife, bursting into tears of joy.

"Then you have no dread of meeting him?" suggested the elder lady.

"'Dread of meeting him?' Dread of meeting my own dear husband? Ah, no, no, no! No dread, but an infinite longing to meet him. Oh! I know and feel how I have wronged him. How deeply and bitterly I have wronged him. But I know, also, how utterly he will pardon me. Yes, I know that, as surely as I know that my Heavenly Lord pardons us all of our repented sins!" fervently exclaimed Salome.

"Heaven grant that you may be happy, my child'" said the lady, earnestly.

At that moment the door opened, and an aged nun, one of the attendants in the Old Men's Home, entered the room.

"Well, Mere Pauline, what is it?" calmly inquired the abbess.

"Holy mother, I have come from Monsieur le Docteur to say that the messenger has come back from L'Ange, and brought an answer to the telegram. Monsieur le Duc d' Hereward will be here by the midday express from Paris, which reaches L'Ange at five o'clock this afternoon," answered Mere Pauline.

"Thanks for your news. Sit down and breathe after climbing all these stairs. And now tell me, how is the wounded man?" inquired the abbess, as the old nun sank wearily into the nearest chair.

"*Helas!* holy mother, he is sinking fast. The doctor thinks he will not outlive the night; and meanwhile he is anxious, so anxious, for the arrival of Monsieur le Duc! He asks from time to time if the duke has come, or is coming; if we have heard from him, and so on," sighed the old nun.

"But have you not soothed him by communicating the message received from the duke, that his grace will be here at five o'clock?"

"No, holy mother! for he was sleeping under the influence of opium, which the good surgeon had felt obliged to administer in order to quiet him just before the message came. If he wakes and inquires about the duke again, we will give him the message."

"Quite right. Has the wretched man seen a priest, or asked to see one?"

"No, mother! but I was not unmindful of his immortal weal. I asked him if he would see Pere Garbennetti. He brightened up at the name, and inquired if le pere was here. I told him yes, and at his service, waiting to attend him, indeed. But then he gloomed again, and said no; he would see no one until he had seen the Duke of Hereward. He would rest and save his strength for his interview with the Duke of Hereward. I will return to my charge now, if my good mother will permit me," said the old nun, rising from her chair.

"Go, then, Mere Pauline, if you are sufficiently rested. Keep me advised of the state of your patient, but do not tax your aged limbs to climb these stairs again. Send one of the younger nuns, and give yourself some rest," said the abbess, kindly.

"*Helas!* holy mother, I shall have time enough to rest in the grave, whither I am fast tending," sighed the old nun, as she withdrew from the room.

"Oh, mother!" joyfully exclaimed Salome, as soon as they were left alone, "he comes by the midday express! It is midday now! The train has already left Paris! He is speeding toward us, even now, as fast as steam can bring him. I can almost see and hear and *feel* him coming!"

"Calm your transports, dear daughter; think of the dying sinner so near us, even now," gravely replied the elder lady.

"I can think of nothing but my living husband," exclaimed the young wife.

"Oh, these young hearts! these young hearts! 'From all inordinate and sinful affections, good Lord, deliver us!'" prayed the abbess.

She had scarcely spoken, when the door opened and Sister Francoise entered the room.

"I came with a message from the portress, good mother. She says that a young woman has come from L'Ange, who claims to be the wife of the wounded man, and insists upon being admitted to see him. The portress does not know what to do, and has sent me to you for instructions," said Sister Francoise.

"The wounded man is sleeping and must not be awakened. Tell the portress to keep the young woman in the parlor until she can be permitted to see the patient, then do you go to the Old Men's Home, inquire for Monsieur le Doctor Dubourg, and announce to him the arrival of this woman, and let him use his medical discretion about admitting her. Go."

"Yes, holy mother," said Sister Francoise, retreating.

"You have not had a moment's peace since this unhappy man has been in the house," said Salome, compassionately.

"No," smiled the lady. "Of course not, but it cannot be helped. We must bear one another's burdens."

The loud ringing of the dinner-bell arrested the conversation.

"Come, we will go down," said the abbess, rising.

They descended to the refectory.

The long hall, that had been the scene of so much horror and confusion in the morning, was now restored to its normal condition.

The plain, frugal, midday meal of the abbess and the elder nuns was arranged with pure cleanliness upon the table, where, but a few hours before, the body of the wounded man had lain. But the awful event of the morning had taken a deep effect upon the quiet and sensitive sisterhood. They sat down at the table, but scarcely touched the food.

When the form of dining--for it was little more than a form that day--was over, the abbess and her nuns arose, and separated about their several vocations.

Later on, the abbess sent a message to the Old Men's Home, inquiring after the wounded man.

She received an answer to the effect that the patient had waked up, and had been told of the telegram from the Duke of Hereward, and the expected arrival of his grace at five o'clock.

The news had satisfied the suffering man, who had been calmer ever since its reception. He had also been told of the arrival of his wife, but he had declined to see her, or *any* one, until he should have seen the Duke of Hereward. He was saving up all his little strength for his interview with the duke.

As the hours of the afternoon crept slowly away, the impatience of the young wife, Salome, arose to fever heat. She could not rest in any one room, but roamed about the convent, and through all its departments and offices, until, at length, she was met in the main corridor by the abbess, who gravely took her hand, drew it within her arm, and led her along, saying:

"Come into my parlor, child. The Duke of Hereward has arrived."

CHAPTER XLVII.
THE END OF A LOST LIFE.

The Duke of Hereward knew nothing of his wife's presence in the Convent of St. Rosalie.

On his arrival, soon after five o'clock, he was met by the portress, who ushered him into the receiving parlor and sent to warn the abbess of his presence.

The abbess dispatched a message to the surgeon in attendance upon John Scott, and then sought out the young duchess to inform her of her husband's arrival.

Meantime Dr. Dubourg hurried down to the receiving-parlor to see the Duke of Hereward. They were strangers to each other, so the portress introduced them.

"I hope your patient is better, Monsieur le Docteur," said the duke, when the first salutations were over.

"No, I regret to say. There is, indeed, no hope. The poor man has been sinking since morning. He is most anxious to see your grace, before he dies, and that very anxiety, I think, has kept him up," gravely replied the physician.

"I am sorry to hear that. Is he in condition to see me now? Will not the interview tend to excite him and shorten his life?" anxiously inquired the duke.

"It may do so; but, on the other hand, his failure to see you might prove fatal to him sooner than his wound would. The fact is, sir, the man is doomed; his hours are numbered, and he knows it. He is eager to see you; he seems to have something weighing upon his mind, which he wishes to confide to you. He has been saving his little strength for an interview with you. He has refused to speak to any one, lest he should waste his forces and be too weak to talk to you."

"I will go to him, then, at once," said the duke.

"Do so, your grace, and I will attend you," said the doctor with a bow.

The duke arose and followed the doctor through the long corridors and narrow passages leading from the Nunnery to the Old Men's Home.

On their way thither, the duke inquired how the patient had received that fatal wound, of which his grace had only heard a vague report from scraps of conversation among the officials at the L'Ange Railway Depot.

The doctor gave him a brief account of the arrest and the suicide.

The duke made no comment, but fell into deep, sorrowful thought, until they reached the door of the room in which John Scott lay mortally wounded.

The doctor opened the door and passed in with the duke.

It was a good-sized, square room, in which had once been placed four cots to accommodate four old men. Now, however, all the cots had been removed except the one on which the wounded man lay, and that had been drawn into the middle of the chamber, so as to give the patient a free circulation of fresh air, and to allow the approach of surgeon and attendants on every side. The walls were white-washed, the floor sanded, the windows shaded with blue paper hangings, and the cot-bed covered with a clean, blue-checked spread. Four cane chairs and a small deal table completed the furniture.

Everything was plain, clean and comfortable.

The doctor, with a deprecating gesture, signed to the duke to wait a moment, and went up to the side of the bed, and finding his patient awake, whispered:

"Monsieur, the friend you expected has arrived."

"You mean--the Duke of Hereward?" faintly inquired Scott.

"Yes, monsieur."

"Give me then--some cordial--to keep up my strength--for fifteen minutes longer," sighed the dying man at intervals.

The doctor signed to Sister Francoise, who sat by the bedside, to go and bring what was required.

The old nun went to the deal table and brought a small bottle of cognac brandy and a slender wine glass.

The doctor filled the glass, lifted the head of the patient, and placed the stimulant to his lips.

Scott swallowed the brandy, drew a deep breath as he sank back upon the pillow and said:

"Now, bring the duke to my bed side, and let everyone go and leave us together."

The doctor signed for the duke to approach, and silently presented him to the patient.

Then he beckoned Sister Francoise to follow him, and they left the room, closing the door behind them.

"I am sorry to see you suffering, my brother," said the duke, kindly, as he bent over the dying man.

"Ah! you call me your brother! You acknowledge me then?" said Scott, half in earnest, half in mockery.

"Most certainly I do acknowledge you, and most sincerely do I deplore your misfortunes," answered the duke.

"Yet I have been a great sinner. I feel that now, as I lie upon my death-bed," muttered Scott, in a low tone.

"I look upon you as one 'more sinned against than sinning,'" said the duke seriously.

"Yes, that is true also," murmured the dying man.

"But let us not dwell upon that. The past is dead. Let it be buried."

"Aye, with all my heart."

"You wished to see me."

"Yes, I did."

"To make some communication to me. Is it a very important one?"

"It is so important that I have risked my soul to make it to you."

"But how can that be?"

"Why, in this way. I have but little strength, I might have used that strength in making my confession to Father Garbennetti, and received absolution at his hands; but I was afraid of exhausting myself so that I should not be able to tell you what I have to communicate."

"I trust and believe that you have more strength than you suppose. Your eyes look bright and strong."

"That is the effect of the brandy. I never tasted better. Ah! they know what good liquor is--these holy sisters--no offence to them, bless them; their care has helped me; but I am going fast, for all that."

"You are at ease--you feel no pain?"

"No; but that is because mortification has set in. I feel no pain: I am at ease, only sinking, sinking, sinking fast. Will you pour out a little glass of brandy and give it to me? You will find the bottle and the wine-glass on the table," said the patient, who was visibly growing feebler.

The duke went and brought the stimulant, and administered it to the dying man.

"Ah! that revives me! How long have you known that I was your brother?" Scott inquired, as soon as the duke had replaced the glass and returned to the bedside.

"Only since our honored father's death. I should at once have claimed you and carried out certain instructions he had left me for your benefit, in the letter in which he revealed our relationship--if--if--if--"

The duke, with more delicacy than moral courage, hesitated, and finally left his sentence incomplete.

"If I had not dishonored my family by committing a crime, and flying the country!" said John Scott, finishing the sentence for the first speaker.

"I did not say so," exclaimed the duke, flushing.

"But it was the truth nevertheless. And now before I begin my confession, will you please to tell me the nature of the revelation and of the instructions that my father left to you concerning me?"

"Certainly. He told me the story of his first fatal marriage; of the divorce sought and granted under lying circumstantial evidence; of your birth some few months later--out of wedlock--although you were the son of his lawful marriage. He told me how impossible it was ever to restore you to your lawful rights, and he charged me to regard you as a dear brother, and share with you all the benefits of the estate, the whole of which would eventually have been yours had not your father's own rash act deprived you of the succession, and forever put it out of our power to restore you to it. I accepted the trust, and should have discharged it had you not left the country."

"Well, I suppose the old man did as well as he could under the circumstances. He too was to be pitied. But now tell me, did *you* help to hark the bloodhounds of the law on my track?"

"No. From the time I received a hint from that wretched man, Potts, the valet, implicating yourself, I refrained from all action in your pursuit."

"I thought so--I thought so. You wouldn't like to help hang your own brother, even if he had deserved it; but he did not quite deserve it; and it was to explain that, as well as some other things, that I brought you here. You know so much already, however, so much more than I suspected you knew, that I shall not have a great deal to tell you; but--my strength is going fast again. I shall have to be quick. Give me another glass of brandy."

The duke complied with the man's request, and then replaced the glass again and returned to the bedside.

"I suppose I should not require that stimulant so often to keep up my dying frame, if I had not been so hard a drinker in late years. However, it is absolutely necessary to me now, if I am to go on. Come close; I cannot raise my voice any longer," whispered the fast-failing man.

The duke drew his chair as closely as possible to the side of the cot, took the wasted hand of his poor brother, and bowed his head to hear the sorrowful story.

In a weak, low voice, with many pauses, John Scott told the story of his life, from his own point of view, dwelling much on his mother's undeserved sorrows and early death.

He told of his own secluded life and education, and of his ignorance of his father's name until after his mother's decease.

He confessed the rage and hatred that filled his bosom on first learning that poor mother's wrongs, greater even than his own.

He spoke of the natural mistake made by the country people at Lone, who misled by his perfect likeness to his brother, had received him and honored him as Marquis of Arondelle.

He admitted that their error flattered his self-love, and believing that he had the best right to the title, he allowed them to deceive themselves, and to address him and speak of him as Lord Arondelle, the heir.

He related the incident of his first accidental meeting with Rose Cameron, who, like all the other tenantry, mistook him for the young marquis, and so had her head turned by his attentions, and followed him to London, where he secretly married her.

This brought him to the time when the extravagance of his companion, added to his own expensive vices, brought him deeply into debt. He knew that his father had placed a large amount of money in the hands of Sir Lemuel Levison to be invested for his (John Scott's) benefit. He applied for a part of this money to pay his debts, but was refused by the trustee. Whereupon a quarrel ensued, which resulted in Sir

Lemuel Levison's resolution to take the money down to Lone Castle and restore it to the original donor, that the latter might dispose of it at his own discretion.

This move maddened the penniless spendthrift. It drove him to desperation. He resolved to get possession of his money by foul means since he could not do so by fair ones; by violence, if not by peace. Circumstances had brought him to acquaintance with a pair of desperate thieves and burglars.

He sought them out, tempted them by the prospect of great booty for themselves, and arranged with them the whole plan of the robbery of Lone, stipulating that there should be no bloodshed at all; but that if the burglars were discovered before completing the robbery, they should seek rather to make their escape than to secure their booty.

But who can unchain a devil and say to him, "Thus far, no farther shalt thou go?" The instigator of the crime had no power over his instruments; on the contrary, they had power over him from the moment he called in their aid and became their confederate.

John Scott continued his confession by relating that he took the men down to Lone, disguised as countrymen, and led them to the castle grounds, where, lost in the great crowd that came to see the preparations for the wedding festivities, their presence as strangers was unnoticed; that at night he drugged the drink of the valet, stole the pass-key from his pocket, and through the secret passage under Malcolm's Tower he admitted the thieves into the castle, and by means of the valet's key passed them into Sir Lemuel Levison's bedroom.

He shuddered, failed, and seemed about to faint, as he recalled the horrible tragedy enacted in the room that night.

The duke gave him another small glass of brandy before he could revive and continue.

"Heaven knows, though under strong temptation, not to say under imperative necessity, I employed thieves and burglars, I was neither a robber nor a murderer in intention. I wanted to get my own money, withheld from me against my expressed desire--that was all. I do not say this to extenuate my crime, but to let you know the exact truth. I cannot dwell upon this part of the dreadful tale. You know already that the thieves murdered Sir Lemuel Levison in his chamber. It seems that he had not gone to bed, but had fallen asleep in his chair. He woke and discovered them.

He was instantly about to give the alarm, when he was knocked senseless by Smith and killed by Murdockson. From the moment that I heard the old man was dead, although I had not intended the awful crime, I knew that I had actually occasioned it, and that the curse of Cain was upon my head! I have not had a happy moment since. I fled the country, and stayed abroad until I heard that my wretched companion, Rose, was in trouble. Then I returned in disguise to see what was to become of her, resolved to give myself up to justice, if it should be necessary to vindicate her. But I found, by cautious inquiry, that she had been admitted as crown's evidence on the trial of the valet Potts, who was discharged from custody, on a verdict of 'Not Proven,' but that she was in prison again, on the charge of perjury, for having sworn--what she truly believed, by the way, poor wench--that the confederate of the thieves who murdered Sir Lemuel Levison was no other than the young Marquis of Arondelle. You were there, sir, and immediately proved an alibi?"

"Yes," said the duke.

"Rose was thereupon committed for perjury. I found her in prison on that charge when I returned to Scotland. I did not see her then. I was afraid to show myself, especially as I knew the girl felt very bitterly toward me, believing that I had willfully betrayed her into danger, when in point of fact it was her own dishonesty that led to her arrest. Her vanity tempted her to purloin and secrete a portion of the most valuable jewels from the booty that had accidentally in the confusion of the thieves' flight fallen into my hands along with the money that was my own. I had intended, secretly to return the jewels upon the first opportunity, but the unfortunate woman secreted them, and denied all knowledge of them. After my flight she was so mad as to wear the watch in public, and to take it to a West End jeweller for repairs. Of course that jeweller, like others, had a full description of the watch, recognized the stolen property, and caused the arrest of the holder."

"We heard all that on the trial. Do not exhaust yourself by repeating anything that has already come to our knowledge," said the duke.

"I refer to this only to explain the bitterness of the girl's feelings toward me as the reason why I was obliged to keep concealed."

"But if the girl had been favorable toward you, would not it have been equally dangerous for you to have shown yourself?"

"Oh! no; my disguise was too complete. Besides, if I had not been disguised--

you see in that neighborhood I had never been known as myself, but had always been mistaken for you--and the people were not undeceived up to that time. Give me a little more brandy. Ah! this spurring up a jaded horse! You see it does not get into my head. It only keeps up my sinking strength," added the man, after the duke had complied with his request.

"I remained in the neighborhood to see the result of Rose Cameron's trial for perjury. It was near the end of the term when she was arraigned at Banff. She would certainly have been convicted, for it was in evidence that she had sworn that the Marquis of Arondelle had been the confederate of the thieves and murderers, and had himself received and delivered to her the stolen booty; and her testimony was rebutted on the spot, not only by the high character and standing of the marquis, but by witnesses who proved an alibi for him. She would certainly have been convicted, I say, had not an unexpected witness appeared in her behalf. John Potts, the valet, who had been discharged from custody, came upon the stand, took the oath, and testified to the existence of a perfect counterpart of the Marquis of Arondelle, in the person of one John Scott, the companion of the accused woman, who had always foolishly believed him to be the young marquis himself. This testimony not only vindicated the accused woman from the charge of perjury, but opened her eyes to the facts of the case--namely, that I had never abandoned her to suffer in my stead while I went off to marry another woman, as she had supposed--that my only sin against her was in having allowed her to deceive herself in believing me to be Lord Arondelle."

The man gasped as he concluded the last sentence, and the duke said:

"You had better rest now. A little rest will do more good than any stimulant."

"You think so? Nay, rest would be death for me now. I must go on while my nerves are strung up; once they relax, I die."

"Very well; I am listening attentively."

"As soon as Rose was discharged from custody I sought her out, and there was a mutual explanation and reconciliation. But the testimony of John Potts, given on the trial of Rose Cameron, had placed my life in great jeopardy: so we secretly left the country. We went away separately for our greater security. I went first. Rose came on a week later. We met by appointment at L'Ange. In the obscurity of that village we hoped for safety; but I was tormented by remorse; for the murder of

Sir Lemuel Levison lay heavily on my soul. There, my wife, Rose, gave birth to a little girl, whom we secretly placed in the rotary basket at the door of the Infants' Asylum attached to this convent. The good nuns received it, and cared for it. They called it *Marie Perdue*, 'Lost Mary.' After Rose's recovery, we went away, because it was not safe for us to remain so near home with such sharpers as English detectives and French police on our track. We took refuge in Italy, in the Sanctuary of the Holy See. We stayed there several months, when, thinking that all pursuit had been abandoned, and longing to see our child, we came on a flying visit to L'Ange. But the police were on the watch for us. I was arrested, as you have heard, on the day after my arrival. Quick work; but you see the chief of police here telegraphed the police in London, and brought the detectives hither within twenty-four hours. You know the rest. I am dying here by my own hand. It was a mad, rash, impulsive act, for which I am deeply sorry; but--I am dying in expiation of *my* share in the tragedy at Lone Castle."

The young duke took the emaciated hand of the failing man and pressed it in silence; he was too deeply moved to trust himself to speak.

"I have but this to say now. I leave a wife and helpless child. They are penniless and friendless. You will not let them starve," murmured the man.

"Oh, no, no, I will care for them, believe me, as long as we all shall live," said the duke, earnestly.

"That is all. Bid me good-by now. And when you go out ask good Sister Francoise to send the priest," said John Scott, holding out his white, cold hand.

"I will. Good-bye. May our merciful Father in heaven bless and save you, my poor brother," murmured the duke, pressing that pale hand, laying it tenderly on the coverlet, and gliding from the room of death.

Ten minutes later, the good Father Garbennetti was closeted with his penitent, administering religious consolation.

When the last sacred offices were all performed, the priest retired, and the wife and child of the dying man were admitted to his presence, with permission to remain with him to the end.

In the meantime, the Duke of Hereward, conducted by Doctor Dubourg, traversed the long passages leading from the Old Men's Home to the convent.

As they went on, the duke gave the doctor instructions to supply the patient with everything that he should require during the last few hours of his life; and after death to take direction of the funeral, and charge all expenses to himself (the duke), adding:

"I shall, of course, remain at L'Ange until all is over."

"It will not be long, monseigneur. The poor man has been kept up by mental excitement and by strong stimulants all day long; there comes a fatal reaction soon, from which nothing can raise him. He will not outlive the day."

"I am very sorry for him," murmured the duke.

"He was, perhaps, a distant relative of your grace. There is a slight family likeness," suggested the doctor.

"There is a very remarkable family likeness, and he is a very near relative," answered the duke, adding; "I hope you will kindly follow the instructions I have given you in regard to him."

"I will faithfully follow them out, monseigneur," said the doctor, with a bow.

At the entrance to the convent proper they were met by an elderly nun, who brought the lady superior's compliments and begged leave to announce that refreshments were laid in the receiving-parlor, if the Duke of Hereward and Doctor Dubourg would do the house the honor to partake of them.

The young duke was tired and hungry from his long journey and longer fast, and gratefully accepted the sister's courteous invitation in his own and the doctor's name.

The nun led the way to the parlor, where a table was set out, not merely with slight refreshments, but with the first course of a dainty dinner, which the forethought of the abbess had caused to be prepared for her noble guest.

The duke and the doctor sat down to the table, and were attentively waited on by two of the elder sisterhood.

Notwithstanding the good appetite of the guests and the delicacy of the viands set before them, the meal passed in gravity and in almost total silence, for the thoughts of the two companions were with the dying man whom they had left in the Old Men's Home.

When they had finished dining, and had arisen from the table, a message was delivered by one of the old nuns who had waited upon them, to the effect that the lady superior desired to see the duke in the portress' room for a few minutes, before his departure.

The duke immediately signified his readiness to wait on the lady, and followed his conductress to the little room behind the wicket appropriated to the portress.

CHAPTER XLVIII.
HUSBAND AND WIFE.

Two hours before this, the lady superior had conducted the young duchess to the private apartment of the abbess, to await the issue of events.

Salome, pale, and trembling with excitement, sank into the nearest chair.

"You do not fear to meet the duke, my child?" inquired the abbess, uneasily, as she also dropped into her seat.

"Fear to meet my own magnanimous husband? Oh, no, no! I do not fear to meet him; but I long to meet him with an infinite longing!" fervently exclaimed Salome.

"I am very glad to hear you say so. And you are sure of his prompt and full forgiveness?" said the abbess, softly.

"'Sure of his forgiveness!'" echoed Salome, with a holy and happy smile. "Yes, as sure of his forgiveness as I am of the Lord's pardon!"

"And yet when he hears the truth and understands all, he will know that he has nothing to forgive. And he should know and understand everything before he sees you. For this reason, as well as for several others, I have brought you here, and I advise you to seclude yourself yet for a few hours. I do not wish you to see the duke, or even to advise him of your presence in the house, until he has seen the dying man and heard the confession of the truth from his lips. That confession will prepare your husband to receive and understand you, better than any explanation you could possibly make would do. It will also save you from the distress of having to make a long explanation. Do you understand me, my child?"

"Yes, dear mother, I understand, and thank you for your wise counsels."

"I have also given directions to Sister Dominica that after he shall have concluded his interview with Mr. Scott, and partaken of dinner, which will be prepared for him in the receiving parlor, he shall be requested to meet me in the portress' room, where I propose to break to him the intelligence of your presence in the house."

"Thanks, dear mother! infinite, eternal thanks for all your great goodness to me," fervently exclaimed Salome.

"You are much too extravagant in your expressions of gratitude, my daughter! You exaggerate like a school-girl!" smiled the abbess.

"Oh! I will prove by my acts that I do not exaggerate my feelings at least!" persisted Salome.

And then, with girlish enthusiasm, she began to tell the lady-superior all she intended to do for the benefit of the convent charities, and especially for the "Infants' Asylum."

The vesper-bell summoned them to chapel, where the evening service occupied them for an hour.

They then went to the refectory, and joined the sisterhood at tea.

In coming from the refectory, they were met in the corridor by old Sister Dominica, who stopped the abbess, respectfully, and said:

"I come, holy mother, to report to you that I have followed all your instructions. Monseigneur le Duc and Monsieur le Docteur have well dined. Monsieur le Docteur has returned to his patient, Monseigneur le Duc has gone to the wicket-room to await madame, our holy mother."

"*Bien!*" said the abbess. "I will attend his grace. Go, dear daughter, and await my return in my parlor. Sister Dominica, lead the way and announce me."

Salome, in obedience to the abbess' orders, went back to the lady-superior's private parlor to await, with palpitating heart the issue of the lady's interview with the duke.

Sister Dominica deferentially led the lady abbess to the wicket room, opened the door, and said:

"The lady-superior of the convent to see Monseigneur, the Duke," then closed the door after the abbess, and retired.

As Mother Genevieve entered the room, she saw standing there a tall, thin, distinguished-looking young man, with a pale complexion, blonde hair and beard, and blue eyes. His face bore traces of deep suffering bravely endured. The gentle abbess sympathized with him from the depths of her kind heart, and for the first time felt glad that he would regain his wife, although by his doing so the convent would lose her fortune.

"Monseigneur, the Duke, of Hereward?" she said graciously, advancing into the room.

"Yes, madam. I have the honor of saluting the Lady Abbess of St. Rosalie?" returned the duke, with a bow.

"A poor nun, monseigneur; who, as the unworthy head of the house, begs leave to welcome you here," humbly returned the lady, bending her head.

"Thanks, madam."

"It is a sad event which has brought you under our roof, monseigneur."

"A very sad one, madam."

"And yet, for your sake, a very fortunate one."

"May I be permitted to ask you, madam, in what way this misfortune can be fortunate?"

"I had supposed that you already knew that, monseigneur."

"Perhaps I do. I am not sure. I do not clearly comprehend, madam. Will madam deign to make her meaning plainer?"

"Yes, monseigneur, and you will pardon me if I enter too abruptly upon a subject at once painful and delicate."

The abbess paused, and the duke inclined his head in the attitude of an attentive listener.

"The young Duchess of Hereward, monseigneur?" said the abbess, in a low voice.

The duke started very slightly, but his pale face flushed crimson.

"Pardon, monseigneur. I am the more deeply interested in the young lady, for that she passed her infancy, childhood and youth--being nearly the whole of her short life, indeed, under this roof--where I stood in the position of a mother to her orphanage."

"I knew, madam, that the motherless heiress was educated here," replied the duke, by way of saying something.

"You will, therefore, understand the interest I take in Madame la Duchesse, and forgive my question when I ask: Have you heard from her grace since she left her home?"

"You knew that she had left her home, then?" exclaimed the duke, in painful astonishment.

The abbess bowed assent.

"I hoped and believed that no one knew of her flight except the members of our own household, and the single confidential agent I employed to find her, and on whose discretion I could implicitly rely," said the duke, in a tone of extreme mortification and sorrow.

"Be tranquil, monseigneur, no one does know of it out of the circle of her own devoted friends, who can never misinterpret it."

"You know something of the duchess' movements, then? You know, perhaps, the cause of her flight--the place of her residence? You know--ah, madam, tell me *what* you know, I beseech you!" implored the duke.

"I know the cause of her flight, and justify her action even though she acted under a false impression. I know the place of her residence, and will tell it to you after you shall have answered one or two questions that I shall put to you. First then, monseigneur, when did you last hear of the duchess?"

"Some few weeks after her flight, I received the first and last news I have ever had of my lost bride. It came in a short and cautiously written note from herself. This note was without date or address. It was apparently written in kind consideration for me, but it contained no word of affection. It was signed by her maiden name and post-marked Rome."

The abbess smiled as she remembered that letter which had been written by Salome to put her husband out of suspense, and which had been sent by the mother superior, through a confidential agent who happened to be going there, to be mailed from Rome, to put the Duke of Hereward entirely off the track of his lost wife.

"I have the note in my pocketbook. You may read it, madam, if you please," continued the duke, as he opened his portmonnaie and handed her a tiny, folded paper.

The abbess took it and read as follows:

"DUKE OF HEREWARD: I have just arisen from a bed of illness which has lasted ever since my flight, and prevented me from writing to you up to this time.

"I write now only to relieve any anxiety that you may feel on account of one in whom you took too much interest; for I would not have you suffer needless pain.

"You know the reason of my flight; or if you do not, my maiden name, at the foot of this note, will tell you how surely I had learned that it was my bounden duty to leave you instantly.

"I left you without malice, trying to put the best construction on your motives and actions, if any such were possible; I left you with sorrow, praying the Lord to forgive and save you.

"I dare not write to you as I feel toward you, for that would be a sin.

"I have entered a religious house, where, by prayer and labor, I may live down all "inordinate and sinful affections," and where I shall henceforth be dead to the world and to you.

"This, then, is the very last you will hear of her who was once known as SA-LOME LEVISON."

"She says you knew the cause of her flight. ***Did*** you know it, monseigneur?" inquired the abbess, when she had finished reading the note, and had returned it to the owner.

"I did not even suspect it, at first, madam. At the trial of John Scott, on the charge of murder of Sir Lemuel Levison, to which I was summoned as a witness for the crown, some facts were developed that first awoke my suspicions as to the cause of my wife's flight. These suspicions were further strengthened by the tone of her letter, received three weeks afterwards, and they were absolutely confirmed by a revelation I have received this day."

"From John Scott?"

"Yes, madam."

"You know the cause of your bride's flight, monseigneur. Do you blame her for it?"

"Under such circumstances, I honor her for it. She nearly broke her own heart and mine; but, as a pure woman, believing as she was forced to believe, she could do no less. Now, madam, I have answered all your questions. Now relieve my anxiety--tell me where she is."

"First tell me where you have been seeking her?" inquired the abbess, with a singular smile.

"In Italy, of course! Her letter was post-marked Rome, though without any other address," said the duke, lightly lifting his eyebrows.

"That letter was written in this house, and sent to Rome to be mailed thence, in order to put you off the true track of the duchess, monseigneur," said the abbess, with a smile.

"What do you tell me, madam!" exclaimed the duke, in surprise.

"Madame la Duchesse is under this roof, to which she fled for refuge direct from London!"

"Can this be possible, madam?"

"It is true! To whom, indeed, could the child come, in her extremity, but to me, the mother of her motherless youth?"

"Oh, madam, you fill my heart with joy and gratitude! My wife under this roof?"

"Yes, monseigneur."

"And safe and well?"

"Safe and well."

"Thank Heaven! Can I see her at once? Does she know I am here? Does she know--"

"She knows everything, monseigneur, that you would have her know, although she has not heard the confession of John Scott, which has just been made to you. She knows everything by means of the agencies I set to work to investigate the truth. And she knows that you will forgive her, through the intuitions of her own spirit."

"When can I see her, madam? Oh, when?" exclaimed the young duke, rising impatiently.

"This moment, if you please. She is expecting you. Follow me, monseigneur," said the abbess, rising and leading the way through the broad hall that stretched between the wicket room and the lady-superior's parlor.

When they reached the place, the abbess said:

"Enter, monseigneur. You will find the duchess alone, within."

And she opened the door and admitted him, then closed it behind him, and paced slowly away from the spot.

As the duke advanced into the room, so silently that his footsteps were un-heard, he saw his wife sitting within the recess of the solitary window. She wore a simple dress of black serge, with a white collar and white cuffs, such as she had worn ever since her entrance into the convent. Her head was turned toward the window and bowed upon her hand in an attitude of meditation. She neither saw nor heard the soft approach of the duke. He stood gazing on her with infinite pity, for a moment, and then laying his hand gently on her shoulder, whispered:

"Salome!"

She started up with a wild cry of joy! She would have sank down at his feet, but he caught her to his bosom, held her there, stroking her hair, kissing her face, murmuring in her ear:

"Salome, Salome, my sweet wife, Salome! Oh, how thankful! Oh, how glad I am to meet you!"

She could not answer him. She could not speak. She was overwhelmed by his goodness. She could only burst into tears and weep like a storm upon his bosom.

He sat down on the sofa, and drew her to his side, keeping his arm around her and resting her head upon his bosom, while still he smoothed her hair with his hands, and kissed her from time to time, until she ceased to weep.

"I can never forgive myself," she murmured at length--"never forgive myself for the deep wrong I have done your noble nature; nor do I ask you to forgive me; because--because your every tone and look and gesture expresses the full forgiveness, you are too delicate and generous to speak!"

"No, sweet wife, do not ask me to forgive you; for you have done no willful wrong that needs forgiveness. And I have no forgiveness for you, sweet, but only love! infinite, eternal love! Our past is dead and buried. Let it be forgotten. You will leave this house with me this evening, love. And as soon as our duties will release us from this neighborhood we will return to England, where a host of friends will welcome us home. And here is something that will surprise and please you, love. Your flight is not known to the world. We are believed to be living in Italy together, where I have been traveling alone in secret search for you these many months. We shall return to society as from a lengthened wedding tour. Come, love, will you go away with me this very evening?"

"I will go anywhere, do anything you wish--for, under God, henceforth I have no will but yours, oh, my lord and love!" murmured the young wife, sweetly, and solemnly, as she turned her face to his, and he sealed her promise with an earnest kiss.

The same evening the Duke of Hereward took his recovered bride to the pretty, rustic inn at L'Ange, and installed her in a pleasant suite of apartments. They remained at L'Ange until after the funeral of poor John Scott, whose body was interred in the little cemetery by St. Marie L'Ange.

The young Duke of Hereward defrayed all the expenses of the burial, and settled upon the widow an income sufficient to enable her to live in comfort and respectability. With the full consent of the unloving mother, who was but too willing to be relieved of her incumbrance, the young Duchess of Hereward adopted little Marie Perdue; "perdue" no longer, but the cherished pet of a fond foster-mother.

Before leaving France, the Duke and Duchess of Hereward richly endowed the charities of the Convent of St. Rosalie, which had been so long the refuge of the lost bride. The duchess took an affectionate leave of the gentle abbess and her simple nuns, who had for so many months been her only companions. She promised to make them an annual visit.

The young duke took his recovered bride over to England, then on to Scotland, and finally to their beautiful home, Lone Castle, where the young couple were received by their tenantry with great rejoicings.

THE END.

The Codes Of Hammurabi And Moses
W. W. Davies

QTY

The discovery of the Hammurabi Code is one of the greatest achievements of archaeology, and is of paramount interest, not only to the student of the Bible, but also to all those interested in ancient history...

Religion   **ISBN:** *1-59462-338-4*   **Pages:132**
MSRP $12.95

The Theory of Moral Sentiments
Adam Smith

QTY

This work from 1749. contains original theories of conscience amd moral judgment and it is the foundation for systemof morals.

Philosophy   **ISBN:** *1-59462-777-0*   **Pages:536**
MSRP $19.95

Jessica's First Prayer
Hesba Stretton

QTY

In a screened and secluded corner of one of the many railway-bridges which span the streets of London there could be seen a few years ago, from five o'clock every morning until half past eight, a tidily set-out coffee-stall, consisting of a trestle and board, upon which stood two large tin cans, with a small fire of charcoal burning under each so as to keep the coffee boiling during the early hours of the morning when the work-people were thronging into the city on their way to their daily toil...

Childrens   **ISBN:** *1-59462-373-2*   **Pages:84**
MSRP $9.95

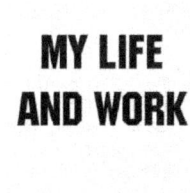

My Life and Work
Henry Ford

QTY

Henry Ford revolutionized the world with his implementation of mass production for the Model T automobile. Gain valuable business insight into his life and work with his own auto-biography... "We have only started on our development of our country we have not as yet, with all our talk of wonderful progress, done more than scratch the surface. The progress has been wonderful enough but..."

Biographies/   **ISBN:** *1-59462-198-5*   **Pages:300**
MSRP $21.95

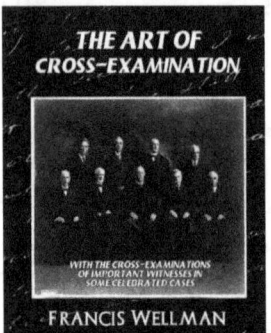

The Art of Cross-Examination
Francis Wellman

QTY

I presume it is the experience of every author, after his first book is published upon an important subject, to be almost overwhelmed with a wealth of ideas and illustrations which could readily have been included in his book, and which to his own mind, at least, seem to make a second edition inevitable. Such certainly was the case with me; and when the first edition had reached its sixth impression in five months, I rejoiced to learn that it seemed to my publishers that the book had met with a sufficiently favorable reception to justify a second and considerably enlarged edition. ..

Reference   ISBN: *1-59462-647-2*

Pages:412

MSRP $19.95

On the Duty of Civil Disobedience
Henry David Thoreau

QTY

Thoreau wrote his famous essay, On the Duty of Civil Disobedience, as a protest against an unjust but popular war and the immoral but popular institution of slave-owning. He did more than write—he declined to pay his taxes, and was hauled off to gaol in consequence. Who can say how much this refusal of his hastened the end of the war and of slavery ?

Law   ISBN: *1-59462-747-9*

Pages:48

MSRP $7.45

Dream Psychology Psychoanalysis for Beginners
Sigmund Freud

QTY

Dream Psychology
Psychoanalysis for Beginners

Sigmund Freud

Sigmund Freud, born Sigismund Schlomo Freud (May 6, 1856 - September 23, 1939), was a Jewish-Austrian neurologist and psychiatrist who co-founded the psychoanalytic school of psychology. Freud is best known for his theories of the unconscious mind, especially involving the mechanism of repression; his redefinition of sexual desire as mobile and directed towards a wide variety of objects; and his therapeutic techniques, especially his understanding of transference in the therapeutic relationship and the presumed value of dreams as sources of insight into unconscious desires.

Psychology ISBN: *1-59462-905-6*

Pages:196

MSRP $15.45

The Miracle of Right Thought
Orison Swett Marden

QTY

Believe with all of your heart that you will do what you were made to do. When the mind has once formed the habit of holding cheerful, happy, prosperous pictures, it will not be easy to form the opposite habit. It does not matter how improbable or how far away this realization may see, or how dark the prospects may be, if we visualize them as best we can, as vividly as possible, hold tenaciously to them and vigorously struggle to attain them, they will gradually become actualized, realized in the life. But a desire, a longing without endeavor, a yearning abandoned or held indifferently will vanish without realization.

Pages:360

Self Help   ISBN: *1-59462-644-8*

MSRP $25.45

QTY

The Rosicrucian Cosmo-Conception Mystic Christianity *by Max Heindel* ISBN: *1-59462-188-8* **$38.95**
The Rosicrucian Cosmo-conception is not dogmatic, neither does it appeal to any other authority than the reason of the student. It is: not controversial, but is: sent forth in the, hope that it may help to clear... New Age/Religion Pages 646

Abandonment To Divine Providence *by Jean-Pierre de Caussade* ISBN: *1-59462-228-0* **$25.95**
"The Rev. Jean Pierre de Caussade was one of the most remarkable spiritual writers of the Society of Jesus in France in the 18th Century. His death took place at Toulouse in 1751. His works have gone through many editions and have been republished... Inspirational/Religion Pages 400

Mental Chemistry *by Charles Haanel* ISBN: *1-59462-192-6* **$23.95**
Mental Chemistry allows the change of material conditions by combining and appropriately utilizing the power of the mind. Much like applied chemistry creates something new and unique out of careful combinations of chemicals the mastery of mental chemistry... New Age/Business Pages 354

The Letters of Robert Browning and Elizabeth Barret Barrett 1845-1846 vol II ISBN: *1-59462-193-4* **$35.95**
by Robert Browning and Elizabeth Barrett Biographies Pages 596

Gleanings In Genesis (volume I) *by Arthur W. Pink* ISBN: *1-59462-130-6* **$27.45**
Appropriately has Genesis been termed "the seed plot of the Bible" for in it we have, in germ form, almost all of the great doctrines which are afterwards fully developed in the books of Scripture which follow... Religion/Inspirational Pages 420

The Master Key *by L. W. de Laurence* ISBN: *1-59462-001-6* **$30.95**
In no branch of human knowledge has there been a more lively increase of the spirit of research during the past few years than in the study of Psychology, Concentration and Mental Discipline. The requests for authentic lessons in Thought Control, Mental Discipline and... New Age/Business Pages 422

The Lesser Key Of Solomon Goetia *by L. W. de Laurence* ISBN: *1-59462-092-X* **$9.95**
This translation of the first book of the "Lernegton" which is now for the first time made accessible to students of Talismanic Magic was done, after careful collation and edition, from numerous Ancient Manuscripts in Hebrew, Latin, and French... New Age/Occult Pages 92

Rubaiyat Of Omar Khayyam *by Edward Fitzgerald* ISBN:*1-59462-332-5* **$13.95**
Edward Fitzgerald, whom the world has already learned, in spite of his own efforts to remain within the shadow of anonymity, to look upon as one of the rarest poets of the century, was born at Bredfield, in Suffolk, on the 31st of March, 1809. He was the third son of John Purcell... Music Pages 172

Ancient Law *by Henry Maine* ISBN: *1-59462-128-4* **$29.95**
The chief object of the following pages is to indicate some of the earliest ideas of mankind, as they are reflected in Ancient Law, and to point out the relation of those ideas to modern thought. Religiom/History Pages 452

Far-Away Stories *by William J. Locke* ISBN: *1-59462-129-2* **$19.45**
"Good wine needs no bush, but a collection of mixed vintages does. And this book is just such a collection. Some of the stories I do not want to remain buried for ever in the museum files of dead magazine-numbers an author's not unpardonable vanity..." Fiction Pages 272

Life of David Crockett *by David Crockett* ISBN: *1-59462-250-7* **$27.45**
"Colonel David Crockett was one of the most remarkable men of the times in which he lived. Born in humble life, but gifted with a strong will, an indomitable courage, and unremitting perseverance... Biographies/New Age Pages 424

Lip-Reading *by Edward Nitchie* ISBN: *1-59462-206-X* **$25.95**
Edward B. Nitchie, founder of the New York School for the Hard of Hearing, now the Nitchie School of Lip-Reading, Inc, wrote "LIP-READING Principles and Practice". The development and perfecting of this meritorious work on lip-reading was an undertaking... How-to Pages 400

A Handbook of Suggestive Therapeutics, Applied Hypnotism, Psychic Science ISBN: *1-59462-214-0* **$24.95**
by Henry Munro Health/New Age/Health/Self-help Pages 376

A Doll's House: and Two Other Plays *by Henrik Ibsen* ISBN: *1-59462-112-8* **$19.95**
Henrik Ibsen created this classic when in revolutionary 1848 Rome. Introducing some striking concepts in playwriting for the realist genre, this play has been studied the world over. Fiction/Classics/Plays 308

The Light of Asia *by sir Edwin Arnold* ISBN: *1-59462-204-3* **$13.95**
In this poetic masterpiece, Edwin Arnold describes the life and teachings of Buddha. The man who was to become known as Buddha to the world was born as Prince Gautama of India but he rejected the worldly riches and abandoned the reigns of power when... Religion/History/Biographies Pages 170

The Complete Works of Guy de Maupassant *by Guy de Maupassant* ISBN: *1-59462-157-8* **$16.95**
"For days and days, nights and nights, I had dreamed of that first kiss which was to consecrate our engagement, and I knew not on what spot I should put my lips..." Fiction/Classics Pages 240

The Art of Cross-Examination *by Francis L. Wellman* ISBN: *1-59462-309-0* **$26.95**
Written by a renowned trial lawyer, Wellman imparts his experience and uses case studies to explain how to use psychology to extract desired information through questioning. How-to/Science/Reference Pages 408

Answered or Unanswered? *by Louisa Vaughan* ISBN: *1-59462-248-5* **$10.95**
Miracles of Faith in China Religion Pages 112

The Edinburgh Lectures on Mental Science (1909) *by Thomas* ISBN: *1-59462-008-3* **$11.95**
This book contains the substance of a course of lectures recently given by the writer in the Queen Street Hail, Edinburgh. Its purpose is to indicate the Natural Principles governing the relation between Mental Action and Material Conditions... New Age/Psychology Pages 148

Ayesha *by H. Rider Haggard* ISBN: *1-59462-301-5* **$24.95**
Verily and indeed it is the unexpected that happens! Probably if there was one person upon the earth from whom the Editor of this, and of a certain previous history, did not expect to hear again... Classics Pages 380

Ayala's Angel *by Anthony Trollope* ISBN: *1-59462-352-X* **$29.95**
The two girls were both pretty, but Lucy who was twenty-one who supposed to be simple and comparatively unattractive, whereas Ayala was credited, as her Bombwhat romantic name might show, with poetic charm and a taste for romance. Ayala when her father died was nineteen... Fiction Pages 484

The American Commonwealth *by James Bryce* ISBN: *1-59462-286-8* **$34.45**
An interpretation of American democratic political theory. It examines political mechanics and society from the perspective of Scotsman James Bryce Politics Pages 572

Stories of the Pilgrims *by Margaret P. Pumphrey* ISBN: *1-59462-116-0* **$17.95**
This book explores pilgrims religious oppression in England as well as their escape to Holland and eventual crossing to America on the Mayflower, and their early days in New England... History Pages 268

www.**bookjungle**.com *email: sales@bookjungle.com fax: 630-214-0564 mail: Book Jungle PO Box 2226 Champaign, IL 61825*

QTY

The Fasting Cure *by Sinclair Upton*   ISBN: *1-59462-222-1*   **$13.95**
In the Cosmopolitan Magazine for May, 1910, and in the Contemporary Review (London) for April, 1910, I published an article dealing with my experi-
ences in fasting. I have written a great many magazine articles, but never one which attracted so much attention... New Age/Self Help/Health Pages 164

Hebrew Astrology *by Sepharial*   ISBN: *1-59462-308-2*   **$13.45**
In these days of advanced thinking it is a matter of common observation that we have left many of the old landmarks behind and that we are now pressing
forward to greater heights and to a wider horizon than that which represented the mind-content of our progenitors... Astrology Pages 144

Thought Vibration or The Law of Attraction in the Thought World   ISBN: *1-59462-127-6*   **$12.95**
by William Walker Atkinson   Psychology/Religion Pages 144

Optimism *by Helen Keller*   ISBN: *1-59462-108-X*   **$15.95**
Helen Keller was blind, deaf, and mute since 19 months old, yet famously learned how to overcome these handicaps, communicate with the world, and
spread her lectures promoting optimism. An inspiring read for everyone... Biographies/Inspirational Pages 84

Sara Crewe *by Frances Burnett*   ISBN: *1-59462-360-0*   **$9.45**
In the first place, Miss Minchin lived in London. Her home was a large, dull, tall one, in a large, dull square, where all the houses were alike, and all the
sparrows were alike, and where all the door-knockers made the same heavy sound... Childrens/Classic Pages 88

The Autobiography of Benjamin Franklin *by Benjamin Franklin*   ISBN: *1-59462-135-7*   **$24.95**
The Autobiography of Benjamin Franklin has probably been more extensively read than any other American historical work, and no other book of its kind
has had such ups and downs of fortune. Franklin lived for many years in England, where he was agent... Biographies/History Pages 332

Name	
Email	
Telephone	
Address	
City, State ZIP	

☐ **Credit Card**   ☐ **Check / Money Order**

Credit Card Number	
Expiration Date	
Signature	

Please Mail to: Book Jungle
PO Box 2226
Champaign, IL 61825
or Fax to: 630-214-0564

ORDERING INFORMATION

web: *www.bookjungle.com*
email: *sales@bookjungle.com*
fax: *630-214-0564*
mail: *Book Jungle PO Box 2226 Champaign, IL 61825*
or PayPal *to sales@bookjungle.com*

Please contact us for bulk discounts

DIRECT-ORDER TERMS

20% Discount if You Order
Two or More Books
Free Domestic Shipping!
Accepted: Master Card, Visa,
Discover, American Express